A ROM

WATERFALL EFFECT

BY THE AWARD-WINNING AUTHOR OF
UP IN THE TREEHOUSE

K.K. Allen

Books

by K.K. Allen

Sweet & Inspirational Contemporary Romance
Up in the Treehouse
Under the Bleachers
Through the Lens (Coming in 2018)

Sweet & Sexy Contemporary Romance
Dangerous Hearts
Destined Hearts

Romantic Suspense
Waterfall Effect

Young Adult Fantasy
The Summer Solstice Enchanted
The Equinox
The Descendants

Short Stories and Anthologies
Soaring
Echoes of Winter
Begin Again

Copyright

For more information, please contact K.K. at SayHello@KK-Allen.com

ISBN-13: 978-1985801516
ISBN-10: 1985801515

To those brave enough to see truth beyond the shadows.

WATERFALL EFFECT

K.K. ALLEN

prologue

Aurora, 18 Years Old

He enters the courtroom with his head down and feet shuffling, the shackles on his wrists and ankles providing minimal room for movement. His wiry body swims in his khaki slacks and blue button down top, appearing far too conservative to be a threat. Untamed salt and pepper hair frames his downturned head and emotionless face, and exhaustion is evident in his forehead creases and the pillows beneath his half-closed lids.

There's a tremor in my chest I don't quite understand. A medley of nerves, confusion, and sorrow. My life has become a circus of law enforcement, nosey media, and probing doctor visits since awakening from a coma nearly one year ago. And it's all supposed to end today. At least, that's what my aunt Cyndi tells me.

A frenzied whisper snakes through the crowd, drawing my eyes to the man the public has branded a monster. A monster with a mental disorder who has been labeled a threat to society—and to me.

Seven disappearances. Seven girls. Three years. The only tie between us, eerie carvings of our initials found on trees scattered around the woods near where each of us disappeared. Beside each one, a checkmark and a tally where he numbered his victims like we were trophies.

Ice fills my veins as it does every time I think of what could have been. They say I was Henry June's seventh and last victim. The only one of us found alive. Somehow, I escaped the same fate as the others. Though the whereabouts of their bodies and the details of what happened remain a mystery.

My eyes steady on the man who slows his awkward gait to my left. My skin explodes with goosebumps. My chest fills to the brim with a panic I'm mostly able to suppress—thanks to my medication—but I'm not immune. Especially not when faced with an accused murderer. I'm seated directly behind the plaintiff's table, between my aunt Cyndi and my best friend, Scott—only a few feet from the man who should riddle me with hurt and rage.

I'm too confused to pinpoint my reactions—the way my eyes bulge at the sight of him, the way my fingers sweep my bare-skinned knees like the flick of a brush, the way my chest feels heavy with fire while my veins still pump ice. None of it makes sense.

Chains rattle as the guard shakes the man's arm to move him forward. The man resists, his whiskered chin tilting toward me as if he senses his prey, but his eyes remain fixed on the floor. Does he feel my presence? Because I'm more than certain that I would be able to feel his. I adjust my posture in an aim for comfort, but the effort is useless under the circumstances.

The man's eyes snap to mine. A hush falls over the room as he leans toward me, his stare dark and empty as a vibration takes over his body. It's like he's looking right through me. Would he hear me if I spoke?

I move to stand, to face him, to ask him if what the others say is true. Aunt Cyndi holds out her arm to stop me. I wish she wouldn't. I need to know. Because if it is true—how could he be so cold, so heartless?

Schizophrenic delusions aside, the reality is that after over six months of court hearings, the evidence presented in the case of the other six victims has only made his guilt more unclear than ever.

"You were dead." It's just a gravelly whisper, sandpaper to my heart. "I saw you. I—I held your limp body in my hands." He peers down at his shackled hands and shakes them hard. "You bled for your sins. You should be dead," he hisses, then squeezes his lids together. His head whips left and right, as if trying to wake from a nightmare. When his eyes fly open again, they land on mine with conviction. "You're not real. You're not real. You're not real." He whispers these words on repeat like they calm him.

Emotion crushes my throat as an unspoken plea fills my mind. *Please make it stop*, I want to scream. *Just let the nightmare end.*

"Let's go, June. Straight ahead." The corrections officer's boom echoes through the room as he continues to wrestle with the man in chains, gripping his arm and tugging him forward. The prisoner gives in, but he keeps his bloodshot eyes locked on me from over his shoulder as he's dragged away. No more words come, but he finally rips his eyes from mine as if the sight of me pains him. Maybe it does. Maybe he knows what he did. Maybe somewhere in that disturbed brain of his lies a man with compassion.

There's a shuffle of feet as everyone settles into their seats again, somber, ready for the judge to read the final verdict. They may not have found enough evidence to try the man for murdering the other victims, but they have me, my blood on his hands the day I was found, and a convincing testimony from someone I allowed too close to my heart. The circumstantial evidence is enough to convict a person for decades, but not for life.

However, with the rumor of a plea deal on the table, who knows what will happen today. Not even I am privy to such information.

Aunt Cyndi's dainty arm snakes around my stiff shoulders, yanking me from my thoughts and pulling me close.

"Are you okay?" Her whispered tone soothes me some. I know I'm not alone. Neither she nor Scott would ever let me go through something like this without a shoulder to lean on.

I don't respond to her yet. I'm not sure how to. *Of course I am not okay.* Nothing about this situation is or ever will be okay.

"He's sick, Aurora." She takes a shaky breath, still doing her best to stay calm, but I detect anger there, too.

"His voices will never hurt you again," she says. *"He's crazy. He's a monster,"* is what she means.

When I return her statement with a blank stare and silence, she gives my shoulders another squeeze. She understands well enough; no amount of comforting words or warm hugs can right the wrongs that led us all here.

They say that under the influence of alcohol, the danger of the man on trial grows, as it did the night of November twenty-sixth. The night I went missing, only to be found three days later in my father's arms, bruised, disoriented, and on the brink of death.

Because the man on trial—my father—tried to kill me.

What's worse? I don't remember any of it.

Not guilty by reason of insanity.

The verdict rings in my ears long after security has forced everyone out of the courtroom. Except for me. They let me stay, my body frozen, as the doors close. I just need a minute to myself.

Eerie quiet settles in the air, bringing a sense of calm to the chaos I've felt since that day I awoke with tubes in odd parts of me and a mind as blank as the day I was born. Aunt Cyndi and Scott started to fill in some of the gaps, but with every kernel of knowledge they bestowed came a dozen more questions. Every day was a challenge, both mentally and physically. The more I remembered, the more painful it became to grasp. I didn't want those memories. I didn't want the pain that came with it. I'd already lived through the death of my mother, my father's downward spiral, and the heartbreak that comes with first love. And with my memory returning in chunks at a time, I was having to relive each heart-wrenching event of my life all over again.

Still, after all that time, three days of darkness remain, blotting out my memory like an eclipse frozen at totality.

It all led to this: my father's arrest, the trial, a sudden change in plea, and now the verdict that will be forever etched in history via public records, newspapers, and even an upcoming made-for-TV movie. I don't think I ever wanted to be famous, but if I had, this would not be the way I'd envision it happening.

With medical testimony that confirmed my father's diagnosis of paranoid schizophrenia, his crimes were explained away by mental illness—but there's no sidestepping his guilt, no matter what he pleaded in the end. It was still my blood he wore on his hands. It was still my body he rocked in a state of shock and denial. And now, my father goes to a mental health facility. Ten years for first degree felonious restraint and committing bodily harm with the intent to kill.

It's over.

The last nine months have been hell. Doctors, police, investigators, psychologists, lawyers, reporters. In an endless frenzy to collect evidence and witness testimonies, I've lost almost one year of my life. And while all I've wanted is for it to end, this isn't the feeling I expected to have. This isn't closure. This is a loss more tragic than death. In the past year, I've lost everything. My parents, my home, my—

The clang of the heavy courtroom door disrupts my thoughts. Loud chatter from activity in the halls fades in, then out as the door closes. I turn to the door, expecting to see a security guard, Scott, Aunt Cyndi...anyone but him.

Jaxon Mills.

Just the sight of him causes a mixture of love and devastation to swarm my chest, latch onto my ribs, and beg for entry. The last time we were left in a room alone together, I told him to leave. I pushed him away. And while it hurt more than I could have ever imagined, it crushed me when he did as I said. But what else could either of us do?

His crisp, black button-down shirt makes him look like a fraud. Even with the sleeves rolled up to hug his forearms and the deep creases where it was once tucked into his gray dress pants, he looks and feels like a stranger to me now. The freckles on his creamy cheeks are gone, leaving only a sprinkling of light brown dots on his nose. His coppery brown hair is longer than when I last saw him, his wild curls dipping below his thick brows and reaching a good two inches past his ears. His normally confident smirk is conspicuously absent. And the fire that's always burned from within him is nowhere to be found.

He looks just as lost as I feel.

My gaze travels up to meet his signature stormy eyes. They're like lightning the way they fill me with the brightest light and zap me with their intensity, making me feel like I'm full of life and dying all at once. And all I can do is absorb every single second of it.

It's funny how our memories latch onto the comfort of an embrace, the warmth of a smile, the tingling of affection when we find love. Those feelings are hard to part with, even when they no longer belong to us.

I exit the row and meet him in the aisle, stopping a few yards away. Any closer and this conversation will be harder than it already is. I tilt my chin downward, my thick, coffee brown hair swinging over my narrow shoulders. What's left to say?

I knew Jaxon would come today. He was the first person I looked for when the Balsam Grove crowd arrived. It took me only a second to spot him sitting among the angry mob beside his parents. Just one glance was enough to undo me.

How can two people so deeply in love fall apart so quickly? My stomach churns acid at the thought of how far we've grown from each other over the past year. He shuffles his feet, showing me he's nervous, too.

Why did he come? Was his intention the same as the others'? To get gratification from the final verdict? To celebrate the conviction of the Balsam Grove Monster? Was the drop of the gavel enough to bring the nightmare to a close for the town? Probably.

But me? I've lost everything.

I look up. "You shouldn't be here," I say, my voice shaking with anger.

"Neither should you." His retort is quick, steaming with the same frustration from our last conversation.

In the past nine months, I've only seen or heard from him a few times. First, on the phone after leaving the hospital when I was too weak to avoid him but too hurt to hear him out. Then at Aunt Cyndi's when he showed up months later, uninvited, to warn me he was going to testify against my father in court. And finally, one month ago, when he sat in front of the courtroom and divulged information about my father's character, situations he'd witnessed, and private conversations he'd had with me—thoughts and fears I was ashamed to have, let alone have made public. And each time we spoke, he pleaded his case for why I belong in Balsam Grove despite the horrific events I was a part of. Maybe he can ignore the reasons I left, but I can't.

Even if I wasn't furious at Jaxon for his betrayal, I would have never gone back to that town. Not with my father's alleged crimes hanging over me like a dark cloud. Not with the harsh whispers of my peers and neighbors nipping at my back. And on top of it all, Jaxon and I weren't on the best of terms when it all went down.

Sighing, he dips his fingers into his pockets and looks at his shoes, a lock of wavy hair shielding his eyes. "I didn't come here to argue." His voice has softened, but somehow the pain in his tone has grown louder. "I'm sorry—about your father. I really am, Auror—"

A bubble of disbelief escapes my throat as tears threaten to follow. "You always hated my father. Don't give me your sympathy, Jaxon. Not now."

His eyes snap to mine. "Then what do I give you? I won't lie to you. I've never told you lies, and I won't start now. Yes, I may have had trouble understanding your father's...actions at times, but I never hated him. He's your dad, Aurora. And that means something to me. But I wasn't going to stand by after what happened without saying a word. Whether he was responsible for his actions or not, you almost died. The man needs help, and now he's going to get it."

I lower my eyes. "It doesn't matter anymore."

"It will always matter." His words come out choked, and he takes a step forward like he wants to comfort me. But something stops him in his tracks as if he senses I'm not ready for his embrace. That his touch would be anything but comfort. He deflates a bit.

"There's so much to say, but now isn't the time. Come home, Aurora. You belong in Balsam Grove. With me."

A sting hits the back of my eyes at the mention of my old home. Does he really think I could just go back to a town filled with rage and live a happy, normal life? Typical Jaxon. Ignoring the issues for the sake of moving on. Meanwhile, the issues never go away. They chip away at us, piece by piece, until we're finally forced to confront them. By then, it's too late.

It's too late now. There's too much damage. Too much left unresolved. Too much history tainted by what my father did. And Jaxon testifying in court only adds insult to injury. Grief for all the above swells within me, like a humidity weighing me down until my breaths are pure vapor, and all that I need to overcome thickens into a dark sea of loss.

I won't fight the current. Not anymore. I take a stuttered breath and regain my composure to speak again. To close this door once and for all. To remind him why this could never work.

"I think you're forgetting the reason I ran into the storm that night in the first place."

That was a low blow, I know, but he's the one who stepped into this courtroom while the wounds of my father's conviction were still fresh. He might as well have stepped into a warzone.

"That's not fair," he growls, his expression twisting with shock.

My chest flames with determination. I feel like I've just found my enemy's weakness in the boxing ring. I don't believe in violence, and I'm sickened with myself for sharpening my words as if they're weapons, but this is just as much about protecting Jaxon as it is about protecting myself.

"Not fair? Let me tell you what's not fair, Jaxon. You keeping secrets from me. You making decisions that affect the both of us, alone. You giving up everything you've been working so hard for, just to wait around for me when your life could be so much better than that."

His face twists in disagreement. "How can you be upset at me for wanting to wait for you to finish school?"

I ignore him, not wanting to admit that there are still parts of that night before my abduction that feel fuzzy. I remember showing up at his house in a rage. I remember our fight. I just can't remember what prompted it. How *had* I found out about his decision to give up his dreams? And why *couldn't* I listen to his side of things? Instead of sorting through it all, I ignore his question.

"You want me to come back to Balsam Grove? You don't even want to be there. Why are *you* still there, Jaxon?"

"I'm there for *you*. I've *stayed* for you."

"I never asked you to."

I know immediately this was the wrong thing to say. I can see it in his pinking cheeks, in the rough fingers that push through his hair and grab the back of his neck as he struggles to find his words.

"You didn't. You're right. You would never ask me to stay, which is exactly why I made the decision without you. You're so damn strong, Aurora, and so incredibly selfless. But I would have never regretted my decision."

His words are a chain wrapped around my heart, and every pleading, soft-spoken syllable feels like he's tugging and tugging, as if force will eventually make me learn to follow him on my own.

"You don't know that."

"I *do*. You're my life." His voice cracks as he takes another step, but he stops just as fast, assessing my reaction. When I don't protest, he closes the distance and takes my face in his palms. I let him touch me. My conflicted heart wants him to touch me. But what I want doesn't change the facts, especially the most painful one of all—that Jaxon is part of the reason my father was convicted of crimes too horrifying to believe.

"Come home." It's a passionate, desperate request that first fills my heart, then breaks it into a million pieces. My knees weaken, and it would be easy to fall to the floor. I can't take this anymore. Nothing feels right. No matter what I choose, it will be wrong.

"I don't have a home," I remind him, my voice thick with emotion.

Jaxon's face crumbles as he leans his forehead against mine. His skin is soft and warm.

"Your home is with me. Anywhere you want it to be. We don't have to go back. We can go anywhere. We can change our names if you want. Disappear forever. You're eighteen now. There's nothing tying you down."

God, how I wish he wouldn't feed me such tempting offers. To disappear. To be someone else. To be with Jaxon. It all sounds too good to be true, which means it probably is.

I shake my head and focus on the reality we're standing in. My eyes catch on the defendant's desk where my father stood not thirty minutes ago.

"What about my father? He'll be alone. I'll need to visit him—"

Jaxon releases me and pushes himself up to full height, a deeper shade of red taking over his expression. "Jesus, you're still doing it. You're still protecting him."

"He's my *father!*"

Jaxon steps back, an incredulous look on his face. "The man took a plea deal today in admission to abducting you. You were there. I watched you when they announced his sentence. Who the hell cares what his mental state is. How can you want to be anywhere near him after that?"

Wrapping my arms around my waist as if the pressure could hold in the ache, I shiver. "He didn't admit to taking those girls."

Jaxon's face falls. "You can't be serious. How is it obvious to everyone but you?"

"If it were obvious, then there would have been enough evidence to convict him. I shake my head hard, forcing a swallow over the lump in my throat. "I can't accept that he did it. I can't even bear to think it." I blink back tears, my eyes hot and stinging. "And if you still do…" I shake my head, unable to finish my sentence, but I don't have to. One thing I know for certain about Jaxon Mills; he knows me better than anyone.

"So, now what?" he says on an exhale. "You can't hold on to your father's innocence forever. You'll never move forward if you do. What will it take, Aurora?"

One year ago, we could barely keep our hands off each other. We'd overcome the distance and time that had kept us apart for two years before finally getting our chance. We surpassed the awkwardness of our first summer together—the summer I was much too young for him but much too in love to care. After that, every moment was as precious as the last grain of an hourglass. As if we knew our time was running out.

Our time has run out.

The door opens behind Jaxon, revealing the concerned face of Scott, my best friend from childhood, from when I led a happy, normal life in Durham, North Carolina. His eyes flick between the two of us. Jealousy has festered between them for years, but Scott has only ever been a friend in my heart.

"You okay, Aurora?"

"Of course she's not okay," Jaxon snaps.

I shoot him a warning glance, then turn to Scott, my face softening. "I'm coming. I just need another minute."

Scott's worried glance drifts between me and Jaxon, his lean frame blocking the view of the hallway behind him. His freshly cut, sandy blond hair is perfectly styled atop his head, a complete contrast to Jaxon's tanned and rugged appearance.

"Okay." He hesitates for another second before sighing, then stepping out and shutting the door behind him.

"You're not seriously going to leave with that guy. I thought—"

Jaxon looks genuinely confused right now, and so damn hurt. Part of me wants to fix it. I've only ever wanted to fix everyone. But clearly, I'm the worst person for that job.

"You thought what, Jax? That my father would be convicted and everything would go back to the way it was before? You think Sheriff Brooks will allow me to step one foot back into that town without a challenge?" I scoff. "Even my father's best friend thinks he's a monster." I shake my head, trying to rid the memory of the town's angry eyes watching me as I entered the courtroom earlier today.

"This isn't about the town. This is about you and me."

I cringe, knowing this conversation will only take us in the same circles, and neither of us is ready to end the loop. I charge toward the door, but I have to pass Jaxon to get there.

As I do, he wraps an arm around my waist and pulls me in, his hot breath heavy with desperation against my ear. "Don't go."

I crumble instantly, his arms my only chance of standing. I've missed his hold and his sweet, whispered words that ignite a heat between us no extinguisher could ever dissipate.

"We need more time to figure this out."

My eyes flutter closed, relishing in his embrace one last time. How easy it could be to fall victim to our love once more, forever. But I can't.

"Let me go, Jax."

He does, and the move is so quick, my lungs deflate with the loss of him.

Jaxon has always been the wild rush of the creek barreling by, a force powerful enough to alter even the sturdiest of landscapes, and he halted me with his eyes. Icy gray orbs with a stormy finish. And I wanted to fall. To let his rapids carry me and take me over the edge.

I wanted to live in his waterfall.

Not drown in his cascade.

Stale air whirls amid a buzz of the fluorescent lights as we hold our gaze and cling to this moment, prolonging our goodbye. That's what this is, isn't it? If we can't be together…if I can't return to Balsam Grove…if I can't forgive him. Goodbye is the only way forward.

SIX YEARS LATER

1

Aurora

The shrill ring of my cell phone comes through the car speakers, breaking through the heavy silence. Scott's name lights up on my dash and my entire body cringes, unprepared to face the consequences of leaving home. Of leaving him.

I tap ignore, and the car is awash in deafening silence again. My heart races and my hands shake as I grip the leather steering wheel. I can't believe I'm only minutes away from the one place I swore I would never go again.

Maybe it was my father's suicide that prompted my decision to return to Balsam Grove. Maybe it was the unease that crept in when I thought about a romantic future with Scott. Maybe it was a combination of the two. All I know is I've been caught in a riptide for years, fighting, never knowing which way to swim. And now that the wind has died down, I can finally relax and trust in the current.

My grip tightens on the wheel as I turn onto US-64 and follow the main road up the winding mountain. I've been driving for over four hours on a mission to haul ass out of Durham, North Carolina. When I left, I hadn't considered that it would be dark when I finally arrive at my destination. Street lights are scarce through mountain terrain. The only extra light comes from a gas station off the main road that looks like it was plucked straight from the seventies. It's dimly lit, its walls and windows cluttered with signs, masking the building's wear. If it weren't for the neon sign blinking *Open* in the window, I wouldn't consider it serviceable.

Is this an indication of what the town has become? Discarded history, abandoned, useless…lost? I force myself to take deep, steady breaths to avoid another panic attack and focus on my drive. There's no way I'm turning back now.

Nestled within Pisgah National Forest in the Appalachian Mountains of North Carolina, Balsam Grove is lightly populated, maintained more for the passersby than locals. Waterfalls, rivers and creeks, camping sites, and hiking trails make up most of the town. In Balsam Grove, everyone owns land, tourists are a necessity, and everyone knows everyone. At least, everyone *thinks* they know everyone.

Eight more miles and I'll be at the cottage in the mountains where I vacationed with my parents every summer growing up. Where my father decided to make his permanent home after my parents separated when I was fifteen. Where I moved two years later, after my mother was killed.

Balsam Grove.

Whenever I think about this place, the memories of my time here rush over me, and in some cases drown me completely. It's part of the reason I've avoided any thought of the small town for so long. A coping mechanism, my therapist called it, and I accepted it then. But I've been fighting the current for too long in an effort to stay still. I lost so much in that town, but there was good there too.

Memories are a fragile thing—how they come and go and distort themselves into something they're not. How they have the power to light us up or cripple us in a flash. As someone who's suffered through short-term memory loss—or dissociative fugue, as the doctors labeled it—the memories I lost during and surrounding the three days of my abduction are a curse and a blessing.

I've come to realize that what's lost shouldn't always be found.

For starters, the three days I was taken and held captive by my own father. My body shakes at the acceptance of this truth that, for years, I couldn't make sense of. But that's another gift that came with therapy—the knowledge that insanity cannot be justified. Whether controllable or not, my father's actions were wrong.

It's taken countless therapy sessions and the six years since my father's trial to make peace with the court's verdict. Not that I've come to terms with what happened that dreadful November, nor do I have any wish to remember those three days missing from my memory. No. As far as I'm concerned, those three days are buried six feet under rock and soil with my father, with no hope of returning. I've wished them their peace. But that doesn't erase the rest of my time in Balsam Grove.

What I do remember about the town now, after years of suppression, comes in small, blurry doses.

Rolling terrain that stretched for miles as my feet pounded against the rocky earth. Splashing water from a nearby creek and skipping rocks across the river. My rubber soles slipping as I hopped across a high stack of chopped wood. The happier memories filter in through a sheet of fog, obscuring the rest from view. But they're still there, fighting to come to the forefront.

I shiver at the memory of Jaxon, at the way I left him standing in that courtroom. His plea still rings between my ears. *Come home.* It still hurts to think about, especially because he was once my happy place. Being with him made everything feel larger than life as he encouraged me to experience all the things nature had to offer.

No responsibilities. No expectations. Just adventure.

I want to feel that again, the whimsical freedom of my childhood before my world turned upside down. Before I lost everything—including myself.

I'm almost there. Moss-covered spruce trees line every dip and curve of the road as they bow to the howling wind. The radio mentioned a storm brewing in the Atlantic, and by the curtain of clouds that's quickly shutting the stars out of sight, I know I'm running out of time before the sky unleashes on me.

Relying on my car's headlights to guide me through the desolate woods, I slow before seeing a sign for Shoal Creek Falls. I drive another half mile down dirt and gravel, and a mailbox with the number 7933 confirms I'm in the right place.

A smattering of raindrops pings the roof, quickly morphing into buckets as I turn onto the private drive that leads to my old home. With a quick flash of my high beams, I spot my father's cottage up ahead, all twelve hundred square feet of dark brown house and fifteen acres of land that I now own.

With a tight grip on the wheel, I park the car in the middle of the drive and begin to gather my things. I left Scott's with only two suitcases containing clothes, shoes, and one family photo album that didn't get packed away in storage with the rest of my mom's things. Just the essentials. Nothing else in the house was mine. Not the pristine furniture, not the pretentious wall décor, not even the fancy tablet he gifted me on my twenty-fourth birthday. It was all getting to be too much.

I take a deep breath and let it out slowly, trying to disperse my rising anxiety. It takes everything in me to not succumb to the emotions that flood my thoughts and cripple me to extinction. Grief, guilt, and confusion terrorize my mind, but I pull strength from the fact that I have no regrets. Only hope.

Hope.

As thick raindrops continue to pummel the roof, I search the passenger seat until I feel the very thing that set everything into motion.

My decision to leave my life in Durham behind didn't develop over a few days or even a few months. It's been in the back of my mind for years. But it wasn't until I received the envelope containing a gifted deed and a key to my father's cottage in the mountains that I knew I had to make it happen.

A single slip of my father's old stationary accompanies the deed. Written at the top of the lined sheet, in a scrawl made with shaky hands and utmost care, are words I can hear my father saying as if he's in the car with me now.

Through smoke and fire, reality awaits—ever-changing, yet always present.

I run the pad of my thumb over the familiar bold, dark blue print before taking the key from the envelope and shoving it into my pocket. I take another deep breath and switch off the ignition.

Ignoring the missed calls and messages from Scott, I swallow against the thickness in my tired throat and reach into the backseat of my Honda Accord. In my hasty effort to pack, I somehow managed to bury my jacket in the tumbled mess of clothes and shoes without thinking that I might need it when I arrived. One, two, three tugs later, I free the fabric from my suitcase and zip it around me before snatching my handbag and stepping out of the car. My phone's flashlight shines against the cobblestone path as I dodge the slanted downpour, careful not to snag my loafers on the uneven terrain.

My father hasn't tended to the cottage in almost seven years. I assumed the worst when it came to the state of his home. Rotted wood. Broken doors. Chipped and faded paint. Weeds to my chin. Maybe even vandalism.

But I was wrong. The cottage looks like it's been cared for. Sure, it could use some TLC, but it certainly doesn't appear to have been abandoned. Unlit garden lights line the mud and dirt-caked stone pathway to the front door. The porchlight isn't on either, which doesn't surprise me considering it's been years since anyone has replaced the bulbs. I can fix that tomorrow. The utility companies assured me the power and water would be on by the time I arrived, but something stirs in my gut, telling me I won't be so lucky.

Wood panels creak beneath my feet as I step onto the covered porch. A set of rocking chairs and a wooden porch swing decorate the front, relenting to the wind as they moan and rattle. As a strong gust engulfs me in the deep, earthy scents of pine and soil, I brace myself for the first memory to come, expecting it to hit hard now that I'm faced directly with my past. Isn't that how it's supposed to work? I see, feel, hear, and smell scenes from my past, and the memories come rushing back like a tsunami?

A crack of lightning jolts through the sky, causing me to jump. I yelp, the wind and rain swallowing my voice as my stomach churns with nervous energy. My pulse quickens, a sign of life I welcome like it's my first breath.

Even though it's June, it's a cool night in the mountains. The wind and the fact that I'm soaked in Earth's cry makes me shiver. Wrapping an arm around my middle, I unlock the cottage door and practically leap inside. My jacket comes off first, my boots second, and then I'm locking the door behind me and patting down the wall to find a light switch.

Aha. Got you.

My fingers find the switch plate settled between a kitchen inlet and the front door, and I flick it on—but darkness remains. *Of course.* I wiggle and toggle the switch a few more times, just in case. Nothing.

Defeated, I lean back against the door and sigh.

On the other side of the room, rain splatters against the sliding glass that overlooks the back porch. The storm clouds have pulled the curtain on nature's glow, stealing most of my light.

After kicking off the door with a bout of desperation, I move through every door and shine my phone's flashlight over every tabletop, taking in my surroundings. I see the bathroom. The office. And a wooden ladder propped at an angle above the kitchen inlet, leading to the loft above.

I circle the room like a shark, inspecting the furniture, touching the walls, and inhaling a burgundy blanket that's hanging over a couch. But familiarity fails to stir within me. *I feel nothing.*

I'm still numb.

I'm still broken.

I'm still empty.

And it's all so goddamn suffocating.

Disappointment settles in my gut like an immovable anchor. This moment is yet another reminder of why expectations are something I try to steer clear of. I didn't realize how badly I wanted to feel *something* until now. But nothing sparks that wick in the dark corner of my mind. I'm afraid it may be lost forever.

My right hand falls to the edge of the kitchen counter as pressure builds in my chest and throat. No tears come. They rarely do. Instead, I'm distracted by the whistle of the wind and the whoosh of the trees as I peer out to the rain-battered balcony. I focus on the sounds as I breathe deeply through the darkness, allowing the panic to dissolve naturally. It usually does once I'm able to accept what's going on with my mind and body, though it's easier when I understand what triggered an attack. Tonight it's the storm and any loud or sudden noise that comes with it.

After another deep breath, I feel some of the tension fall away from my body. I turn to the ladder and test the first couple steps before climbing to the top. My father's bed rests there, still dressed in the neutral tones he wore best. The dim glow of the mostly obscured stars shines in through a floor-to-ceiling window behind the bed. I still rely on my phone's flashlight to navigate the top floor.

Inside the bathroom in the corner of the room, beside a small closet sans door or curtain, I flip the switch, and in an instant, my dream of a warm shower is shattered. I sigh. If there's water, it will be cold, but that won't stop me from washing this grime off after driving for hours.

The shower knob squeaks in resistance, and after a few croaky moans, the head releases several strong spurts before a powerful stream of water splatters against the tile floor. I step into the tub, gasping at the shock of the cold pelting my body. My lungs work hard while I adjust to the temperature, my body quickly coming alive beneath its spell.

Without soap or shampoo, I do my best to wash away the stress of the day, making a mental note of all the things I'll need to pick up in town tomorrow. I can't imagine needing much. Without social obligations filling my calendar or a job to dress up for, there's no one here to impress. I can focus on me.

Freezing cold, I step out of the shower and fumble around in the dark bathroom cabinet, relieved to find a clean towel. After drying off, I change into a loose, faded red *The Walking Dead* tank top and leggings. Fitting, I suppose. The similarities between my favorite fictional apocalyptic universe and this graveyard of a town are not lost on me.

As the wind continues to whistle and howl, throwing trees left then right, snapping branches and leaves and tossing them who-knows-where, I grab a blanket from the bedroom closet to avoid having to crawl into bed with old, unfamiliar sheets. Another item to add to my shopping list.

A calm begins to settle around me while my mind and heart react with a flutter. What am I doing here? What was I thinking? I had a good life. I was moving on.

And just like that, the doubt creeps in. Doubt I managed to suppress on my drive simply by distracting myself with a goal of getting here.

I could be at home with Scott. Going to the movies. Spending the evening at a nice restaurant with his coworkers in Raleigh.

I let my mind drift back to nights with Scott, us showering in separate showers, meeting in the hall to kiss goodnight, and then padding off to separate rooms to sleep. We'd been friends for so long, I couldn't seem to get comfortable with the idea of anything more. So, while I felt Scott's need for me rise, my need for him didn't. Perhaps our relationship was doomed to stay in the friendship zone forever.

It didn't help our situation that I'd been in love before. That full, deep, soul-crushing love. I understand how something so powerful, so real, can consume someone. What it's like to be abuzz with passion and allow all inhibitions to fall away, no matter the consequence.

That's how things were with Jaxon. It was all dark corners and stolen kisses. Hidden waterfalls and abandoned cottages. Our need increasing with each touch, each kiss. I didn't feel that love with Scott, and I knew it would never be fair to hold him to some type of fairytale standard based on a forbidden love that ended so cruelly.

I had to face it. With Scott, there are no sparks, no burning from within or pooling in my belly. He's simply my best friend. Someone to talk to, to laugh with. He's safety. And unlike with Jaxon, when I laugh with Scott, I don't laugh from my gut. My words don't flow in an endless string. It isn't all Scott's fault, though. And the numbing effect of my anxiety meds doesn't help, either.

Shit. *My meds.*

I rip the sheets off me and jerk to a sitting position. In one leap I reach my handbag. I unzip it and toss the contents left and right. They should be here, but I can't find them. *I didn't pack them.* No, I refuse to believe that. I wouldn't forget my pills. I've been taking them every single day for over six years. Even if they weren't on my list, I would have grabbed them and stuffed them into my bag without even thinking. Maybe I tossed them in one of my suitcases. I look out at the rain, knowing there's no way I'll be venturing back out there tonight.

My mind backtracks to earlier today when I stopped in the bathroom for my toothbrush and that damn telemarketer called, rerouting me from my mission. My heart sinks, knowing I completely forgot to check the medicine cabinet for my newly refilled bottle. I search my handbag again, checking the tiny crevices and secret pockets, hoping to be surprised.

Nothing.

For heaven's sake, what is wrong with me? I'll have a panic attack just thinking about having a panic attack. There's no pharmacy in town, either, which means I'll have to drive halfway to Asheville *if* I can even get my doctor to fill me a new order.

Groaning, I crawl back into bed, blood pumping from my adrenaline-fueled search. A light glows brightly on the nightstand, and I turn my attention to my phone, sitting unplugged with a low battery warning illuminating the screen. *Great.* It will die any minute. Pulling it to me, I scroll through the messages one final time before shutting it off in hopes of reserving some battery life in case of an emergency.

I am in the middle of the woods. What once felt like home now feels strange. I want to sleep, but every creak and groan is amplified in the midst of the storm, promising little chance of rest.

With a slight pillow adjustment, my eyes find the window behind me, and I stare blankly into the night. Checking my phone again was a mistake. Scott's name continues to be the blinding force in my thoughts. Leaving him. Coming here. Hurting him. I don't even have a good reason why.

I smile sadly, imagining the epic tantrum he would throw if he were here to witness this disaster of a night. He's always been more of the five-star accommodation type. Pressed suits, weekly dry cleaning, and vacations consisting of spa days and fancy restaurants. Never once has he even entertained the idea of a camping trip. It's like he's devoted the rest of his life to rebelling against the place that almost took my life.

Balsam Grove is the last place Scott will ever look for me, and I made sure to leave no trail behind. Our bank accounts and cell phones aren't connected. I've never been on social media. I left him information to continue paying my share of the bills. And I quit my job at the law firm after my father's death, so there weren't any loose ends to tie up there.

Two years ago, I subtly mentioned visiting Balsam Grove. I was curious. Naturally. But Scott put a firm foot down and refused. I didn't push the subject. He'd known my father for the length of our friendship. He'd witnessed the change in my father's behavior from normal, fun-loving guy to paranoid schizophrenic. Scott was in that courtroom with me when my father was convicted after pleading not guilty by reason of insanity. And he remained my friend after my father was sentenced to the mental health facility for ten years, minimum. Beyond all that, Scott would feel isolated in a place like this. Bored. Restless. He's been talking about moving to Raleigh for years. A bigger town. Taller buildings. Better nightlife. He's tired of the commute. Maybe now that I've left Durham, he'll make it happen. Working in the corporate world gives him financial and social rewards he never had growing up. As an accountant for a well-known hotel chain, he loves the thrill of deadlines, after-work happy hours, corporate parties, and travel. But his hustle and bustle is my boredom. His networking is my hell. And his planning is my anxiety.

I sigh. How I wish my heart was something I could manipulate, to feel for Scott what he feels for me. How I wish my deepest desires weren't chasing after fallen memories, so I could be free to love again. Is it possible? To love again after losing the love of my life? I was seventeen, for Christ's sake. Certainly there's got to be someone else out there for me. Preferably someone who isn't tangled in my past. Because clearly, Scott wasn't the problem. He never was. It was me and my obsession with the boy I once knew and loved with all my heart. And if I'm being honest with myself, that's why I had to leave Scott.

While I've never intentionally compared my feelings for Scott to those I had for Jaxon, it was inevitable. Thoughts of Jaxon come as easy as breathing, even now, years later. I can't even think of what I would do or say if I saw him again. But I've already convinced myself that he won't be here. There's no chance in hell he would have stayed. Jaxon had other dreams, and once I wasn't around to hold him back, he would have pursued them.

The same feelings I've had for years begin to churn inside me. Emptiness. Numbness. Desperation for something more. Here, there, my reality is the same.

But being here is step one. I don't know why my father left me the keys to the cottage, or what I'll do now that I'm here. All I know is that out of all the decisions I could have possibly made, this was the one that felt the most right.

The rest is up to the wind.

2

Aurora

I'm somewhere in between dreaming and sleeping.

Water ripples with each heavy bang as a strong force pulls me forward, my body weak against the pressure. I let myself be taken, pulled through deep then shallow water, gasping once I've reached the surface. The pounding continues to rip me from my slumber every few seconds. But it's not a simple knock on the door. It's as if someone is heaving their entire body into it, shaking the sturdy wood from its hinges.

My mind races, rushing to make something of the noise. The darkness still handicaps my senses as I look around the room, slowly remembering that I'm in my father's cottage in the middle of—somewhere. I can't even think straight. Blood pumps through my veins, and I swear I can hear the dull thump of my heart.

Not a panic attack. Please, not now. It's been so long since I've tried to control them on my own, but luckily my meds from this morning should still be flowing through my system. *I'll be okay.*

A heavy thud below jerks me fully awake. My eyes snap to the window at the head of my bed to find the swirl of debris and the whiplash of the trees as wind whistles and screams like a tea kettle's warning. Wood cracks, then creaks beneath me, like a great force is smashing into it. I remind myself that this little cottage is surrounded by hundreds of acres of trees. If anything is trying to break in, it's a fallen tree, or a squirrel, or…I don't know. Clearly, I should have checked the weather before choosing tonight to arrive. If this cottage caves, then my search for enlightenment was a waste.

I slam my lids closed to focus on drowning out the noise. *It's just the storm.* I release a long, steady breath and repeat the words like I'm soothing a scared child in my arms. But instead of relief, I feel starved of air. Usually it's the darkness that helps me feels safe. But tonight, it seems to be making my panic attack worse. I need light.

Ripping the sheets from my body, I grab my phone and take the ladder to the bottom floor, then turn in a slow circle, checking out the rest of the house from here. Everything appears to be intact. I power on my phone and wait, but nothing happens. It's dead.

A flicker of movement catches my eye from outside the kitchen door's floor-to-ceiling window. I step closer, squinting and seeing nothing but the trees thrashing in the wind. My heart is pounding so hard and so fast on my retreat into the living room, I think it might explode.

A rumble of thunder shakes the house, followed immediately by a crash of lightning slamming into the ground right outside the cottage. I near the sliding glass doors to check the locks. I'll feel safer once I double check every window, every door.

There's nothing to be afraid of, I remind myself. No one even knows I'm here.

But the darkness finds me again, and everything tilts—my focus, my balance. My palms hit the glass door to steady me. My breaths come in gasps as I force my eyes to stay open, my only savior the orb of light exposed between two looming clouds.

The only way out of a panic attack is through it. My therapist's words filter through the haze of my mind. Doctor Rohls taught me how to control the crippling anxiety as it washes over me. He trained me not to run from it. Running only makes it worse.

Breathe through it, he said. *Feel it. Let yourself react to it. Your anxiety is normal, Aurora. Everyone has bouts of it, but what it manifests into is all in your mind. You want to encounter your triggers like you would any other fear. Stand up to it, breathe through it, and one day your mind will become immune.*

There's power in knowing I can take back control of my body when drowning feels so much easier. Once my breathing returns to normal, I give the handle a shake to confirm the latch is secure. There's even a thick cylinder of wood wedged in the bottom slider for added security. A somber smile lifts my cheeks ever so slightly as a memory comes. A memory of my father securing the house each night before bed. The last thing he would do was check on the sliding window in my room downstairs, safeguarding it with a similar wooden dowel.

I turn in the direction of my old bedroom, which was also my father's office. I slept on a pull-out couch that I could never pull out because the room was filled with so much stuff my father refused to organize. Every night, I'd wait for my father to go to bed before removing that piece of wood. My body hums at the reason why.

Jaxon Mills.

Here I go again. More thoughts of Jaxon. It's been like this ever since my father's death, when the attorney showed up on my doorstep with the gifted deed. Since my first visit to the cottage when I was eight years old, I considered Balsam Grove and Jaxon a package deal. But I didn't come back here for him. That would be ridiculous. After the way we ended things, the reasons why, and the time it's taken for me to even consider coming back... I'd be a fool to think there could be anything left between us. He's probably long gone, anyway.

Another boom of thunder steals my attention, making me jump and turn my focus to the window. A flash illuminates the night, revealing a tall figure cloaked in a navy jacket, his head low with rain streaking down the front of the hood. A dark beard masks his face. I gasp as the man's head tilts up, and his stormy eyes lock on mine.

Those eyes. I'd remember them anywhere.

"Jaxon?" The whisper slips out on a breath that comes straight from my heart. Could my mind be playing tricks on me? The man doesn't look like Jaxon. At least, not like the Jaxon I left in that courtroom.

But those eyes...

Nature's lightshow is just a flickering tease before darkness falls again. The figure backs up from the porch, trips down the steps, and stumbles off into the darkness, leaving me questioning everything I've missed over the past six years.

What happened to this small, tight-knit town after my father was convicted? What kind of people live here now? Will I remember any of them? Will they remember me? How long will I be here before I outstay my welcome?

My vision blurs. The pressure in my chest is too strong. I'm beginning to lose my balance, so I feel around to grasp something that can hold me up. My fingers brush against a wood cabinet beside me, but I miss my chance to grip it. I fall backward, my head hitting the floor in a thud.

The ache in my head is nothing. At least I can feel it. And this time when everything fades to black, I'm still conscious. Still aware. That's good.

I'm not sure how long it takes for my breathing to even out again, but when it does, the storm has calmed and I'm able to stand back on my feet. Shuddering, I make my rounds, checking all the windows and locks before climbing the ladder and getting back into bed. I pull the covers up to my chin and conjure up the image of the man outside again. A man I desperately want to believe is Jaxon. So desperately, I could have easily imagined him.

Sometimes darkness settles over me like a blanket, quieting the noise and protecting me from exposure. Other times, when there's too much to drown out, darkness becomes my mind's prison. Complete solitude. No escape. My thoughts run rampant, chewing away at my peace like tiny insects. And in these moments, I'm reminded of just how alone I am.

In the six years since my father's conviction, my life has been about rebuilding, settling onto a new path, and moving on. I thought after all this time, I was ready to take that final step and confront Balsam Grove. To ignore the demons dormant within me and stand on the soil of my past. But it's clear to me now. In the last six years, I've been avoiding, and every step has been a step in the wrong direction. I know that now. Hopefully it's not too late to find my way back, to move forward, and to feel right with myself again.

As I finally begin to sink into the haze of sleep, the man in the storm holds the spotlight in my mind. I can't get over his eyes. They were the last thing I saw before he tripped off into the night and the last image that flashes through my mind before a yawn pulls me down. Eyes that lit up so clear, so gray, striking me right in the heart and reminding me of everything I once loved and lost.

Only now, I think they should terrify me.

3

Aurora

Light filters in through my eyelids, and it takes me a second to sort out my surroundings. The sheets are stiff and colder than I'm used to. The surrounding air carries a rich humidity scented with alpine and a hint of dust, without a fan to soften the heat pouring in from behind me.

I'm in Balsam Grove.

In the cottage.

There was a storm last night.

My eyes open wide as I recall the familiar gaze that stared back at me in the flash of lightning, like the universe wanted me to see him. I shiver at the glimmer of hope buried deep in my chest that he was real and not a figment of my dreams. But if that was him, he made it pretty clear he didn't want to see me.

Shame washes over me. He bolted just like I did six years ago.

Moaning, I make my way to the bathroom. Thoughts like these will only distract me. I need to focus on why I'm here: to heal and to move on. Nodding with conviction, I turn the knob at the sink, fill my palms with cold water, and lean down to splash my face.

After managing to lug my suitcases inside, I sort through it all downstairs. My clothes are a jumbled mess from last night, but I manage to find a pair of khaki shorts and a flowy white blouse with short bell sleeves. After strapping on a pair of sandals, I hop in my car, and it only takes a few seconds to remember the direction I need to head to reach the small section of shops in town. It's interesting how some parts of my memory are so clear, like I never left, and some are held hostage in a black box I can't access.

A few minutes later I pull in to a parking lot at the end of a block of shopping centers. Nestled between a sprawling incline of the mountain and the French Broad River are several short blocks of two-story brick buildings in assorted colors and sizes. The river is narrower in this part of town, and the water flows hard and fast as a result of the storm last night. I want to capture it. Frame it. And carry it with me always so I'll never forget it again.

It's easy to lose sight of the beauty that lies in simplicity. A small town like this has so much to offer, all of it free: the landscape, the natural resources, the adventure, the quiet. Yet there are those who have lived here their entire lives who feel restless, trapped, and want nothing more than to leave. I always appreciated my small summer doses of Balsam Grove, but now that I'm here taking in the air with eyes wide open, I realize how much even I had taken for granted.

My steps slow as I peer in the windows of the three dozen or so shops that line the main drive. The grocery and hardware stores look familiar, their hanging signs unchanged—paint worn and in need of straightening—but most of the sidewalk shops seem to be new.

A sign in one window calling attention to a weekly waterfall tour with a few spots remaining catches my eye. My heart beats fast as I push through the door, my curiosity winning out.

Balsam Grove was always a great tourist town, off the beaten path but worth the drive for those who're looking for a challenging hike or a day lounging at the falls. I've never taken a tour, though, not in all the time I spent here. Mostly because there was no need to hire a tour guide when I was busy exploring the woods with Jaxon.

A woman in her mid-fifties sits behind the desk and acknowledges me with a distracted smile when I enter. She's nodding into a bright blue phone receiver, the kind with a spiral cord attached.

"Absolutely," she says. "You're all booked for Saturday, and I just emailed you some forms. You'll need to bring them in when you arrive so we can clear you for the group hike." Her smile brightens. "Wonderful. Then I'll see you Saturday, Mr.—"

The voice on the other end of the line distracts her again. I turn to the rack of pamphlets against the wall and leaf through them. Balsam Grove sure seems to be thriving. There's a tour for just about everything. Mountain biking, leisurely scenic hikes, fishing, horseback riding, waterfall adventures, whitewater rafting, tubing down French Broad River. Geez. The options are endless.

One flyer in particular catches my eye, advertising Canvas and Wine classes, whatever that is. I smile when I see a waterfall hiking brochure beside it that describes the history of the changing landscapes since the first hiker documented them in the early 1920s. I don't have to read it. I remember the landmarks well. I spent hours staring at each one, memorizing every jagged edge and concave, noting at what points the flow increased or calmed in speed. I remember the crescendo of water at the lips of the falls, the sound of the powerful water being swallowed by the pool below.

It's true what they say about experiencing the world through a bigger lens as a child. The colors are brighter. Senses are new. Dreams aren't limited by roadblocks and failures—they are infinite. But when you're a child, the shadows are also darker. Vulnerabilities are raw, unprotected. And the weight of a single disappointment can be crushing.

Still, no matter what life handed me over the years, good or bad, the falls became my safe haven. From a deteriorating home life. My rising doubts about my future. My love life gone awry. The falls were always there. Despite their changing landscapes, they were the sturdiest place for me to stand.

Or so my young mind thought.

The receptionist's phone clatters onto its base, bringing me back to the present.

"Thank you for your patience, dear." The woman smiles. "Are you interested in a tour? If you give me an idea of what you're looking for, I can point you in the right direction."

"I-I'm not sure." My gaze drops to the brochure again. "Hiking, maybe? I'd like to get to know the area again." I bite my tongue and cringe. She doesn't need to know I've been here before. "I mean, it was a long time ago, and I don't really remember much."

She smiles again, her small, almond-shaped eyes piercing me with their brightness. "Well, then you have some options. We have hiking tours daily. One stops at the waterfalls for lunch, and one goes a bit further up the mountains. We have weekend and weekly tours that leave on Fridays and Mondays too if you plan on staying awhile. Otherwise, we can book you on a half-day or day-long hike."

"Any tour is fine." I can't handle the plethora of options.

There's a curiosity in her expression now as she looks me up and down. I'm not dressed the part of a hiker. I'm not even sure what I'll wear when I go on this hike. The wardrobe I brought is scarce and simple in style, but I figured I could buy what I needed when I arrived.

She turns to her computer. "How long will you be in town?"

How do I answer that? The decision to come back here to mend the wounds of my past didn't come with a manual. There's no end date. No deadline. I'm just here to figure out what's next for me. Balsam Grove is a pit stop on the way to the rest of my life. When I'm ready, I'll sell the cottage and put a deposit on a place of my own…somewhere.

"Oh, I'm not sure. Maybe a month." The idea of being here for more than another day knots my insides with live wires. After experiencing the storm last night and the rise of panic that came with it, not to mention the man who appeared on my back porch… I'll need to take this one day at a time.

"I see." She taps away on her keyboard. "I can put you on a waterfall day hike next Wednesday. You'll leave at ten in the morning and arrive back at base at eight."

That sounds perfect. A tour of the land to bring me back to that state of mind where anything felt possible. When the rush of the river lived in my veins, and when the storm wasn't a warning but a celebration. I'm desperate for a taste of it all.

I hand her my card with a smile. "Great, I'll take it."

But as she's entering my information into the computer, I see the recognition register on her face. For a moment, her eyes lock on the screen and I swear her fingers tremble on the keyboard. At first I think I'm imagining it, but when her face crumbles and she looks back at me like she's preparing me for bad news, I know she recognizes me.

"Oh dear." She shakes her head dramatically, failing to meet my eyes. "This is quite the unfortunate event. It looks like the last slot for the waterfall tour just got booked up. I can put you on a waitlist for another tour. No guarantees, though."

"Wait," I lean in trying to glance at her screen. "You just said there was an opening."

"It's been filled." Her voice is colder now, less friendly.

My mouth opens, shock slicing through me. "I've been standing here the entire time. How did someone take my spot?"

The woman's faded red lips shake for a second, a tell that she's not being completely honest. If there's one thing I've learned to do over the years, it's how to read people. Their mannerisms, their ticks. I've become quite good at it.

"It was an online reservation." She's still not looking back at me. "It happens all the time, really." She waves her hand in the air. "It's something we intend to fix, but unfortunately, we're all filled up for the next few weeks."

My jaw snaps shut, and I push away from the counter with a huff.

"Let me just get you onto our waiting list…"

She drones on in a nervous rush while I'm quiet, too busy assessing her every flinch and tremor, certain she refused me a hiking spot on purpose. But now that I'm examining the older woman's aerosoled blonde hair, her light blue eye shadow, and the long tap of her cherry red acrylic nails, familiarity sparks in my chest. I can't put my finger on how or why, but I know this woman.

The click and creak of the door followed by heavy footsteps averts my attention. I swivel toward the sound. A man in a dark brown suit and tie with a decorative patch on his arm walks in. He's wearing a gold badge in the shape of a star above his lapel, and his eyes flicker between the woman behind the counter and me.

He studies me hard, as if I'm a mystery he's piecing together. Chills shoot down my spine, making me shiver.

The deputy's eyes move over me, the scowl on his face growing like he's just made a connection. I swallow. No, I am not being paranoid. He knows who I am. And he is not happy to see me.

My heart is lodged in my throat but that doesn't stop me from matching his once-over with one of my own. He's young, just a few years older than me, with short, sandy blond hair, bangs cut too short, and hazel, almond-shaped eyes. In fact, he eerily resembles the woman behind the counter.

That's when it hits me. "Tanner." My voice may come out small, but there's confidence in my tone.

I didn't have many friends when I lived here, but the few acquaintances I made were thanks to Jaxon. Tanner was one of them. He was Balsam Grove's sports hero, competitive to a fault about pretty much everything. He was also the definition of entitled, being that his father was the town's sheriff. He was always getting into some kind of trouble, but he'd get away with it every time. Pranks, theft, loud arguments with anyone who dared ruffle his feathers. A few times his rage got the better of him, and his fist would wind up buried in someone's cheek. Sheriff Brooks would always pull some strings and get him out of trouble.

How the hell did he end up on the other side of the law? I guess it's obvious, but it's still hard to imagine the people of Balsam Grove take their orders from *him*. It's laughable, really.

"Aurora June. *Holy* fuck. What's it been, seven years? You have some nerve showing your face in this town again." It's an odd thing to say with a shit-eating grin, but that's Tanner. Awkward humor at the most inappropriate times. And he revels in it.

I know he said it as a joke, but I have to fight the twist of discomfort in my chest. It's enough verification that I'm unwanted. Unwelcome.

I look back at the woman behind the counter. Now that everything is beginning to click, I know she's Tanner's mother.

Sighing, I turn back to Tanner, taking in his attire one more time. "There is no way your pops gave you a gun and a badge. Who in their right mind would let you protect them?"

His lip curls with the competitive flair I remember all too well. "You bet your ass they do. Balsam Grove has never been safer. And now that we're finally booking tours again, we intend to keep it that way."

"Booking tours *again*?" What an odd thing to say.

"That's right." His brows pinch together. "Hiking wasn't so popular around here for a bit. Rumor got out about the hiker disappearances, and it destroyed business around here. A lot of locals went out of business. A couple years ago when all the smoke had cleared, we started offering new tours and accommodations, and slowly but surely things started picking up again."

My skin crawls at the way he's looking at me now, testing me, like he thinks I'm my father reincarnate.

"Yeah, well, congratulations." My voice is dry as I shift with unease. "I'm just passing through. I have some things to take care of at the cottage, and I don't want any trouble." I hope Tanner knows this is a request as much as a statement.

Tanner exchanges a worried glance with his mother over my shoulder, triggering my eyes to roll before I start to move forward with annoyance. "Never mind. I need to get going."

"Wait, Aurora," he jumps in, stepping in front of me to block my exit. "Look. You should know…the town—these people—they don't forget. And, well, things are finally going well again. With Pops out a lot helping search and rescue teams around the state, I'm second in command. It's me who's running things now."

He pauses, as if uncertain how to phrase what's coming next, an uncharacteristic move for Tanner. But then again, Tanner did always treat me like a little sister. Like he was trying to protect me from something—or someone. I always thought it was because our fathers were good friends.

I sigh. "I'm not here to stop any progress. Just let me be. I'll stay out of your way. Everyone's way. No one needs to know I'm even here."

He calls me on my bullshit with a tilt of his head and raised brows, zeroing in on me with his eyes. "Seriously, Aurora? You think they won't recognize you? You're still carrying the June name, aren't ya?" He leans closer, lowering his voice to a controlled whisper. "What are you doing here? The town will be up in arms when they realize you're back. I'm trying to be nice here, but I'm not joking around about that. They won't feel safe with—" He cuts himself off with a shake of his head.

My gut churns with a blaze. I don't think I want to hear the rest of that sentence.

"If you don't leave on your own, these people—they *will* run you out of town."

"Let them try."

He narrows his eyes. "It won't be pretty."

I adjust my stance, leveling him with my stare. A challenge. "And I'm sure you'll just stand by and watch."

He grows taller, ears reddening in anger. "This is *my* town. And I will do *anything* to protect the people here."

Anger bubbles up inside me with his words. "You say that like I'm a threat."

His silence and his hardened jaw tell me everything I need to know. Maybe Tanner isn't the misunderstood boy I remember from my childhood. He's clearly jumped on the June hate club bandwagon.

"He's your blood. I'm sorry, Aurora. Like I said, I have nothing against you. I'm telling you all this so that you'll be prepared."

"Well hear me, because I'm only saying this once more. I will leave when I'm good and ready, and not a second before."

The cold glare he shoots me in return fills my veins with ice. He leans in, the heat from his anger wafting toward me in warning. "I imagine staying in your daddy's old cottage must bring back some feelings." His voice is low, almost menacing. I hate the way my body trembles in response. "Doesn't it? Especially being there alone at night. When darkness creeps in and you're left isolated with your thoughts, those old memories must destroy you. After what he did to those girls. To you."

This time my body shudders, visibly.

"I'm not alone," I lie. After everything he said, that's what I respond to. I feel compelled to arm myself with something he can't control, even though it isn't true. I am alone, but no one needs to know that. "I'm here with someone."

Tanner looks out the door, searching—for someone or something. "There's no one with you."

I try to hide my swallow by raising my chin. "I came to town to get some things. He's back at the cottage."

"He?"

"A friend," I blurt out, but it's not enough to say *friend*. He needs to know I'm protected. "My fiancé." The lie twists through me, knowing how happy the statement would make Scott. I saw the ring box in his computer bag when I borrowed a pen to scribble him a quick goodbye. Seeing it only hastened my departure. But I can't think about that right now. I can't think about how awful I was to him, leaving without a warning or an explanation.

But I hope the excuse will buy myself some time and hopefully get Tanner off my back. The last thing I need is to give him a reason to rile up the town. If he thinks my stay is temporary, *which it is*, and he knows I'm with someone, *which I'm not*, maybe he will keep his distance.

"I'm going to assume that fiancé of yours is aware of the situation we have here. You're making a mistake, Aurora."

His words hit me deeper than I'll show. He wants me gone. Truly. To heed his warning and leave before I disrupt the financial progress of the town. But I can't for the life of me see how me being here will disrupt anything. And as easy as it would be to pack my things and head back to Durham, I can't leave. Not until I'm able to accomplish what I came here to do. To find peace. To face the past I've kept locked away for so long.

A pressure builds in my throat. "I didn't do anything wrong, *Deputy* Tanner."

"No, not yet. But you are a reminder of the hell your father rained down on this town. You should know, the talk hasn't died just because your father has. We're in a better place here now," he says, straightening his stance. "*Everyone* is."

The way he says *everyone* triggers erratic thoughts to spiral through me, winding and weaving through my chest. I get the feeling he means *Jaxon* is in a better place without me. And that fucking hurts.

While Jaxon and I kept our affection for one another on the down low, it was hard to hide from those we were closest to. No one approved. For so many reasons—our age difference and my father's bad reputation, to name two.

Crossing my arms over my chest, I take in a deep breath. "Well, *everyone* is just going to have to get over it. I'm here.

My dad's cottage is mine now. And I won't be driven away by a bunch of Balsam Grove assholes who feel the need to bully me out of town."

Tanner dips down, lowering his face so his nose is almost touching mine. I flinch in surprise but hold my ground.

"I wish you would reconsider. I'll be watching you, sweetie. Every wrong turn, every establishment you step into, every acquaintance you make. I'll be watching that fiancé of yours, too."

I chuckle, feeling the opposite of amused. "You're going to spy on me, Deputy Tanner? I can't imagine that's legal, not even in Balsam Grove."

His lip curls upward. "Don't say I didn't warn you."

I walk toward the exit, my entire body radiating an uncontrollable heat. I need to get out of here before I say something I'll regret. I reach the door and wrap my hand around the cold metal knob, squeezing it beneath my palm. I turn it and take my first step out the door.

"Hey, Aurora." Tanner's voice crawls over my skin like a swarm of ants. I freeze and turn, meeting his cold-as-ice smile with an expressionless one of my own.

"Welcome back to Balsam Grove." He winks. "Be careful out there."

Aurora

Just minutes later, still flustered from my exchange with *Deputy* Tanner, I'm back to window shopping, slowing my stroll since I've nearly made it to the final block of town. I almost forgot just how small this place is.

None of the shops are familiar, but an empty storefront with an aged, crooked For Sale sign and a green metal park bench out front catches my eye. Beside it is Creek Canvas, a cute shop I recognize from a flyer I saw back at the tourist center. There's an easel painted on the window, the words "May Classes Sold Out" scrawled on in a rainbow of colors.

Heart beating fast, I press my face against the glass to find three rows of easels, a long cabinet along the back wall, and a metal desk in the front corner of the room. The lights are off, and I can't help but imagine what the studio looks like during the day when it's filled with people, colors, and laughter. A wave of nostalgia passes over me, pushing my thoughts back, deep in time, to one of my first interactions with Jaxon Mills.

Aurora, Eight Years Old

I was lost, the woods of a new town still a world of excitement and terror all at once. My parents had warned me to stay close to the cottage, but the further I traveled down the river that passed by my house, the more my curiosity grew.

It was a spotted deer grazing on the tall weeds that caught my eye and had me inching my way deeper into the woods. By the time I realized how far I'd traveled, it was too late. I was lost. Fear filled my lungs as I spun in a circle, kicking up the leaves at my soles as the wind whipped my sleeveless arms. A sob began building in the back of my throat.

There was no way of knowing which direction I was walking, so I'd start in one direction, decide it was wrong, and then turn in another.

After what seemed like hours, I spotted a cottage twice the size of my parents' place, its front door wide open and rock music streaming from within. Hope bloomed in my chest.

The chaotic guitar riff drowned the sounds of my approach. I prayed there was someone in that cottage. Someone who would be nice enough to help me find my way home or call my parents.

It never occurred to me to be afraid of whatever—whoever—I'd find within those walls, but the moment I crossed the threshold, I knew I shouldn't be there. Everything about it felt wrong. Losing my way. Wandering into a stranger's home—uninvited, no less. But I didn't turn around. I couldn't. Not after I saw him.

The boy was facing a long wall when I spotted him, his arm strokes long and wide. His entire body moved in time to the music like he was the conductor of the grandest orchestra. And just like that his symphony began to spring to life before my eyes.

I must have stood there for a good hour undetected. I wasn't trying to hide. The boy simply never took his eyes off that wall. Colors masked the space before him, greens and blues, shaded to form the landscape just outside the cottage door.

There was a wide, winding river that seemed to stretch into infinity beneath the trees and wildlife that came to life on the wall. The mural managed to take up the entire space, and I stared in awe at his creation.

The boy with the wild curls didn't need to face me for me to recognize him. I'd met him and his parents one week before when my family arrived in Balsam Grove. Jaxon Mills was his name. The moment his eyes met mine I understood what it meant to get butterflies. I got them everywhere. In my tummy, in my chest, in my throat, even in my arms and legs.

He wore a beanie on his head, which was odd, considering how sticky hot the air was at the start of summer. The rest of him fit the season. He wore black board shorts and a loose-fitting tank top. We stood a few feet apart, him clueless to the light he'd lit inside me, and me, wide eyes on him, feeling like at any moment I'd begin to fly.

There was only one problem. Jaxon was older. Four years older, to be exact.

Our parents chatted for what seemed like hours. They encouraged him to show me around, so we walked to the French Broad River at the bottom of the hill in our back yard. He skipped rocks. I tried, but because I couldn't swim and was terrified of drowning, I stayed too far back from the edge of the stream to be successful. There were awkward stares and a string of mumbles in return for the only questions I could think to ask—none of them significant. He never once offered a smile, and words were clearly not his favorite.

Standing in front of his masterpiece one week later, I started to understand him a little bit more. Jaxon didn't need words to communicate. He only needed art.

The music stopped abruptly, ripping me from my daydream. My eyes turned from the wall, landing on Jaxon's hard stare and heaving chest. He looked like he'd just run a marathon.

"What are you doing here?" His question boomed, the empty room echoing his words.

"I got lost." I gestured to the door. "It was open. Is there a phone? I need to call my parents."

"Your parents told you not to go far from the cottage. How long have you been lost?

"I-I don't know. A few hours maybe." My cheeks burned with embarrassment.

"You should have stayed close to the stream," he grumbled.

I nodded and swallowed, hating that this cute boy was lecturing me on how to stay safe. "I didn't think I went far, but I guess I did."

"You're about a mile out." He sighed heavily. "I can take you home."

I nodded, thankful despite my humiliation. I watched as he started to clean up his paints and blankets, tossing brushes onto pans. My eyes locked back on the mural. "This is incredible, Jaxon."

With a huff, he stomped the few feet to his iPod stereo and snatched it from its base. "Yeah, well, take a good look because it won't be here long."

"What? Why?" I didn't understand, but panic stretched through me. His art belonged there. In that space, on that wall.

He tossed a brush onto the drop cloth and swiped at the sweat on his forehead. "Eggshell white. That's the color I'm supposed to paint it. I was just messing around."

My jaw dropped. "You're going to paint over it? No, you can't." I was horrified. How could he destroy his own work? It was beautiful. Unique. Any guest would be lucky to have it as part of their stay.

His next glance cut straight through me, so sharp and so cold, I felt it like a swift blade. "I can and I will. Look, I'll walk you home, and your parents will never need to know you disobeyed them. But you need to promise me two things."

I waited for his terms, knowing I'd already agreed to them, whatever they were.

"Not a word about my painting. And do what your parents say. You can't wander off into the woods, Aurora. It's not safe out here. Even hikers travel in pairs or groups."

I forced a nod in agreement, grateful for the deal but still not understanding why he had to destroy his creation. If only there was another way he could keep his art. "Of course," I mumbled in a voice that sounded meek to his boldness. "I promise."

His expression softened almost immediately, and then he stuffed some things into a bag while storing the rest under the sink in the kitchen. When he was finished, he stood and walked toward the door. "All right, let's go."

Aurora

I'm still peering around the studio, trying to make out a piece of unfinished art on an easel at the front of the room, when the ding of a bell followed by the scent of freshly brewed coffee draws my focus to the café next door. Even with the glare of the sun on the window, I can make out a bench seat overlooking the intersection and a long bookshelf beside it.

Yes. Coffee. I'm not sure if a cup will settle my nerves after my run-in with Deputy Dickhead, but it's sure worth a shot.

The bell dings again as I cross the threshold of Creek Café, a homey coffee shop with a long counter and a glass case filled with mouthwatering baked goods. The café is empty except for a pixie-sized woman with short, bright red hair styled in an angled bob who's facing the back counter. She swivels at my approach, revealing a large, rounded belly, sparkling blue eyes, and flawless skin. Wow. She's stunning, and while there's something about her that sticks out like a sore thumb in this town, she also looks like she's right where she belongs.

She wipes a spot off the back counter before her big eyes lock on mine. Her entire face lights up. She tosses the rag to the side and clasps her hands in front of her, resting them on her belly. "Well, well. You must be staying awhile." Her voice is syrupy sweet but strong.

"Um." I look around to confirm that we're the only two in the café. We are, so I let out an awkward laugh at her greeting. "Excuse me?"

She nods toward the front window of the café. "I saw you down the street, eyeing the shops, taking your time like you were memorizing everything. We mostly get passersby around here. No one cares to really take in the town, not unless they're planning to stay awhile."

She must notice the way my wary eyes examine her as she continues to assess my intentions.

"Out of towners," she clarifies. "Hikers, campers—they stop for coffee, sometimes stay for a night, then head for the camp sites and hiking trails. No offense, but you don't look like you're going hiking anytime soon." Out of my periphery I see her check out my sandals, khaki shorts, and white blouse. "You just look like you're planning to stay awhile."

I press my hands on the counter, considering her words while searching the menu written in chalk above her head. "And *you* sound like you've lived here awhile."

"You could say that. Five years, in fact. What's your story?"

"Just moved here." My eyes flicker to hers, almost expecting her to know who I am. "Not sure how long I'll be staying, though. Guess it depends how good the coffee is."

Her laugh is soft and airy, her fair-skinned cheeks now a pinch of pink like she was worried she'd assumed wrong. I return her smile.

"The pressure is on. Pick your poison. Just don't make me blend anything." Her face twists. "That shit's premade and weak. You look like you're here for the strong stuff, anyway."

That I am. "Americano. Let me see what you got."

The barista smiles as she focuses on the metal contraption behind the counter. I know nothing about making coffee, but the tap-tapping of old coffee grounds falling into the trash mesmerizes me. I watch in fascination as she presses a button to grind the beans, simultaneously catching steaming water in a cup. Then she starts the espresso drip.

"Would you like something to eat? There's a full breakfast menu." She nods to a container of trifold papers on the counter. "And fresh pastries." She gestures to the glass container at the other end of the counter.

The woman continues talking, letting me have time to think as she turns a lever and slowly pours the espresso over the hot water.

"You may have seen the bakery across the street," she explains. "Meg and I have an arrangement. I give her fresh coffee grounds, and she gives me some goodies from her shop every morning. Since you'll be here for a while, you should stop by and meet her. You'll probably leave a few pounds heavier, but trust me when I say, it's worth it."

She winks as she places a steaming, pale yellow coffee mug on a saucer and slides it to me. She rests her elbows on the counter, leans in to hold her face in her palms, and waits. I stare at the coffee, drinking in the smell before I even taste it. She continues to smile expectantly, confident in her skills. I examine the cup in my hands, enjoying the anticipation on her face before tilting my head. "What is your name?"

She stands, pulling her shoulders back, eyes shining. "Claire. And you are?"

I've just put the cup to my lips, but I pull it away to respond. "Aurora." And then it's back to my lips, and I'm sipping my first taste of Claire's Americano. "This is incredible."

She shrugs, but it's the joy she's trying to hide with pinched lips and sparkling eyes that says the most. Claire is every bit as endearing as her café.

"And I'd love a pastry. A chocolate croissant, if you have one."

Her laughter comes out light and bubbly. "We have one left. It's all yours."

"Why the laugh?"

"Oh, it's nothing. My friend is the only one around here who orders those. Meg makes them special for him. It's love. What can I say?"

I hold up my hands. "Please, let him have it. I can order something else."

But Claire's already moving behind the glass case and reaching inside it for the lonely chocolate croissant. "Nonsense. First come, first served." My mouth waters as she heats it for a few seconds, then places it on a square dish and slides it in front of me. Moving her hands to her hips, she shrugs. "Besides, there's more where that came from at Meg's bakery."

I unzip my phone wallet. "What's the damage?"

Claire rings me up, and as she does, I let my eyes wander around the room. The interior walls are alternating white brick and grayish blue sheetrock, the vintage chandeliers a matching blue with crystals dangling on short strings. There's a living room set up on the other side of the room with plush, blue plaid couches and oversized chairs surrounding a fireplace, and there's a reading nook beside a bookshelf filled with books and magazines near the front window.

The café is cute and cozy, but it's not until I look around and see the silver-framed art on the walls that I fall completely in love. A striking painting near me depicts an odd-shaped tree casting shade in the woods. The sunshine peeks through the clouds above a rolling, luscious green landscape. An uphill dirt road rests between a narrow section of tall trees.

This place has captivated the very essence of Balsam Grove. Its rugged coziness, its natural appeal, its earth-soaked tones. But the oil paintings on canvas displayed around the room are where the real stories are told. There's history here, and I want to immerse myself in all of it.

I don't even realize I've walked a few feet to the nearest wall to examine one of the paintings until my nose is only inches from its intricate lines and vibrant colors. Everything about the art comes to life as my eyes roam over it.

Only one person could have painted this.

"Incredible," I breathe as a feeling of pride swells in my throat.

"If you stare at that painting any harder, I might make you buy it."

Claire's voice makes me jump, transporting me back to the present, back to Balsam Grove and back to Creek Café, which officially has me under its spell.

I'm about to gush to Claire about the painting and ask her who painted the series—not because I don't know, but because I need to hear it—when her eyes fall to my chest.

"Aurora, oh my God."

I look down, and it's only then that I feel the sting of hot coffee seeping through my thin, white cotton blouse and onto my chest. "Oh!" I exclaim. "I didn't realize..." Looking into the nearly empty cup, I frown. "I'm so sorry. I'll buy another."

Claire waves a hand in front of her face. "Absolutely not." She takes the cup and saucer from my hands and moves back around the counter. "There's a bathroom over there if you want to clean up." Her head nods to the other side of the room, near the living room setup. "I'll have a to-go cup ready when you're done." She winks. "Can't do much damage with those."

I know better than to argue with kindness. With an apologetic look, I step into the bathroom and flip on the light. I shut the door behind me, then look back at myself in the sink mirror.

For the first time in years, I left the house without a full sheet of makeup on my face. Without eyeliner circling my light blue eyes, without exaggerating my natural pout with my favorite deep rose-colored lipstick, without painting on my eyebrows and layering three thick coats of mascara before curling my long lashes. It's like I'm staring back at a stranger.

Scott is all about keeping up appearances. Since we often traveled into Raleigh where he works, he expected me to fit in with his crowd. Suited to perfection, makeup a requirement, shiny jewels to complement every look. There was always someone to impress, so there was no such thing as a casual night out.

At first I didn't mind. It was nice to dress up and enjoy an expensive glass of wine, but when monthly events became weekly events and eventually started slipping into our weekday evenings, I feared this lifestyle was becoming the new norm. I'd already lost so much leaving Balsam Grove. My father getting placed in the institution was the final nail in the coffin. Except I still existed within the tight spaces of that coffin, a thin stream of air tethering me to my old life as I slowly slipped from one world to another.

I appreciated Scott for adopting me into his world without question, for showing me the ropes in a high-class society that embraced me right back. To them, I wasn't my father's daughter. I was Scott Turner's best friend-turned girlfriend. The legal assistant with the sharp style, the beautiful smile, and the stilettos that made me appear five foot four instead of my natural five foot one.

Living with a mask made it easier to be accepted but harder to breathe. No matter how many dresses I tried on, no matter how many smiles I wore, none of it ever felt right.

Is that why I'm here? To feel free from the masks? From the charade? Things with Scott aren't *that* bad. He loves me. He takes care of me. For heaven's sake, we've been friends practically our entire lives. That's got to count for something.

And if I'm being totally honest, part of me misses him, even after only one night of being away. But it's the *him* before all the romantic complications that I miss. The friendship. And there's no going back. He's already admitted to waiting a decade to make any sort of move with me, which tells me it was never about friendship with him at all. The friendship part was the façade to keep me around in hopes that one day I would feel the same way for him that he feels for me.

Maybe that's harsh. Everyone wants to be able to fall in love with their best friend. He just wasn't the one.

Shaking my head, I grab a paper towel and wet it, then pat down my coffee-scented skin. I take my time, thinking and dabbing, quickly giving up on trying to remove the stain from my shirt. Maybe it's time I shed more than my makeup.

With quick contemplation as I chew on the corner of my bottom lip, I give in. I unbutton my top, peel the stained shirt from my skin, and toss it in the trash, leaving me wearing only my cream camisole that was luckily left unharmed. It's like I've shed a layer of skin, and I'm just now realizing how heavy it was.

For the first time in years, I *really* breathe—a full inhale that fills my lungs to capacity. Then I exhale.

Away from Durham, I'm finally on my own. No expectations. No responsibilities. I have enough money saved up to take a break and figure my shit out before I'll need to get a job. I'm going to remember who I was before my future was destroyed and replaced with investigations and courtrooms and conspiracy theories and psychologists.

I've come to the right place.

I'm finally ready to exit the bathroom, grab my coffee, and head to the general store when a telephone starts ringing from the front of the café. Claire's tiny but powerful voice greets the caller. She sees me and waves, looking apologetic and mouthing "I'm sorry" before she slips into the back room.

We could be friends, Claire and me. She's nice and chatty, but not annoyingly so. Curious, but unobtrusive, and that alone is refreshing.

Suffering from brain trauma came with an extensive care plan I wasn't prepared for. Years of hospital visits, rehabilitation, and psychiatric evaluations took their toll on me.

So the fewer questions people ask, the better, and I'll pay them the same respect.

As I wander around the living area of the café, I take in more of the art displayed on the walls: an old, lonely mill with its front door ajar; a red house on a hill with a silhouette in one of the windows; an odd flower after a rain shower; a capsized rowboat wedged between a log and a creek rock.

Each piece captures a simple but unique moment in time, and there's something breathtaking about that. An untold story with a single focal point, bright and alive, as if it's proving a history that once existed. It's proof of life. Of something real.

But out of all the beautiful paintings, it's the largest one that holds my gaze captive. Just the sight of it framed above the fireplace takes the wind from my lungs.

A familiar bridge sits over a deep and quick-moving river, releasing into the falls below.

Hollow Falls.

I pull in a sharp breath, awakening from my daydream to find myself still immersed in the incredible detail of the art on the wall. I take in every imperfection in the wood, every trace of wear telling the age of the structure. I drown in the smooth water that runs over rock and land beneath the arc that brings movement and thrill to the art.

Hollow Falls is by far the most beautiful waterfall I've ever seen—both in real life and on canvas. It's as if it's living and breathing right before me. The rapids slamming into rock and running over the lip of the falls. The freefall down into the plunge pool below, creating an explosion of mist and undertow in a powerful collision. It's as dangerous as it is beautiful. Feared as it is admired.

I've never been so afraid of a still object in my life.

And that's when I realize I'm shaking. But why? The image isn't a new one. Hollow Falls is where I learned to swim. I spent countless days frolicking in its waters, climbing and jumping from its rocks. But staring back at the canvas now, it's like I've been struck and injured.

I'm still staring at the image when the familiar chime of the door sounds, so muted in the background of my thoughts that I don't react right away.

My heart recognizes him first and it beats firmly to his approach. With every step, I'm awakened by his presence, just as I was that night I jumped into Hollow Falls and found him drifting there alone.

My chest squeezes as I remember how my world flipped upside down the summer of my fifteenth year, all set to that same backdrop.

5

Aurora, Fifteen Years Old

I was only eight years old when my parents first brought me to their new vacation home in Balsam Grove. They promised a picturesque cottage in the mountains, sitting among tall, rolling foothills, dirt paths that led to a plethora of waterfalls, hiking trails we would traverse as a family, and the guarantee of making new friends. It was a promise of perfection. Quality time. Adventure. And I believed their lies. Every single one of them.

A war waged on between my parents for years due to my father's schizophrenia and his refusal to seek treatment. I wasn't as oblivious as they thought, and eventually, their fighting became harder to ignore. The arguing was bad, but the silence was worse. Their emotional distance stretched canyons, and the tension became a constant, a void weighing down the cottage to damn near suffocation.

I was fifteen when I experienced the first rise of a panic attack, though I didn't understand what was going on with me at the time. But when the walls began to cave in around my heart and squeeze my chest, I knew I couldn't take another second of their hate-filled voices. I flung the wooden dowel from the sill, slid open the window, and slipped into the darkness.

I ran, losing air with each step, but instead gaining something more valuable. *Peace.* I chased it, stumbling on the twigs and rocks my flashlight failed to warn me of. I let it wrap me in its embrace, dodging trees and branches that seemed to spring from nowhere, traveling along the river and letting my flashlight guide me to the one place I knew would bring me back to life.

Hollow Falls is one of the many hidden jewels in Balsam Grove. It was a popular hangout for the local high school kids, but even they were respectful and cleaned up after themselves after a late night of partying. I may have watched them from a distance a time or two, thanks to a particular neighbor boy who held my interest.

But that night, I was alone. Hollow Falls belonged to me. I stepped onto a rock perched above the water, testing its sturdiness. I'd jumped from the same rock before—only ten feet high compared to the lip of the falls at thirty-five feet—but never when surrounded by so much darkness.

Before I could lose my nerve, I stripped down to my underwear, took a deep breath, and jumped.

The crisp bite of the water awakened something in me, bringing me to the surface and giving me that first deep breath after nearly drowning back at the cottage. That breath—it saved me, bringing clarity when my eyes finally opened to the wading body of Jaxon Mills. I swallowed against the instant thrumming in my chest. The boy I'd only spoken to a handful of times, who I'd often watch from afar, was now watching me. Waiting.

I'd known him for years, though our four-year age gap made friendship seemingly impossible. He spent most of his time working for his parents, anyway, moodily tending to the rental cottages at all hours of the day. As far as I could tell, Jaxon rarely made time for friends. Even when he was surrounded by others, he somehow seemed to be alone.

But there he was, outlined by the moon, beads of water rolling down the deep crease between his eyes as starlight gleamed off the tops of his cheeks. His full lips were masked with a thin coat of river, and the attractive slope of his nose scrunched as if there was an itch he didn't dare scratch. His exhale was long and slow as he assessed me, the intruder to his quiet night.

"Your parents know you're out here?" His tone carried curiosity, but it wasn't at all threatening.

My cheeks warmed as I laughed to mask my shame of being far too young to traverse the woods alone. I was sure that was what he was thinking. He saw me as a child with a curfew. Still a little girl, though my curves spoke differently.

If only Jaxon knew how I saw him. If only he could feel how my heart slammed the walls of my chest at his nearness. My gnawing crush on Jaxon that began when I was only eight years old never faded, but it was easier to manage when I wasn't treading water mere inches from him. Temptation lashed at me like an untrained beast. Boys didn't look like

Jaxon in Durham. They weren't made from the mountains like he was. They were scholars, bred from the wealthiest families. They were clean-cut, meticulous in their appearance. They were phonies in comparison to what I saw in this boy with few words.

Embarrassed to be caught, I righted my stance and leveled him with my eyes, trying to project confidence I didn't own. "They were preoccupied when I left. Are you going to tell them?"

Silence stretched and rippled between us, the stillness of the night balancing me. I knew in that moment, despite the awkward run-in, everything was just as it should be.

"No," he said, and I released a light breath in relief. "But it's dark. Anything could happen, and no one would know where to start looking for you."

He was right, but my pride refused to let him know it. I huffed in annoyance, pulled my eyes away, and focused instead on the thirty-five foot drop at Jaxon's back.

He didn't ask me to leave. In fact, he didn't ask me any other questions that night. We swam slow circles around each other while an understanding grew through a comforting silence. And in that silence, an invisible line was drawn between us. An admission that there was something sparking that shouldn't be. A piqued interest. A mutual curiosity.

Although my fear of water had diminished once I'd learned how to swim, I knew I was already in way too deep. And I wasn't sure if Jaxon was someone who would let me drown, or someone who would save me.

The night Jaxon and I found ourselves swimming together beneath the falls became the first of many. A friendship budded there. An unspoken understanding. A forbidden attraction.

From that night forward, he stopped glaring at me when we'd spot each other in the woods. Instead, he'd invite me along from one cottage to the next as we tended to his list of duties. He didn't mind that I talked his ear off about philosophy and my desperation to spend a summer in Italy under the Tuscan sun. He simply smiled at the way I lit up about my dreams and continued with his chores in silence.

Until one day when everything changed again.

"What is all this?" I asked him as I climbed off his motorcycle and assessed the backpack he made me carry as we zoomed through the woods.

We'd arrived at a small clearing on the other side of Hollow Falls. There was a hill there with unique branches and vines that fell over a round clearing, like a secret alcove beneath the trees. He set up a canvas, and suddenly it made sense. He wanted to paint. But when it came time to sit down and begin mixing the colors as I'd often seen him do, he handed the brush to me instead.

"I'll teach you."

My heart quickened in my chest. My eyes batted between him and the blank canvas. I shook my head, already terrified of failure. "Me? I'll mess up."

"You can't possibly mess this up, Aurora. I promise."

I moved forward despite my fears and took the brush from him anyway, excited to try. Trusting in his promise. He smiled, knowing all too well what was going on in my head.

And so it began: my first art lesson. It stretched for hours as he taught me the basics of painting. He taught me how to translate the scene before me onto canvas in a way that had always seemed like magic when I'd watched him do it. And when my brush hit that canvas for the first time, I was hooked.

He treated me as if I was meant to be there, in turn creating an impossible feat for my heart. I couldn't combat my attraction, but I managed it well...at first. But as the days blended into nights, and the nights back into days, I found my control slipping. I became a pebble in a stream, facing an impossible river after the heaviest storm. My only hope was that Jaxon would be there to greet me once I finally fell.

But he wouldn't.

By the end of the summer, I had fallen for Jaxon completely. And with five days left before my family ripped me from the woods to head back to Durham, I wanted every extra second I could get with him. But while I was trying to get closer to him, he was subtly pushing me away.

I should have taken the first hint when he walked straight past me during my morning walk upstream toward his house. Without a word, without a look, he kept walking.

Had I done something? Said something? Become too annoying for him to handle? I had no idea, but I was far too in love to give up the chase after such a perfect summer. Surely, despite our age difference, he felt it too.

But then the next clue came, and then the next. Until we were down to the final week of our stay, and I was beginning to itch with anxiety, every nervous emotion becoming too much to stifle.

One day in town, I ran into Jaxon's best friend, Danny. He was home from college for the summer and let it slip that there would be a party that night at Hollow Falls. Desperate to see Jaxon again, I asked if I could come along. Danny, being the nice guy he was, said okay.

That night, Danny and I met at a crossing in the trail where a path to his house joined mine and walked the rest of the way there together. His eyes kept darting to me suspiciously. "You and Jax have been hanging out a lot, yeah? That's what I've been hearing, anyway."

My cheeks heated, and I shook my head. "Not so much lately." My eyes shot to his. "Who's been talking?"

He gave me a wry smile, like I could have easily guessed. "Tanner's been running his mouth, of course. He doesn't like the idea of you two together, Little A. Anyway, just warning ya. The last thing you both need is his dad catching wind of whatever's going on."

Danny was referencing Tanner's dad, Sheriff Brooks. An old fashioned gentle giant of a man who'd struck up a friendship with my father. But my heart sank with his words.

"Nothing's going on, Danny. Honest." I hated how true that was. "We were just friends."

"Were?"

I shrugged, feeling I'd said enough.

"You think Jax will be okay with you coming tonight? I mean, you are pretty young and there's going to be booze—"

My laugh was loud, cutting him off. "How old are you again?" My challenging smirk made him laugh and nod in concession.

"Alright, well don't say I didn't warn you. It might get kind of wild out there tonight, and I'm sure you have a curfew or something."

I hated the regret in his tone. The urgency to get me to change my mind like I was the little sister he never had.

"It's fine," I assured him. "Let's just go."

From there, I could see the party at a distance. It was nearing sunset, the skies crisp with a blend of orange and purple tones filling the horizon, but the party was already well-lit by a half-dozen floodlights hooked up to a generator that surrounded the pool of the falls.

Danny didn't argue with me again, though he did walk a few steps ahead of me so he could enter the scene of the party first. As if he didn't even know I was there.

When Jaxon saw me, his expression filled with shock and anger. His eyes darted between Danny and then me, narrowing when he realized his best friend must have invited me.

"Go home, Aurora," he demanded from his rock a few feet away.

Embarrassment radiated through me, causing my throat to tighten with emotion. All dozen or so pairs of eyes seemed to be on us. And if that wasn't enough, the raven-haired girl with the tiny black bikini and perfectly bronzed skin who was sitting beside Jaxon giggled.

Was that why he had been avoiding me for the past week? Because his friends were home? Did I embarrass him? Or was he just busy spending all his time with someone else? Someone older. Someone prettier. Someone who could give him things he thought I couldn't. Things I could only dream about.

My chin trembled as I avoided the blaze of his eyes, fearing his next words would be just as fiery.

"It's late. Go home now while you can still find your way." This time he spoke gentler, like he cared.

I stepped forward, ignoring his request, and ignoring the hurt that stirred within me. "I think I'll stay for a while." He tensed as I stepped onto the rock and sat beside him, opposite the girl whose name I didn't care to learn.

Eventually, everyone started partying. Cans of beer were passed around, music played from someone's speaker, and everyone was in the river. Everyone except for Jaxon and me. We were still perched on our rock, the lights filling the space below us and the trees blanketing us in the shadows of the night.

Danny's distant voice reached us from where we sat. "You sure your old man won't be sneaking up on us tonight?" he asked Tanner as he approached him in the water.

Tanner rolled his eyes and shook his head. "No way. Not tonight. There's some block party going on in town, so he'll be hovering around Main Street all night."

Relief left my chest in a soft sigh. I didn't need my parents finding out I was partying in the woods with a bunch of college-age kids.

"You really shouldn't have come." Jaxon's words broke through my quick second of peace—his regret apparent.

"Why?" I asked it boldly, wanting the no-bullshit answer. The one I doubted Jaxon would give.

He remained silent.

"I leave in a week." The hurt in my tone reeked of desperation, I knew it. I looked at him, trying to read his expression in the dark, but his profile was all I got. "I don't want the summer to end. I don't want to leave."

His head dropped as a sadness filled the air.

That's when I knew it wasn't just me. Jaxon would miss me too. Maybe he'd been keeping me away because he knew I was going to leave anyway. Everything ached—my heart, my soul. Everything felt so clear, yet so wrong at the same time.

I swallowed my nerves before reaching for his hand, just the tips of his fingers to mine. He allowed it—the touch innocent—but the look he gave me next wasn't. He stared at me in a way that pinned my heart to the walls of my chest. His fingers wove through mine, fully, pure with intention, and they squeezed.

And then he leaned in, eyes darting to my mouth as I wet my lips in anticipation. I'd waited eight summers for this moment. For that kiss that would change everything. For my feelings to be returned. It didn't matter that there was a river filled with Jaxon's closest friends below us. It didn't matter that The Black Eyed Peas' "I Gotta Feeling" wasn't the most romantic soundtrack to our first kiss. All that mattered was that his lips touched mine, my eyes fell shut, and I let Jaxon take my very first first.

My insides exploded with fireworks, leaving me light-headed and quivering with nerves as I leaned in for more. I was aching for him and wanting him to know. "Jax," I murmured against his lips.

I wish I had known that my voice was all it would take to break the spell. I would have happily become mute. Suddenly, he was ripping his mouth from mine and pulling his hand away like he'd been burned. "Shit. What the hell are we doing?" he hissed. "We can't, Aurora. Fuck. You're too young."

My eyes stung with unshed tears. "Who cares?"

"I care!" His angry whisper zipped across the space between us, stinging me with his poison. He growled and shook his head. Then he ripped off his shirt and stood. "Go home, Aurora." He leapt, arms first, body arched, fingertips piercing the water first.

That splash was like a sledgehammer to my gut. And that wasn't even the worst part. When he surfaced, he swam straight for the pretty girl with the perfectly bronzed skin whose name I'd learned was Presley. Time slowed as my heart hardened, preparing to be shattered as he sidled up to her. She giggled, oblivious to the girl in the shadows who he'd just kissed, and wrapped her arms around his neck as his gaze shot up at me, signaling his final farewell.

This time I listened. This time I left.

I arrived back at the cottage in tears, hiccuping each breath as it came. I slid through my window at close to two in the morning, just as my mom burst through the door, her eyes ablaze with anger.

"I don't even want to know where you've been, young lady. It doesn't matter. Pack your things. We're leaving first thing in the morning."

She retreated with a slam of my door.

It wasn't until the next morning that I learned the reason for her outburst and for our early departure. My parents sat me down to announce their separation and that my father would be staying in Balsam Grove, alone, while I returned to Durham with my mother.

Those two days should have been the worst days of my life. Unfortunately, the worst was yet to come.

6

Aurora

Breathing becomes a foreign concept as I try my best to ground myself back into reality. I watch the man tense as his hard eyes meet mine and my ears become the subwoofer to the pounding in my chest. Although there's no lightning to accompany his gaze this time, shock zaps through me.

Jaxon Mills.

My savior. My destroyer.

He's here.

The coffee shop has gone silent, save for the sound of my sharp intake of air, the rustle of my shorts as I run my palms against them, and the AC unit on full blast. I swallow to reign in my hammering heart, because although I regularly punch fear in the face, this feels like something else.

There's a casualness in his stance as he waits, assessing me as if he can't believe I'm really here. I'm assessing him right back, and like an addict, I can't get enough.

The natural curls of his thick, reddish-brown hair hide behind a slouchy, navy knit beanie, and a full beard masks his strong jaw, calling attention to the overcast sky of his eyes. My heart grows full knowing that he's kept his hair long, the way I always loved. I can't believe he's here.

I had almost convinced myself that last night was a dream and that Jaxon wasn't really still in Balsam Grove. I even lied to myself, told myself I didn't want him to be here. I know now there's nothing I wanted more.

The treble in my heart quickens.

His athletic build is thicker than I remember, harder, cut with age and his outdoorsy nature. The strong lines of his thick arms are visible under the short sleeves of his solid red shirt. Tattered jeans splotched with paint cover his legs and lead to the brown flip flops on his feet.

He's different than I remember in more ways than one, but the feelings swarming in my chest are all the same. I'm gutted at the sight of him, yet magnetized by his presence. My senses awaken at the nearness of it all.

Not knowing what to do next, I do what comes naturally when it comes to confrontation. I step directly into it, closing the gap between us as my hands move to my hips, my fingers curling into fists. I tilt my head to let out a breath.

"I thought that was you creeping around my place last night."

His jaw hardens, eyes shining with anger. "Nice to see you, too, Aurora."

Everything about his rough voice fills me with the same shame I felt walking away from him after my father's trial. He must hate me. But the way he curls his tongue on the first "r" of my name, transports me right back to our last day together. Back to the courtroom. Back to his pleading, desperate eyes I failed to get lost in. If I had, there is no way in hell I would have walked out that door.

Or maybe I would have walked out that door no matter what. I knew there was nothing I could do to repair the damage and embarrassment that riddled my soul. That day in court, I officially became the daughter of an attempted murderer. Unofficially, I was the daughter of a serial murderer who had taken the lives of six innocent people.

But my father wasn't the only guilty party. Jaxon should have never confessed my secrets. He had no right. And because of that, two hearts broke that day.

Fast forward to today, and nothing has changed. The debris from the destruction so many years ago still exists. We're ruined.

Still holding my gaze, Jaxon finally breaks the silence. "Let's get one thing straight. I wasn't creeping around your place last night."

I let out a laugh, nerves rattling my chest. "So you just happened to be traipsing around my cottage on my first night here? C'mon, Jaxon." My attempt at playful comes off all wrong, more accusing, and I instantly regret it.

"Don't flatter yourself," he growls, his face darkening in color. "I had no idea you were back." After a few heart-pounding beats, he shakes his head and looks away.

"So that *was* you last night. I thought maybe I'd dreamed it." His eyes flicker to mine, spreading heat up my neck and into my cheeks. "What were you doing walking around in a storm?" I ask, quickly trying to cover the fact that I do still dream about Jaxon, even if that's not how I meant it. "A tree could have taken you out."

He lets out a sarcastic breath. "I can manage the woods just fine. But I had no choice last night. My dog gets spooked during the storms, and sometimes she runs off."

Does he still live with his parents? The air grows cold. The town's opinion doesn't worry me so much, but I was never good enough for Jake and Diana's son.

"And you think your dog found my cottage last night? Why?"

He shrugs, his thick lips pursing in annoyance, bringing my attention to his perfect mouth. There was a time I knew every inch of Jaxon well. There was a time when those lips belonged to me.

"Your cottage has been empty for a long time. She slips through the doggy door and sleeps there sometimes, especially when there's a storm."

"What? What doggy door?"

My heart is beating fast. How has everything changed yet stayed exactly the same? He doesn't respond, but in the seconds that follow, realization dawns on me way too fast.

How could I have forgotten?

Aurora

A few weeks after I'd moved in with my father I hadn't even had time to adjust to the fact that the cottage was now my permanent home. After my mom died, my world blackened. I didn't speak. I barely moved. I certainly didn't eat. Voices penetrated the sound barrier to my brain like waves of white noise.

Aunt Cyndi tried to keep me with her in Durham, pleading with Child Protective Services to allow me to spend the final year of high school with my friends where I'd lived my entire life. She tried to tell them that my father wasn't well, but just because a person has a mental disorder doesn't make them an unfit parent. There needs to be proof that they're dangerous or neglectful. My father had never harmed a single hair on my head, and his distance over the last two years had everything to do with my mother keeping me away from him.

So I moved to Balsam Grove, locked myself in my room, and made no plans to come out. But that day, instead of ignoring the sound of the doorbell, I pushed myself to stand…to walk to the door…and to open it.

My father stood there, a smile plastered on his face as he stared down at a white and black puppy. She had sharp, foxlike ears, stubby legs, and ice blue eyes, and she was playing with an old pair of shoelaces, pawing them into her mouth. I looked back up.

He was smiling. That was the first thing I thought. Before thinking about the puppy he held close to his chest—before remembering that I had spent the last three weeks dwelling in unspeakable grief—I thought about my father's smile and how I hadn't seen it in years. A pang hit my chest. I missed his smile, but I missed him more.

He handed her to me. A Siberian Husky, he told me. Lacey, I named her as we played tug of war with the shoelace. And suddenly, my world wasn't so dark. I had my dad back. I had a new friend in the form of a little yelping puppy. I had distractions.

Unfortunately, I'd already learned that distractions come and go, but the darkness always remains. It was up to me to keep the light that still burned inside me from flickering out.

Aurora

"Oh my God. Lacey."

Swallowing, I force myself to breathe against my quickening heartbeat. "How is she?" Heat and tension waft between us.

"She's happy. Just has a thing about storms, that's all."

And now I get it. Totally. Completely. My chest swells with sadness, and a sting pricks the backs of my eyes. How could I have forgotten about my Lacey? The last time I saw her there was a storm, just like the one we had last night. She didn't seem afraid of it then, though maybe I was too busy being angry with Jaxon that night to notice much else.

Panic works its way through me. "Did you find her last night?" I ask, praying for an answer that will stop an attack in its tracks.

"Yeah." He says it like it's no big deal. "It happens all the time. If she doesn't go through the doggy door in your kitchen, she hides under the back porch. That's where I would have checked, but then I saw you in your window, and, well…she came home this morning."

My chest ripples with heat, realizing he wasn't there for me at all. What did I expect? Jaxon and I haven't spoken in years. And besides, how could he have possibly known I was back?

"Just do me a favor and knock next time." My annoyance seems to fuel his arrogance, and a glare lights up his face.

"Sure thing," he spits back, angrily. "But I did knock. Pounded pretty hard, actually. Saw a car in the driveway and figured someone was there. I didn't want to scare whoever it was since it was past midnight and all. And by the way"—my laser beam of a glare hits him right between the eyes—"you should really put that thing under the carport. You're lucky a tree didn't take out a window."

When his white smile flashes wide, I have the distinct urge to stomp on his toe. It's a ridiculous thought. Childish, even. But I can't help but think how good it would feel to wipe that condescending look right off his face.

Instead I step up to him, toe-to-toe. It all feels so forbidden, just like my feelings for him when I was too young to have them. "Look. I'll tell you the same thing I told Tanner to give you some peace of mind. I'm not here to cause trouble." I take a deep breath, gathering my cool before opening my mouth again. "I'll be in and out of town before you know it."

"That's probably for the best," he says, not even a smidge of hesitation.

Who knew the pieces of my heart were still whole enough to break again? But they do. They crumble and fall to my feet at his words.

His expression softens. "I didn't mean it like that."

I let out a laugh. "Yes, you did."

My eyes flicker away, attempting to hide the hurt I still feel when he looks at me with those blustery eyes, the ones made from marble and magic and a little bit of mystery. I wish I could say they do nothing to me. I wish I could say that staring back at this gorgeous man confirms that the numbness I've felt for years is permanent. But I can't. I'm captivated by everything he is, even though he's a stranger to me now.

The sound of the door alarm breaks our staredown. After a rocky step backwards, I look toward the entrance to see Tanner approaching the counter with a nod in my direction. "Miss June, I see you've discovered the best coffee in Balsam Grove." He nods at Jaxon. "Morning, Mills."

"Deputy," Jaxon greets in return, never taking his eyes from me. He quirks his lip. "Don't you mean the *only* coffee in Balsam Grove?"

Tanner flips around when he gets to the counter, leaning back and folding his arms. "I guess that's true, now, isn't it?" His eyes move between us for a few beats before frowning at us both. "Well, this is awkward."

My jaw tightens. Did he follow me in here just to harass me? Or is this his normal morning stop?

"Not sure why you care." Jaxon cocks a brow. "Nothing better to do today, Deputy?"

Tanner's lip tilts up as his eyes narrow in on Jaxon. "Sure as hell nothing better than this, Mills. I'm claiming my front row seat to watch this shit show from start to finish. Is this what they call a love triangle? Or maybe I'll get lucky and find myself with a front row seat to some full-on ménage a trois action."

"What the hell are you talking about?" Jaxon growls.

My cheeks flame with embarrassment, and Tanner tosses his head back with a laugh. "Balsam Grove's tragic love story continues, with a twist. What does your fiancé think of you getting reacquainted with your ex, Aurora? That why you kept him home today?"

Everything freezes, and all I can hear is the pounding in my chest.

"I'm coming, I'm coming!" Claire's voice cuts through the silence as she rushes in from the back door. "I'm so sorry. You have to forgive my—" She rounds a pillar and almost jumps when she sees the three of us, stopping in her tracks. "Oh my. Aurora, it looks like you've made some friends."

My skin tingles at the word *friends*. I look at Jaxon, whose eyes have hardened in Tanner's direction. A wave of unease fills the air.

"Why do I feel like I interrupted something?" she asks with nervous humor, glancing between the three of us. No one answers as she places her apron around her neck and starts to fix a couple coffees.

Feeling the flush of my cheeks heat beyond reason, I slide past Jaxon, trying to ignore the gale of his eyes as I grab my to-go coffee and toss my pastry into the thin paper bag Claire left for me.

"I better get going," I say to no one in particular. "Thanks again, Claire. It was nice to meet you." After a quick nod to Tanner and a fleeting glance at Jaxon, I make fast work toward the exit.

As the door shuts behind me, I hear Jaxon's faint voice speak to Claire. "Wait a second. Was that the last chocolate croissant?"

7

Jaxon

"Can one of you *please* tell me why my customer just walked out of here like she saw a ghost?"

I don't even have time to process what just happened before Claire starts in on us. She stands behind the counter wearing an incredulous expression, her head cocked to the side and a hand pressed to her hip.

I swallow as my eyes flit back to the door just as Aurora's petite frame slips out of view. My heart lurches in my chest, toward her, and I'm not opposed to chasing after it.

Aurora June. With her round-shaped face and prominent, deep-set blue, she's still a vision of innocence and beauty, with a defiant edge. I've never met a more curious girl in my life. I always did feel like she could see right through me, too.

Just like last night as she stared back at me through the window. And today, the moment our eyes locked.

"That's all your boy here," Tanner says, tipping his coffee at me with accusing eyes. "Seems nothing has changed. Am I right?" He raises his brows at me in a challenge. I clench my fists and roll my eyes. Now is not the time for Tanner to start shit with me.

He must notice my agitation because he lets out a knowing chuckle and shakes his head. "I need to run back to the station, doll. Let me know if you need anything while Danny's covering for Pops."

Tanner tips his hat at Claire and then leaves—without paying, as usual. By now, she's used to it, so she doesn't even bat an eye. The dick could at least leave a tip.

Claire's husband and my best friend, Danny Andrews, has been working round the clock for three days while Sheriff Brooks helps a rescue team up north search for a helicopter that crashed somewhere in the woods. When Danny got the call from Sheriff Brooks to cover him, he didn't hesitate one bit. I imagine Tanner's pretty peeved about that, since they're both in the running for sheriff once Brooks hangs his belt.

I look up to find Claire's eyes trained on me. I'm not sure what to tell her, so I aim for humor. "Seriously, though. Did you really just give her the last croissant?"

Claire rolls her eyes and shoves my coffee at me. It splashes through the hole of the to-go lid and lands on the counter. "I sure did. Paying customers first, Jax. You'll have to get your fix from Meg."

I groan. "Seriously, Claire? You know I can't step foot in that bakery."

"Why not? C'mon. Meg's a sweet girl and she really likes you. Like, *really* likes you. Just take her on another date and see how it goes. Give her a chance. For God's sake, give *someone* a chance. It might as well be her. You'd be a hell of a lot better for her than Tanner. And she'd be a whole lot better for you than that Valerie chick."

I cringe at the mention of Valerie. I'd almost managed to forget my fling with the socialite from Asheville. It was fun while it lasted, but it was never meant to be more than a stolen fuck in a hotel room every few weeks. And Claire can't stand her. I think that's why she's been pushing me off on Meg, which I don't understand at all. Just because Meg and I are both single doesn't mean we belong together. I've been single for seven years. In fact, the reason why just walked out that door.

"Just drop it with Meg, okay? Tanner is insanely in love with the girl."

"And she's insanely in love with *you*."

"And she'd probably be insanely in love with Tanner if you'd stop filling her mind with unicorns and rainbows."

Claire lets out a breath of annoyance. "You, sir, think far too highly of yourself."

Shaking my head, I step back. "C'mon, Claire, give me a break. I'm on two hours of sleep and I've got other stuff on my mind. You're going to have to play matchmaker with someone else."

She sighs dramatically. "Fine. Tell you what. You explain what just happened with Aurora, and I'll get your precious croissant for you while you watch the café."

Now she's speaking my language. "Deal." I hop onto the counter and take a sip of coffee.

"What are you doing?" Claire squeals. "Get your butt off. I already sanitized this morning."

"No one's here," I say, gesturing with a wave of my hands.

"That's because you scared our only *real* customer away." Claire's eyes harden. "Now get off."

She grunts as she leans her entire upper body into mine, shoving me, but I won't fight a pregnant woman. I hop off the counter and spin around to find Claire already wiping away my invisible ass print.

"Lacey got freaked by the storm last night and ran off. I went to Henry's old place to find her, and Aurora was there. She thought I was lurking around. I wasn't." I shrug. "All got cleared up. Now, hurry off to the bakery while I watch your empty café."

Claire stops her circular motion at some point, my words clicking together in her brain. "Wait. Aurora was at *Henry's* last night? Why the hell would she be there?"

Claire didn't grow up in our small town, but she's been like a sister to me ever since she moved here five years ago with Danny. There isn't anyone here that doesn't know the name Henry June, and Aurora's name often trails in conversation. For almost four years, the June family made our dot on the map as close to famous as it'll ever get. Every now and then a group of hikers would come along to search the woods for the bodies that were never recovered, but they wouldn't pay for a guide or a tour. They'd go off-trail and scour the woods on their own. The June Expedition became its unofficial name.

There's a stigma attached to the June name that I'm not sure Aurora's even fully aware of yet. No one wants to remember that time. And when word gets out that their local celebrity has graced them with her presence—well, let's just say they won't be bringing her fruit baskets.

"Aurora, as in Aurora June. Henry's daughter."

Claire's hand covers her mouth. "Oh." Her eyes become soft as realization hits. "Oh my God. She's *your* Aurora."

I look away, knowing my expression would reveal every ounce of pain that's ailed me over the past seven years. "She hasn't been *my* Aurora in a long time. She's someone else's now." I swallow, the words sticking to the surface of my throat. "A fiancé." That shouldn't hurt, not after all this time, but the thought of her with anyone else is like a knife twisting in my heart.

"I'm sorry, Jax." -

I wave away her sympathy, feeling the walls of the room slowly moving in on me. It wasn't supposed to be like this. I imagined seeing Aurora again, but this was not how it played out in my head.

"It's fine," I say with a shrug. "It's not like she's sticking around." My words sound hollow as I speak them. "Aurora never sticks around for long. This time, it's for the best."

And that's the truth.

The faster Aurora leaves Balsam Grove, the better.

Aurora

Everything is different in the daylight.

I'm on my way back from shopping after the disastrous run-in with Jaxon when I really notice it. I take in my surroundings with new eyes. Everything is crisp, lively, and colorful. Woodland creatures are awake, singing and fluttering around while river water runs tranquilly in the background. Debris from the storm—nothing more than damp leaves and twigs—fully covers the walkway to the drive. The intoxicating scent of wet earth and wildflowers triggers a calmness I miss. And as I roll onto the drive leading to my father's cottage, I take in the mountainous terrain backdrop with the widest eyes.

Last night was about the destination. Trusting in my gut and taking a leap of faith. Getting here without looking back.

Today brings reality. Staring at it all now, I realize painfully, I have no idea what comes next. Part of me imagined it all becoming so clear the moment I stepped foot back in Balsam Grove. I see now, that's not how this will happen.

"Your mind is suppressing painful memories, Aurora. Sometimes it's okay to forget."

Doctor Rohls' voice rings in my ears. After my accident, I saw him weekly, and his gentle words helped ease my troubled mind. He encouraged me to explore but not push. To be curious but not greedy.

"Your memories will continue to come," he promised, *"so long as you give them a safe space to come back to."*

Eventually, I understood. Eventually, I stopped searching for my past in my present. It took two full years of therapy to begin to let go and focus on my future again. To rebuild, although it wasn't like I had much of a past to build from. My past was locked in a padded room, sharing a ten-year sentence with my father.

Gravel crunches beneath my tires as I pull in to the small carport to the right of the driveway. I had completely forgotten it was here until Jaxon mentioned it today.

My backseat and trunk are filled with bags of all the essentials I could think of: sheets, towels, trash bags, toiletries, cleaning supplies, food. I make a few trips, dumping everything on every available surface, then begin replacing the old with the new.

There's still no electricity, but I've made the calls, and all should be restored today. After another cold shower, I make my way downstairs to start exploring the cottage, determined to go through every room, every drawer. What better way to become reacquainted with my past?

The cottage is spotless, unlike when my father lived here, complete with all the makings of a home. A couch with a large, red blanket tossed over it faces a television set in the corner of the room. A black freestanding stove is set against a tile backsplash, a stack of wood and a set of iron tools beside it and a large, white throw rug on the floor.

Spinning my wet hair up into a knot, I start with the bookshelf in the corner of the room above the old, square television. I can't help but smile as I run my finger along the worn spines of the titles. I'm not surprised to find the works of Plato, Aristotle, Russell, Descartes, and Nietzsche.

I close my eyes, basking in a rare moment of happiness as I recall a time that feels precious. Safe. Like home. I open my eyes. *Nothing like this place.*

At my childhood home in Durham, my father kept his office in the den. His library was massive, taking up all four walls of the room. Just to spend time with him, I'd waste the days dusting and organizing the books as he worked. He didn't mind my presence, and I didn't mind the silence. Sometimes I'd stay so long that my parents would have to carry me to bed after I'd fallen asleep.

At twenty-six years old, my father, a certified genius, became the youngest professor of philosophy to ever teach full-time at Duke University. He was a wise man who spouted wisdom like it was gospel. My mother, a former student of his, lapped up every word like they were aphrodisiacs. She relished in his sophistication and delighted in his wild philosophies.

Their daily banter usually stemmed from passionate thoughts and questions boomeranging between them.

"There are no definitive answers. Only endless possibilities," my father would boast.

Always questions. Never answers.

He was adamant about his words. He lived them, breathed them. And we were convinced of his musings as well, because he was Professor June—her love, my father. Our hero.

Even heroes have their weaknesses.

The knock comes abruptly, yanking me from my reminiscence. I set down the copy of Plato's *Republic*, then inch around the couch and peek through the window to find Claire's face pressed flush against the glass. Despite recent events, I laugh at the absurdity of her smooshed face and open the door to welcome two coffees and a giant smile.

"Wow. You deliver, too? That's quite the service."

She rolls her eyes and shoves a cup in my hands. "Don't get used to it. This is my peace offering. You know, to make sure you're not going to pack up and leave town after the way Jax spooked you."

"Well, I did take his chocolate croissant."

We both laugh, easing some of the tension.

I shut the door behind her and remain planted as she continues to the living room. How much does Claire know? How well does she know Jaxon? Probably better than I do after all these years.

"Serves him right," she says as I join her on the couch, mirroring her cross-legged position. "Don't worry about him. Jaxon can march his two pretty legs over to that bakery whenever he wants. Meg would happily whip him up a dozen more for free."

My heart dips into my stomach. I desperately want to know if Jaxon is spoken for. It sounds like he is, but I'm not about to ask outright.

When I was eight years old, I stared at Jaxon like he was the model for male beauty, and he seemed to only get better looking with age. And now? Six years since seeing him, seven since we were a couple, Jaxon is sexy as hell. And admittedly, as much as I need him to be taken, I pray that he's not. I pray that there's still a part of him deep down that remembers what we had. And misses it.

It's so goddamn selfish of me, I know.

I should leave Balsam Grove now and never look back.

"Well, thanks for checking on me, but I'm fine. Really."

"Are you?" Claire's expression softens as she presses her cup to her lips and watches me over the lid. "You ran off pretty fast earlier."

"I think being back will just take some getting used to."

Claire's smile is faint, empathy clearly written in her expression. "So, it's true. You're *the* Aurora June."

Discomfort churns in my gut. "You know who I am?"

"You're kind of a celebrity around here. It didn't even dawn on me that it was *you* when you introduced yourself earlier." Her eyes light up. "And then your ex-boyfriend was stalking around your cottage last night like a psycho. What is that all about? Girl, I would have had a heart attack."

We laugh despite the peculiar conversation. "Right? He was wearing a hood, too!" I'm happy to slide past the subject of my father. "It's not a big deal. It was just a misunderstanding. Lacey was my dog before I...moved. I guess she still wanders off during the storms, poor thing. It's amazing after all these years she still comes here. I'd only had her a few months before our last night together."

She shivers with her whole body and takes a sip of her coffee. "You know, you should have tased Jaxon. Taught him a lesson. Or at least had Officer Tanner cuff him and drag him down to the station. Leave him in a cell for a couple hours." She winks. "That would have made everyone's day."

I laugh. "Next time. Since it sounds like there will be a next time." As the laughter dies, my smile goes with it. "I'm glad that was all cleared up. I'm not here to cause any trouble."

"Why are you here?" As soon as the words are out of her mouth, she cringes, and twists her face apologetically. "I'm sorry. That didn't come out right. Not many people would choose this town to live. I'm here because of my husband, Danny. You know him?"

I nod with a smile. Out of everyone Jaxon hung out with when we were younger, Danny was my favorite friend of his. A great guy with a level head and big heart. He always managed to reign Jaxon in when needed. It's nice to know he ended up with someone like Claire.

"I love it here," she continues as if trying to convince herself. "It's small and safe, and I love the people. The café is my dream. But if it weren't for Danny, I never would have chosen this place to put down roots."

"Trust me. I get it. But I didn't choose this place either, Claire."

She nods in understanding.

"Look. I have a past here. I get it. My dad was the bad guy in town. I get that too. I'm not here for redemption or to relive my past. I'm just...figuring things out. Hopefully people can respect that. I don't think there are any other choices for me at the moment."

This answer only seems to confuse Claire more. She sets her cup between her legs and tilts her head. "What are you trying to figure out? I know I'm a stranger and all, but I'd love to help, if I can."

I shake my head. "This isn't something anyone can help with."

"Why not? Look, I'm not like the others. Whatever past you have here is null with me. I'm the pregnant outsider"— she laughs like her pregnancy is an absurdity instead of a blessing—"who happens to be a deputy's wife and runs a cozy café. People here are forced to smile when I walk by, and trust me, that's no better than throwing stones. You and I should stick together."

Claire means well, but she has no idea what she's committing herself to. "You have enough to worry about with your baby and your café. Don't go tacking on obligations to the new girl in town." I give her a teasing smile, but a cloud passes over her eyes, dimming them momentarily.

"I'll be honest, Aurora. Jax didn't share the gruesome details of your split, but I know enough about what went down. I can't for the life of me understand what would bring you back here." She scans my expression and tilts her head a smidge. "But honestly, Aurora. What does any of that have to do with us sticking together?"

"I got the sense from Tanner that I'm not welcome here, and I'd be stupid to believe my father didn't leave a mark. But I didn't think me showing up here would be an unwelcome reminder of it all. Not to the extent I'm realizing now. You should consider all that before you offer up friendship."

She reels back slightly while shaking her head. "Dang, girl. You've perfected the art of pushing people away, haven't you? All I'm saying is, if you need someone to talk to, your secrets are safe with me."

I open my mouth to speak and then think better of it. Why I feel compelled to tell a stranger everything leaves me dumbfounded. But looking back at Claire, I see her sincerity. Her willingness to listen. To help. And if I'm honest with myself, that's something I want. A friend. Someone who won't return every confession with a question, forcing me to explore the root cause. Sometimes roots are too complicated to be worth the dig.

I'll give her the short version.

"My dad passed away a couple weeks ago, and everything I thought I wanted changed. Here I was, feeling lost, like I'd been walking in place for years. The idea of coming back intrigued me. I didn't have to think hard about it. I packed my bags and drove here last night." I shrug. "For now, that's all there is to this story."

"For now?"

My nod overshadows my swallow. *For now.* Who knows what will happen now that I'm here. Maybe there's a part of me that wants to face Jaxon and the pain between us, but I've talked myself out of that possibility, trying desperately to focus on healing this gaping hole within me first.

"Did your dad really—?" Claire pauses, but I know what she wants to ask.

"He committed suicide at the facility he was in."

Her hand flies to her mouth. "I'm so sorry."

Shaking my head, I give her a light smile. "It wasn't his first attempt. He wouldn't let me visit, but I'd get reports. He wasn't doing so well there at the end."

"At the mental facility? Aren't they supposed to help people like your father?"

I nod. "I think they tried. But schizophrenia is an unpredictable beast. It can deteriorate the mind, similar to dementia. It didn't help that he refused medical treatment when he was diagnosed. I was twelve when my parents sat me down to explain it all. Later on, it made sense why he stopped smiling, laughing, hugging me..." My throat tightens and my eyes burn at the reminder. I still fight to remember the sound of my father's deep chuckle at my awful knock-knock jokes. I frown, the feeling of disappointment still an ache in my gut. "The stress of it all wore on my parents for years until they decided to separate. He just...didn't want to be around people anymore." I shiver, remembering that awful morning my parents split. "There's no telling what triggers a schizophrenic or what can prevent episodes from occurring. I think eventually the voices became too much for him."

Claire's hand lands on mine, squeezing it tight. I can't believe I've just divulged the details of my father's mental disorder to a total stranger. But as the firm hold on my hand spreads calm through me—mind, body, and soul—I know I can trust her.

"And what about your fiancé? Jaxon said you were with someone."

I groan and then laugh, shaking my head. "I should have never said that to Tanner, but he was treating me like the townspeople would gas my house as soon as they found out I was back alone."

"What do you mean? So you don't have a fiancé?"

I shake my head and cringe. "No, I don't."

My response satisfies Claire. Her eyes shine as she runs a finger around the rim of her coffee lid. "Well, that's settled. What are you going to do now that you're here? You'll be bored out of your mind without a job."

Her eyes flick to mine and I realize there's more to the reason she stopped by my house.

"You can only hike the trail and swim under the waterfalls so much before you start to get restless around here," she continues with a smile.

I laugh. "I haven't thought too much about how to keep my calendar full, but you're probably right."

"Come work with me at the café," she suggests. "I only have one other girl, and she's taking summer classes, so I'm drowning with all these hours." Claire rubs her rounded belly. "And this little girl will be coming in less than eight weeks. I could use a backup for when that time comes. If you're still here, that is."

She holds up her hands. "No pressure, honestly. Hiring has been on my list of to-dos, but I haven't listed the job yet. If you're interested, you can start as soon as you want."

Claire just might be even crazier than I thought. "I have no experience at all."

"That's okay! I'll train you. You'll be a pro in no time."

"Really?"

"Yes, really! Are you considering it? I should warn you, the pay is dismal."

A job wasn't even on my mind when I left Durham, but Claire's right. I might drive myself insane trying to fill my days hanging around the cottage or hiking the woods. I *am* here to try new things. To find myself—whatever that means.

I shrug. "Already considered. I accept." I beam.

She squeals and throws her arms around me. "This is great! I can't believe how perfect this is. You can start next week after I put a new schedule together, and I have a new shipment coming in so I can teach you how I manage all of that." She claps her hands as she stands to leave. "I'm a fun boss. Promise. And the tourists will love you," she winks. "You're a lifesaver, Aurora."

I take a sip of my coffee and sigh, leaning back as she grins at me from above. "If you can teach me how to make coffee like this, *you* just might be the lifesaver."

ONE WEEK LATER

9

Aurora

I'm feeling restless within these cottage walls, just as Claire predicted.

By eight a.m., I'd already downed an entire bottle of water. By nine a.m., I'd confirmed the hole under the back porch does, in fact, exist. And by ten a.m., I had showered, dressed, and started pacing the living room floor with no clue what to do next.

I curl up at the edge of the couch, scrolling through messages from Aunt Cyndi and Scott. I'm replying to Aunt Cyndi's text when my phone starts ringing and Scott's name flashes across the screen, and I groan. I've been avoiding him for too long.

Tapping *Answer,* I place my phone to my ear and squeeze my lids together before pulling in a breath. "Hey, Scott."

As soon as the words escape, I bite my lip and shake my head. I know I sound regretful, but the only thing I regret is being too weak to have this conversation in person.

There's a quick huff of air on the other end of the line. "Jesus, Aurora. I've been worried. Are you okay? Where are you?"

Silence is all I give him as my mind splits off in a million different directions. If he learns where I am, he'll come after me. He won't understand. He'll be hurt. And he'll try to convince me to leave. I need to do this on my own.

"Aurora." His voice is soft, pleading, making it that much harder to respond. My insides furl with guilt. "Whatever is going on, whatever I did, just come home and let's talk about it."

I inhale through my nose and exhale from my mouth, slowly, like I was taught to do when the pressure around me becomes too much. When the world becomes dark. When the cries within me scream too loud and anxiety swallows me alive.

Scott doesn't understand. I have no home, or at least not a place that feels like home. But he doesn't deserve to feel like this is his fault.

"You didn't do anything, Scott. You're wonderful. You've always been wonderful. I can't explain it exactly. Just trust me when I say I'm okay, and...I can't come back."

I hear a heavy sigh on the other end of the line, and I don't need to be there to know that Scott is pacing our small house—well, *his* house.

Two years ago, the thought of rooming with my best friend sounded exciting. But I had no idea that moving in would lead to an avalanche of expectations and guilt.

After spending the first two years following my father's arrest obsessing over the three days of memories I had lost, I realized how much time I had wasted on something I couldn't control. I had to move on. So, I buried myself in my studies and completed my undergraduate degree in philosophy from Duke in just three years. That same year, Scott received his degree in finance and was offered a great job as an accountant in Raleigh. He purchased a beautiful, cozy, two-bedroom house with a two-car garage and invited me to move into the guest bedroom to help cut down on living expenses.

Scott respected my privacy, and while I always knew he had a thing for me, I ignored it until I couldn't anymore. Gradually, our roomie situation turned into a dating situation, and although I'd allowed for things to develop before I was ready, I felt as if I owed him a chance.

From that point on, it was like I'd boarded a train with no end in sight.

Four weeks ago, Scott attempted to take our relationship to the next level. We'd only ever kissed up to that point. But with flowers, jazz music, dim lights, candles, the works, I knew the expectation was that there would be more. The second his hand touched my breast, I had a full-blown panic attack, each dizzy, staccato breath bringing me closer to a blackout.

My father passed away the next day.

"You're upset because of your father," Scott tries, reasonable as always. "I knew this would be hard for you. I get it. If it's time and space you need, I can give that to you. I can find a place to stay while you sort things out for a few days—or weeks. Just don't leave."

His voice cracks, and that's when I feel the stinging behind my eyes. "Scott—"

"I love you, Aurora. I know we haven't said those words, not in that way, but you need to know. You can't just walk away and tell me it's over. It can't be over. It just started."

I can feel my chest tighten and my face crumble at his confession. Even though I could have guessed, the words are too much to bear. Scott is the type of man women dream about. He's determined, trustworthy, financially secure, smart, and confident. His admirable traits were hammered into my mind by Aunt Cyndi until even I believed he was perfect. And maybe he is. But then, why do I still feel this incorrigible need to chase my past, no matter what darkness still lies there? And why can't I explore my past while feeling confident enough to move forward with my future?

After years of trying to do just that—move forward—I've realized that maybe I need to start listening to my own wants and needs. And that's why I came back.

When I made the decision to end our relationship, I knew Scott wouldn't understand. Everyone expects me to fit into the picture he's created in his mind—childhood friends destined to be together. He makes it all sound so simple.

"You're a wonderful person, Scott. You've been my best friend all these years, and you know I love you too. Me leaving doesn't change any of that, but I'm just—I'm not the one for you, and this isn't something that will fix itself."

"So let's fix it," he pleads. "Together."

"I can't."

"Why not?"

"I'm suffocating." My whisper comes quickly, and I cringe when I realize it was loud enough for Scott to hear. He doesn't deserve that. I clamp a hand over my mouth. I'm such an idiot.

I shake my head, immediately wishing I could take back my words. Scott and I have never argued. He's always gone above and beyond for me to make up for all that I lost. And I've gone with the flow, loved him for who he is, been the doting girlfriend he needed me to be. But it kills me to think about staying.

"I've loved you my entire life." His voice cracks, worn with emotion. "I waited for you. After everything. I thought you felt the same."

I want to sink into a hole. We may have only made our relationship official two months ago, but that doesn't matter. To Scott, we've been together for a lifetime.

"I'm sorry, Scott. I need to go."

"Just tell me you're okay," he jumps in before I can hang up. "If I call, will you answer? Because I need to know that you're okay and not dead in a ditch somewhere."

All goes silent, and the air catches in my throat. "What did you just say?"

"Oh, God. Jesus, no, Aurora. I didn't mean that. I just— *fuck*. I'm an idiot. I'm sorry." He stumbles, but it's too late for a recovery. "Will you call? Text? Can you promise to at least check in with me from time to time? Just so I know you're okay? Wherever you are. Maybe I can visit…"

The bubbling anger in my chest reduces to a simmer as I slowly forgive him for his slip. Scott isn't a mean person. He wants what's best for me, but almost in the way that a parent tries to control their child. Scott has always tried to mold me the way he wants others to see me. I realize it now—or I may have always realized it, but now, I know I'm done.

"I don't think that's a good idea. I'm sorry, Scott. My letter tells you everything you need to know."

"Your letter tells me you're leaving to *find yourself*. Why do you need to leave to do that? You can do that here. You can go back to school, get a different job. I'll *help* you. Running away never solves anything. You should know that."

Again, it's like he's slapped me. Is it possible to know someone practically your entire life and never see the ugly in them until their future is threatened? I suppose.

Scott's a planner. He knew he wanted to work with numbers by the time he was eight. He planned to intern for his dream company, date a girl in college, get engaged after graduation, and then marry, have babies, and live happily ever after. Not a bad plan, and with us being childhood friends, I guess I fell into that plan seamlessly.

He almost got everything he wanted.

I've just ended our relationship. Our friendship. Our *plans*. He has every right to be upset, but for the first time in a long time, I'm doing something for me and not because someone else told me to.

I wipe a tear from my eye with the back of my hand. "Can you give me some time? I'll call you, okay? Just know for now I'm fine."

"Wait."

"I need to go. Goodbye, Scott."

"Auror—"

With a deep breath, I end the call and silence my phone.

A heavy tear falls onto my cheek. As confident as I am in my decision to be here, there's no possible way to make this situation better. While I should have been honest with Scott before I left, I know he would have hounded me to make things right. He would have tried to fix it, and I would have eventually relented. Nothing would have changed.

I couldn't let that happen.

Going back to Durham would mean being confined to a life I never chose. I'd end up marrying a man who says he loves me with all his heart and soul, but I don't know why. His reasons for loving me are that I'm smart, attractive, and funny, but doesn't love flow deeper than that? Shouldn't he love me for all the reasons why?

Maybe Scott's right to an extent. Maybe I'm solving nothing by leaving Durham—by running away—but I can't keep fighting what I feel is right.

And Balsam Grove feels right.

10

Aurora

As I approach the edge of the winding river less than a minute's walk from my cottage, it's like someone has injected me with life. The effects are instantaneous. With a lift of my chin, I close my eyes and inhale until I'm no longer dulled and disoriented. Everything becomes clear. In Balsam Grove, I breathe the air with new lungs, feel the breeze with new skin, and see the land through new eyes. It's divinity at its finest.

It's not hard to understand why I fell in love with this place when I was younger. In a world so busy, so full, and so totally reliant on technology, there's an incomparable serenity when you come to the mountains. Wandering alongside the river, finding perfect flat stones to skip across the wide divide of water, stopping every so often to memorize the simplest things. I've fallen completely under its spell once more.

I don't try to navigate my path. I hike beside the river, around every curve and bend, uphill and against the current. It's a familiar path, but my focus isn't on the destination. Every now and then I stop to take a drink from the stream, pluck a fiery pink flower, and tune into a wild animal scampering across fallen leaves. But it's not until I reach a steeper incline that I take a moment to assess where I'm headed.

The river has significantly deepened and increased in speed since I began walking a few minutes ago. A steeper incline forces me to distance myself from the water's edge, onto a more manageable path through the woods. My thighs burn from the steady climb, and my throat aches from dehydration. I never planned to journey this far, but I could have at least thought to bring water. I'm ready to turn back, find the river, and drink from it when I spot the top of a familiar red house peeking over the hill. Hummingbirds unleash in my chest as I inch forward.

Mere seconds later, I'm standing on flat land again, taking in the two-story home that overlooks a waterfall, an old millhouse beside it. It's like it came out of nowhere, but this house—it's home to some of my best memories, my biggest dreams, and the beginning of the horrible nightmare that ended life as I knew it.

"Ah, that's my girl," a voice booms in the distance. "Bring it here, Lacey."

Shit. Jaxon?

My eyes sweep left, to the source of the river. Two waterfalls coming from different directions spill into one body of water where Jaxon treads. He's patting the water as Lacey paddles over with a stick in her mouth.

My Lacey.

My chest constricts at the sight of her, no longer a puppy.

Jaxon takes the stick from her mouth, then rubs her head before she continues paddling to the edge of the river. After she climbs out and does a full body shake to dry off, he tosses the stick to the side and turns back to the water, swimming lap after lap until I've lost count. Every powerful stroke reveals inches of well-cut muscle and betrays his familiarity with the water.

Jaxon always loved everything about the water. Diving, swimming, fishing...sex. I shiver at the memory of how well our slick bodies fit together. Of his delicate fingers stripping me of my bikini top so he could see all of me as he inched his way into my body, my heart. Of his hot mouth wrapping around my pebbled nipple just to hear my whispered cry. Of the way he watched me with hooded eyes as I came for him, my back pressed against a boulder and the plunging falls above us swallowing my cries.

He took everything good from me, but it was me that handed it over for the taking.

He's still mesmerizing, and I can't take my eyes off him now. With every stroke, I imagine him swimming away from me, away from our past and deeper into the rushing swell of the stream. How long has he been swimming? How far?

I swallow my anxiety as he finally breaks from his exercise to catch his breath. When he does, I'm as breathless as he is.

I'm not sure how long I've been staring when he uses the slick rocks to pull himself from the water, but I'm completely captivated by the droplets coursing down his naked back and arms. He's all strength and agility, effortlessly pulling himself to his feet. I should turn away, but I don't. Instead, I watch as water glides from his long hair, down his narrow waist, and then over the most beautiful ass I've ever seen.

Is he...?

I gasp, my hand clapping over my mouth. But it's too late. One slip of my breath is all it takes for Lacey's snout to jerk in my direction and sound off the first menacing growl. Jaxon's head follows in a swivel just as I slam my body onto the ground, hiding myself from view. Something sharp cuts through my skin at the top of my arm. I groan, knowing blood will follow, but there's no time to inspect the damage. I need to get out of here before Jaxon sees me.

And then guilt hits me. Jaxon isn't mine to ogle. He's with *Meg.*

Lacey is still growling, and she lets out a bark just before I hear the click of paws scraping against the rocks. *Shit.* She's coming. I wince, managing to keep my cry silent as I army crawl my way down the hill.

I make it about halfway when I hear another growl, this one much closer. My head snaps up, and I find myself staring into the ferocious, light blue eyes of the most beautiful creature. Lacey stands on top of the hill, detonating bark after bark, her teeth bared and angry.

She doesn't even remember me. My sad heart cries.

"Lacey! Get back here. Now!" Jaxon's voice booms.

The cuddly giant lets out a half-bark, half-yelp before whining and backing up at her master's command. Relief floods my veins while I watch, wide-eyed, as Lacey retreats, thankful Jaxon decided not to chase after her. I think I might literally die if he saw me this way, lurking around like some predator.

And that's when I realize, lurker to lurker, Jaxon and I are now even.

11

Aurora

It's two o'clock when I show up at Creek Café for my first training shift. The events of this morning weigh heavy on my mind, and guilt obstructs my thoughts. Claire is busy fixing a coffee for a customer while three more wait their turn. I hover nearby for a minute, completely useless with zero coffee-making skills under my belt, looking around at the café filled with customers.

Huh. I guess I understand the reason for the rush. Everyone's fitted in their hiking getups, complete with boots, backpacks, and rolled-up sleeping bags. From the looks of their matching yellow shirts adorned with logos, my guess is they're a team of some sort.

Claire tosses me an apron, gesturing for me to come around. "There she is!" She greets me with a distracted smile.

"Wash your hands. You can work the glass case while I make the drinks. You'll learn the register, too."

By the glass case, I'm assuming she means the pastries. That, I can do. I tie the apron at my waist over the Creek Café tank top that Claire gave me last night, the fresh cut on my arm hidden under a bandage.

"Were you expecting this crowd?" I'm toasting a bagel and reaching for the cream cheese in the mini fridge when I get another look at the line, which is now stretching to the door. Every seat and window ledge is spoken for.

She shakes her head, her smile never leaving her face. "Nope. Sometimes we don't know when these big crowds are going to blow in, but I sure am grateful for them." She nods at the group of hikers closest to us. "This group is an independent tour. They don't book through our city, and a lot of their hikes take place off the paths. We warn them away from it, but like I'm always trying to tell Danny, it's the mountains. Once upon a time, there were no trails. Anyway..." She winks as she places two drinks on the counter and shouts out a name. "Glad you're here."

I'm about to respond when a flash of blonde hair crosses my line of sight. The door to the back room is still closing when the girl gives Claire a quick wave and a smile. "See you tomorrow, boss."

Claire waves back without looking up from the register. "Bye, Amber."

When the girl's eyes fall on me, there's a moment of pause and a flicker of curiosity, but it's replaced with a brighter smile in the blink of an eye.

"That's Amber, the other barista I was telling you about," Claire tells me as she rings up another order. "I'll introduce you another time when this place isn't slammed."

Two hours go by before the crowd finally dies down and there are only a handful of customers lingering about. Claire doesn't waste a second to start showing me how everything works. I've been watching her on the register, so that doesn't take much training, but the coffee preparation does. It's not easy to remember how many espresso shots for each size drink, which machine to use for what, what ingredients can be substituted.

And here I thought life was simpler in the mountains.

Claire tells me we'll be getting another rush tonight, this one planned, so we spend the next hour stocking up on supplies. I've just taken inventory of the needs for the glass case when she entrusts me with the café for the first time and runs off to Meg's bakery. Almost as soon as the door dings on her exit, it dings again to signal a new customer.

Panic sets in immediately at the sound. If they ask me to make anything, I'm screwed.

My hand is full of a cleaning rag as I make circles around the surface of a table, scrubbing something sticky from the dark wood. Maple? Caramel? I can't be sure. But damn it, I need to acknowledge this customer. I may be new to baristaing, but customer service is a no-brainer.

Feeling the heat above my brow, I move the back of my hand across the beads forming on my forehead. I plaster a smile on my face and open my mouth to greet whoever just walked in.

The air freezes in my throat when I see a handsome, bearded man with smoky eyes and broad shoulders approaching—fully clothed this time, with a brooding frown etched on his face. Somehow, Jaxon manages to get better looking every time I see him, even though right now he's covering his beautiful curls with a burgundy knit cap.

My surprise at seeing him walk through the door morphs into mortification as a vivid image of his bare ass flashes through my mind. *He didn't see me.* He couldn't possibly know I was the object of Lacey's rampage from earlier. Or could he? Maybe he was storing up for a big ol' laugh later because that is something Jaxon would do. He's great at hiding his true feelings until he can't possibly stand it anymore, as I learned quite well when I was seventeen, when he eagerly peeled my clothes from my skin in his parent's basement and pushed into me for the very first time, greedy and rough, our bodies colliding just as our hearts already had.

What I would give to be beneath Jaxon during his loss of patience again.

I shiver. The way he's staring me down, his hard-set jaw, and the gleam in his eyes speak volumes. I could dig a hole right here and bury myself in it for eternity. *He knows I was there today.*

"Hello again," he greets me, eyeing the rag in my hands. His brows turn down in the middle, confusion transparent.

Again? He means last week, right? Not today, when I saw him fully—*Jesus.*

Giving up on the sticky substance, I swipe the rag from the table before moving away from him to stand behind the counter. Thank God there's a barrier between us now— anything to stop the stampede in my chest.

"What can I get you?" *That's right. Straight to business, Aurora.*

"I'm sorry." He steps forward, pressing his palms on the counter across from me as he leans in, bunching his shoulders. "Since when did you start working here?"

I consider his questions, also contemplating if I should quit right now. He must be a regular here, which means I've just encroached on his space. I'm not here to cause Jaxon any more grief than what I left him with. Suddenly, my new job at the café isn't as exciting a prospect as it once was.

"Since today," I respond with a swallow.

"Claire hired *you*?"

Why does it feel like we're playing tug-of-war? I fight to mask my anxiety, tugging the rope in my direction as I speak. "Yup," I say with more confidence than I'm feeling. "Is there something I can get you?"

He peers up at me through long lashes, the blues and grays of his eyes becoming my favorite hue of marble-magic as a ray of light hits them. My hold on the rope loosens.

"Let me think about it." He sounds irritated, and his brows are still pinched together as if he's deep in thought. It's enough to make my insides furl.

"Take your time." I swallow, doing my best to deflate some of the tension. My eyes dart from him to the espresso machine behind me before I clear my throat. "I can make pretty much anything, but I'm still training, so *anything* might suck." I blush at my confession. "And I don't know your *preferences*, so I probably won't be memorizing your drink anytime soon like Claire. But I promise to do my best."

He just nods, his frown deepening before peering up at the menu again.

"I'm sorry, do you have a problem with me working here? It's obvious you do. You might as well just come out and say what you're thinking. Let's get it out of the way."

There's a tick of his jaw and a tightening of his knuckles against the counter's edge. "I don't think you want to hear what I'm thinking."

I lean forward, my palm slapping the counter. "Yes. I do."

His head snaps forward, eyes locking on mine and pinning me there with his glare. I tug my gaze away from his face and move down his strong neck, landing on the cream v-neck shirt he's wearing beneath a plaid button down with rolled sleeves. I swallow at his intensity as heat rolls off him in waves.

"Alright, fine. I'll just say it," he grumbles. "Claire needs someone she can count on. Not someone who will be in and out of town before she knows it."

The force of my own words getting tossed back at me is a hard slap in the face. I let out a shaky breath. "Feel better now?" I'm still standing tall, but I can feel my insides crumbling. "Not that it's any of your business, but Claire is fully aware of my situation." Now it's my turn to pin him with my glare. "So, now that we got that out of the way, what can I get you?"

He blows out a breath then looks around the room. "Where is she, anyway?"

My cheeks heat again at the thought of him and Meg. "She went to your girlfriend's bakery to prepare for the rush she says we're getting tonight. Meg, right?" Could I be any more obvious? He's going to see right through me.

His expression twists into confusion. "What did you just say?"

I swallow hard, pushing the lump down my throat. Is he going to be angry with me forever? Geez. I'm just here to make some damn coffee. "Meg is your girlfriend, right? Claire said she's in love with—"

My eyes lock on his as I speak, and then something happens. The stale air sparks, and Jaxon laughs. A good-natured chuckle that relieves some of the tension built up between us. At that moment, everything I'd envisioned about Jaxon and Meg vanishes, and reality takes its place. He doesn't need to confirm that my assumption was wrong. That while Meg may be in love with him, the feelings aren't mutual. Nerves pop off in my chest.

"No, Aurora." Jaxon's tone is filled with exasperation. "Claire thinks she's everyone's cupid, but aside from her own love life, she's clueless."

"That's harsh."

"It's true." His eyes narrow in my direction. "Not that it matters to you, but *Tanner* is in love with Meg."

I ignore the first part of his sentence with an internal cringe. "Deputy Tanner?" There's only one Tanner in town. And I'm not sure why I'm referring to him as *Deputy* Tanner either. Even wearing a badge, I still picture him as the troublemaker from our youth.

Jaxon nods, a slow nod that forces me to turn my annoyance into a blush.

"Oh." Suddenly, everything begins to click into place. The guilt I had been feeling all day for my unlawful attraction dissolves completely, and I'm left feeling raw. Opened and dissected for all to examine. Jaxon is very much single and very much as forbidden as he ever was, given our history. I squirm under my skin, and I know he sees it.

"Ah. Well," he says standing upright. "Looks like I'm making my own drink today."

"Wait, what?"

My jaw drops as he presses one palm against the counter and then swings his feet over in one hop. A second later he's standing directly in front of me. I gasp as his palms land on my shoulders and his fingertips press into my skin. He turns me toward the espresso machine, his touch burning through me just the way I remember, lighting me up from within. My breath hitches in my throat.

"I'll show you how."

I swivel to face him, causing him to release his grip. I look up to meet his eyes. Jaxon towers over me by more than a foot, his six foot three frame to my five foot one. I used to love it. The way he peered down at me like somehow I was the one with all the power. The way his strong arms would wrap around my waist and lift me to steal one sweet, lingering kiss—at least that was the intention. But my legs always managed to wrap around his hips to pull him closer, resulting in him pressing my back into the nearest wall.

"You're not supposed to be back here." My voice feels small. I take a shaky a breath to start again. "It's my first day." *That's better.* Another breath. *You can do this.* "You'll get me fired." I place my hands on his chest and push, but he doesn't budge. He simply looks down at my hands with an unreadable expression.

"Please." It's my final plea, but his eyes snap to mine before he seems to consider my words—I mean, *really* consider my words as his gaze traces from my hands down the length of my arm, stopping briefly on my bandage before landing back on my face. They linger for only a second before he nods and backs away. "Okay, miss independent. Knock yourself out. Large coffee. Black."

He retreats slowly, just like Lacey did this morning, only his eyes carry a twinkle of amusement now. Such a strange contrast to moments before.

Letting out a relieved breath, I set a to-go cup beneath the nozzle and push the button to grind a fresh batch of beans. Black coffee isn't something I could possibly get wrong. If I'm being honest, I'm slightly disappointed. I could have benefited from a challenging order before Claire unleashes me.

I set his coffee in front of him and start pushing buttons at the register. "It'll be two-fifty."

He slides a five-dollar bill toward me. "No change."

Nodding, I complete the sale, purposely not returning his burning stare. I can feel him watching as I slip the tip money into a jar on the counter and turn away, busying myself by shaking the milk containers to see if they're empty enough to be disposed of. I would literally do anything to avoid having to make small talk with Jaxon. That was never our style. It was either all or nothing. Deep and meaningful or complete silence.

He hasn't moved. I can feel his eyes practically digging into me as I accidently dump the unused grounds into the trash. "Shit," I swear under my breath the moment I realize what I've done. Rolling my eyes, I shut the lid to the machine and exhale heavily.

"How long will you be in town?"

His question has a prickling effect on my exposed skin. I look up, my eyes flitting away as soon as contact is made. "I'm not sure yet."

"So you're here just, what—taking a vacation with your fiancé? Selling Henry's place? What's the deal, Aurora?"

I stop distracting myself with odd jobs behind the counter and face him. I owe him that much. I owe him everything, but right now, all I can give him is the truth—at least part of it.

"There's no fiancé." I can't read his expression, and he doesn't offer any words. "Tanner was giving me a hard time about being back, and it just came out."

"It just came out that you had a fiancé when you don't?"

When he asks like that, it makes me sound delusional. I don't want to explain Scott to Jaxon, so I shrug and skip the explanation all together. "Anyway, the timing was perfect. I wanted to leave Durham. Even before my dad died I was feeling...unsettled, I guess. I'm not really sure. I needed a place to stay for a while—a change of scenery—so I came here." I pause, looking around for something else to do.

In my periphery, I see him lean forward into the counter again.

"I'm sorry about your dad...passing." His voice holds its usual gruffness, but it's softer now. I'm not sure how to respond.

No one has been sorry about my father's death. It's like they all assumed I would be okay with it because of what he did and because it was he who ended his own life. It's the assumptions that have been the hardest thing about all of this. I'm presumed to hate him. The attempted murderer, the monster, the crazy man. I'm presumed to have banished him from my heart like my love for him was ever a choice. Even with all that happened, I loved the man who raised me. The man who wanted to care for me even though he was struggling with his mental health. He was determined. He was loving. But at some point, something went wrong.

Luckily, the ding of the door ends our conversation. I look up to find Claire grinning, her hands filled with packages that almost reach her chin.

"Wow. You got the motherlode," Jaxon teases as he takes the bags from her and deposits them on the counter.

"You keep selling out, I'll keep the supplies up," Claire quips.

What are they talking about? Selling out? Of what? They're speaking a language I don't understand as she winks at him and then turns to me with a grin. "How'd it go? Did we get any customers?"

I look at Jaxon, who's now emptying the bakery contents into the glass case. Confused, I nod my head and point. "Just him."

Claire's laughter floats, light and airy, across the room. "I hope you made him pay."

"She did." He grins, and Claire's laughter grows louder.

"For future reference, Jax doesn't need to pay. He's kind of the owner, but we don't like to give him too much credit for that."

Again, mortification weaves through me. *Owner?*

"Part owner," he corrects her with a slap and squeeze of her shoulder. "Which reminds me, I thought we were supposed to talk about all potential hires before we commit to new baristas."

I know he's teasing by the quirk of his lip, but my cheeks still heat with embarrassment.

Claire waves a hand in the air, dismissing him. "You worry about your half of the business and I'll worry about mine."

He chuckles and shakes his head. "Fine with me." He points to the boxes of unopened pastries. "Looks like you two can figure this out." He winks. "I better start setting up the studio, anyway. See you girls soon."

Half of the business? Studio?

Jaxon crosses the room, leaving me with one final glance before he reaches a set of double doors I hadn't noticed before. In shock, I watch as he props each French door open and walks into the next room—into the canvas shop with the *Sold Out* sign painted in the front window.

I look over at Claire, who's taken over for Jaxon sorting items onto the shelves in the glass case. "What is he setting up?" I ask, my heart beating way too fast.

"Huh?" she asks before registering my question. "Oh. Jax owns the art studio, Creek Canvas, next door. Hence the whole co-owner thing."

"Really? The Canvas and Wine shop?"

Claire's eyes shine with pride. Apparently, this place is so much more than I originally thought. "Exactly. So you're familiar with it?" she asks.

"Well, yeah. It's where people drink wine and paint." I think that's what the brochure mentioned.

"Yup. The art is tailored to Balsam Grove. It's easy and so much fun, and they can order wine and food from us. Our job tonight is to make sure his customers are fed and happy. And then they get to walk out of here with masterpieces of their own making." She giggles. "And the ladies love Jaxon Mills. He's practically a celebrity around here. I wouldn't be surprised if they talk about him in Durham."

I try not to react to her words, but my stomach knots. If anyone spoke Jaxon's name in Durham, I definitely didn't hear it. Him owning a paint class is something I would remember.

"But—this town is so *small.* How can he possibly fill up a class?"

Claire's brows shoot up as she points to the room next door. "You've seen him, right? The brooding hunk of meat that just swayed his ass into his *art* studio? Don't tell my husband I just said that, but it's true. The man is a hot commodity for miles. We're talking people who give up their Friday nights in Asheville just to drive here and take a class. It doesn't hurt that he's a creative genius, either. If Jaxon listened to anything I said, he could turn that paint class into an art gallery, but he doesn't paint as much as he used to."

Looking around again, I take in the art as if for the first time. "Did Jaxon paint these?" I already know the answer, but I need to hear it for myself.

Her gaze travels with mine. "Every single one. I don't think I could afford them otherwise. These are the ones he refuses to sell." Her eyes crinkle in the corners when she smiles.

I love how close she and Jaxon seem to be. And I'm happy to know Danny found someone special to share his life with.

"Anyway, we usually sell tickets for the classes online, but sometimes people come in hoping to find something new for sale and end up getting tickets for his class as a consolation prize." She winks. "He's booked for the next month, though, so the only way anyone can get a ticket is if there's a cancellation. We've had to turn down more people than I care to acknowledge lately." She rolls her eyes, as if there's some discontentment surrounding that subject.

"Why doesn't he raise the price of tickets? Or add another instructor? If the demand is that high—" But Claire's already shaking her head.

"He won't. No one can teach like that boy, and he doesn't do any of this for the money. The price he charges pays for the materials and overhead. Every tip gets donated. His profits are zilch."

"That doesn't make any sense. How does he live?"

"You don't know the story?"

I shake my head. "It's been a long time, Claire. And we've barely spoken since I've been back."

A flicker of guilt crosses her expression before she lowers her voice and responds. "I don't know the whole story, and it's really not my place to say, but Jax and his parents had a falling out years ago. He wanted to focus on art, and they wanted him to go to school. When he refused, they left him the money they'd saved up for his college and their estate, which includes a dozen rental cottages. They left him everything of theirs that had to do with Balsam Grove, told him it was his to do as he pleased with, and took off. After— well, you know—I guess they wanted zero reminders of this place…and they never came back."

"Jesus."

There was tension between Jaxon and his parents before, but as far as I knew, nothing that could tear their family apart.

Claire nods. "You're telling me. Danny and I met in college, and I didn't even hesitate to move here after graduation. After living in the city my whole life, I wanted simple." She laughs as if something crosses her mind as she says the word simple. "I don't think I realized how small this town really was, but I was blinded by love." She shakes her head, her heart eyes practically throbbing in their sockets. "Tanner's daddy, Sheriff Brooks, happened to have an opening for a recruit, so it all worked out like it was meant to.

"Jaxon was the definition of a starving artist when I met him. He had money and all that, but you wouldn't have ever known it. You could either find him at the bar or in front of an easel. He was definitely less talkative and even more of a grump than he is now." She smiles fondly at the memory.

I can already tell Jaxon has come a long way from the guy she's describing.

"But he's always been a good guy." Her tone becomes softer. "Wants nothing more than to live and breathe his art, even if he doesn't paint as much. Teaching others seems to make him happy." She drops her chin onto her fists, which are resting on the counter. "We got to talking one day, and I told him about my dream café that would be a place customers wanted to stay awhile. With art like his on the walls. Homey. Warm. With this being a hot spot for hikers, I wanted to give them a home away from home.

"I didn't realize he'd really been listening until he brought me here one day. Both suites were for rent, and that's when we came up with this crazy plan to have him teach art next door. The Canvas and Wine idea just sort of came naturally after that. It was all so perfect. His dream and mine, with Danny working down the road."

My heart feels full after hearing her story, but there's also a twinge of sadness there. Passion can create anything. I had it once. That *thing*. That feeling that felt as easy as breathing. That vision. It was all within my grasp. That same passion lived in me before a nightmare cast a permanent shadow over my world.

I'm not sure if I can ever get it back.
I'm not sure if I want to

12

Aurora

"I'm opening the doors in five minutes." Jaxon pops his head in to deliver the message, then leaves before I can check him out again. He's wearing a red beanie tonight. It pairs well with his worn denim jeans and cream v-neck shirt, plaid removed. Not that he probably put any thought into it. Jaxon was always a "toss on whatever is clean" kind of guy.

Claire moves to the doorway between Creek Café and Creek Canvas, spreading her arms in a flourish. "Welcome to Canvas and Wine."

I walk past her into the studio, and I'm frozen, a multitude of emotions coursing through me. Maybe I should have prepared myself for this better. My senses are on overload. My body feels light. I'm drifting in a haze as it all hits me at once.

Jaxon is a real artist. He did it, and I missed it all.

Claire places a serving tray in my hands and leads me around the studio, explaining the culture of Balsam Grove like there will be a test later. "In a small town like this, we have to think about our neighbors," she says. "The studio brings the café business while the café brings the studio a service it couldn't otherwise offer. When we close down for the night, customers usually flock to the bar down the street." She grins, bursting with pride for her and Jaxon's creation.

She nudges me and points to the front window, where a line has formed, starting at the front door and extending past where my eyes can see. "Three nights a week for two hours, *we* are the entertainment."

My eyes scan the line of eager customers waiting to be let in the door, the end nowhere in sight. "Geez. They're all out-of-towners? Coming to a painting class?"

"Paint by instruction," Jaxon corrects as he breezes past me to get to the door, alpine and maple scenting the air around him. "And there will be a few locals tonight, too. Consider yourself warned."

Claire throws me a sympathetic but amused pout while wrapping her arms around my elbow. "They'll try to chat you up and ask *all* the questions because they have nothing better to do. Just keep busy, and be polite." Then she winks. "Good luck."

The room is filled with four long tables covered in black cloths, two dozen easel stands and canvases atop them, and white paper plates dotted with a variety of colors. Jaxon's easel sits on a desk at the front of the room beside a canvas of what I'm assuming the finished piece should look like: a wine bottle filling a glass in one long stream, swooping around to form an incomplete heart.

Unlike the Hollow Falls bridge painting in the café, this one lacks detail and life, but it's still beautiful. Jaxon couldn't mess up a painting if he tried. I often joked he could build a masterpiece from a trash bin.

Loud chatter begins to fill the room, and I look to see that Jaxon has opened the door. A flood of women and a few men walk in and take their seats.

"It's time," Claire sing-songs beside me.

And time it is. We're taking orders right out of the gate and filling them before the start of the lesson. We work like a machine, seamlessly taking orders, ringing them up, and serving.

I'm in the back room filling up my tray when I hear Claire come in behind me, her peach-scented perfume alerting me to her arrival before the soft patter of her Converse.

I shut the fridge with my toe and place the two beers down.

"Hey." My eyes narrow with concern as I glance over at Claire. Her face looks pale, and her hand falls to her stomach. "Are you okay?"

She nods, her eyes widening. I know she doesn't want me to worry. "Oh, yeah. I swear I've had the best pregnancy, but this last trimester has really been getting to me with the dizzy spells and the heartburn. Not to mention my feet manage to swell to the size of Texas if I'm standing for too long." She laughs, though I can tell she's in pain. "And whoever told me women eat more when they're pregnant was on crack. I can't seem to keep anything down anymore." She sighs and slips off her apron. "Do you think you can cover? I could use some rest."

"Of course. Go home. I'll be fine."

I keep the snacks and drinks flowing after she leaves, which means more time in the studio and unavoidable stares from the locals when I cross their line of sight. I'm sure this is just the beginning of it. By tomorrow, the entire town will know I'm here, and I'll be grateful for a harsh glare or two. I expected some tension because of my father, but they seem to be forgetting that I was a victim too.

With around thirty-six students, mostly girls around my age, the night has turned into something resembling a party. Pop music streams from the surround sound speakers, and the room is filled with tipsy chatter. I don't mind it, except for the fact that Jaxon seems to spend more time warding off his fan club than instructing.

I shouldn't be noticing things like that, I know, but ninety minutes into the two-hour painting class, my focus has started to drift to him. It doesn't help that Claire calls me to tell me she always brings him a glass of wine toward the end of the night. "Sounds rowdy in there. Jax will need a pick-me-up by now." She laughs on the other end of the line.

"Thanks for the heads up. Now go rest."

"Definitely. I'm already in bed. I'll see you tomorrow, Aurora. Thanks, again. Oh, and great job today."

I thank her and smile as we hang up the phone.

With Jaxon's wine in my hand, I stall in the back of the class, not wanting to disrupt his lesson as he works his brush against the canvas. I never thought I'd see this sight again. I'd almost forgotten the effect his quick and effortless movements have over me. My eyes move from the canvas to his forearm to his back muscles rippling through his white shirt. The man is still as sexy as his art. Maybe even sexier now.

I take a deep breath before continuing forward. Jaxon turns at the same time I swipe the lonely beverage from my tray and hand it to him.

"Claire thought you could use this."

He accepts it, his eyes never leaving mine. "That was nice of her."

There's something incredibly sexy about watching Jaxon drink wine. The way he holds the stem delicately between his pointer finger and thumb. The way he moves the glass so it's circling the air, the dark red liquid swirling as he takes in the scent with a pull of his nose. The way his lips part for the glass, tipping it into his mouth. The way he swallows.

Jesus. Even Jaxon's neck has changed—thickened—and it warms the space between my thighs.

"All right. That's time," he announces to the class, setting his wine glass on the table beside him and thanking me for the drink with a nod. He stands at the front of the room to give the next instruction.

Giggles and moans fill the room as paint brushes are set down. Surprisingly, even when drunk, they all listen to Jaxon.

"What's next, teach?"

"Patience, Julie. I need to check out your masterpieces first." More giggling ensues.

My back is against the wall as I watch Jaxon circle the room to give his feedback. He's less broody when he's teaching art, I notice. Approachable, even. He smiles and laughs at the appropriate times, and he even manages to crack a few jokes. None of this is out of character for the Jaxon I fell in love with. But compared to Claire's version of him when she first met him, this version makes me happy.

My muscles lock up when a warm body comes to stand beside mine. When his arm brushes against my shoulder, I know I could combust right here. I take a moment to tamper down my nerves, taking deep, slow breaths as we stare at his painting.

A beat of silence passes before he speaks. "So." He shoves his hands in his jeans pockets. "What do you think?"

My eyes scan the painting again, fighting for something brilliant to say. I'm at a loss. "It's…good. Great use of colors."

He chuckles. "Ah, that's right. You never could lie well. You should remember, an artist's ego needs stroking."

"Not all artists." Peering up at him from the side, my lips tilt in his direction. "Besides, I think you have plenty of women here more than willing to stroke whatever you ask of them."

Heat rushes up my neck as I realize how that just sounded. But my words are all it takes for the energy between us to change from awkward to far too intense.

His eyes narrow and darken before he gives me a teasing glare and nudges my side. "Tell me the truth. What do you think?"

He always manages to make me feel exposed. "I'm no art critic…"

His brows twist as he glances at me again. "Okay. But you have an opinion. I'd like to hear it. Genuinely."

My entire body sighs as I examine the painting once more. "Great colors, great use of lighting." I shrug. "I don't know. It just doesn't wow me like the paintings in the café. Like the Hollow Falls piece, for example." I gesture to the wine painting in front of us. "This one is imaginative, I guess, with the way the wine pours in. It's cute. Romantic even. But it's not realistic."

He examines his own work again. "If I taught this class how to paint Hollow Falls, we'd need a lot more wine."

I fail to hold back my smile. "Fair enough." I give him a sideways glance, biting back my amusement. I love that I can make him squirm, but maybe I shouldn't have been *so* honest. Art is a sensitive subject for both of us.

"Besides," he adds on a breath. "Some art can never be replicated." His words skim over me like the tip of a brush, slowly, fluttering on its finish. "Any imitation would be a lie."

I try to ignore the hum of his words reverberating through my body and fixate on his painting once more. "You're good, okay? You know you're a great artist, Jaxon. This painting is no exception."

This time, he laughs on a breath. "Don't patronize me, Aurora." His eyes cut to mine as his chest builds with air. "You've always been honest with me. I'd hate for you to stop now. This is shit and you know it. But this class could never pick up a paint brush the way you did." My heart beats faster with his words. "I've never seen anything like it. Not before, not after. Tell me you're still painting." The desperation in his voice sucks the air entirely from my lungs.

Balsam Grove has always been my open sea. Overwhelming, deep with history and uncharted knowledge, and infested with mysterious creatures from my past. After six years of avoidance, I came in on a life preserver. So why do I feel as if Jaxon is a wave pushing me into a raging storm?

Just then, a student calls for his attention, and I take the opportunity to rush around the room for last call. I'm at the register when the phone rings, and I smile when I see Claire's name on the caller ID.

"How's it going?" For a sick pregnant lady who can't eat, Claire seems to have a hard time speaking around whatever is in her mouth. She sounds chipper.

"Just closing out the last of the orders. Easy peasy."

She wants to know the sales numbers, so I run them off to her.

"Wow. Great job tonight, doll. That might be a record number of orders in a single night."

"Really?" I'm genuinely surprised. I didn't do anything special. "It was fun." And it's true. I'm actually surprised by how fun tonight was. I didn't think about my panic attacks, or the reasons why I'm here, or that I don't belong. And it wasn't because I was distracted. It was because I was surrounded by so much of what I used to love. The art. Jaxon. Okay, so maybe that's only two things. But it's progress.

"I'm so glad you loved it. I was thinking. It's going to be tough for me to work most of those with the amount of standing. I'll happily give up the awesome tips to veg out on chocolate-drizzled potato chips and binge on Netflix. Danny's been grumbling that I work too much, anyway, and with his schedule we barely see each other as it is."

My face twists. "Did you just say chocolate drizzled potato chips?"

Claire rolls her eyes. "I can feel your judgment, Aurora. Judgment is not allowed."

Stifling a laugh, I slam the register closed. "So, you want me to take the Canvas and Wine shifts?"

"I mean, if you want the extra hours and tips, they're yours."

"By myself?"

"You can totally do it." She doesn't give me time to respond. "Anyway, just think about it. I posted the rest of the week's schedule on the cork board in the break room. If you have any conflicts, just let me know."

"Sounds good." I eye the clock on the wall, seeing that class is just about over.

"I need to get going. Go ahead and lock up the café first, then you can help Jaxon clean up. I can close out the till in the morning. Just leave through the studio when you guys are done."

We hang up, and I head back into the studio as everyone starts to shuffle out the door. Jaxon holds it open, distracted by a burgundy-haired girl in the back row. Pouty lips, flirtatious eyes, drop dead gorgeous body. She flips her hair and gives him a wide smile as she closes in. Too close. The moment her palm rests intimately on his chest, my own chest tightens. *I can't watch.*

All my energy goes back into cleaning, wiping down every surface I can reach, scrubbing in places that don't need to be scrubbed. The room is almost spotless before I hear the click of the door, signaling that the last of Jaxon's groupies have officially left the building.

Claire warned me. Jaxon is practically famous around here. These girls go crazy for him. I saw it for myself tonight. Whatever feelings have been resurfacing need to stop—now. I'm in Balsam Grove for me. To reclaim the bits and pieces of me that were stolen long ago, and the last thing I need is Jaxon distracting me from my mission.

My pulse races when I spot a lonely wine glass, still half-full, sitting on Jaxon's desk at the front of the room. Jaxon is there, wiping down his station and organizing his supplies. I brave it toward the front of the room, my sights set on the last wine glass. But as soon as it's in my hands, I find myself stopping in front of the finished canvas and tracing the heart-shaped stream of acrylic paint with my eyes.

"I charge by the hour, you know."

I jump, my heart leaping out of my chest at the sound of his voice. Wine splashes onto my hands and I turn to the side with a laugh. "That did not—"

My words are halted by my gasp when the wine in my hand slams into Jaxon's brick wall of a chest. Deep red wine splatters onto his freshly painted canvas and his cream-colored shirt just before the glass shatters at our feet.

"Oh, shit. Oh, shit!" My heart rate spikes as I swipe a rag from my back pocket and crouch to mop the tile. And to think I almost made it out of this place unscathed. Shaking my head with embarrassment, I mop up as much wine as I can before my rag is dripping.

"Hey," Jaxon squats to face me. "There's glass everywhere. Let me get this."

Acknowledging him with a shake of my head, I continue to wipe at the mess. "No, this is my mess. Let me clean it."

"C'mon, Aurora." He reaches for my hand to stop me, but I yank it away, losing my balance and teetering off the balls of my feet. I throw my hands back to catch me, realizing too late what a shitty idea that was. My palms hit the slippery floor, but that's not all. What feels like one thousand tiny shards of glass pierce my left hand, and pain shoots straight up my arm.

Before I can assess the damage, Jaxon's pulling me to my feet. "Let me go, Jaxon. I need to clean my mess." My throat is tight, my eyes sting, and I have to fight for my next breath. Why won't he just let me clean?

"You're bleeding, Aurora. Stop fighting me and let me take care of you."

I try to resist his hold, but every time I tug away from his grasp, he pulls me closer and closer until I'm officially struggling for air. I take it in in sips and hiccups, fighting like hell for my lungs to expand to feel some relief. But it's not working, and my vision begins to fade from blurry to black.

"Let me go, Jaxon." I squeeze out the words between each tiny breath.

He releases me, but that just seems to make it worse. I latch onto him without thinking, and his arms circle my waist, holding me tighter, steadying me.

"Hey, it's going to be okay." His calm, strong voice is my life preserver, and I cling to it desperately. "Can you focus on something for me? The painting. Anything. Just focus and try to breathe, okay? Deep, slow breaths."

My eyes flicker to his lips, and my ears devour his deep rasp as it surrounds me. Meanwhile, my nose finds the slightest hint of crisp cedar in his scent while my fingers grip the edge of his shirt and tug, doing my best to ground myself in reality. And as my world threatens to fade to black, I use his strength to pull me back to the surface, trading darkness for light.

"You've got this, Aurora. Can you take a deeper breath for me?"

His command brings on a quick, deep breath that fills my insides, and my body goes slack in his arms. "There she is." He's rubbing my back as my body becomes a ragdoll in his hold. I can feel him move me, guiding my disoriented body toward the back room. "Fight me again and I'll toss you over my shoulder."

Under normal circumstances his growling tease would make me blush, but these are not normal circumstances. What in the world just happened to me? My panic attacks have never been like that—like I was being yanked from my body and plunged into the deepest part of the earth. Then it hits me.

My pills. My full bottle of anxiety meds that I left at Scott's.

Shit. I thought I could try to go without them for a little while. To see if I could handle my attacks on my own. Turns out I can't, and I'll need to get them replaced pronto.

Once we're in the back room, which extends the length of the studio and café, he leaves me at the breakroom sink and begins to search a wall of shelving between the bathroom and breakroom.

"Stay here."

A spark warms my chest as I glare at him over my shoulder. "You're so bossy."

"Yeah, well, technically I'm your boss, so…"

I could scream at his arrogance. Instead, I let out a forced annoyed breath and fight back a smile. "*You* are not my boss."

My arms wrap around my waist, holding tight as I continue to regain my equilibrium. What I find in the mirror over the sink is frightening. Disheveled hair, half out of its ponytail holder. Smeared eyeliner that makes me look like a bandit. A streak of blood across my cheek.

But then I catch Jaxon's eyes in the mirror, and none of it matters. He's standing behind me, the top of my head barely reaching the top of his chest, and I shiver again.

With Jaxon, I feel every silence like it's a calm before a storm. Anticipation twists through me as I wait for his next move. I don't have to wait long. It's as if a vacuum has come along and sucked up all the air in the room when he presses his chest against my back and leans forward to switch on the faucet.

Leaning down, his breath dangerously close to my neck, he examines my hand. "Hmm. We'll need to wash this blood off. It will sting, but I need to get the glass out."

As much as I want to be stubborn about this, he's right. So when his strong hands cup my elbows, I let him push me forward, easing my left palm under the water. At the first bite of cold, it's like tiny needles are stabbing me. I wince.

At some point, his hands slide from my elbows to my forearms and he grips me tightly, maneuvering my hand under the water like I'm his puppet. Unnecessary, but I get the feeling he needs this. To play a part in helping me. He's slow, careful, washing me gently until the last of the blood has left my hand and swirls down the drain.

Jaxon switches off the water and gently lifts my injured hand. Curious, I peer over my shoulder. As he examines me, I examine him back—the hard lines of his face, his unshakeable concentration. His even breathing. His jaw, cloaked with an inch of thick, dark beard I already love. His stormy gray eyes as they zero in on something in my palm.

It's not until I feel a pinch that I realize he's taken the first piece of glass out of my hand. Snapping my head down, I watch as he plucks out another shard and places it on a napkin beside the sink. Mesmerized, I'm glued to his every move. I'm thankful when he's done but disappointed when he steps away after wrapping my hand in a light bandage.

I look at him over my shoulder, and we lock eyes again. There's something unspoken there. Something that causes my eyes to drop to his mouth and my lips to part just slightly as I think, just for an instant, what it would be like to kiss Jaxon again.

Before I do anything stupid, I flip around so I'm facing him. My bandaged hand finds the edge of the sink, control quickly filling my body with each new breath. "Thank you."

Mortified doesn't even begin to describe how I feel right now. Between stumbling around all night serving drunken college girls with big, fat crushes on Jaxon, spilling that damn wine, cutting open my hand, and having a panic attack in front of him, tonight has been a disaster.

"May I?" He's gesturing toward the sink so he can wash my blood from his stained hands. We swap places so I'm now standing behind him. My eyes follow the movement of his arms as they flex and move against each other, rinsing and scrubbing until his hands are clean.

I almost miss the hint of a smile on his face as he glances at me over his shoulder. "Did you really dislike my painting *that* much?"

Heat scales my body. That's right. I ruined his painting, too. "I'm so sorry, Jaxon. I wish I could replace it." Trying to ignore the fact that my face is probably as red as the wine I spilled, I step closer as he faces me. "And you shouldn't put weight on anything I say about your art. You know you're talented beyond measure."

"Yeah, well. So are you."

"Were."

He shakes his head, his jaw hardening and lips tightening as he dries his hands on a towel. "I can't forget what you said earlier because you were speaking the truth. Aurora, you don't have to love everything I paint."

"But I do." *I'm such an idiot.*

He laughs, a beautiful laugh I didn't realize how much I missed until now.

Sighing, I see that he won't let this go. "You know better than anyone that art means something different to everyone. I guess I just prefer my art to have a story. But that doesn't mean that piece out there isn't beautiful."

He studies me, tilting his head slightly as his gray eyes shimmer in the overhead lights. "Everything I create has a story. Did you ever think that? Even if you don't remember the story, it still happened."

I try to ignore the insinuation that his art has anything to do with me and watch him with pleading eyes. "I'm not explaining myself well. I wasn't judging your art."

"Of course you were. That's what art is for. To judge, to critique. There's no right way to *see* art. It's aesthetics." He pauses, his eyes still on mine. "If you're spending any time thinking about how your senses are reacting, then we're both doing our jobs—as artist and critic."

I groan now, hating how much I love his words. Hating the effect every syllable has on my skin. "Don't tell me you've forgotten this about me. My father was a philosopher. It's ingrained in me to question everything. The paintings displayed in the café—those make me feel something. That's all I meant."

"And tonight's painting doesn't evoke anything? Not a romantic bone in your body, huh?"

That question sounds like a trap. Instead of answering, I turn toward the back cabinet filled with branded shirts for the café and art studio. I grab a black one that looks to be about Jaxon's size and toss it to him. "Sorry about your shirt."

He glances down, assessing the wine stains. "What? I was hoping you would autograph it later."

"That's not really my thing anymore." It's a confession, though I know it's a bit abstract.

His eyes hint at acknowledgement. "You never did answer my questions earlier."

I shrug, averting my eyes.

"Aurora." He speaks softly, but in a scolding tone that rings my heart. "Are you seriously telling me you haven't painted since you left?"

I nod, swallowing to steady my nerves. "I'm going to wait for you out front."

Placing my palm on the door, I pause before opening it. His stained shirt is lifted, covering his face and revealing a tight, rippled chest and narrow waist.

Jaxon catches me staring as he flattens the new shirt against his sculpted frame. He gives me that look. The one from the very beginning when we found ourselves treading water together. It's just a look, but it makes me feel like we share a secret.

Pushing my way out the doors and back into the café to compose myself, I press my back against the nearest wall and move my palm to my chest, trying desperately to stop the race of my pulse. I need to get Jaxon out of my head. It's the least I can do, because there's no way in hell I'll ever get him out of my heart.

13

Jaxon

My eyes stay glued to the taillights of Aurora's car until they round the first bend, disappearing completely from view. After everything—the pain, the distance, the anger—my chest still aches when I watch her leave.

Since the moment I saw her standing in that window at Henry's cottage, I knew I was in trouble. It was more than the way she lit up in the dark, her dark brown hair a tangled mess and her wrinkled nightgown clinging to her soft curves. It was the rise and fall of her chest as if she was fighting to pull herself out of another panic attack. Like nothing had changed.

Nothing. Not even the impulse that swept through me to remove the glass barrier between us and take her in my arms. To soothe her. To let her know she wasn't alone.

Tonight I had my chance. The fear that glistened in her big blue eyes wrapped my heart with cold fingers and squeezed. I refused to let her push me away, not when my need to protect her felt as necessary as breathing. Seven years didn't change the perfect fit of her body in mine. Her olive skin still felt baby soft beneath my touch. She still smelled of orange blossoms and wild berries, a perfect pairing to her natural exotic beauty.

Aurora's father immigrated to the United States from Ukraine when he was a child with his parents, both doctors. Just a short few years into his young teaching career, he fell in love with Aurora's mother, Frieda Santos, who was raised in Portugal by an American mother and a Spanish father until she moved to Durham, North Carolina for college.

I always thought Aurora was a perfect blend of charm and seduction, and nothing about that has changed. And that does nothing to ease the temptation that runs through me when she's near, the need to know everything about the past six years of her life, and the desire to help her find her way back to her art.

I grip the handle and twist back on the bar of my bike. The engine roars, and I consider my next move. A few seconds later, I shut off the engine, swing my leg over the bike and walk back toward Creek Canvas.

I have no idea how things will end with Aurora in town, but I have an idea of how they can begin.

14

Aurora

I'm stacking fallen logs from the wood pile beside the cottage when I hear the crunch of leaves and twigs behind me. My heart does a little flip in my chest when I look over my shoulder to see Jaxon approaching with Lacey.

"Whoa, girl," I say, the back of my knees slamming against the wood pile as Lacey bounces up to me, her nose pushing directly into my crotch. *Well, okay then.* At least she's not threatening to tear my head off like yesterday. "Um, Jaxon," I call, slamming my legs shut. That doesn't stop Lacey as she plows into me again. "Think you can help me here?"

"Oh, so now you want my help?" he teases.

Lacey continues to sniff around while Jaxon laughs.

"What is up with her?" I ask, amused but a little annoyed.

"She's trying to get to know you again."

"Well, can you tell her she's going about it all wrong?" I place my hand on Lacey's nose and try to push her away.

"Tell her yourself."

I look up, ready to snap at him when I see his playful smile.

"Seriously, Jaxon?"

His laughter softens. "Okay, okay." Narrowing his eyes, he crouches down slightly. "Lacey," he commands with a clap of his hand on his thigh. "Come."

She pulls away from me with a hanging smile and wide, happy blue eyes before trotting back to her owner.

I'm straightening out my denim cut-offs while Jaxon lectures Lacey about how to approach women. He looks good, dressed in khaki-colored cargo shorts that hit just below his knees and a solid gray t-shirt covered in paint splotches. There's also something in his hands, which I'm guessing is the reason for his visit. It's rectangular and thin, wrapped in brown paper, about the size of the canvases from last night.

"Don't tell me," I tease, my eyes shooting lasers at the package. "A housewarming gift?"

He returns a smile so charming that I'm not sure I could move forward to greet him without my legs turning to putty. "Something like that."

But he doesn't hand it to me. Instead, he props it against the side of the house and tips his head. "Open it later. Let's go for a walk."

Dusting my hands against my jeans, I turn back to the rest of the fallen wood I've yet to stack. It's not going anywhere anytime soon.

"Okay, but you need to keep an eye on Lacey. I can't decide if she really likes me or if she's looking for a reason to make me her next meal."

Jaxon laughs. "She likes you, I promise. I can't say she felt the same way yesterday, but you're good today."

My eyes go wide as I stare back at him, completely mortified. He knew I was there. But how? And why is he just telling me now? *Asshole.*

"I don't know what you're talking about," I try.

"Liar."

Crap. "Fine, but I didn't see anything. I swear."

His eyes narrow in amusement. "*Big* liar." He takes a step, patting his leg for Lacey to follow. "You could have warned me you were there. Otherwise, it kind of seems like you were peeping on me in the woods. And that's a little creepy."

Heat rushes through my body, filling my cheeks with transparent mortification. "Oh my God, Jaxon, I wouldn't do that. I wasn't even paying attention to where I was going or how far I'd gone. I just kept walking up the river. And then I saw your house, and by then it was too late. I looked down and you were—"

"Naked."

I swallow. "Yeah. Sorry." Then I tilt my head. "You aren't worried a tourist will wander onto your property and see you?"

He shrugs. "Hikers are pretty good about sticking to the trails. Don't you remember all of this?"

"It's been a long time."

There's a pause, a beat too long as his eyes pin me in place. "Let me show you around the woods again. Lacey and I walk the old trails every day. And if you're sticking around for a while, you should know your way. But here's a quick tip: if you get lost, just keep walking in one direction. It might take you an hour in some areas, but eventually you'll arrive somewhere. A road, a business, a house. We're not that deep in the mountains that you couldn't find your way."

"Why didn't you tell me that when I was eight?" I laugh lightly, and he smiles in return.

"I didn't know the woods as well as I do now. I've probably explored every square inch of it at this point."

I laugh again. "Why? That sounds uneventful."

He shrugs, but he doesn't return my laughter with his own this time. Instead, his jaw ticks and his eyes harden. My insides twist as a disturbing thought comes to me, remembering the missing bodies probably buried somewhere in these woods. Has he been looking for them this entire time? I can't bring myself to ask him the question out loud. No good could possibly come of it.

I decide to change the subject. "I just figured if I followed the river, I'd easily be able to find my way home."

He nods. "That's a good plan. Still, I'd like to show you around. In case there's a next time and you happen to stray away from the water or encounter a bear."

"A bear?" I screech. Jaxon just laughs.

"It could happen."

"And what? You've got tips for bear encounters?"

He shrugs. "Sure. And deer, and skunks."

Lacey plows ahead of us, probably bored of our bickering. As she sniffs her way along the water's edge, stopping every so often to mark her territory. I feel like it's my turn to speak, but I'm having trouble initiating anything more than another awkward conversation.

We walk in silence for a few minutes before he takes my hand, squeezing tight like he thinks I'll pull away, and looks around like he's checking for something. "Let's cross here." He helps me jump from one slick rock to the next until we've crossed the shallow stream.

"Lacey," he shouts, getting her attention. She bounds across the stream to join us. Once on land, she shakes her body, throwing water everywhere before taking off ahead of us into the woods.

When I realize I'm still holding Jaxon's hand, I release it, tingles radiating through my palm. My legs begin to burn, and I look around to find us in the same spot I was in yesterday, except on the opposite side of the river. "Are we going swimming?" I ask when we reach the top of the hill.

"No. Not today. There's somewhere I want to take you. We're taking a shortcut."

He hands me a canteen I had no clue he was hiding, and I drink from it, thankful for the cold relief against my throat. He takes a sip next and then pats Lacey's butt, signaling for her to continue. "Go on, girl."

Lacey trots off ahead of us, her bushy tail wagging behind her. "She knows where we're going?"

"Uh huh."

"You two speak a secret language I don't know about?"

I love when Jaxon smiles. His steely eyes shine bright, and a small dimple appears in his cheek above his beard. "Lacey and I walk these woods a lot, but we rarely head south of French Broad River. There's only one cottage up that way. Remember that one?" He smiles as he references the cottage where I caught him painting for the first time. "I haven't touched the place in years, so it's falling apart. The wild animals tend to roam there, just in front of Hollow Falls. I let them have their space, and they stay away from the other rentals."

"Let me get this straight. You manage your parents' old properties. You have some weird telepathic language with my dog. And you're a famous local artist. You've really stepped up your game since I last saw you, huh?"

Another smile, this one bigger. "You've been paying attention."

Quiet falls around us as my mind begins to wander. This fascination I have with Jaxon is not something I've felt in a long time. It was never like this with Scott. I've never had to work so hard to get to know someone. To be fair, I've never *wanted* to work so hard to get to know someone.

The thought of Scott sends a huge wave of guilt rolling over me. It's hard not to compare every conversation and situation to him. For so long it felt like he and I lived in isolation. It was hard to make new friends after my father's sentence. Trust wasn't an easy thing to come by, and I never socialized enough outside of my friendship with Scott to get to know other men.

My thoughts fade as I notice that Lacey has stopped walking and is now sniffing around aggressively. The stream has gained power and sounds like it's in surround sound. I swallow, a familiar feeling skittering up my spine.

We've come to a clearing in the woods, and we're back along the edge of the river. I must have been so deep in thought that I completely missed our approach.

Looking up, I gasp. "Is this—?"

But I don't need to finish the question. It looks just as it does in the painting and in my memory. A long stretch of dark brown wood arches from one side of the dangerous water to the other. Each splash slams and slips over boulders, pushing away the smaller rocks and spraying the air with mist.

I wish I brought my phone so I could capture this moment. The way the sun peeks through the trees, bathing the bridge in its light. The way nature's shadows cast down, cloaking parts of the wooden bridge.

"It's still here," I breathe.

Jaxon comes up behind me, standing just inches from my back. For a second, I close my eyes, trying to catch his crisp alpine scent mixed with the earth tones of my surroundings.

"Well," he encourages, "go check it out."

I look over my shoulder. "Really? It's still safe to walk on?"

He nods. "Of course."

Feeling the crunch and sink of dirt and rock beneath my shoes, I'm giddy with memories—the best of the best. It's like a greatest hits album is spinning on a loop in my head, bringing back scenes of the friendship we never saw coming. I think about our painting sessions where we would haul our canvases, tripods, and supplies into the woods and paint until we'd bled our hearts onto the backdrop. We painted everything we felt, heard, saw... It was a race against the clock to accomplish everything we could before the sun began to dip and we had to rush home.

The moment my hand lands on the top of the rail, I feel a sense of peace wash over me. It's the exact feeling I was searching for when I first arrived in Balsam Grove and got to the cottage one week ago. When I was desperate to feel something familiar.

I walk from one end of the bridge to the other and back again, running a hand over the rounded rail that was handcrafted long before I ever stepped foot in this town.

Jaxon doesn't approach until I take a seat at the center of the arch, letting my feet dangle over the edge. The wood is soft and sturdy beneath my palms as I curl my fingers around the rail. Staring out at the scene before me, I watch the river rage and feel the cool spray of water hit my legs. And I smile.

At first I think the laughter I hear is coming from nearby, but then I close my eyes and I realize it's all in my mind. All in one simple, slow-building memory.

This was home. Right here. Jaxon and me. This was our happy place, and that's why he brought me here today. He wants me to remember.

My mind is spinning when I give in to the memories of the boy that made my heart beat against my chest the way the water beats against the boulders. At fifteen, I couldn't tell him he made me feel that way. I couldn't tell anyone. Instead, I watched him toss rocks as far as he could throw them, admiring the jut of his jaw and the rounded peaks of his cheekbones as the sun poured down on him, painting him in the most glorious light.

The memory fades away and I open my eyes, leaving my heart crashing against my chest once more. Peering to my right, I find Jax just as he was in my memory, tossing rock after rock after rock over the most powerful peak of the waterfall. Until he looks over at me and pauses.

After all this time, could he possibly still want me? What we had was strong, but the forces that kept us apart felt stronger. Could I forgive him for what he did?

He sits beside me on the bridge, remaining quiet, like he knows this is my moment.

"Why did you bring me here?" I ask after a moment.

His eyes remain fixed ahead. "I thought maybe you'd want to see that nothing much has changed. It's still here, right where you left it. Maybe that's why I haven't been able to paint as much as I used to. I've kind of seen it all." He swallows.

The events of the last few days flip through my mind like a picture book.

Jaxon looking for Lacey at my house during the storm.

My attraction to his paintings in the café, then seeing him again just moments later.

Spying on him under the double falls.

His new life.

His attentiveness during and after my panic attack.

Him showing up at my house today, unannounced. It was like he knew I needed him. Jaxon always knew. Jaxon always cared.

When he confessed my secrets in that courtroom six years ago, my heart shut down. Not just toward him, but toward everything I once loved. Who would have known that the things I shut out to survive were the same things that could bring me back to life? Because that's how I've felt since coming back here. Like I've been waking up, trading darkness for light.

"I was happy here." I can feel the quiver in my words.

"You were," he says. "*We* were happy here. You and me."

Oxygen fills my lungs as I attempt to steer around his words. I'm not ready to have that conversation. "It's amazing what you're doing with your art, Jaxon. I know I didn't say anything before, but you should know I'm proud of you. You're making things happen."

There's a downward tilt of his lips as he picks up a rock and tosses it into the river. "Shutting myself off from the world to paint until my fingers feel like they might fall off has always come easy. I might be going through some sort of painter's block right now, but I can't remember a time when I didn't know what I wanted to do with the rest of my life, you know?"

"Not really," I say with a shrug. "I wish I did, but I don't. It was easy for me to give it up."

"You can do it again. Just pick up a brush. That kind of talent doesn't just disappear."

He doesn't understand. No one does. "I tried once, but I—" Looking up, I almost collapse from the heat behind his eyes. Jaxon's always been good at making me feel like the only other person in the room. Like I'm the only one on this entire planet that means anything to him. Maybe that was true once, but it can't possibly be true now. There's too much history. Too much time spent apart.

Still, he stares at me like we're tethered together by infinite possibilities. And what I wouldn't give for that to be true.

"I can't paint," I admit. "M-my fingers shake, and my hand doesn't move. My vision gets all blurry when I try to mix colors, and I cry, Jaxon. I cry for hours. It's just...not the same."

He leans in. I can feel his breath scrape my cheek. "Let me help."

I glue my eyes to the river. "No."

"Why not? You helped me when I needed it most," he says.

Turning my eyes down, I catch the movement as his knee slides closer to mine. I sigh, knowing Jaxon is making this into a bigger deal than it is. "All I did was buy you a canvas and some paint so you could create something you didn't have to cover up."

"You were eight." He says it like that meant something to him.

"I earned an allowance."

He shakes his head in frustration. "Aurora. You changed my life when you handed me that canvas. I finally realized why I'd been so miserable. Because while I may have been lost in all the moments I painted, it was like everything I'd created and covered ceased to exist the moment I slapped that damn eggshell semi-gloss over it. You set me free."

"It was nothing."

"It was *everything*."

I look up and suck in a sharp breath. He's so close. Mere inches away, and all I want to do is grip his shirt between my fingers and tug until his mouth falls on mine.

"You're lucky to be able to live your dream." My words come out soft, but by the jerk of his head, I know he hears me.

"So can you. If I can do it, so can you."

Shaking my head, I recall another painful memory. "No, Jaxon. You seem to be forgetting how different our dreams were. You settled because of me, and I was angry for it."

That same intense heat rips through my insides, just as it did the day I found out he turned down the biggest opportunity of his life because of me.

Jaxon's true dream was to leave Balsam Grove and take his art with him. He wanted to travel, painting the world's landscapes, not just this one. What he said earlier about running out of things to paint—it's true. And it's all because of me.

"I wasn't going to leave you here. Not alone. Not with—" Jaxon slaps the back of his neck and grips it. "No, we are *not* doing this. If you still think I was in the wrong, then I guess that will never change. I did what I had to because I loved you, and I never once regretted it."

"You would have."

"No. I wouldn't have."

"You can't possibly know that."

"I do know that. You still don't get it. Dreams change. I would have never been happy leaving you here while I chased old dreams. I wanted to take you with me. I wanted to make new plans."

I shake my head, refusing to be pulled back into that awful fight. "I could have gotten over that. We would have been okay. That's not the reason I stayed away for the past six years, and you know it."

"Stop, Aurora." He pulls away, fearing what I'm about to say.

"You gave the cops everything they needed to book my father, based on my confessions to you. My secrets. You might as well have handed over my diary. There was no evidence, but they didn't even care. They had your word that he was a monster." My chest is on fire. "Just because a man has a mental disorder doesn't make him a monster."

Jaxon's eyes widen and his face turns a disturbing shade of red. "No evid–?" He stops short and shakes his head. "Aurora, you were nearly a corpse when that deputy found you in your father's arms. I saw the photos. I wish to hell I didn't because

I will never get those images out of my mind. They haunt me to this day. All I did was tell the truth."

"It wasn't your truth to tell!" Heat lashes through my body. I've walked into an inferno with no exit in sight. Apparently, time doesn't heal all wounds. Time seems to have only made things worse.

"What did you want me to do?" Jaxon lifts his arms and drops them like he's exhausted. "Should I have lied when they questioned me at the station? Or in a court of law? Would that have made you happy, Aurora? I had to tell the truth. I had to protect *you*. Your father was mentally ill. You and I both know that in itself isn't a crime. But do you remember how many nights you crawled out of your window and in through mine just to get some sleep? You were terrified of him."

"I didn't understand what he was going through. There's a difference."

I'm shaking from the inside out, my head spinning at the dark memories that ambush my mind. Memories of my father's nightmares that would wake him with the most heart-wrenching screams. The sudden explosions of anger that would burst from him at any memory of my mom, which grew more frequent over time. But it was the volatile way he ripped my art from my possession that the lawyers latched onto.

The fear I had of my father was embarrassing. I never wanted anyone to know, but Jaxon knew everything about me. I trusted him, and then he betrayed my trust by revealing my darkest confession to everyone—strangers, neighbors, family, friends. Everyone.

He doesn't respond, and the pain of the past bleeds into my veins like poison, spreading, thickening, and filling my heart with a rage I find incomprehensible. Why is my anger directed at Jaxon when my father is the guilty one—when he pleaded insanity for unimaginable crimes?

"I loved him." My words are soft and true, and I know it's something Jaxon won't be able to understand. How could a girl still love a man who would do that to her? To others? Why don't I hate him? I should hate him. Sometimes *I do* hate him, but it's not enough to make me forget Jaxon's betrayal. But for the first time in six years, I can admit to myself that I want to.

"What happened that night, Jax?" Emotion grips my throat as I speak. This is the first time in years I've broached the subject. But maybe there's something more to it all. He looks at me like he doesn't quite understand what I'm asking. "The last thing I remember about that night was leaving you. We had just argued about you not accepting the offer to join the workshop. Lacey was with me. I remember sobbing as I left, and then—nothing. I woke up over a week later in a hospital bed and no recollection of anything."

Jaxon finds my hand and threads his fingers into mine. "I should have never let you leave that night. We were both so angry." He drops his head. "I'll never forgive myself for what happened to you."

I squeeze his hand and face him with tear-filled eyes. "Stop. I can barely handle the guilt I carry for my father. We argued. Couples argue all the time. I just wish I could remember what happened after I left you. It was rainy and windy. Lacey was with me. And then everything just fades to black." I take a deep breath. "During my father's trial, they realized that all the girls went missing during a storm."

Jaxon breathes through his nose. "Don't you think it's better that you forgot what happened that night?"

I squeeze my eyes together, knowing exactly what he means. I've been there, thinking the exact same thing. But forgetting hurts.

"I've been forgetting for years, Jaxon, and losing pieces of myself while doing it. I'm tired of forgetting. If I'm not careful, I'll lose myself completely."

"Let me help you."

"How?"

"Everything is connected," he says. "Every event, every painting. Everything. You want to know why you were happy in Balsam Grove when you visited? You experienced life, Aurora. You were open to its charm, and in return, it surrounded you. You lived it, you breathed it. And you can do it again. No one will ever be able to recover your memories for you. Those are yours. And your theory that you could ever lose yourself completely is bullshit. That could never happen, and the proof of that is here with you now."

My lungs balloon with air as I look around at the bridge and at the waterfall below me. He's right. As soon as I stepped out into nature again, I felt it all. It was as if nothing had changed.

"Then where were you when I woke up?" My voice quivers. I can't believe I'm asking him the question that's been twisting my heart since the day I came out of my coma.

"What? I was there. I never left your side until you forced me away." He swivels to face me, his knee bending and resting against the wood. "I was there when they put you in that ambulance. I rushed to the hospital behind them. I called your aunt Cyndi to tell her where you were and what happened. I lied to the hospital and said you were my cousin just so they would let me stay with you, and I stayed until Cyndi arrived with that Scott kid and they told the nurses I was lying. I was there. I never left. Not even for a minute. Not until Scott came out of your room and told me you wouldn't see me."

"Scott said you left." I swallow, confused and trying to make sense of what he is saying. My memories are all a blur, but the pain feels far too fresh, a wound reopened.

He must catch the confusion in my expression because he shakes his head, eyes brewing with the storm that's always ready to blow in. "I'll never lie to you, Aurora. Just like you'd never lie to me."

I stand, and he stands too. Looking around again, I suddenly feel off balance. This bridge, these woods. It all used to be so familiar. My home away from home. And now I'm a stranger.

"I think I should go back to the cottage."

He steps toward me but I back away, knowing there's nothing that can help us now. I don't stay and wait for him to think of something more to say. I turn and start back down the hill along the river.

"Where are you going?"

I keep walking.

"Aurora, you can't walk through these woods alone."

I flip around, heat raging like an inferno through me, blazing through my eyes. "Why not?"

He lets out a breath before opening a mouth to speak. "It's not safe."

"Isn't it? What's there to be afraid of now?"

"Don't be stupid. We're in the middle of the fucking Appalachians. It's never safe to be out here alone. You know that."

My jaw clenches, and then I take four long strides toward him until I'm under his nose. "You think these woods scare me after what happened? I may not remember those three days, but I know I was strong enough to survive them."

I turn around, swallowing against the lump in my throat. "Goodbye, Jaxon."

15

Jaxon, Twenty-One Years Old

Two years had gone by since our kiss—two years since she walked away from Hollow Falls in tears and I was told by her father that she was never coming back. I should have felt relief. The kiss was wrong. My feelings for Aurora were wrong. But it was loss that filled my chest, leaving an ache I tried to bury instead of confront.

She was gone, but she was everywhere.

When I finally saw Aurora again, it was by accident. It was nearing midnight, and I was standing at the bridge overlooking Hollow Falls when I heard the first crunch of leaves as someone approached. I sensed it was her before I saw her. It was like I'd been standing in this same spot for two years, waiting for this moment.

We both carried giant flashlights to guide our way, and we shone them on each other from opposite sides of the bridge. My heart trembled at what I saw. Aurora's eyes streamed with fresh tears, and her attire was completely inappropriate for nighttime in the woods—tiny shorts and a pale pink tank top that somehow hid nothing and too much at the same time.

I was twenty-one. She was seventeen. And although she was still too young, I could no longer pretend I wasn't attracted to her. Especially when I dropped my gaze to find her nipples brilliantly hard, thanks to the windy summer evening. My thoughts roared with imagery of what Aurora June would look like with her clothes on the ground, her legs wrapped around my waist, and her supple flesh in my mouth. Even after the hideous way I had treated her two years earlier, my mind was filled with years of caged lust.

She was standing in front of me again, invading my space, and I wanted, in every way imaginable, to invade hers.

The bridge at Hollow Falls had become my sanctuary. At all hours of the day, I'd find myself in the same exact spot, dreaming of a future that felt so far out of reach.

I'd been stuck in Balsam Grove my entire life, tending to the cottages since I was ten years old. My parents had always planned for me to take over the properties when I was old enough. They would retire, move to their dream home in the Canadian Rockies, and leave their estate to me. When I was younger, this all sounded like a dream. It sounded easy.

But things changed when I found my passion for painting. I dreamed of traveling the world with nothing but a backpack, some canvases, and my paints. My parents, on the other hand, felt art was a distraction from my future. And so the arguments commenced, along with the resentment. The older I got, the more Balsam Grove felt like a prison.

When Aurora arrived in the woods that night, I was concocting a plan for my escape. I'd submitted my art to a professional workshop led by one of my favorite artists, Dante Addario, where we would paint and sell our work around the world.

What I didn't realize at the time was that the girl standing in front of me with the sad eyes and crumbling expression would change everything I knew about my world—for better, for worse, forever.

She hesitated to approach, like I might shun her the way I did when she was fifteen. But there she was, standing in front of me on the same bridge that towered over us two summers before, a puppy nipping at her heels. I felt a pang of relief in my chest. We had another chance. I couldn't let her leave again.

I called out her name like it belonged with the night. "Aurora, don't go."

She stopped and turned, then searched around me with her light.

"It's just me. Jaxon," I confirmed, not wanting her to think I was a stranger in the woods.

"I know who you are."

She continued her turn. My heart fell.

"Wait," I called out, this time louder. "I heard about your mom. I'm so sorry."

I wasn't sure if that was the right thing to say. Death wasn't something I'd had any experience with, but she turned again and raised her flashlight to me. I started walking, not knowing if she would stay or go. She started walking too, and we met in the middle.

In that moment of silence, we were nothing but two spotlights in the dark, converging at the center of the bridge.

"I was going to come by and see you. I just didn't know if you wanted to see me."

"It's fine. I've only been back a few weeks—"

"I should have come by."

Her agreement shone through her silence, making me feel like an even bigger prick than I already did. "Is that a new dog? A husky?"

Despite the pain I'm sure Aurora felt, she managed a smile as she stared down at the black and white furball on a leash. "Her name's Lacey. I thought she might want to check out the woods."

"It's late—"

Aurora's heavy sigh cut me off. "Don't give me a lecture about being out here alone. Please, Jaxon. Not tonight."

I dropped it. I wouldn't tell her the gruesome reality that had become Balsam Grove—that six girls had entered these woods and never returned home—but she would learn.

"You still come out here?" She shone her light over the edge of the bridge.

"Almost every day."

We sat, setting our flashlights on either side of us, and I stared at her silhouette in the darkness.

"Are you still working for your dad?" she asked.

I laughed. "My father wants to give it another year and then hand over the keys and move far away from this place. He wants me to sign paperwork and commit to taking over by the end of next summer."

"That's great, Jaxon."

"Is it?"

A sigh fell from her lips. "I don't know. Maybe it's not what you want."

My chest burned. Aurora knew about my art, but she didn't know how important it had become to me over the past years. She didn't know about my plan to leave Balsam Grove.

"Things have changed a lot," I confirmed. I knew I was being vague, but I couldn't bring myself to tell her my plans.

"Yeah, it has." Her voice was so sad, so lost. I wanted to hold her, but I knew part of her sadness had to do with me, with the way I'd treated her. She was my best friend, though I'd never told her that. How could I? Being four years her senior, I was embarrassed.

More silence snaked between us before she spoke again. "You're still painting?"

"I am. Are you?"

"It's complicated."

"Aurora—" I started. It was a warning, another lecture, and she could hear it coming from a mile away. Painting connected us from the first summer we met, and its threads were still deeply buried. We were tethered, no matter the distance, no matter the time apart. That connection was once so innocent, but after seeing her again, even in the darkness, I knew all innocence was lost.

Aurora shifted. I could feel her bare skin slide against my jeans, and I wished I had worn shorts too so I could feel her, skin-to-skin.

"My dad threw everything away." Her voice cracked.

Her words caught me by surprise. "Threw what away?"

She couldn't be referring to her paintings. Art was everything to Aurora, and her parents had always embraced that. Philosophy and art. Their family thrived on those things.

"Everything, Jax." Her voice quivers. "My canvases from two summers ago are gone. And everything I brought from my mom's—all my tools, too. Everything."

Still, I was confused. "Maybe your father put everything in storage—"

She let out an exasperated breath that I could feel swirl with the next gust of wind. "No, Jax. They're all gone. They came this morning with the rest of my stuff from back home and my dad completely flipped out. He told me he destroyed them. H-he screamed at me." She pinched her eyes shut to keep herself from crying. "He said he hated me for painting them."

"What? Why?" I couldn't help myself. I placed a hand on her knee and squeezed, hoping to provide some comfort when she needed so much more. Her father had always been a little off, but tossing her art? That crossed the line.

"I thought everyone knew."

"Knew what?"

There was a long pause. Aurora's body started to shake. "Some of my paintings were in an art show at school. M-my mom was on her way to my show when she crashed." She blinked up at me, fresh tears spilling from her lids and down her cheeks. "She died because of me. Because of my art." Her voice cracked again before she let out a sob. "And my dad hates me for it."

"He said that?" I asked incredulously.

She nodded. "He says my art is the work of the devil inside me."

Darkness unleashed through me like a wild fire I had no hope of containing. "Jesus, Aurora. He's delusional." My arm moved around her shoulders, squeezing and letting her cry. "I'm sorry. He's probably grieving, but that gives him no right to say those things to you. Or to touch your stuff."

She sniffled. "He's upset and dealing with this the best way he knows how."

I didn't want to tell Aurora what I knew about Henry June. That in the two years she'd been away, he'd garnered a reputation for himself as the town drunk. That he'd gotten into more trouble than I could keep track of. And this talk of the devil wasn't the first instance I'd heard of something like that coming from his mouth.

I gave her shoulder another squeeze. "Are you going to be okay?"

More silence invaded the next two seconds, stretching time and filling it with doubt. "Just let it go, Jax. Okay?"

As much as I hated the idea of letting the subject go that night, I would have done anything she asked of me. But I couldn't let it go forever. Not until Aurora found her smile again.

Jaxon

She walks away from our spot at the bridge with determination, blazing a trail behind her, and I follow closely behind. Not even a minute later Aurora freezes in her tracks. The movement chills the air, and my steps falter behind her.

Suddenly, a squirrel shoots up the tree in front of us. As it takes off along a branch, rustling its leaves, my gaze falls back down to the familiar initials and tally engravings that mark Henry June's seventh victim.

Aurora's shoulders begin to shake. Her lip trembles, and a crease appears between her brows. Without thinking, I move toward her and put my hands on her shoulders, but she jerks away. Then she stomps off in the same direction she started, without a word.

I follow her the entire way home, keeping my distance but also keeping my eye on her. When Aurora nears the bottom step of her porch, she whips her head around, strands from her ponytail flying between her lips and sticking there, but she doesn't move a strand. "You didn't have to follow me home."

I step a few feet to the side of the house and lift the package I arrived with earlier, handing it to her when I get close. She looks down at it, her face telling me she completely forgot about the gift I brought with me.

"Whatever this is, I can't accept it." She lifts her chin high and crosses her arms in defiance.

"You know what it is, Aurora."

"I can't take that, Jaxon. Did you hear anything I told you earlier? I'm a lost cause."

Grinding my teeth, I step around her, lifting the package up the stairs and leaning it against the sliding glass door. "I heard everything. All the more reason for you to take it."

When I turn, she still hasn't moved from her spot. There's something about the way she stands there with the sun beaming down on her rigid stance and tight jaw that injects my veins with a dosage of her. Of my past. Of the one who's never stopped consuming my present.

Aurora lost some of her memories, and she left me with some I wish I could forget.

"If it helps, don't consider it a gift." I slip past her again, hopping off the last step and stepping forward.

"Then how much do I owe you?" she snaps back.

"Bill you later."

I don't look back. If I do, she'll see how easily she still gets under my skin—but not in a way that makes me want to yell at her. No, I want to pick her up and press her back against that sliding glass, press my mouth to hers, and drive into her until she has no other choice but to use my strength to keep her upright.

I flip her a wave over my head and shove my hands in my pockets before whistling for Lacey to follow.

"Go on, girl." Aurora's gentle as she speaks to her. "Go keep your daddy safe. He's going to need it."

My chuckle cannot be contained. She may be mad now, but she won't stay that way for long.

16

Aurora

It's been three days since I've seen him. Three days since our trip to Hollow Falls. Three days of staring blindly at a gift that would have once thrilled me.

What am I supposed to do with these?

The canvas is as blank as I am, mocking me. Beside it lie five tubes of paint, a scraper, three brushes—all different sizes—and a wood palette to mix my colors.

He just wants to help, Aurora. He's always just wanted to help.

But he knows how I feel about painting. I've told him what it does to me. How I've tried and failed. And still, he handed me the wrapped canvas like I'd know what to do with it.

There was a time I wouldn't have questioned my next move. I would have gone straight to work, painting whatever landscape swept the distance in front of me. Minutes would have turned to hours and hours to days, and I wouldn't have noticed the change. Inspiration was everywhere, especially with Jaxon as my mentor.

Sometimes tragedy strikes us in the most unusual of ways. When my mom died, I got my first taste of how cold the darkness could be, but art helped me through it. Well—art, Lacey, and Jaxon. My lifelines. Everything changed when I woke up in the hospital. I became so far removed from who I used to be and started living in a parallel universe—no light, no guide, no explanation…no end goal.

For so long, I was okay with the numbness. The darkness. In a way, it was all I knew. It was my way of shutting out a past that would otherwise haunt me.

I'm still staring at the blank canvas hours later when there's a knock at the door. Sighing, I lift myself from the stool and peer out the glass at the entryway. I see Claire standing there, wearing a bright smile, tight jean shorts, and a low-cut black tank top that showcases her perfectly rounded belly. If I'm ever pregnant, I want to have a body like Claire's. Curvy in all the right places, and somehow still thin despite her habit of sneaking pastries from the glass case when she thinks no one is looking.

Twisting the knob, I pull open the door and grin. That's when I get a better look at the whole ensemble. Silver, bohemian style earrings dangle from her ears, a matching bracelet wraps her wrist, and her cherry red hair is freshly cut, giving her bob a sharper angle in the front.

"Look who's trying to get laid tonight," I tease.

Claire raises her eyebrows and points at her belly. "Girl, have you seen this sexy belly? Danny has no problem getting it up when I give him the come-hither finger."

"Come-hither finger?" I laugh, watching as she sticks her pointer finger up toward her, bending and straightening to demonstrate. But it's the extra eye wiggle that has me laughing.

"Okay, I get it. Your belly is sexy, but I was commenting on your outfit. Aren't you closing the café tonight?"

She shakes her head. "Nope. Amber's got tonight." Then she slips past me, her eyes roaming the space and locking in on the blank canvas. "Care to explain this fascinating piece of art?"

"It was a gift from our friend Jaxon Mills." I tilt my head as she sits on the stool and turns toward the counter that faces the kitchen. "Did he tell you he taught me how to paint when I was fifteen?"

She draws an invisible doodle on the counter as she opens her mouth to respond. "No, he didn't. But Danny mentioned some stuff. He just said you and Jax have a history that only you two could understand." Her eyes shine when she looks up. "But it involved a forbidden romance and a love for painting. I totally swooned."

Laughing, I walk over to the fridge and stare into it, not quite sure what I'm in the mood for. I could go for a large glass of wine, but I've run out and I'm not about to head to the store now. Peering over my shoulder at Claire, I frown at my hosting skills. "Would you like something to drink? Water, tea? Can pregnant women drink tea?"

She shoots me a pointed look. "Yes, but no thanks. You and I are going out."

I let out a laugh and reel back from my hold on the fridge door. "Um. You mean *you* are going out. I'm going to bed."

She bats the air with a tiny wave. "Nope. It's Danny's birthday, and we're going out. To a bar. Well, to *the* bar. It's the only one in Balsam Grove. We're going to dance. You're going to get drunk. And I'm going to be the best designated driver you've ever had." She points to her tummy. "You can thank the baby for that." She flashes me a grin, then narrows her eyes just as fast. "Get dressed."

I scan her outfit top to bottom and decide that she's not joking. "I have nothing to wear."

She sighs heavily and stands. "I highly doubt that. Where's your closet?"

I jump to my feet, stepping quickly between her and the ladder staircase. "It's upstairs, and there is no way in hell you're going up there with that baby inside you. I'd die if you fell off that ladder. Give me a minute. I think I have some jeans and a tank top or something."

"Perfect," she says, all smiles. "I'll just…keep myself entertained."

With a roll of my eyes, I climb the ladder and reach my closet, pulling out a pair of jean shorts first. But staring down at them, I know they're not right for tonight. Jaxon is Danny's best friend, which means he will probably be there. I don't want him to see me in the same old shorts I wear every day. Balsam Grove isn't the place for designer threads or my mother's pearls, but I should still be able to throw on something nice for a night out.

Shifting through my closet, I eye an outfit I bought on a whim a few months ago. Something about it caught my eye, though it doesn't quite match the conservative style I've been sporting since living with Scott. It's playful, fun, and sexy—and when I saw it, it just felt like me. But when I got home, tried it on, and looked at myself in the mirror, something felt...wrong. I was ashamed of myself for wanting to wear something that might draw attention to me. So I buried it in my closet, and then it traveled here with me.

Something sparks in my chest, an acknowledgement that maybe I'm ready to be a little bit daring. I've come all this way to break the chains that have been trapping me in darkness. Maybe it's time to step out of my comfort zone.

I slip into the white and black striped chiffon one-piece. The shorts fall just below my ass, and I can feel the air graze the sensitive skin there. Feeling exposed, I grasp at the thin straps, ready to rip the outfit off and exchange it for something safer—and then I catch my reflection in the mirror. My shame melts away as I realize I like what I see.

Slowly, I release the hold on my strap, reach for the black velvet buttons that run from the dip in the neck to my waist, and begin to button them. When I'm done, I pull in a breath. My eyes drift down the white chiffon, my fingers skimming the skinny, vertical black stripes. I swallow, taking in the matching tie around my waist. The bruise on my arm from my fall in the woods is still visible, but I let it breathe in spite of the dark yellow skin.

I prop the door to my bathroom open so I can chat with Claire while I apply a light coating of makeup. "What are you doing going out anyway? Aren't you like, fifteen months pregnant or something?"

"Ha, funny! Danny's been working a lot since the sheriff's been helping out a rescue crew a few towns over. He hasn't seen his friends in a while, so I suggested Franco's. The whole town's coming out."

My stomach knots as I visualize an angry mob surrounding me at the stake, fiery torches in their hands. I could fake an illness, but she'd know I was lying. I could tell her I don't want to go, but that would be rude. Or I could go and face whatever comes my way, because that's exactly why I came back to Balsam Grove. I won't let the people in this town dictate my future.

I swipe on some mascara and then climb back down the ladder, my black sandals dangling from my fingertip. "What do you think?"

Claire, who has been staring out the back window, turns to face me.

Her smile grows wide. "Damn." And then she points to me. "You realize all the men in this town are married, right? Well." She quirks her lip. "Except for a couple, but I don't think you're dressed like that to impress Tanner."

My face floods with warmth. "Let's just go before I put my pajama pants back on."

She laughs and turns toward the door, then glances at me again over her shoulder with a grin. "The moment he sees you, he won't be able to take his eyes off you."

He doesn't even see me.

Jaxon's leaning against the brick wall on the other side of the room, a beer tipped to his lips and his eyes focused on the glowing Asian beauty who's chatting him up. It's impossible to miss him, especially with the red beanie he wears on his head. When we were younger, his hats were reserved for keeping the hair out of his eyes when he painted, but now it seems they're a staple. Except for that time he was swimming under the falls, I don't think I've seen him with his hair down since I've been back.

Franco's is a far cry from the hole in the wall Claire described on the way over. With its brick walls and dim lighting, it's got a rustic ambiance. A jukebox plays a nineties rock song I can't remember the name of, and there seems to be more than enough room for the thirty or so people milling about, shooting pool, throwing darts, and tossing beanbags into the corn hole board on the low stage.

I don't know where Claire thinks I come from, but I get the distinct feeling she was trying to warn me Franco's wouldn't be up to my standards, as if I have standards for bars. I don't.

Aside from the social events Scott would drag me to, I stayed in. His idea of a fun time was speaking in jargon to his buddies over import beers and fancy appetizers. I was content with my quiet—reading, cooking, bubble baths, and enjoying a glass of wine. Again, more differences between Scott and me. But the differences weren't all bad. Without Scott, I probably would have become the world's biggest hermit. He never let me stew in my self-loathing for too long before forcing me back on my feet. He was good for me, but wrong for me in the end.

Does that make me selfish? My chest pangs with guilt. No matter what happens, I can't ignore the fact that Scott has been a part of my life for as long as I can remember. My sweet and awkward best friend who grew up too fast, becoming far too serious and neck-breakingly handsome. I need to call him. We may not be a right fit romantically, but the thought of throwing away twenty years of friendship crushes me.

Claire and I link arms as we dart through the crowd, heading toward the other side of the bar. My stomach churns. With every step, another local throws a hard glance my way. I stick out like a sore thumb in this place, and clearly, word has already spread. Henry June's daughter is back.

Jaxon is still posted against the wall as we head his way, his intense eyes on the same girl. She's smiling up at him as she speaks, standing far too close for comfort. My skin crawls. He still hasn't seen me. He's too busy looking at her.

I hate it. I hate it as much as I hated him talking to that girl on the rock at Hollow Falls when I was fifteen.

I yank my eyes away, my gaze falling on the face of an insanely gorgeous man. With mouthwatering mocha skin and the richest light brown eyes, Danny Andrews doesn't look like the stereotypical small-town deputy. With his tall, lean frame and confident grin, he would look right at home on the cover of a fitness magazine or a romance novel. Hell, maybe even that *Bachelor* show all the ladies go crazy over.

Danny matches Jaxon in height and build, but that's where the similarities end. Stubble masks the lower half of his face, but the dimples on his cheeks peek through when he smiles. His eyes smile all on their own, and his dark, curly hair is cut close to his head. I couldn't have pictured a better husband for the little vixen sitting in front of me.

As if hearing my thoughts, he looks back at me and lights up with recognition—but then he sees Claire. His focus is completely stolen. In one smooth step, he's sweeping his wife into his arms and practically swallowing her in a kiss.

Wow. The heat in the room just rose to blistering. Her arms wrap around his middle, and it's like I've just entered the best part of a sizzling adult flick.

I step back, feeling like I'm intruding on their intimate moment, and turn my attention to the bar. It's long and narrow, with beer taps lining the back wall. I smile at the older woman sitting on a stool beside me. She does a double take before giving me a hasty once-over, lip curled, like my appearance disgusts her. She barks out a laugh as she tosses her eyes forward without a word.

Well, that was dramatic.

Ignoring her, I lean into the counter to get the bartender's attention. He's an older man, with silver sprinkled into his hair and heavy bags below his eyes. At some point, he looks right at me, a scowl already fixed on his face, but he doesn't take my order, even when I lean forward a little more. Instead, he serves the woman with the rude stare beside me and the already drunk man on my other side.

With a frustrated breath, I push away from the bar. I don't need to be here. I don't need to watch Claire and Danny's lovefest while Jaxon chats up some girl. I refuse to spend the night getting mean-mugged for the blood I carry, but before I can turn around to leave, my back slams into something hard.

I swallow, already knowing what—*who*—I'll find behind me. It's his body, his tall frame that molds firmly against my back like it was made for me. It's his crisp cedar scent, like he's just ridden his motorcycle through the woods. And it's his silence that always seems to be heard the loudest.

"Two Godfathers." Jaxon's voice carries across the bar to a female bartender. She nods at him in acknowledgment, her rainbow-colored hair falling in front of her shoulders. Less than a minute later, two drinks, amber in color, slide beneath my chin.

Jaxon tosses her a bill, but she pushes it back with a hard look, gesturing for him to keep it. "You testing him, Jax? What are you doing bringin' her here?"

"Just ordering a couple drinks on my buddy's birthday, Shelby. Let's not make this a problem."

Shelby's eyes narrow, then she turns to me, her pointer finger aimed at my face. "I got no beef with you, but you should know the rest of the bar does. And that man—" she looks over her shoulder at the bartender who ignored me earlier. "That's the owner. Name's Franco, and he hated your pops. Not a fan of you either. He ain't gonna serve you tonight or any night ever, dollface."

I straighten, my mouth open to let her know I really don't give a shit, but Jaxon leans over me to lift the drinks from the bar, blocking my view of Shelby. "We get the picture. Thanks for the warning, but maybe Franco should stop being such an asshole if he wants to keep this place afloat." Then in a softer growl aimed at me, he says, "Come with me."

I do. I follow him, only because I have nowhere else to go. I could walk out of here, but then how would I get home? I wish I could just leave. I'm angry. Angry at that woman sitting at the bar. Angry at Franco for ignoring my order. Angry at Shelby for making things so clear. But most of all, angry because Jaxon thinks he can step in and defend me like he actually cares.

Frustrated, I move past him toward Claire and Danny, who are no longer making out. Instead, they're standing with Tanner and the girl Jaxon was talking to earlier. She's laughing at something as her gaze drifts to me, curiosity blossoming wide in her sable eyes.

When I get close enough, Claire reaches for my hand and pulls me into the circle they've created. "Aurora, this is my good friend Meg. She owns the bakery down the block." Claire throws me a sly wink over her shoulder, and everything starts to click.

Meg. Meg's Bakery. As in, the Meg who has a crush on Jaxon, who is also the Meg that Tanner has a crush on. Understanding fills me at once.

"I told her about your chocolate croissant obsession."

"It's nice to finally meet you." I smile, and Meg returns it warmly.

"It's nice to meet you too. My croissants have never been in such high demand. Thank you for that." Her voice is sweet and melodic.

I like her, I can tell already, and I'm softened by the fact that nice people besides Claire and Danny do exist in this town.

"And you remember Danny, I'm sure." Claire smiles proudly between us.

"Of course." I meet his gaze, and his warmth wraps me like a blanket. "Happy birthday, Danny."

He tilts his head, affection radiating from his expression. "It's Deputy Danny now, Little A. And don't you forget it." He winks and pulls me in for a hug.

His arms are strong. Confident. They squeeze me like they're asking me to trust and forgive him all at once. Like he knows he's part of the town that shuns me and understands how out of place I must feel coming back. Yet Danny knows, just like I do, that this is the only place I belong.

"It's great to see you again, Aurora. You've been missed."

I laugh into his shoulder, feeling the strength of his hold which causes a squeeze in my throat. "By who, exactly?"

"Me, for one. And you know who else, Little A. Don't let his grumpy ass fool you." We pull apart, his hands still clasping my shoulders.

"I think we need a celebratory shot, don't you? My birthday. You coming home. Claire handling that little pumpkin in her tummy like a champ."

"You getting a night off for once," Claire adds to his list with a coy look in his direction.

Danny raises his arms out wide. "There's so much to celebrate!"

Before I wave off another drink—I haven't even started the first—Jaxon's handing me the two drinks he already ordered and moving back to the bar. Claire drags me to a booth nearby and starts telling me about her latest 3D ultrasound.

"I swear, Aurora. I rubbed my belly and asked her to smile for me, and she did."

"I told her our little peanut probably just had gas," Danny jokes with a chuckle.

Claire smacks his elbow, then chuckles and turns back to me. "Anyway, she's perfectly happy baking away until it's time to face the world." She sighs as her eyes drift to the ceiling. "Can you believe there's a person in here?"

I look down at her stomach, amazed. "It's incredible, Claire. You're going to be such a great mom." And I mean it. Even though we've only known each other for a couple of weeks, I've seen Claire handle stress like a saint. She's had incredible patience training me, and I love the way she glows when she speaks about her baby.

"Thanks, Aurora. I'm trying not to think about how scared shitless I am." She laughs.

I place my hand around hers and squeeze, wishing I had some sage advice, but I've never even held a baby. She's going to be just fine.

Jaxon arrives with the drinks, Meg following and Tanner on her tail like an unusually quiet caboose. He's not even blowing smoke tonight. I'm surprised by how different Tanner seems without his deputy uniform on. He's nervous. I see it in the way his eyes watch Meg when she's not paying attention, but then flit away when she turns toward him. Interesting.

I squeeze in closer to Claire to allow room for Meg and Tanner in the circle booth. Disappointment pangs my chest when I see Jaxon at the end of the table, still standing with a tray full of shots. Danny must notice our awkward arrangement because he pulls Claire out of the booth to let Jaxon in next to me. They climb back in beside him.

Yup. Awkward.

We could easily be mistaken for three couples, but the truth is so much more complicated than that. Meg in love with Jaxon, but Tanner in love with her. Me in love with Jaxon, but Jaxon in love with no one—not anymore, anyway.

But then why does he sit so close to me, his jeans pressing against my thigh? I swallow against the kick of my heart.

Jaxon raises his brows at me once he's passed out the shot glasses. "You cool with this?"

It's a fair question. Jaxon's never seen me drink, but he saw my father drink, and that was never a pretty sight. My father would spend hours a day at this bar for months on end, racking up chatter about what a hopeless mess he was, with a motherless daughter at home, no less.

My father was a hated man in Balsam Grove. Clearly, he still is.

Diluting my thoughts might be the best thing for me now. Not to mention, Claire is driving. I respond to Jaxon with a nod and pick up the shot glass to take a whiff. "Tequila?"

"Patrón. You don't need the lime, but take it if you're not sure about the stuff." A crease parts his brows. "You've done a shot before, right?"

Pinching back a laugh, I hold the shot to my mouth and shrug. "I guess you'll find out."

Everyone is poised with their drinks in their hands—Claire with her club soda and the rest of us with our tequila.

"Let's do this!" Danny yells, pounding one fist on the table while he tips his glass to his mouth.

"Happy birthday, buddy," Jax says.

"Happy birthday, douchebag," Tanner grumbles.

"Happy birthday, baby!" Claire screams.

"Happy birthday, Deputy," I say before tipping back the shot. Liquid sears my throat as it slides down. I take the burn with bulging eyes. Grabbing the lime, I wedge it between my lips and chomp down to cool the burn as fast as possible.

The truth is, I haven't done a shot since college, and even then, it was a rare occurrence. Since graduating, I've only had the odd mixed drink, beer, and wine. Tequila shots? Never.

A throaty laugh beside me burns my cheeks and I turn. Jaxon is watching me, tossing the straw from his Godfather and angling the liquid into his mouth. "Here." He pushes something in front of me, and when I look down, I frown.

"Water?"

He shrugs. "Do you want something else?"

I eye the second drink he ordered, pointedly—he never technically gave it to me. He grins, pushing it my way. "All yours."

I take a sip—more like a guzzle. I know his eyes are on me. I can feel them burning my skin like lasers, but I don't look back at him.

What would I say? The truth? That I'm embarrassed for holding on so hard to the past when I was dying in it? I need to find a way to let go, to move forward. I know that. But I'm not sure if I can do it with Jaxon pressed up against my body like he is now, sharing the same air and drinking the same drink. All I can think about when I'm near him is getting closer.

"You okay there, Aurora?" his voice jolts me.

"Yup." I look around, trying to find the best way out of this booth, but I'm trapped between Jaxon and Claire.

"You can't avoid me tonight, Little A."

"Don't call me that," I snap. My cheeks heat. I didn't mean for it to come out like that, but I always hated when Jaxon called me Little A. It felt like an insult coming from him. Like he wanted to remind me of our age difference.

There's too much silence now. My feet shuffle against the floor, and my fingers slip around the condensation of my glass. I take another drink.

"You've been avoiding me since our walk."

My eyes pinch close. "Jaxon—"

I look up to find his brows arched. I haven't even spoken, and he already doesn't believe me. I sigh. "It's been a convenient circumstance, that's all."

"Ouch. A *convenient* circumstance?"

I swallow. "I've been working mornings."

"And why is that convenient?"

Heat flames in my chest. "Can we please not do this now?"

He grits his teeth with a wrinkle of his nose. "Sure, fine. Some other time then. Maybe in another seven years." With a lift of his glass, he's dumping the rest of the liquid into his mouth before slamming it back on the table.

I'm not sure how to handle his reaction. My throat burns with emotion as I lean in, lowering my voice so only he can hear me. "You're not being fair. Do you think it's easy for me to be here? To let these people disrespect me? To feel your indifference toward me whenever we end up in the same room? Jesus, Jaxon. When I'm around you..." My eyes flicker up, locking on his as my breath hitches in my throat. My pounding heart flutters. He's so goddamn gorgeous.

"When you're around me *what*, Aurora?" The rasp of his voice coats my body in chills.

I'm not sure I could articulate it if I tried. I'm confused. I'm hurt. I'm angry. I'm sad. For everything we had and lost. For everything we should be but can't. For a beautiful future that was poisoned by a horrific event that stole so much more than three days of my memory.

I push away from him, sliding toward Claire and Danny, who break apart from their kiss to move out of the booth and let me out. But before I can get away, Jaxon is on my heels. "Why can't you answer my question?"

I spin around, my eyes moving over the room to see we've already caught the attention of a handful of people. Sighing, I shake my head. My cheeks darken as the answer to his question forms in my mind, then drips to the tip of my tongue. "When I'm with you, I remember what home feels like. What *hope* feels like." Emotion squeezes my neck. "And then I remember how it all ended. I'm as angry as I am guilty. I don't know how to get past it. I don't think you do either."

"Of course I don't know how I'll get past it. I don't even know how long you're planning to stick around. Why mend something if it's just going to break again? I don't know anything about the last six years of your life, Aurora. I was shut out, remember? And then you just show up here without a reason, without a plan." I shiver at his words. "Look at you. It's only been a couple weeks and you're already trying to put distance between us. Why did you even come back?"

If that isn't a punch in the gut, then I don't know what is. Why *did* I come back? I'm starting to forget. I thought I came back to close the door to my past, but I'm starting to think my subconscious had other ideas. "What do you want me to say? That I came back for you?"

Maybe that's exactly why I came back.

"You're here because this is where you belong." His conviction rings loud as people around us begin to stare. "This has always been where you've belonged."

My heart is pounding as I look around. Drowned out by the jukebox tunes, the onlookers can't hear us, but they sure as hell can see us. Another June, getting heated in the bar. Surprise, surprise. This will do nothing to prove that I'm not a threat to this town's peace.

Stepping back, I try to gain distance between us, but Jaxon reaches out and clutches my forearm with a strength I can only define as complete and utter desperation. It stops me. It stops my heart, and I know for absolute certain I will follow Jaxon anywhere.

He guides me to the middle of the room just as a familiar acoustic cover song spills through the overhead speakers. One by one, the people dancing around us shuffle off the floor, leaving just the two of us in the center of the room.

He pulls me in and wraps a strong arm around my waist, laying a palm flat against my lower back. No one else— nothing else—matters. Not the curious eyes of those who surround us. Not my heart hammering straight into his chest. Not the gaps in my memory. None of it.

My dance moves are lackluster, but in Jaxon's tight hold, I feel like I'm a princess at the ball. We don't move much, just a small step right, then a small step left, his palm slipping lower until the pads of his fingers dent the skin just above my ass.

I inhale slowly, taking in the intoxicating mix of crisp earth and tequila that wafts from his skin. And when his head dips low, his lips brush my ear, and my lids flutter closed. I melt.

"I don't know why you decided to come back," he murmurs lowly. "All I know is that you're here now." My heart squeezes. "You may feel like you've lost yourself, Aurora. That you've grown distant from the things you once loved. But it's not too late to reclaim your life. Let me help you."

There it is again. *Let me help you.* Those simple words cast a ray of warmth over me, prickling my insides and reminding me I've been numb for too long. Maybe he's right. Maybe it's time to reclaim my life, and maybe Jaxon is the perfect person to help me. Aside from Scott, he knows me better than anyone. The real me. The me before I was lost to the darkness.

"What the hell is she still doin' here?" a man barks.

Jaxon moves in front of me just as Franco approaches, but I step around him just as fast. I don't need Jaxon fighting my battles. "Excuse me?"

Jaxon wraps a stiff arm around my waist so I can't move forward. "Leave her alone, Franco." Jaxon can't help himself. He still fights for me, declaring his position loud and clear for the entire bar to hear.

It's then that I notice the music has died, and all eyes are on us.

"You don't scare me, boy. You don't see me causing a scene in your paint shop, now, do ya?"

"No one is causing a scene except for you."

Franco scoffs, his eyes darting to the crowd and back. His eyes are so red, I doubt he sees anyone but me. He leans in. Jaxon tightens his hold.

"You think you can waltz back into this town after we spent seven years cleaning up your pops' mess? I let you have your fun tonight, but no more. It's time you pack your bags, sweetheart. Be on your way, back to wherever you came from because you ain't welcome here. Not in my bar. Not in my town."

My jaw drops.

"That's enough, Franco. Jesus fuck. She didn't do anything to you, old man."

Franco's finger comes up, jabbing it an inch from Jaxon's face. Jaxon doesn't even flinch. "Get her out of here, Mills, or

I swear to God, I will see her out myself. The law's on my side with this one."

I look up to find Tanner in the same spot we left him in, still in the booth, but now his arm is around Meg. His eyes flash with conflict, like he's not sure if he wants to watch or help. If I'm being honest, it hurts.

Claire and Danny are weaving through the crowd toward us, but the damage is already done. I feel like my chest might burst as my eyes travel around the crowd, meeting gazes that match the seething hate in Franco's.

He's just looking out for his town. But why do I have to be the bad guy?

"What is your problem?" I manage to hold back the tears, feeling the rage of my pain.

"You, sweetie. You are my problem. You and your batshit crazy father."

Jaxon's hand lands on Franco's shoulder, the tips of his fingers whitening from the pressure. "Back off. Whatever beef you had with Henry *ends* with Henry. Jesus Christ, man. Aurora just lost her father. Have some goddamn respect."

Franco's jaw tightens and his nose flares. "Respect?" he barks. "You're going to regret this, Mills. She was trouble for you then, and she's trouble for you now. Don't let those perky tits and pretty eyes fool you."

Shit. Jaxon steps away from me and toward Franco, his elbow cocking back and springing forward faster than I can even blink. My breath catches in my throat. My palm covers my mouth. But just as Jaxon's fist is about to meet Franco's jaw, it freezes in mid-air.

My breath slides out in a whoosh. Danny's hold on Jaxon's elbow is firm as he pulls his friend back.

Jaxon pushes him away and swivels around. "What the fuck, Danny? This asshole deserved that and more."

"I agree, but you need that pretty hand of yours. Let me deal with Franco."

"I don't give a fuck about my hand. This is my fight," Jaxon growls.

I step forward again resting a hand on Jaxon's chest. "Actually." Our eyes meet. "This is my fight."

Franco lets out another laugh. "Well, look at that. The June orchard blossomed, and the apples are all alike. You're as crazy as he was, aren't ya, little June?"

I'm fuming, my fists balled tight, and I can feel the pressure in my neck rise to my cheeks. Franco sees it. He knows he's gotten under my skin. So he goes for another lick at my open wounds.

"I won't let you fuck things up for me the way he did. I'm older now, lost a great deal of patience over the years." His eyes turn to Jaxon, who's still being held back by Danny. "Just you wait, Mills. Her colors will start shining through soon, just like her dead pops."

It's like a vacuum just sucked up all the sound in the room. I inhale sharply, my eyes on Jaxon. His fists are balled up, his face is red, and I swear his left foot kicks back like a bull about to charge the streets of Spain. He lunges forward again, catching Danny off guard and making him struggle harder to hold him back.

"What the hell is going on here?" booms another voice.

An older man with a shiny head, a tan shirt near-bursting at his rotund waist, and a star-shaped badge over his breast pocket comes barreling over, his face red with confusion and anger. I remember that face. The face of the man who would toss my daddy into the back of his cruiser and drive him home after he'd gotten too drunk at the bar. Sheriff Brooks.

He looks between us all, his eyes lingering on me a little too long, but he doesn't address me. "Someone mind telling me what all this yellin' is about? I could hear y'all from outside."

Jaxon steps forward, Danny finally letting him out of his hold. "Franco's kicking Aurora out because he's got a grudge against her father."

"That's right. My bar, my rules." Franco spits, stepping closer to Jaxon and staring up under his nose. "She's got to go. Now."

"Whoa, whoa," Sheriff Brooks calls, placing a hand on Franco's shoulder and yanking him back. "Leave Miss June alone. As far as I can tell, she ain't done nothin' wrong."

Franco turns to face the sheriff. "Are you shittin' me? C'mon, Brooks. You know she don't belong here. I want her out. Law says I can refuse service to anyone. Well, I'm refusing service to her."

"You know what?" I raise my hands, waving the white flag. I've had enough. My body is shaking. I knew it wouldn't be easy coming back here, but I didn't expect this. "I'll see myself out, thank you very much." I start to walk away, then turn back around. "Oh. And you should really wash your hands after you take a shit. Your drinks taste like ass." I walk away, the crowd parting as I pass. "Fuck you, Franco," I call behind me.

"Fuck you, Aurora June," he screams after me.

I'm still shaking as I step out the front door of the bar, but I feel liberated after standing up for myself. Sure, Franco won. I left. But I walked out on my own two feet with my head held high.

Jaxon's on my heels, curling his hand over my shoulder and twisting me into his hold. Instantly calmer, I wrap my arms around his middle and lay my cheek against his chest. We're hugging. I can't remember the last time we hugged. Despite the subtle changes that come with age, we still fit together perfectly. *God, I've missed him.* Tears climb the back of my throat, building into a ball and threatening to escape. My fists clutch his shirt.

I sigh and open my eyes. They land on the gleaming silver motorcycle parked against the curb. "Is that yours?"

He nods into my hair without loosening his hold. "Yeah, the old one bit the dust too many times. I got tired of bringing her back to life."

I laugh softly, loving that there are still pieces of us that are connected through memories. The number of times Jaxon had to haul his bike back home on foot to fix her was truly impressive. But Jaxon loved it. Along with painting and traversing the woods, he loved fixing up that old bike.

Loud chatter blasts through our quiet night as the door to Franco's opens and our friends tumble out. Well, *friends* might be the wrong term. Tanner's still got his arm over Meg's shoulder, and his eyes narrow when they find mine. He doesn't want to be my friend. He wants me gone, just like the rest of the town.

"Aurora," Claire gasps, charging to my side. "Franco was such an ass. Are you okay?" She looks between me and Jaxon, exchanging concern for a slow-spreading smile. "Never mind. Stupid question."

I nudge her and roll my eyes. "Shush."

Brooks walks out of the bar next with a polite wave in passing. "Y'all okay to drive tonight?" Jaxon, Tanner, and Claire assure him they're fine. He tips his hat, gets into his cruiser, and drives off.

Once he's gone Claire loops her arm with mine. "You ready to head home, or do you have a ride?"

My eyes grow wide. "Wait, you're going? You guys don't have to leave because of me."

Danny shakes his head in assurance. "Nah, Franco doesn't deserve our money. We're going to head back to the house and have a few beers. Play some pool. You guys should come." That's when I see the rest of Danny's party guests spill out the door behind him.

Jaxon looks at me, then shakes his head. "Aurora and I have plans. You don't mind do you, dude? You're kind of old to be celebrating your birthday, anyway."

Danny socks him in the arm. "I'll remember that when it's your turn." He winks. "You kids have fun."

I catch the flash of disappointment in Meg's eyes, but she gets over it quickly, wrapping an arm around Tanner. Tanner, who still hasn't said a single word.

"Be safe," Claire sing-songs to me with a wink as Danny literally sweeps her off her feet to carry her to their car. She yelps, then throws her head back and laughs. Meg, Tanner, and a few people I don't know walk off toward another car down the sidewalk, and then finally, it's silent again.

Jaxon looks over to me. "What do you say?" he asks, his voice a soft rasp against my heart. "Want to go for a ride?"

Warmth spreads in my chest and I nod. "Yes, but on one condition."

"Anything."

I smile, my gaze settling on his. "Don't take me home just yet."

17

Jaxon

Aurora's arms wrap around my waist as if they never left all those years ago, and all the familiar fluttery feelings come back with a vengeance.

She's pressed against me, her legs straddling my hips, my back to her chest, her palms flush against my abdomen, and her fingers digging into my skin through my shirt. I groan and shift against my arousal pushed up against my jeans. Having Aurora's curvy frame strapped to my body again feels even better than I remember.

I rev the engine—once, twice—to distract the flow of blood, then glance at her over my shoulder. "Ready?" She nods, my helmet swallowing her entire head, and my lip curls in response. There's nothing sexier than a woman strapped into my gear, especially this woman. "Hang on tight," I say before I gun the engine with a final warning.

She will hang on tight. Aurora will clutch onto me like her life depends on it, just the way I used to love. When she was fifteen, it was the closest she could be to me without us crossing that forbidden line. As much as she loved the thrill of the bike, part of her was always a little terrified. Her arms hugged me a little too tight and her thighs squeezed me a little too hard, but nothing felt better.

I pull out onto the deserted street, and we just ride. I steer us up the mountain passage, and we weave down the narrow streets for miles. It's the perfect night—a slight chill in the air, a light breeze, a clear sky, and a crescent moon hanging big and bright in the sky. Nightlife croaks and sings, and the scent of burning wood from a nearby campground tangles with the aroma of pine and oak.

As much as I've always wanted to leave Balsam Grove to travel the world, I still love everything this town has to offer—its simple lifestyle, the familiarity of it all. And with Aurora wrapped around me again, I find myself drifting in and out of memories. Memories of waking up every morning with a kick in my heart at the thought of spending time with her. Of our adventures together. Of teaching her how to paint until eventually the mentor became the pupil. And of how easy it was to fall in love. Deep, soul-crushing, heart-murmuring, mind-bending love. I'm not even sure when the switch went off in my heart, but I'll never forget the way she made me feel about my own art when she was just eight years old. Maybe it started then. The seed was planted. And every summer after would bring me closer and closer to delivering her first heartbreak.

I'll never forgive myself for that. For shunning her at Hollow Falls when she was fifteen. For making her think I wanted anyone but her. I didn't. I wanted no one else, and that scared the shit out of me. She was four years younger, and her feelings for me weren't subtle. Around my friends, especially Tanner, that was dangerous. That night haunted me for two damn years—until I saw her again and could finally make up for everything we'd lost. Can we do it again? Yet another tragedy has brought her back to me—first her mother's death, and now her father's.

But will she stay this time?

I'm lost in all things Aurora when I see oncoming lights rounding the bend up ahead, highlighting the sway of the fir trees that line the road. Aurora tightens her hold around my middle, causing my heart to jump in my chest. Why is she holding on so tight? Is she scared? Excited? Does she remember how she went from clinging to me in fear when she was fifteen to hollering into the wind at the thrill two years later? She changed so much over those two years, growing more and more beautiful while sprouting wings of her own. Her love for the mountains grew. Her art flourished, and her level of stubbornness was far superior to anyone I'd ever seen before. I loved it all.

I loved how she soared despite the pain of her mother's passing. She flew, and I fell madly in love.

My fingers unwrap from the left handle as I place my palm against the back of her hand, pressing it into my abdomen. I want her to know I remember. I want her to know I could never forget. Her fingers curl into my shirt, and I wish for a moment there was no fabric between us.

I exhale heavily, closing my eyes just for a second, embracing every bit of this moment before it's ripped away from me like before. There's so much to say.

The headlights up ahead are growing brighter, forcing me to squint from their blinding light. Shit. My heart jumps up my throat as I realize how much distance we've closed since I first spotted the car in the distance. The gap is closing...and the car is not in its lane. It's in mine, barreling too close and too fast.

"Jaxon, watch out!" I hear Aurora scream just as I swerve right to avoid the oncoming vehicle. It zooms past us, missing us by inches as pebbles fly out from behind the tires. Aurora grips me tighter, slamming her cheek between my shoulder blades as my breaths punch the air.

I pull over onto the dirt shoulder, as far away from the road as I can get, and I follow Aurora as she scrambles off the bike and clutches her chest.

"Are you okay?" I bend down, assessing her under the half-lit moon. "Hey," I say, taking her hand in mine. She's shaking. "Look at me, Aurora."

She looks up, and it's as if she's squeezing my heart in her tiny, innocent hands. Her eyes are thick with tears, red from trying to hold them in, and so incredibly panicked. Every urge and feeling I've ever had for Aurora comes rushing back at once.

My thumb catches her first tear, but my heart catches the next. I'm reminded all too well of the Aurora that came back after her mother passed away, the girl who quickened to a panic at any loud noise or sudden movement. She changed after her mother's life was taken too soon. Over the next summer, as she fought to take control back from her anxiety, her father's behavior grew more and more erratic, hindering any chance for Aurora to heal herself. As Henry June began to steadily slip from one reality to another, Aurora's energy went toward him.

Aurora's panic attacks aren't new to me. I've seen the suffocation in her eyes. I've held her through them, just like I did the other night after the explosion of wine and glass in the studio. I've done it dozens of times, but that doesn't make it any easier to deal with now. I hate seeing Aurora in pain.

I press her cheek against my chest, my arms wrapped tightly around her as she breathes through the panic.

When I feel her breathing return to normal, I pull away to get a good look at her. "I'm sorry. I didn't even realize they were in our lane until we'd rounded the bend."

She looks back to the road with concern. "I'm fine. Do you think they were drunk?"

I shake my head, wondering the same thing. "I don't know. It's like they didn't even see us." I don't want to admit the discomfort in my chest at the fact that the driver never even swerved out of the way. Either they never saw us, or they were trying to hit us. I shudder. I can't think like that, and Aurora doesn't need any other reason to worry.

"Should we call it in? Did you get a description of the car?"

"I didn't see much, to be honest. But I'll call it in." I whip out my phone and call the station. No one's there, so I wait for the transfer and get Brooks' voicemail. Frustrated, I shove my phone back in my pocket and look around at where we are. "You okay to get back on? We've got maybe a mile or so until we're there."

She nods. "Yeah, I'll be fine."

A couple minutes later, we arrive at an inconspicuous dirt trail. I know it's here because it was my buddies and I who paved the path to Mountain Look, a secluded clearing that looks out over the edge of a cliff. Yes, we did it with dirty teenage intentions, but I only ever took Aurora there.

I park the motorcycle near a tree and let the headlight beam toward the cliff. After grabbing two blankets from the storage compartment, I take Aurora's hand to lead her down the short trail to the edge of the cliff. Her warm hand in mine feels natural, familiar, like we never stopped holding on. A chill sweeps through me. Clearly, I never stopped.

"I can't believe you're bringing me to Mountain Look." She laughs when she makes the connection. I smile.

"You fell in love with the stars out here."

"That's not all I fell in love with out here."

I swallow and turn toward her, my chest thick with the weight of her words. How can someone who exited my life so coolly still warm me in the only place that matters?

We lay a flannel blanket down over the dirt and stone a few feet from the edge of the cliff. I sit beside her, close enough to let my knee brush against hers as we stare into the wide-open space.

"Try not to let them get to you." I glance at her and catch her face flash with doubt. "I know it's easier said than done, but they don't know shit, Aurora. What you've been through, the reasons you're here... It's no one's business."

She sighs and kicks off her sandals. "I've told myself the same thing, but it still hurts, Jax."

Jax. I think that's the first time she's called me that since she's been back.

"I can't win with these people."

"It's not a competition, and you have nothing to prove. You're not him."

I cringe at my own words, knowing exactly how a similar conversation like this went years ago. The last thing I want is to dredge up a bunch of bad memories and move backwards. Aurora's here. We're alone. And we're talking. But she needs to understand what I'm telling her, and I'm not sure she does.

"Yeah, well. I may not be him, but I have my own issues. These panic attacks are no joke. Before my dad was sentenced, they got pretty bad. I tried to learn how to control them naturally. Meditation, yoga, exercise—but I couldn't get a handle on it. I finally gave in and went on medication, but I haven't taken a single pill since I got here."

"Why?"

I see the hesitation in her silence. "I left them by accident, but that's not the only reason." More silence. "I wanted to see how it felt to go without them after so many years."

"And how has it felt?"

"It's felt...okay. So far I've mostly been able to control the attacks on my own."

"That's good, right?"

She shrugs. "I think so. For the longest time, I was happy to numb it all and forget. I don't want to be numb anymore." Her eyes flick up to mine like she's scared. Like she thinks maybe she's doing something wrong.

"I get it."

"You do?"

I nod. "Sometimes it feels like six years have passed, and all I've done is stand still against the rush of time."

She glances up, her eyes scanning me like she's curious about all those years, those passing moments. What has she missed? Who am I today? I want to know those same things about her.

My eyes lock on hers. "Ask me anything."

She inhales sharply. "I've seen how women practically fling themselves at you. I guess I'm surprised you haven't settled down with anyone by now."

There's a question in there somewhere, but she hasn't asked it. When I don't respond, she sighs. "Has it ever been the same for you? What we had together? Has there been anyone—?"

A fire builds and licks against the walls of my chest. Does she really think another woman could come into my life and compare in any way to her—to what we had?

My jaw hardens again, because as much as I want her to know there's only ever been one love of my life, I'm not sure she deserves that peace of mind.

"Never mind," she whispers after too much silence. "I don't want to know."

"I've dated others," I tell her anyway. "Casually. But nothing like what we were. Is that what you wanted to know?"

Her expression softens and she tilts her head as her hand finds mine in the dark. "It's never been the same for me either."

"But you've dated?"

I hate myself for asking. Of course she's dated. She's beautiful and smart and sweet. She's talented too, but if she's given up her art, then she's most likely hidden that fact about herself. Men would go crazy for Aurora if she put herself out there. I don't want to find out that she has.

She starts to let go of my hand, but I grab it tightly. She looks down, then back up at me, the most heartbroken expression on her face.

"Shit, I wish I never asked."

She scoots in, her face inches from mine as her free hand moves to my face. I love the way her fingers run against the hair on my jaw like she doesn't know what to do with the texture. The scruff is new for her, but the feeling in my chest as she grips me is the same. Like my heart is breaking and falling for her all at once. The intensity of wanting her mixed with the fear of losing her all over again is incapacitating.

"There was someone else. We were friends and then dated."

Her words are a punch in the stomach. "Like us."

Her mouth opens again, and her brows scrunch like she's in pain. "No, nothing like us. Jax, I left him to come here. I didn't even tell him where I was going." She swallows, and I try my best to stay quiet so I can hear her out. "After my dad died, I realized how much of myself I'd lost. I didn't want to settle. I didn't want to feel numb anymore. So I came back. And it's the only thing that's felt right in years."

I need to be careful around Aurora. I realized this when I saw her standing in the café, looking more beautiful than ever. I could fall again so easily, and it would take nothing to get there. She's everything I remember and more. There's a sophistication about her now that's hidden well behind her mountain roots. She reminds me of her dad in that way. The good parts of him.

"Do you think you made the right choice coming back here?"

She nods without any hesitation, filling me with relief. My head closes the gap between us to rest against hers.

How does she do this to me? After seven years, she's still my everything. Despite the pain, the loss, and the agony of being apart, my love for her has only grown.

And for reasons only I know, that makes everything harder.

18

Aurora

He's been here for two hours nursing the same black coffee, flipping through the June edition of the same magazine he always had rolled up in the back pocket of his shorts when we were younger: *Art World Magazine.*

"See something you like?"

I inhale sharply and turn to face an amused Claire. She doesn't miss a thing, I swear.

"What? No." I shove off the counter and turn around to the sink to wash the remnants out of the last blender concoction I got stuck making. Claire was right to warn me away from these things. Addicting in the worst way and a nightmare to clean up after.

She doesn't approach, but I can feel her eyes on me. "You've been awfully quiet since you clocked in. I thought you'd willingly fess up to where you and lover-boy revved off to last night, but I guess I'm just going to have to coax it out of you."

I shut off the sink and dry my hands before turning and tilting my head at her. "He took me to Mountain Look."

Her eyes grow wide as saucers, and I bite back a laugh.

"I know. Crazy, right? It was like we'd never been apart." I sigh dramatically and watch as Claire's eyes narrow at my sarcasm.

"I hate you."

"What?" I laugh. "That was what you wanted to hear, wasn't it? You probably wouldn't believe me if I told you we took a drive up the pass, almost got run over by a damn drunk, and then spent the next two hours *just talking* up at Mountain Look."

She shakes her head, her eyes accusing. "Nobody just *talks* at Mountain L—"

"See!" I exclaim, hopping onto my toes and then letting out a laugh. "Told ya you wouldn't believe me. But it's true. We used real words. He didn't even try to cop a feel."

Claire's face bunches in annoyance and she whips the white rag in her hand at me. I manage to turn away, but it still swipes me across the cheek. "You're such a brat. You can tease me all you want, but don't even try to tell me you weren't just undressing Jax with your eyes, you little perv."

The bubble of laughter that bursts from my throat comes as a surprise. I clap a hand over my mouth to stop it, but it's too late. Jaxon's eyes find mine as I'm trying to control myself. His expression softens, his cheeks lift, and a twinkle appears in his eyes. My heart gives a little kick in response, and as cheesy as it is, I wouldn't be surprised if his could feel it in return.

"Oh my God," Claire says in a scolding whisper after Jax turns back to his magazine. "You two are like cats in heat. And don't deny it. I'm pregnant. I know how babies are made."

She's ridiculous. "Claire, really. Stop. Things between Jax and me are complicated."

"Not from where I'm standing."

I sigh and cross my arms across my chest. "Feelings like what Jax and I had don't just go away. Seven years is a long time, but he's still my first...everything." I feel a blush coming on, but I ignore it despite the amusement that appears on Claire's face. "We hurt each other, and we were young. People change, you know? There's a lot to work through."

"So, you're working through it?"

I sigh. "No. Yes." I shrug. "I don't know. Up until last night, I thought Jaxon wanted me gone just like the rest of the town."

Claire softens. "Aren't you the least bit curious about why he's been hanging out in the café for the past two hours?"

I shrug, not wanting to acknowledge the live wires that just sparked in my chest. I didn't want to get my hopes up. "He owns the place. I just figured—"

She levels me with one look, holding me captive. "You figured he always hangs out in the café?" She shakes her head. "Never." Her lips curl into a smile. "And he hates—*hates*—black coffee."

My jaw drops. "What does he usually drink?"

Claire laughs and points behind me. I already know she's staring directly at the blender before I confirm it. "You've got to be kidding me."

"Nope. The superhuman genes are strong with that one. He could put anything in that body of his and never see a bad result." I flush. She shakes her head and places her hands on her hips. "Did you hear what I said about—? Ugh, never mind. You two are totally hopeless."

She raises her arms as if she's finally given up, which I highly doubt, and backs away with a smile. "I'm going to work on organizing the back room since you've got this under control out here." She wiggles her eyebrows. "I'll be back."

I make a face at her back as she walks away.

Aurora

I've only been skimming the pages of the magazine. I keep getting distracted by Aurora tossing her hair into yet another high ponytail, as if the dozen before it were getting on her nerves. The polite smile on her face as she greets each customer. Her laughter, light as wind chimes in the fall as she talks to Claire. She steals my focus and knocks the air right out of me.

The coffee, cold and bitter, slides down my throat, and I cringe. I should be used to this by now. They say black coffee is an acquired taste, but my taste buds disagree. I lean forward to set the cup on the table in front of me when someone snatches it from my hands. It's replaced by another, this one cold and icy, with a dollop of whipped cream oozing from the half-dollar sized hole in the plastic dome lid.

Looking up, I'm met with Aurora's amused smirk. "Thought we weren't lying to each other, Jax."

The playful taunt of her tone catches me off guard, and then I register her words. *Fuck.* My eyes roll back with annoyance toward my best friend's girl, who I'd love to strangle right about now. Claire and her loose lips. "It wasn't a lie."

She tilts her head. Another challenge. Fuck if it doesn't rile me up. I used to love this—the back and forth quips that always carried a dose of teasing with the anger. One of us conceding and the other winning a kiss.

Neither of us minded losing.

"It wasn't a lie, Aurora. Think about it." I wait for her to respond, but she crosses her arms instead. "I didn't tell you black coffee was my favorite."

Her obstinate expression settles into defeat. "You're right."

Now it's my turn to be surprised. I squeeze my lids shut and shake my head. "Did you just *concede?*"

A blush lights up her cheeks, and I know she remembers too. Before I can tease her again, she plops onto the couch beside me and snatches the magazine away. "Mind if I join you?"

She settles in and turns to look at me. "You know what I think?" she asks, like whatever it is has already been decided.

"What, dare I ask?"

She hands the magazine back to me. "I think you should close your eyes, flip the pages, and then stop on a random page. Whatever you land on will tell you where you'll visit next. No hesitation. Pick it. Book it. Do it."

"What are you, a travel agent?" It occurs to me in this moment that she very well could be. I don't know much about the last six years of her life. Bits and pieces I was able to figure out. Our conversations last night were mostly about asshole Franco and vague information about our dating history. I know where she went to school and where she lived, but beyond that, I haven't really pushed to learn more. Honestly, I think I'm too afraid of what I might find in her new life.

But at least in this way, she's still the same old Aurora, thinking she knows what's best. Still thinking that leaving Balsam Grove is the answer to everything missing in my life. She still doesn't get it. But I do. Aurora still harbors guilt for my decision to stay when I had an opportunity to leave.

Her hand covers mine, surprising me. Her voice is soft when she says, "Don't read into what I just said, please. I just thought it sounded like a fun game."

I shake off all thoughts of the past and hand her the magazine. "Then you do it. Pick your next vacation."

Aurora bites her lip, staring down at the open page like she's considering. Then she shrugs. "Okay."

She does exactly as she instructed me to do—closes her eyes, leans her head back slightly. The angle gives me the perfect view of her profile, from her chin to the rise and fall of her next breath. I lean toward her, inhaling her familiar scent of orange blossoms and wild berries.

She's blindly flipping the pages of *Art World* one by one, a smile curling her lips. I keep thinking she's about to choose a page, but then she goes again, and again, until she lets out the tiniest giggle, bites down on her bottom lip, and points to the page beneath her chipped nail.

"This one," she says looking at me instead of the photo of Iguazu Falls. I can feel her intense eyes burning through me, but I can't lift my gaze from the page she chose. What a dream trip that would be, to stand in front of one of the most beautiful natural wonders in the world. How I'd love to make that the subject of my next canvas.

"Hey, Aurora," Claire calls, making us both jump. "Do you mind making sure the fridge is stocked for tonight? I think we're all set, but it wouldn't hurt to double check."

"Sure thing." Aurora tosses me the magazine with a grin before lifting herself from the couch and walking off.

I eye Claire suspiciously as she heads my way.

"So." She says the word slowly, as if still figuring out what she's going to say. "Guess who I just got off the phone with?"

Claire has always been like a sister to me. Mostly the loyal kind, sometimes the bratty kind. But protective Claire is surfacing now, and discomfort swirls in my chest.

"I don't want to know," I say, looking down and flipping the page of my magazine with a slap.

But Claire won't let up. She plops down beside me where Aurora just was and sighs dramatically. "Let me give you a hint. Her name starts with *V* and ends in *alerie*. Ring a bell?"

I stiffen. "Clever," I mutter without expression.

"Don't you want to know what she called for?"

"Nope. I told you two months ago, I have nothing to say to her. If she calls, just take a message and throw it in the garbage. I don't need to know about it. She'll get the hint. Can we not talk about this?"

Claire rips the magazine from my grip and tosses it on the table. She waits until I meet her gaze to speak. "Jesus, Jax. What happened with Val?"

"Just leave it alone."

"No! I won't leave it alone. You need to tell me what's going on. She's calling my café now, so I'm involved."

I groan. "It's nothing, Claire. I promise. We had a thing. It's over."

"I told you she was bad news bears, didn't I?"

I shove my fingers through my hair and pinch my eyes closed. "Don't start. Please, just don't."

Claire let's out a sarcastic laugh. "You're in this position because of what you started. I'm just the messenger."

"And I don't want the message."

"Don't you want to know what she said?"

My eyes cut to Claire. "No."

I hate the look she throws me next—a warning that tells me Valerie is up to something. That doesn't surprise me. Valerie has been up to something since the day we met.

"Fine. Tell me. But I swear to God, Claire. There better be a good reason—"

"She's coming to class tonight."

And just like that, it's like the wind has been knocked out of me. "What? How? We've been sold out for weeks."

Claire cringes. "The Salingers canceled."

Damn it. The Salingers are a local couple, both vocally upset at Aurora's return. In that case, I'm not worried about the empty spots.

I shrug, trying to hold my shit together. A larger storm than a town filled with assholes is brewing if Valerie decides to show up tonight.

The solution is simple. She can't come.

"So," I start while the ideas shuffle through my mind. "We have two vacancies. Can you call Val back and tell her you made a mistake? Tell her we're booked. I'm not up for any of her games tonight."

"She said she's coming to collect."

The way Claire says that, the way she's looking at me now, she knows exactly what Valerie means by that phrase. It's not exactly subtle. That's not Valerie's way.

My history with Valerie is complicated and not something I want Aurora anywhere near. My decisions over the last six years haven't always been the best. Nothing could ever fill the gaping hole she left me with, but I carried on the best I could. My art kept me company in my darkest days, the sad, lonely man I had become. It was my safety, the thing I could run to when I had nothing else. But when it came to women, I checked my sanity at the door and gave in to that need without any regrets. At least, I did until about two months ago.

It turns out a one-night stand wasn't all Valerie wanted from me that night we met. She had heard about Creek Canvas from one of her friends and stopped in for class. That's back when I was lucky to book six to twelve students per session. She observed the class activities, eye-fucked me from across the room, and never even picked up a brush. So I did the only thing I could think of at the time and invited her to Franco's for a drink, and then joined her at her hotel for a nightcap.

It wasn't until the next morning that I found out Valerie owned the largest art gallery in Asheville. She had money, she had connections, and she wanted to help. It all seemed too good to be true, but what other choice did I have? Probably plenty, but I convinced myself I had none and took the deal.

Valerie did me a solid with the business. We needed the boost, and I was so grateful, I offered to return the favor however she'd let me. At the time, yes, I meant it sexually, if that's how she wanted to take it. Val is attractive, and there was something deeply encouraging in the fact that she's a little older. More experienced. Plus, she lived far enough away that there would be no expectations. No labels. No commitment. It was perfect.

I made the mistake of repaying her generosity casually and continuously before I found out she was married. She never wore a ring, never spoke of a husband or kids, and I never asked.

No strings attached, that was the deal. When I found out the truth two months ago, I cut it off. Told her it was over. Stopped responding to her calls and texts. It was the easiest thing I'd ever done.

"I don't want her here," I grumble, already feeling defeated.

"It doesn't matter, Jax. She was already on her way when she called. Are you going to tell Aurora?"

My mouth opens, but no words come out. There's no reason she needs to get dragged into this, and even though we haven't been together in years, the sight of a woman I'd once fucked might not bode well for me. She'll be hurt.

With my jaw clenched tight, I exhale deeply to get a handle on my frustration. As much as I hate it, Claire did the right thing. She's thinking with her business hat—thank God someone is. This is my mess, anyway. A mess I should figure out how to clean up quickly. Aurora's presence is the only distraction I want in my life right now. And good or bad, I need her here to figure out what that means.

19

Jaxon

Valerie's convertible pulls up to the curb twenty minutes before class starts—too early for there to be a line, but late enough that there's no time to have the talk I've been mentally preparing for. Aurora and I are circling the stations, placing supplies and paint when Valerie breezes in through the café entrance. I only notice because Aurora greets her when she walks in.

"Hello," Aurora says kindly. "Are you here for class? We'll be opening in twenty minutes."

The crimson-lipped smile Valerie gives her is rich with scorn. I almost laugh at how out-of-place she looks in her red wrap dress with its plunging neckline that reaches her waist and her diamond studded earrings heavy on each ear. Her raven black hair is shorter than when I saw her last, with her bangs falling so close to her lashes I fear her next blink may swallow them.

Her eyes flit from Aurora to me and then back again. Her smile widens.

I may not know much about Valerie Louise, but I know a challenge in her expression when I see one. Aurora is a threat, and Valerie is locked and loaded.

"No, dear. I'm here to visit a friend." Her eyes return to me, softening slightly. "Hello, Jaxon. Long time no see."

I feel Aurora's probing eyes on me. Valerie doesn't present herself like someone who would be *just a friend* to any man. With her cat-like eyes as she surveys her surroundings, she's on the hunt, and it's clear her prey is me.

"I'm just going to help Claire out in the other room," Aurora says, backing slowly toward the door, her narrowed gaze filled with warning and questions directed at me.

"Claire's fine in there." I speak quickly, not wanting Aurora to get the wrong idea. "Stay."

But with a locked jaw and a look telling me she doesn't want to witness whatever is going on in this room between Valerie and me, Aurora bows her head and clears the door.

I sigh heavily, reaching for the back of my neck and squeezing it with my palm.

She needs to go. Now.

"Well, aren't you going to say anything? What's it been, Jax? Two months?"

I swallow against the heat scaling my shoulders and back. "Good to see you, Val." My voice is flat. "Claire mentioned you're taking a class tonight."

She winces, and it's clear she feels my indifference, but she recovers quickly, plastering a smile on her face. "I thought I'd come and check things out." She throws her eyes around the room before resting her eyes on me. "We're still using those old marketing materials to promote you in the gallery, but perhaps you're in need of some new images." She takes another step into the room. "Mind if I take a look around?"

Relief fills my chest. I'm not naïve enough to believe that's truly why she's here, but so far she's all business.

"Go for it. You have fifteen minutes."

I watch Valerie begin her cruise around the room, starting toward the back. Low cupboards line the entire wall with framed examples of Canvas and Wine paintings above them. She takes her time, eyeing each piece of art like she would one of her prospective gallery pieces. A single sunflower against a bright blue backdrop. Rock stairs leading to a creek. An owl perched upon a tree with curled branches and a bright orange sunset.

Not even one of these would make the cut. Valerie's taste is too rich for simplicity. I see right through her. She's putting on a show for me. She wants me to remember her influence in the art world. Unfortunately for her, I don't value it the same as I used to.

"I think we should open up another studio in Asheville," she says slowly, as if testing the waters. She doesn't look at me. "What do you say, Jaxon? Your success here is astounding given the population. Let's continue to build."

I make a face, glad she can't see me. "You suggest that like you have some stake in all this."

This time she stops to turn, pinning me with her eyes. "Don't I?"

A light laugh leaves me without meaning to, but I don't care. Val is ridiculous, always has been, but this visit takes the cake. "No, you don't. You're not even an investor. You promoted my class in your gallery and passed out some brochures to local businesses. And it was incredibly nice of you, but that all came with a price. A price I'm no longer willing to pay. You have no right to come here and proposition me...again."

She chuckles but pivots with a roll of her eyes, meandering around the room and pretending her interest lies in my craft. We both know that's not why she's here. "I'm offering you more, Jaxon," she says, her tone growing harder. "More opportunities, customers, profits. The whole thing. You've always wanted to travel, and that's exactly what you should be doing. Traveling, gathering inspiration, and delivering that inspiration to the studios. We hire instructors. We put studios near the colleges and work out some kind of program with the art school."

"The answer is no."

She whips her head around again. "You haven't even considered it."

"And I won't."

Her eyes narrow as her patience wanes. "I would have never started helping you if I didn't see a potential partnership here. I'm not done with you yet."

"But I'm done with you," I spit the words back, slowly, so she can digest them. I'm past the point of subtlety.

The sight of bright red hair in my peripheral catches my attention as Claire enters the room with a perky smile on her face. "Can I get you something to drink, Valerie? Beer, wine, water?"

Valerie doesn't even glance at Claire. She simply waves her hand in the air, still stewing from my words. "Chardonnay is fine."

"Coming right up."

"Where's Aurora?" I whisper for only Claire to hear.

"Working the register while I tend to your special guest," she whispers back. Her eyes flicker between us. "Thank me later." And then Claire walks out.

I will thank her later. It's not like I've been saving myself for Aurora all these years, but I certainly don't want her to know about Valerie. It would only complicate things. But with Claire watching my back and Aurora in the other room, maybe tonight won't be as bad as I thought.

"You've been staying away, Jax. It's clear now that was on purpose." Her voice reaches me from the other side of the room. Her tone says she's ready for a challenge.

I know what this is. Smart women leave men little room to turn them down. Val thinks she has me by the balls because once upon a time, her promotion single-handedly saved this studio and the café from an early demise. But times have changed.

Who knows what Val has up her sleeve tonight, but one thing is certain. Whatever business she thinks we're still doing together needs to end tonight. I walk toward her, ready to lay down the law.

After a few seconds of leveling my planned response to something less hostile, I stop, just inches from her. She's leaning with her back against the front of my desk, her shoulders pushed back, a wicked glean in her eyes. A couple months ago, this would have turned me on. It would have been so easy to promise Val that I'd meet her in her hotel after

I finished working. We'd share a bottle of wine and go at it all night long.

"It's for the best. You know that, Val. You shouldn't have come."

Her raspy chuckle is like sandpaper to my ears. "C'mon. You don't even miss me a little?" she urges, pushing off from the desk.

"Stop." My voice is gruff, hard, but I don't give a shit. "Don't make me answer that."

She laughs again, tossing her head back as she steps in front of me. "Let's get out of here, Jaxon. Just you and me."

My teeth scrape together firmly. "I'm *working*."

"Not now, sugar." I always hated when she placated me, but I allowed it before because I was numb. Dark. Empty. Things are different now. Even before Aurora returned, I could feel a difference. Learning about Valerie's marriage felt like getting a bucket of ice dumped on me. I woke up. I realized how unhappy I must have been to have completely missed something everyone else seemed to already know. I could have ruined a marriage.

She drags one of her long, dark red fingernails across my sternum and up to my collar, but I take a big step back. More grating laughter permeates the air. She loves this. Me pushing her away. It's like foreplay to her.

"Let me buy you a drink when this thing is over. Like old times. Loosen you up a bit. What do you say?"

"The answer is no, Val. No."

She pouts. "You're a bit more wound up than I remember. You know I can take care of you, sugar." She's practically purring when her smile fades, as if aggravated by my rejection. "I need your cock."

A loud gasp comes from the other side of the room. I turn to find a shocked and angry face to match, followed by an explosion detonating in Aurora's eyes. And as she puts the puzzle pieces together over the next few seconds, wind stokes her flames.

Aurora whips forward until she's standing next to me. "I'm pretty sure he already gave you your answer."

As proud of her as I am for being bold and stepping into the ring, my insides shake when I realize what Aurora just witnessed. What will she think of me now? Clearly, I'm not the same man she left broken and alone in that courtroom. I moved on in ways I'm not proud of, and now we both must face the consequences.

Still, the fury in Aurora's eyes somehow gives me strength. I toss my shoulders back and point to the door, glancing at Val one final time. "It's time for you to leave. I'll make sure Claire refunds your money."

But she doesn't flinch. Instead she stands there, still shooting daggers at Aurora. "Who the fuck are you?"

Aurora moves forward until she's toe to toe with Val, but I wrap an arm around her waist to stop her from pouncing. My nose falls into her neck on instinct, and I'm instantly high from her scent. "Just let her leave."

I expect her to fight against my hold or to stiffen at my touch. Instead, she relaxes and curls into my arms like my touch was all she needed. I can feel the shivers of her body, the heat soaking from her skin and seeping into mine.

"You're going to regret this, Jaxon," Val hisses as she slams her heels against the tile.

"I don't think I will, Val," I call after her. "Have a good night." Val tosses me a glare over her shoulder, and I can't resist hammering one more nail into the coffin. "And don't contact me again."

She yanks open the door, revealing a line of people who all seem to have their amused eyes on us. She huffs, probably embarrassed to have witnesses to her rejection, and pushes her way through the crowd until she disappears from view, hopefully for the last time.

20

Aurora

I'm still shaking minutes later while the attendees settle into their seats. I was completely unprepared to overhear the exchange between Valerie and Jaxon, but my entire body caved with relief in knowing that he wanted no part in what she was offering.

And the way he held me. The way he wrapped me in his arms and wouldn't let me go. An avalanche of "what ifs" begins to pile up in my head. Regrets. Wrong turns. What if he had held me tighter in that courtroom and refused to let me walk out that door? Would I have responded the same way?

But no matter how many moments I try to alter in my mind, the truth remains the same. I should never have let him let me go.

Jax is at the front of the class, his back to me as he chooses a brush from his collection when Claire steps up beside me. "Where's Val?"

I let out an amused breath. "Jax sent her on her way."

Claire's jaw drops. "He did not." I can feel her excitement radiating around us.

"He did."

Her eyes linger on me as she sucks in a slow breath. "Okay, then. You know, Jax hasn't had an empty seat in the class in..." She thinks about it, tossing her head back and searching the air. "Over a year, I'd say."

"Because of Val?" When I'd asked Claire who the bold brunette was that charged into Jaxon's studio, Claire had mentioned Val was a business associate. She was vague, but it was enough to understand Jax had been mixing whatever that *business* was with pleasure.

She shakes her head. "No. He might think that, but he'd be wrong. They come to see *him*. Because he's talented. The devastatingly handsome and broody parts are just a bonus." She cocks a brow at me. "But you know all that, don't you?"

Rolling my eyes, I nudge her with my elbow. "You forgot 'great with his hands' and 'smart.'"

She laughs and nods to the front of the room. "He is all those things. Which is why I would hate to ruin his streak today. I was able to fill one seat with a girl on the waitlist. You should take the other."

"Maybe *you* should sit in. I'll cover everything else," I suggest. Claire has already warned me that after tonight, I'm on my own during the events anyway. Might as well start now.

After another pause, she shakes her head. "Nope. You should definitely sit in."

I don't need time to think about that one. "I don't paint anymore."

Jaxon stalks over, a confused look on his face. "You realize there's a room of thirsty customers waiting for someone to take their orders, right?"

"Sure do," Claire says before backing away. "I'll go take care of that. Aurora is going to sit in and take the class. We're considering it part of her training." Clare winks.

I swear when I see her again, when we're alone, she's going to hear what I have to say, and it's not going to be pleasant.

Jax, however, seems thrilled. "Really?" he asks, his eyes focused on me.

That word. It's filled with surprise and hope, expanding my heart in a way I never expected. I take a breath and look up at him.

"I guess so." I shrug. "I'm free to just sit there and paint nothing, right?"

Jax smiles and shrugs. "The rules are, there are no rules."

I grin, remembering our favorite line of one of the movies they played during the town's old movie nights. "This isn't *Grease,* tough guy."

A chuckle leaves his body and reverberates through me, a smile lighting up his face. I love the way his eyes drink me in. The way just one look could pull me to him and steal my breath.

"Maybe not," he agrees, "but the rules still apply." He winks and reaches for my hand, loosely grabbing onto my fingers and turning so he has me in tow. "Come on. I'll get you set up."

Class begins, and despite my constant fight against my anxiety, I'm a good sport. I take my time getting reacquainted with the objects in front of me like they're old friends. My pointer finger feathers over the canvas, feeling its texture one pore at a time. I pick up a brush and run it across my palm, its edges prickling my skin.

Today's painting is of the bridge at Hollow Falls, but a simplified version, void of textures and layers of depth usually found in one of Jaxon's creations. I don't hear a word as Jaxon leads the class. Instead, I'm lost in the feel of it all. The thrill of easing perfect drops of color from their tubes, the faint odor euphoric to my senses. The heaviness of the brush as it quivers in my hold. The excitement of mixing colors to get to that desired hue—the one that belongs only to me, the creator. And the relief of dragging the paint-filled brush across the canvas in one wicked swipe to mark the start of a new journey.

I'm in the corner in the back of the class, where only the wall can see me and my lack of progress. Jaxon gives me space, but every now and then his eyes find mine, lingering long enough to rile my heart. Even Claire is respectful as she brings me wine, never making a move to peek at my canvas. She just smiles and moves on to the next customer.

Before I realize it, an hour has passed, and I've managed to fill in the background with the light brown hue of the sky. None of it comes easy. My hands still tremble and my breaths feel forced, but it does get better. Whatever has been stifling my wings for so many years has got to go.

My canvas is still one color and one color only by the time Claire closes down Creek Café and takes off for the night as the final students make their way out the door. It's all I've accomplished, but it's more than I have to show for the last seven years.

Jax approaches, a curl of brown hair flipping outward beneath his gray knit cap. I look up with a blush. I'm not sure if I'm nervous because my canvas is all but empty or because I'm finally taking in more of Jaxon with my eyes. I wouldn't allow myself to be so greedy before. After everything that had happened, I didn't feel deserving. He was mine once, and I made the decision to let him go. To free him of the stigma that came with dating Henry June's daughter. Because even though he said he didn't care, I didn't believe him.

"Can I?" he says, dragging me out of my damaging thoughts.

I take a deep breath as I nod. "Sure. I didn't get very far. It's literally just one co—" He steps forward, and I can't finish my sentence. My stomach flips at his nearness. This is so embarrassing. There's nothing for him to see, yet somehow, I know he'll make me feel like it's everything. I laugh through my nerves as he stops behind me. He's not even touching me, but I can feel him everywhere.

Seconds go by, maybe minutes, and I'm intensely aware of the silence as he stares over my head at a canvas filled with nothing but a burnt sky. The sound of metal scraping the floor comes next. I turn to find him pulling a chair up beside me. He sits, his eyes still focused on the painting but his hand moving to cover mine.

"Show me."

My heart kicks, chills erupt over my skin, and my breathing begins to shallow once again.

"Sh-show you?"

Why did I think I could do this? *Because he asked.*

His hand squeezes mine, and I feel it in my heart. My lungs inflate with my next deep breath.

"Paint something."

"Jax," I beg, on the verge of tears.

He waits, not saying a word. His patience makes me want to try. For me. For him. For us. Whenever there was too much to say, we'd let art do the talking. We'd let the brush plot the story while the colors brought it to life.

So I try...because I really want to.

I swallow. My shaky hand moves the brush to the dollop of white on my palette. Clouds. I'll dab in some clouds and call it a day. Easy enough. But when I lift the brush just inches from the canvas...I freeze. My vision blackens, and I hear the words that always come during a state of panic. *"To understand truth, one must find courage to seek light in the darkness."* My father's words.

I move my shaky hand to drop the brush on the table and open my eyes. "I can't. I'm sorry. Maybe it's just not in me anymore."

"Of course it's still in you. You just need to try." His tone is somewhere between encouraging and frustrated.

"What do you think I've been doing for the past two hours?" I gesture to the canvas, returning his frustration with my own. "It was never this hard before. I'd get inspired; I'd paint. That was it. It was all so simple. And now..."

"And now, what? Aurora, talk to me."

Standing, I move away from the canvas and back up to the wall. I just need some space from him. Being so close to him has this strange effect on my thoughts. They get all twisted and tangled, but I know how important this conversation is. He wants to understand, and I need to find a way to deal with this fear I have of painting.

"It's not that I don't want to. I do. It's just—I freeze. I wish I could explain it better, Jax."

"Can you try?"

My breath stutters again before I speak. "I don't know." I shake my head, hating how hard it is to wrangle the words to help him understand. But he's patient, waiting in silence, his eyes relaxed as he stares at me from his stool.

"You know those three days I was missing?" I cringe at my own words, but Jaxon just nods.

I take another breath, letting it out slowly before continuing. "It's just a dark spot in my memory. All the important pieces that could shed light on the darkness are missing. But I know they're there somewhere." I look up again. This time I don't break eye contact. "That's the part I don't know how to explain. The memories are there. I just can't see them." I take in a shaky breath, then swallow. "But I sense them."

Man, this is harder than I thought. I twist my body, trying to gain comfort but finding none. I know I must sound crazy to Jaxon. My therapist never used the word crazy, but I'm sure he thought I was too. How can I not be? Three entire days are missing from my memory. It makes no sense. But Jaxon wants to know, so I'll tell him. I'll tell him everything I don't understand.

"When I lift a brush to canvas and get a hit of the oncoming rush...something holds me back. Something keeps me in the dark. It doesn't help that I've been doing this to myself for seven years. The longer I stayed away from my art and this place and *you*, the more boulders I put up to deter myself from ever returning.

"My therapist used my love for waterfalls to explain how I coped with life after the trauma. He called it the Waterfall Effect. I was the riverbed, trying to hold steady in the roughest water. Time was the river, and it continued to move over me, fast and furious on its way to the drop. He said that every boulder I set up was me trying to stop time—stemming from a fear of moving forward and a fear of returning to where I came from."

I take a long, slow breath as I lean against the wall for support. Jaxon hasn't moved, and his expression hasn't changed. He's just listening, patiently.

"But with every boulder came a consequence, Jax—elements that messed with my landscape, my mind. Because sometimes the current was just too strong to keep out. Still is."

I bite my lip and track his movement as he stands and moves toward me. I press myself further into the wall, rushing to finish, because I don't know what will happen if he comes any closer. "That's where the darkness comes in. The panic attacks. Sometimes, there's just too much to process, and it feels like I'm drowning."

I push off the wall, feeling anxious in my own skin, my heart pounding in my chest. "A stream is unforgiving, unrelenting. It doesn't stop moving. It pays no attention to the direction it's headed. To the damage it's causing. To the lives it's changing. To the path it's carving. And despite the changes, I still stood there, losing more of myself while time stripped pieces of me away."

My confession stirs between us in the silence until he moves a tentative hand to my waist. "You fear you're lost, but you're not." He speaks firmly, his tone low even though there's no one around to hear us. "There's a reason you came back, even if you don't completely understand it. You've always trusted your heart to guide you, and that's why I trust that your intentions have been and always will be driven by something good." He lets out a breath and closes the small gap between us, his warmth a familiar comfort as his front grazes mine. "You survived, Aurora." His confidence strikes me right in the chest. My body quivers at his words. "If that's not moving forward during your darkest days, then I don't know what is."

Deep down, I know he's right. But what about our lives between then and now—the time and distance? How does it affect us? How have we changed? How do we fit?

He's been with other women, and as much as it kills me, I knew it would happen. I just never thought I'd be back to face the consequences. And now, there's so much I need to accept. There are so many questions I want to ask, but I'm not even sure how to begin.

"That sounds like just the type of thing your father would go on one of his tangents about."

I shrug, brimming with emotion as I turn my head to look at Jaxon, tears building in the back of my throat. "My therapist used the Waterfall Effect metaphor when speaking about my father's disorder, too. He could sense I had never come to terms with losing my father. The man on trial was someone else entirely." My eyes flutter to his. It feels good to talk about my father again—the man I loved, not the accused murderer. "When I was twelve and my parents sat me down to explain that my father had been diagnosed with paranoid schizophrenia, I didn't understand what that meant. I didn't see anything wrong with him at the time. He didn't seem *insane* to me." I shrug, forgiving my younger self as I speak. "I explained that to doctor Rohls, and he went on about how the mind is affected by knowledge, time, and the environment, the same way waterfalls affect the landscape around them."

My eyes catch his to make sure I'm not losing him. He's staring at the canvas, deep in thought. "And for the first time in my life, it all clicked. If water represents knowledge, and knowledge produces energy, and that energy runs through the stream—" I pause, feeling a blush creep up my cheeks as I remind myself of my father. Sometimes he could be a bit much, but I still devoured his every word—and at times like this, it shows.

"Keep going," Jaxon urges, filling my chest with warmth.

I nod, swallowing before I continue. "The mind manifests based on all the elements combined, and time, velocity, and knowledge impact the mind, just like waterfalls transform landscapes over time. Doctor Rohls believed in the transfer of knowledge between all beings—and how that knowledge changes over time. Good and bad, until it overflows into a pool of knowledge. The plunge pool." I smile at the mental image.

"Everything is connected," he says.

I nod again, thrilled that Jaxon gets it. "Well, when it comes to the mind of a schizophrenic, the force of nature is a bit rougher on the mind, and completely unpredictable. In the end, that pool of knowledge shallows, providing less energy, less knowledge, to the mind." I bat my eyes away again, unwilling to give into my fears about my own pool depleting one day. "Not every case of a schizophrenic is the same, but doctor Rohls wanted me to understand what happened and why." An ache creeps into my heart, squeezing it tight. "He wanted me to know that no matter what happened from my father's diagnosis and on, he loved me, even if he wasn't able to show it the same way anymore."

Jaxon squeezes my side again, and the comfort I felt as we spoke about my father, about the Waterfall Effect, melts away. I pull away from him, not wanting his comfort. Not with the hours previous poisoning what this talk could have been.

"Jax." I swallow, hating myself for my next question. But I have to know before all of this gets even more complicated than it already is. "Who is Val?"

He pulls his hand from my waist like he's been burned. "What?"

I cringe at his surprise. Obviously he's not interested in Val now, but they have a past just like we do. Is it awful that I want to know what happened between them? Why she decided to show up tonight? What if there are more women like her?

Jaxon's expression morphs from surprise to irritation in less than a second. "Why does it matter?"

I swallow and shrug, turning my eyes away. "I don't know. Never mind. It was stupid."

He stands, towering over me. Shit. I struck a nerve. "Aurora. Jesus Christ. Are you jealous of Val? After I kicked her out of here? Did I not make it clear enough to her? To *you*?"

"I'm sorry. I just hate that there have been others." My voice shakes, and my body quivers.

Jaxon's hands lift and drop, slapping his thighs in defeat. "Casually, yes. I told you that last night."

He's right. And I deserve everything I'm feeling. The tightness in my chest, the rot in my gut, and the clamminess of my palms. "Did you love her?" Just saying the words wracks my body with chills. I know he'll be upset by the question. We are where we are because of decisions I made for the both of us. But maybe I deserve the pain that comes with his. Maybe I want him to know I care.

"Did I what?" Jaxon's eyes flash.

My mouth opens to repeat the question, and then snaps shut again when I see his face.

"It was sex, Aurora. That's all," he roars. "What the fuck?" His face twists, and I realize my question hurt him. "Are you trying to make something more out of this? Because that would be pretty shitty considering you left me no other choice but to move on when you walked away from me in that courthouse." Letting out an incredulous laugh, he shakes his head in frustration. "Newsflash, Aurora. I loved *you* with everything I had. This"—he grips his chest, pulling the fabric of his shirt—"was all yours. And I never wanted it back even when you ripped it out of my chest. So, no, Aurora. I didn't *love* her. I *couldn't* love her, not even if I wanted to. How could I when there was nothing left to give?"

Tears prick the backs of my eyes as his words sink in. When I walked away from Jaxon, and I left him with nothing. He was empty, just like me. Except he found a way to cope.

My tear-filled eyes scan the art on the walls. He did this. He created all of this, while I did nothing with my life. Nothing that means anything, anyway.

Heat licks at the walls of my chest. "At least you had your art. I had nothing."

Jaxon's mouth closes, his jaw tenses, and he pushes a breath out of his nose. "You think I wanted any of this without you?" he roars. Then, with a quick swivel, he grabs the canvas from the easel and tosses it across the room. I jump at the clatter it makes against the tile but recover quickly when he stalks away. The anger and disappointment he carries as he leaves is so heavy I want to run, but I think I've done enough of that.

I hurt him then, and I'm hurting him now. It's up to me to stop the cycle. I just don't know how.

Without another word between us, Jaxon wipes down the stations while I gather the abandoned wine glasses. I try to not pay any attention to his locked jaw, hard eyes, and the fact that he conveniently works his way around the room opposite me. But I notice everything.

I wash the glasses in the kitchen sink, working slowly. I know when I walk into the studio again, it will be time to leave and maybe mutter a goodbye before Jaxon and I go our separate ways. In this moment, it feels like the chasm between us has widened. And I'm not ready for another goodbye, even if it's just for the night. I don't want every moment with him to be filled with tension, anger, and regret. But we're filled to the brim with it.

The last dish is put away and the dirty rags are in the hamper when I finally slip back into the studio. The lights are out, but I see Jaxon clearly lit by the glow of the street lamps streaming through the windows. He's sitting on his desk, staring down, shoulders pressed forward and hands gripping the edge, his knuckles white.

My chest squeezes at the sight of him. His face carries pain I've ignored for far too long. For a second, he reminds me of that same lost boy painting his dreams on cabin walls. I longed for him to look at me the way he looked at his paintings.

Now, I just want him to look at me.

When too many moments pass, I brave the journey across the room and stand in front of him. He still doesn't move, so I press my palms into his legs and apply the slightest pressure for him to part them. He does.

I step into the narrow space he left for me, his inner thighs brushing firmly against my hips. He's not making this easy, but he's not putting up a fight either. My heart pounds furiously as I slide my hands forward. They move up his thighs, stopping just before they reach his waist. "Jax, look at me."

His long lashes whip against his lids, and I'm transported into his storm. Jaxon's world was always filled with chaos, with constant responsibility masked with words like *opportunity* and *future*. He was ready to flee the country the moment he got his chance, despite what his leaving would do to his relationship with his parents. I'm reminded of that boy when Jaxon looks up at me now, every inch of his features calling attention to his pain. The deep creases in his forehead. The pout of his lips. The heavy breaths that move his chest.

Desperately, I search his troubled eyes for that anchor he promised. This time it's me who needs to pull him back to shore. I have that power.

My chest pushes into his with each breath as my hands firmly slide up his arms, over every ridge of terrain until they meet his shoulders. I squeeze, then cup his neck, my thumb brushing up into his shallow beard. His scruff is new to me, and there's something intoxicating about the way it scratches my skin. I imagine the way it might feel if he were to kiss that tender spot in the crook of my shoulder…or in between my legs.

I shiver. I've only ever imagined him tasting me there. Jaxon was always so careful with me, never wanting to move faster than he thought I was ready for. Little did he know, I wanted it all. I was just too afraid to tell him.

His arms are still locked and pressed into the desk, but I swear I feel them shaking, relenting, so close to giving in.

I lean in and press my lips to his ear. "I'm sorry, Jax." He shivers, and my breathing grows heavier. "For leaving. For staying away. For coming back." My voice croaks at my words. "All of it."

Guilt chooses this moment to swarm in. I should have thought about what coming back would do to him if he were still here. I should have never felt I had a right to return. Not without an invitation.

Maybe the town is right to hate me for what my father did. Maybe I'm not as innocent as I want to believe.

Suddenly I feel his strong hands on my back, pulling me close so our chests meet. My head falls to his shoulder, and it feels so damn good to be this close to him. He smells intoxicating, too.

I lift my head to search his eyes, waiting for a signal to tell me what to do next, because all I can think about right now is how heavy my breathing is, how close our mouths are, and how none of it is enough. I can already feel the force building between us, ready to spark. All I know is that if it feels this good just to be in his arms, I might die if our lips ever touch again.

His eyes fall to my lips like he can hear my thoughts. He circles his palm against my lower back as we linger in this embrace, swallowing our fears and filling the space with years of unspoken words and feelings. It's simply too strong to deny.

My lips find his first.

My tongue slips out and skates across his thick bottom lip, trying not to shake on the outside the way I am on the inside. He groans and his arms tighten, crushing me to him in a possessive hold. And just like that, our mouths fuse together.

My next breath catches in my throat as a shiver crawls over me and panic trickles through my veins. I'm desperate for a taste of the past, but I'm terrified of all that comes with it. Darkness tumbles in, and I try to shove it away. We're so close, I want to cry. I need him as much as I am terrified.

But Jaxon would never let me drown. "Are you okay?" he murmurs into my mouth.

I completely melt, my body molding into his, fitting into him just like I was meant to. I nod as I kiss him again, this time unrelenting.

Once we're settled in each other's arms, his firm lips take the lead in a slow dance only the two of us know. I remember his demanding mouth and the way it used to part mine, just like it's doing now. Naturally. Hungrily. The stroke of his tongue as it dips and tangles with mine.

I'm lost in all things Jaxon when my fingers slide through the loose tendrils of his hair to slip off his knit cap. It falls to the desk and his thick curls tumble out. His hair is longer and wilder than I remember. There's more to run my hands through. More to clutch for support as my pulse quickens. More to tug when I feel the bulge between his legs press hard into my belly.

My hands play out their fantasies. They weave through his thick locks, gripping from the root and pulling him deeper into the kiss. I moan, and he groans in return, his arousal rubbing against me, so needy. His hands start to travel over my black jean skirt until his fingers grip the bottom hem, skimming the skin just below my ass.

I gasp, pulling me from his mouth. Jaxon doesn't miss a beat. He moves to my neck, his scruff tickling my sensitive skin and releasing chills all over my body. He tastes me, samples me, sucks me, until my mind is spinning and my skin feels raw to the touch. My hands continue to comb through his hair, tugging when he sucks, and scratching when he draws his tongue from my neck to my ear.

He nibbles on my earlobe, sending a zing of heat coursing through my body. "Fuck, Aurora. I could get drunk off you."

Our lips connect again. I haven't forgotten the way it feels to be wrapped up in Jaxon Mills, but it's even better than I remember. His hold is stronger and his kisses more urgent yet somehow paced to perfection. He's taking his time, but his need is thick and hard against me. He groans like he's on the verge of stripping himself bare to climb inside me.

Panting, I pull my mouth from his and reach for my shirt, lifting it over my head and tossing it to the floor beside us.

Jaxon's pained eyes slip down to my breasts as his hand moves to a strap of my bra. But instead of sliding it off my shoulder, he traces the edge of the fabric with his finger, down the strap, around the cup, and over the swell of my breasts. He moves a finger back and forth, teasing my sensitive skin until I think I'm going to lose it.

"You were always so beautiful," he says, and my heart stops. His eyes reach mine, but his fingers are still moving over my skin, never quite reaching the places I want them to. "You always felt so soft, like silk." I gasp when he hooks a finger beneath the fabric and slides the cup from my breast. "Your nipples were always so hard for me." He looks down as if to confirm that nothing has changed and sucks in a breath, blinking hard. "Goddamn, you're still so beautiful."

I feel the heat of his mouth on my skin just before it wraps around my nipple. His tongue swirls. Desire pools in my belly and aches between my thighs, and I moan when he begins to suck me into his mouth. As if that isn't enough to make me almost explode, his fingers tug at the bottom of my skirt, yanking the fabric up over my ass so it's bunched at my waist. He palms both cheeks, squeezing, then lifts me onto the desk to straddle him.

Fuck. My core hits his length just as he bites down lightly on my nipple. I cry out, tossing my head back and feeding my breast to his hungry mouth as I rub against him.

Bang. Bang. Bang. A heavy beating on the glass from the front window of the studio breaks us apart. I look over Jaxon's shoulder to see a flashlight, bright and aimed directly at me.

"Shit," Jaxon says as he replaces my bra and slides me off him.

How reckless were we to be so exposed, to do this somewhere anyone could walk by? But in the heat of the moment, I didn't care.

"Everything okay in there?" a voice calls from outside.

Jaxon's head snaps toward the sound. He frowns. "It's the sheriff doing his rounds. Let me go tell him we're not robbing the place." He hops off the desk, adjusts himself, then scrambles to grab my shirt and throw it to me. He takes two giant leaps to the front door, unlocks it, and pokes his head out.

"It's just me, Brooks. Closing up for the night and heading out. Everything okay?"

"Ah, Jaxon. Thought I saw some movement. You alone in there?"

"Uh, no. Aurora's closing the café, so I'm walking her to her car."

Sheriff Brooks grunts in understanding. "Got it. Glad you're both safe. Make sure she gets home okay tonight. There's been some suspicious activity in the woods over the last week or so. Just be cautious. You know how kids are when they're home from school and stir-crazy. Pullin' pranks and gettin' naked in the woods." Brooks chuckles.

"All right. Thanks, Brooks." Jaxon shuts the door and leans against it, staring back at me with a light chuckle. "That was almost as much fun as getting caught by him under the waterfall."

A laugh bursts from my mouth. Now *that* is a memory I could never forget. How erotic and embarrassing all at the same time. Jaxon swore no one would be able to see us if we made love behind the sheet of the falls. I trusted him, like always. So there, under Hollow Falls, my back propped against the rocks, Jaxon stripped me completely bare and entered me. Just as soon as we'd started, Sheriff Brooks shone a light on us through the cascade, directly on us. He must have seen Jaxon's motorcycle and known it was us because he called out our names and warned us to leave or he would call our parents.

Jaxon wouldn't have cared, but he knew I did. My father was sensitive to us being together, mostly because of Jaxon's age. A seventeen-year-old with a twenty-one-year-old was a forbidden affair in my father's eyes. Legally and emotionally, though, we were doing nothing wrong.

A heavy sigh brings me back to the present. "We should get going," Jaxon says. "You have everything?" His reluctance is relief to my ears. He doesn't want to go. Neither do I.

I nod, feeling a pout begin to form on my mouth. "Yeah, just let me grab my things."

I'm still dizzy from his kiss as I walk into the café and grab my things behind the counter. There's a missed call and a text notification I decide to ignore. I won't be getting back to anyone tonight with Jaxon's scent dizzying my thoughts and the memory of his kiss burning its way through my insides.

I shiver, zipping up my phone case, and meet Jaxon at the door where I left him.

He locks up and shoves his hands in his pockets as we walk toward the parking lot. After the kiss we just shared, I can't help but feel disappointed he didn't take my hand. "You working tomorrow?" he asks, his head down.

Small talk. I can handle that.

"No, not tomorrow. I was planning on going for a hike. I've been here for two weeks and the only falls I've seen are yours."

He cocks his head at me and raises a brow. "Hiking alone?"

"Would you like to come with me?"

"Can I?"

I smile. "Yes. Be my tour guide."

We're at my car, both of us wearing smiles, and Jaxon catches me off guard by sweeping down and taking my mouth with his. He steps forward, backing me up to the door, his knee finding a home in between my thighs. His mouth is so firm and demanding, I can feel the bruising of my lips before he pulls away. Still, I want more.

"I'm sorry Sheriff Brooks interrupted us," he says against my mouth.

I blush and give him a peck on the mouth. "Me too."

He backs away, his fingers clutching mine until the very last moment. "Tomorrow." And it's all he says before he climbs onto his bike, sets his helmet on his head, and starts his engine. He waits for me to leave first, and I try to hide my smile as I go.

Tomorrow.

21

Aurora

I hear the purr of the engine outside just as I'm pouring coffee into my mug. I look up over the sink and out the window to find Jaxon shutting off his bike. A tingle runs through me at the sight of him, all strength and long limbs, his skin darkened slightly from the sun, hair ruffled and tangled from the ride. I can almost smell his crisp, earthly scent from here.

I'm opening the front door as Jax takes the last step onto the porch, a black helmet in his hands. White swim shorts grip his hips, the bottom hem falling just below his knees, and a sleeveless gray shirt clings freely to the carved muscle beneath it.

A tiny earthquake erupts in my chest upon his approach. From here, with his back lit from the sun, he wears a halo of light that blurs the focus of everything but him.

After our kiss last night, I went to sleep with my lips still tingling and the scent of him on my mind. I woke up not much different. And now he's here, his gray eyes shining at me. I almost can't believe it.

"I know I had a few glasses of wine last night, but I don't recall inviting you over for breakfast," I tease as he steps inside.

"You said you wanted to go for a hike."

I laugh. "Yeah. Later."

He laughs back, and I love how easy it is to banter with him. Meanwhile, excitement shoots off like fireworks in my chest.

"Besides," I tease, "you're not dressed for a hike. You're dressed like you're about to go waterfall hopping."

He grins.

I clasp my hands with glee. "We're going waterfall hopping?"

The smile that lights up his face makes my insides bloom.

He hands me the helmet. "Let's go."

"Wait! No. Not yet. I just woke up, hence this giant mug of coffee in my hands." His eyes fall to the mug and then slip down to my attire, his eyes shining with interest. I'm braless in a white camisole and tiny pink night shorts that barely cover my ass. Shit. My free hand moves to cover a breast, but as it grazes over a hard nipple, I'm not sure that was the best idea. The hard tips ache under his gaze, as if he needed any extra confirmation how worked up I get just at the sight of him.

My mind immediately moves to the gutter, remembering the way his mouth felt on me last night, swirling and sucking until breathing became a chore. The aim of his dark gaze tells me he's remembering the same thing. His eyes snap to mine, and I see his fight for control within them.

"You have five minutes to drink your coffee and get your ass on my bike." It's like his voice has been rubbed with sandpaper. Still, he makes no move to close the distance, and this makes me a little bit bolder.

"Fifteen minutes. I need to shower."

"Ten." He grins. "Unless you want to come just like that."

Rolling my eyes, I set my mug down on the counter and turn toward the ladder. "Not a chance, Mills."

"Fine," he calls after me, ignoring my attempt to rile him up by using his last name. "Fifteen minutes. Not a second later."

I throw him a testing look over my shoulder when I reach the ladder to the loft. "Or what?"

This time, he's not even trying to hide the fact that he's admiring my ass. "Or I'll have to come after you."

With a shake of my head, I'm pulling myself up the ladder. "I'm locking the door."

He laughs.

Jax hands me a helmet when I approach, and I strap it on, taking note of all twenty-five minutes he allowed me to get ready. I'm glad I took his lead on my attire and dressed in white jean shorts and a loose, flowy blue tank top. It's a warm day, but it's still breezy thanks to the thin clouds rolling overhead.

I take a seat, squeezing my legs around Jaxon's hips and sliding my arms around his waist. This time, I'm unafraid to explore the rigid terrain through his shirt, and I'm more eager than ever to shift forward, pressing my chest flush against his back. There isn't a sliver of air between us as I press my cheek into his shoulder blades.

"Ready?" His voice is soft, but I can feel the rumble of his words through his back, warmth radiating from him, and I smile. He always was my furnace.

"Ready," I call back, just loud enough for him to hear over the purr of the engine.

Jaxon's hand finds mine over his stomach. He weaves his fingers, thick and strong, through them and squeezes. The simple gesture sends a rush straight to my heart.

With another rev of the engine, we're off, leaving dust behind us as we zoom down my driveway and out onto the main road. The mountain pass is long and winding, the stretch of road taking us past campsites and resort entrances. We continue to climb with the rising sun. My head is lifted now, my eyes wide open as I hungrily take in everything I missed while I was away. I'd almost forgotten the thrill of strapping myself to Jaxon as he steers, the bike purring powerfully beneath us. The landscape whizzes by, the rich scent of earth and pine lost to the wind as I remember to breathe through my nose.

Our ride seems to last forever, and it feels just like it used to. There wasn't a single day after Jaxon and I admitted our feelings that we didn't try, in some small way, to run away together. To hide in the falls, wander deep into the woods, and paint our way into another existence entirely—always together. Often we would ride, just as we're doing now, making stops along the way to explore or eat snow cones and fresh fruit from the roadside stands. And then we'd continue on, letting the wind whip around us and the sun warm our exposed skin as the memories overtook us. Because this was it. And it was everything.

We finally pull in to a gravel parking lot I recognize as belonging to Skinny Dip Falls. I bite back a smile as I climb off the bike and pull off my helmet. Jaxon reaches for it, and our fingers brush. Warmth spreads across my cheeks as he grins. Jaxon and I never went skinny dipping here, but we always joked about it.

A laugh bursts from me and I tilt my head at him. "Dream on, Jax."

He shakes his head, amusement still lighting his face as his curls shake loose around his head, his wild hair falling around his gray eyes.

He holds out a hand. "Come. First stop of the day."

Warmth spreads in my chest at how much Jaxon still holds on to the past just as I do.

My obsession with waterfalls started on my first visit to Balsam Grove. I'd follow every river, creek, and stream, often getting in trouble doing it, in hopes that eventually I'd find my way to one. The time I found Jaxon painting the mural on the cottage walls when I was eight years old wasn't the only time I'd gotten lost. It happened often, and Jaxon was rarely there to save me.

Something changed when I was fifteen. After that jump into the falls, when I looked up to find Jaxon staring at me, we had a connection. Suddenly he was always there. Always watching. Always waiting.

The very next day, I was skipping over the creek, fearlessly hopping from rock to rock. I enjoyed the small thrill of rebellion. I thought it made me brave. When the sound of a loud engine stopped me, I almost slipped on a rock. Jaxon was pulling up on a royal blue dirt bike, yelling words I couldn't make out until he got closer. "Get out of the stream," I heard faintly over the roar of the engine.

I'm not sure why I listened. I didn't feel like he had any sort of authority over me, but I knew I didn't want to disappoint him. So I hopped back to land and approached him. He offered me his helmet, which I took and placed on my head. Then I climbed onto the back of his bike and wrapped my shaking arms around his waist, my heart beating fast and hard against his back.

"Hold on," he yelled so I would hear him.

I did.

I figured he'd take me home. Tattle on me to my parents. Lecture me again about getting lost.

But he didn't do any of those things. It was like he knew I didn't want to go back to the tension and unpredictability waiting for me at the cottage. Instead, he took me far away, up the mountain pass, where he pulled over and parked. We parked and hiked the short distance to a grand view overlooking the waving treetops and ravines. My chest shook with excitement, and I batted away the fear I knew I should be feeling. I knew of Jaxon, but I didn't know him. I had no right to be on the back of his motorcycle, but rational thoughts weren't the ones I reached for that day when it came to the boy up the river. He was a thrill to be with. A forbidden fruit I could only wish to taste. He gave me adventure when the rest of the world gave me rules.

Jaxon didn't say a word as he pulled the large, military green burlap pack from his back. He flipped it open and went to work, setting up his easel, canvas, and paints.

I watched in awe as he painted the sky and the treetops as we were witnessing them. He even captured the broken yellow flower I'd accidentally trampled when we first arrived. Every line, every detail was meticulous, shadowed to perfection and loud with color.

I'd grown up loving art class, always knowing I was sort of good at it, but I'd never created anything like that. Nothing that felt real. It was as if Jaxon's mission was to expose the earth just as he saw it rather than trying to conceal its imperfections with a vision of what should be. Jaxon made the imperfections perfect.

I fell in love with Jaxon that day. He didn't say much, but I didn't need words to see his beauty. His heart bled into his art, and that's how I knew.

When he started bringing an extra backpack for me—complete with an easel, canvas, and paints—he taught me the basics, but also encouraged me to explore on my own. I became addicted, often begging for Jaxon to take me to a new waterfall. And once we'd get to one, before even unpacking my things, I'd strip to my underwear and dive in.

My parents would have murdered me if they knew what Jaxon and I were up to. Hell, Jaxon's parents would have murdered him too. His father expected Jaxon to be running the property, fixing every leak, every rotted board, every nick in the paint. If they'd only known that we met at the Hollow Falls bridge every day to take off on another adventure together, they would have put a stop to it, and maybe my heart wouldn't have ended up broken that summer. Maybe there wouldn't have been anything about Jaxon worth remembering.

When we reach the clearing before the falls, I squeeze Jaxon's hand. "Thank you for this."

He turns to me, and something in his eyes tells me I don't need to thank him. This isn't just for me. It's for him too.

"C'mon. Let's get you to your waterfall."

It's practically a race to dump our things on the nearest rock and strip down to our suits. Jaxon's eyes are appreciative as they sweep over me. I can tell he's trying to be sly, but I catch his gaze as it settles back on my face. Caught, he winks and takes off, tossing himself off the rock, tucking his legs, and falling into the deepest part of the pool.

We're not alone, unfortunately, but I'm not surprised. This is one of the most popular tourist spots in the area. People love climbing the rocks of the falls, a series of tiered rock beds that carries the cascading water into the swimming hole below.

The way waterfalls form and change over time has always intrigued me. The way unforeseen forces come along and erode the land, transforming what was once there. *Like my memory.* Darkness creeps in with the thought, and I shudder.

I used to believe my mind was nothing like a waterfall because a waterfall never loses its beauty, no matter how it changes. I felt as if I had lost all the good parts of me after those three days of darkness. But being back here in Balsam Grove, surrounded by all the things I used to love, inspires me just as much as it used to. Perhaps it wasn't the darkness that kept me from remembering. Maybe I was just avoiding the light.

Now, I believe anything is possible. Just because pieces of me were lost along the way doesn't mean they're gone forever. They're here, right where I left them.

I'm standing on the same rock Jaxon jumped from just moments ago, taking in the scene before me with the fullest eyes. I pull in a deep inhale and let out a satisfying release, and the full weight of the world dissolves around me. The fresh breeze feeds me the scent of pine and wildflowers I didn't even realize I was craving. The air, crisp but warm, hits me deep in the chest.

"Jump, Aurora."

I smile and peer down at Jaxon, who's now wading in the water below, staring up at me with curious eyes. Not questioning or accusing, just curious. Like he knows everything about today is a hit of nostalgia I need to take at my own pace, and he's allowing me to. But he wants to experience it with me, not watch idly on the sidelines.

A sudden rush of adrenaline carries me to the edge, and I jump out from the rock and into the plunge pool below. For a moment, I'm soaring through the air, and then I'm plunging deep into the ice cold water. That's when clarity hits.

This is why I came back.

After so many years of trying so damn hard to find my way back to myself, I was only distancing myself further. I needed this place and its many simple offerings to be the guidance that would bring me home. And finally, I'm here.

I gasp when I reach the surface, the sting of the cold finally hitting me, my numbness dissolving like an ice cube in the sun. I see Jaxon swimming toward me with shining eyes.

"Finally," he says gently as his eyes lock on mine. "Where'd ya go?"

"Sorry it took me so long." My words are soft and honest, holding so much more meaning than a simple apology. Maybe Jaxon and I needed the years apart to become who we are today. Maybe we needed to fall apart to find our way back to each other. Maybe we had to chisel away the soft rock to find a platform sturdy enough for us to stand on—together.

In the past, our streams were always colliding, always forbidden. It was exciting, but it never could have worked out in the long run. We would have destroyed each other with the thrill of it all, without truly understanding our own paths. But I can feel something new forming between us. Whatever it is carries the strength of yesterday along with the knowledge of today. And it's sacred.

"What is it, Waterfall Eyes?"

The nickname steals my breath. I'd forgotten. How could I have forgotten?

Jaxon closes the distance between us, his fingers dipping into my sides, gripping my waist, and pulling me to him.

"I loved when you called me that." I wrap my arms around his shoulders and smile.

His eyes fall to my lips, and he nods. "I know," he says. "Your eyes still light up when you see one. I'm glad I was here to witness that."

I turn my gaze to the waterfall behind him.

"When my therapist used the Waterfall Effect to explain my memory loss, he'd just gotten done listening to my story of how quickly I fell in love with nature, waterfalls especially." I look down sheepishly. "And with you." I feel a squeeze at my waist. Maybe it won't come as a surprise to

Jaxon that I never stopped loving him, but explaining it all is harder than I could have imagined.

"I guess that's why he started telling me about the Waterfall Effect. He thought it was something that would resonate."

He pulls me closer and listens intently.

"He told me my mind was like a waterfall. Unsteady and altering because of everything that happened. Because of the trauma, a part of me was impacted, struck so unnaturally it altered the way I see things. My past. My present. Even before he said that, I worried I'd completely lose my grip on reality one day. Like my father did."

Jaxon lets out a heavy breath as if he finally understands. "You're not him, Aurora. Not at all."

I can't help but think of Scott when he says that. Scott, who knew me in my darkest days.

"What about my panic attacks?"

Jaxon moves his hand to my cheek, using his thumb to stroke my cheekbone so tenderly. "What about them, babe? They're normal. Everybody deals with anxiety to some extent, and some have it worse than others. Especially considering what you've been through, your panic attacks are justified. There's nothing wrong with being afraid every now and then."

I shake my head, wanting to tell him he doesn't understand. Nothing has ever been that simple for me. "I've seen the statistics, Jaxon. Schizophrenia isn't something that can be prevented or even predicted. Children of schizophrenics have a ten percent chance of developing the same condition as their parents. And even if I don't develop my father's condition exactly, my panic disorder is already a part of me. The odds of it becoming something more terrify me." I don't think I've ever admitted that to anyone. Not even Scott. I shudder. "The reality is, maybe I'm not much different than him."

"No, Aurora. You don't see what I see. Besides, weren't you always the one that was constantly reminding me that just because a person has schizophrenia doesn't mean they're a monster? And you were right."

"Was I? I held onto that belief for so long, but look at what happened, Jaxon. Look at what he did."

Jaxon tightens his grip on my waist just enough to snap me out of the darkness I find myself falling into. "Yes, Aurora. I believe it. You are not your anxiety. Your father was not his illness. He should have been on medication, and he should have never added alcohol to the mix because it made him even more unpredictable. He lost his shit in front of the entire town. He lost his shit on you. But he never even tried to hang on to reality. He gave up on himself. He gave up on you. It's important that you understand the difference. *You* haven't lost your sense of reality."

"Haven't I, though?" This is where I struggle with all that I lost along with my memory. "Three days was all it took for me to forget who I was."

He sighs, shakes his head, and peers into my eyes like he's found my soul. He speaks straight to it. "Aurora, I hate using the word 'normal' because you are not normal in the best way possible, but when it comes to your fears, you are fine. When it comes to the memories you've suppressed, that's what tells me you are far from the evil your father was capable of."

I bite the corner of my bottom lip, knowing I should just agree. That I should accept my attacks and stop fearing them. But it's a fear that's run through me for years. It plays on a loop in my mind with no end in sight. Call me stubborn, but

I've always felt like the attacks were trying to tell me something. Like it wasn't just a coping mechanism, but a warning.

"C'mere," Jaxon says, pulling me to where we can both stand. I let him lead, allowing him to wrap me in his arms.

He turns me so his front hits my back, and we look up at the climbers, the brave souls making their way to the top of the watery cascade. I smile through my tears. I smile for so many damn reasons. Mostly for the way Jaxon holds me with a strength that promises to never let me go. Never again. But also because I feel like we're staring up at a reflection of our younger selves.

A young girl slips, and the boy she's with reaches out a hand to grab hers. He doesn't let go until they reach the top.

It's funny how love sneaks up on you in the most innocent of moments. How a friendly gesture transforms into something so much more.

Love snuck up on me.

And then I was screwed for eternity.

22

Aurora

We visit Sliding Rock next, one of my favorite landscapes.
It's just a long slope of wide rock with a thin stream that flows
into the basin. The slippery rock makes for a perfect
waterslide. Tourists are already lined up on either side, taking
turns sliding down with squeals of delight before diving toes
first into the water.

It's our turn before we know it. My heart is racing as I grip
Jaxon's hand and sit. We dig our heels into the rock to wait
for the water below to clear.

"One, two, three!" Jaxon calls when it's our turn, and we
push off, sliding down the rock. My smile stretches wide as
we descend and plunge into the water.

"Let's do it again!" I say, grabbing Jaxon's hand and
pulling him to the edge.

And we do, not stopping for a breath unless we're forced to wait in line. I've lost count of how many times we've taken the slide down when Jaxon turns to me with a squeeze of my hand. "You hungry? I was thinking we could check out Looking Glass next and chill for a while."

And as if on cue, my stomach rumbles. "Let's go," I say with the brightest smile.

Without another word, we're gathering our things, hopping on his bike, and then he's whisking me away to Looking Glass Falls.

Looking Glass Falls is by far the most crowded site yet. With its deep, wide plunge pool and ideal sunning spots, it's one of the hotspots for tourists. I frown at the idea of searching for a spot to sit among the chaos. And selfishly, I want to be alone with Jaxon. He must see my expression because he gives my hand a tug.

"I have an idea."

We hop back on the bike and he takes us deeper into the woods, down a narrow dirt trail that doesn't seem like it's meant for tourists. And suddenly, I know exactly where we're going. I smile.

Hollow Falls is an unbelievable sight. Hidden in the mountains, off the beaten path, it remains practically untouched, the best kept secret of Balsam Grove. We'll never be bothered by tourists here. It's ours unless a local decides to crash our party.

He pulls to a stop at the base of the falls, and I stare up at them in wonder. The thirty-five feet of raging water pours into a deep pool with a heavy splash. Above it, the bridge where he brought me just the other day. A bridge that had become our meeting place on so many occasions before he'd steal me away for a day of adventure.

"Jax." His name is all I can manage.

"Incredible, isn't it? The tourists still haven't found it," he teases. He helps me off the bike with a grin. "C'mon, I saved the best for last."

We find the perfect flat rock just above the water and lay two towels down to sit. We're silent as we eat our late lunch, a random assortment of sandwiches and mixed fruit, and we stare out at the falls. At some point, I sneak a look at him and blush when I find he's already watching me.

Caught, Jaxon smiles, drops the remains of his sandwich into the bag, and stands. "Time for a swim."

I follow his lead, brushing my hands against a napkin and throwing my trash into the bag before reaching for his hand. We cannonball into the water, swim until we're exhausted, and then lie in the sun until our cheeks turn pink. I sit up, feeling sweat roll down my back. "Maybe we should get out of the sun."

He flips up his hands to shade his eyes and opens one in a squint, then drops his gaze down my side. Smirking in amusement, he pokes a finger at my arm, turning my skin white before it fades back to color.

I glare and slap his hand away as he chuckles. "Watch it," I warn with a finger wagging in the air.

His grin is full-blown now. It's obvious I didn't get much sun in Durham, but geez. "Fine. Let's find some shade," he relents, sitting up and stretching.

After we've settled into our shady spot beneath a tree closer to the falls, Jaxon speaks. "I was thinking about what you said earlier."

I turn to him, curious.

"You may have forgotten some stuff, but it didn't change you." He shoots me a look, then turns forward again and nods at the falls. "It didn't alter your landscape." His response to my therapist's explanation of the Waterfall Effect warms my insides.

"But that's the thing, Jax," I say gently. "It did alter my landscape. It changed me." I swallow as his eyes meet mine. "What I'm realizing being back here is that even though it changed me, that doesn't mean I need to forget where I came from. And it doesn't need to stop me from where I'm going. I'm just…different."

"I get what you're saying. I agree. All I'm saying is that you're strong," he says, taking my hand. His confidence is infectious. "You've always been strong. Even now—you coming back here after everything that happened—that takes bravery. Not many would do the same."

"It felt like a sign."

His brows lift. "What did?"

I shrug, realizing I never did tell him the full reason I came back. "My father left me the deed to the cottage. His attorney delivered it after his death, and it couldn't have come at a better time. It was a sign, Jax. At least I took it as one. I'm not so sure I would have been able to come back and face this place if he were still alive."

"Why?"

This isn't something I've told anyone, and it's not easy to say. "I guess when he was alive, it was like I was locked up too. Not physically, of course. But when he got convicted that day, so did I."

"Aurora, no," Jax says with a swallow. He squeezes my hand, but I shake my head to tell him not to come closer. I don't know what comes over me in this moment, but I'm realizing things I've never even admitted to myself before.

"I blamed myself for what he did."

"No, babe. Why? Aurora, he was sick. You had a hard time believing that then, but there is no way in hell any of that guilt should fall on you."

"You don't understand. I don't even understand it, Jax. I'm just telling you what I was going through when I left that courthouse. I felt guilty, like I had done something to cause all of this, and him getting convicted became my life sentence too. And then he died, and I—" I shake my head, forcing back a sob. "I woke up, I guess. That intense guilt I'd felt because of everything that happened, it didn't feel as heavy. It was…closure. And that's the only way I've really been able to explain it to myself."

Jaxon grips my cheeks, glides a finger across my jaw, and places his forehead against mine. "We all suffered for your father's sins, but babe, you are not to blame. You are a gift, the most beautiful gift in this cruel fucking world. These past six years have been the best and worst of my life. I somehow managed to build something I'm so proud of, but doing it without you was the worst kind of hell. I don't care why you came back; I'm just glad you're here. And you're not leaving."

I smile, rolling my forehead against his. His lips are so close that his breath mingles with mine. My fingers stroke the warmed skin of his thighs. "That's not your decision to make."

His eyes darken, falling to my lips. His head shakes. "The hell it's not," he rasps. Then his lips are on mine, and somehow it's even better than last time. As fast as my heart is beating, I'm not paralyzed by his touch. I feel everything. The air that whips around us like it's holding us together. The sensation of his fingers sliding up my side until they hit just under my right breast. The feel of his thumb caressing my cheek as his teeth nibble my bottom lip.

My head dizzies and my chest swirls with excitement, with anticipation, with hope. I'm completely lost in Jaxon Mills— my favorite place to be.

I part my mouth just enough for his tongue to sweep in to tangle with mine. His palm still cups my neck as he dips me back even lower. I reach for him, digging my fingers into his sides with a fearless hunger.

I miss him. There were so many nights over the years when I allowed my thoughts to travel back to how it felt to be wrapped up in his hold with him deep inside me, his breath in my ear, his whispered confessions of love slipping into my heart where I trapped them forever.

I've always felt greedy with Jaxon, like I could never get enough, but I finally have the confidence to show it. My fingers skate over his ribs and up his chest before I grip his neck, pulling him even closer. But it's the guttural moan that slips past my lips that causes him to growl and pull me onto his lap, cradling me as my ass presses down on his arousal.

We both gasp, and then I'm feeding into his kiss, clutching and nipping while shoving my fingers through his curls. The pads of his fingers dig into my hip and I move, just slightly, greedy for the friction that's started a buzz low in my belly.

It's been so long since I've felt this kind of passion—the flames that threaten to erupt with the friction caused by two souls desperately clawing their way to one another. That was always us. Still is. Innocent with intention, yet anything but as I grind down onto his lap and swallow the next rumble that escapes his throat.

"Fuck," he growls, placing a finger at the top of my bikini bottom and dragging it across my skin as if asking permission to enter. "Do you have any idea how bad I want to touch you right now?" His voice is in my ear as I try to catch my breath. My lids squeeze together. "To feel you again, Aurora?"

I quiver, my breath coming out in pants, but I can't speak. I can't think. I just *want* with so much desperation. My nipples pucker and my breath catches when a finger dips under the fabric and continues its journey back and forth, teasing me.

"You're wet for me, aren't you?"

I can feel the slickness between my thighs as he breathes roughly into my ear.

"You used to love my fingers in you. Remember that, Waterfall Eyes?" He bites his lower lip as his eyes slip down to where his hand is. "You'd squirm so much I'd have to pin you there with my hands." A coy smile lands on his lips before he kisses me again, breathing me in deeply. "And you were so damn loud when you'd scream for me. I'd have to muffle your sounds with my mouth, remember that?" His lips move to my neck as his fingers dip lower, stealing my breath. "But I never got to taste you."

My legs part instinctively, waiting for his touch. My hips lift as I grip fistfuls of his hair.

What is he waiting for?

Just as the thought enters my mind, I feel the drag of his finger as it moves lower, slips deeper beneath my bikini bottoms and finds my center—his delicate touch to my wet warmth. I almost shatter right then. My heart catches in my throat before I remember to breathe. He's rubbing me slowly, feeding me kisses as he teases the bundle of nerves that zings and tightens at his touch.

"I missed you," he rasps his voice almost swallowed by the whistling of the wind.

My forehead falls to his, but just then, the whistling turns into something else. It seems to be coming from somewhere deep in the woods. Jaxon hears it too, beyond the roaring of the falls. I know because we both freeze at the same time, ears turned toward the sound.

Our mouths are a breath apart as we listen for the noise again, his hand never moving from between my thighs. Just as I think we both imagined it, the whistling starts all over, followed by the sound of sticks crunching against the forest floor.

Jaxon's brows furrow.

"It's just an animal," I say, eager to get back to what we started. I use my hand to turn his face back toward mine.

He smiles knowingly before kissing me hard on the mouth, his fingers eagerly continuing their massage against my sensitive bud.

Then another whistle sounds, this one louder and clearer than the two before it.

Our heads twist toward the sound again, my heart beating fast as Jaxon grips me tighter. My legs close as Jaxon slips his hands from my bikini bottoms. His eyes narrow as he searches the space around us. "We're not alone, babe. Someone wants the falls."

"W-what? Is that like a call of possession or something? They whistle and we're supposed to just leave?"

Jaxon laughs lightly, then kisses me before lifting me from his lap, still holding me close. "Let's get out of here. It's getting dark anyway." His voice softens, and my heart follows his lead. It's always followed his lead.

Jaxon was always the one to calm me. Always the one to save me. The moment I lost him, everything went wrong. Everything. I've never believed in relying on a man to save me. No man should ever be the center of a woman's universe. But Jaxon gets that, and he fits into my world just as I always felt I fit into his.

I throw on my clothes, water instantly soaking my shorts and tank top. Jaxon remains topless, dressed only in his swim shorts, and we take off on his bike, zooming through the woods until we're back on the paved road and heading toward his house.

23

Aurora

We pull up to Jaxon's driveway and hop off the bike in front of the two-story house that once belonged to his parents. I swallow back the nerves that come with the memory of the last time I stood at the end of this driveway, so angry at Jaxon for turning down an amazing opportunity just to stay in this town with me. But just as it always has, that memory feels broken, like pieces of it are missing and there's more to the reason for my anger than I could ever remember.

I look over at Jaxon. He's giving me a crooked smile that fills my heart with love. Those damn flutters erupt in my chest again, completely obliterating any negative memory I have and replacing it with the good. So much good.

He takes my hand and tugs me toward him. His finger cups my chin as he stares down at me with my favorite storm, the kind I want to experience rather than run from. The difference once confused me, but not anymore.

"Hey." His voice reaches the deepest parts of me, like it's the bass of my body, making me vibrate deeply in response. "Let me impress you with my newfound culinary skills, and then I'll take you home. I promise I won't kidnap you tonight."

"You won't?" I ask, my pout uncontained, and Jax laughs.

He shakes his head, his lips brushing mine. "Not tonight, babe. Soon. I promise. But not tonight. I have a business thing in Asheville tomorrow and I have to get up early, but I'm not ready to take you home yet." He moves my hand to his chest and dips to kiss me.

I smile, biting the inside of my mouth to keep from grinning like an idiot. "It kind of sounds like you just asked me out on a date. I don't think we ever went on one of those."

He groans and rolls his eyes. "That was all you, and you know it."

It's true. It was my fear of getting caught together by someone who would tell my father. My father, who had already threatened Jaxon with a rifle after he caught Jaxon outside my window early in the fall. My father, who I knew had mental issues I didn't want to aggravate, even if I never understood them completely. My father, who I loved.

"So, you know how to cook now?" I say, fighting against the dark thoughts that have begun to creep in.

He presses his lips to mine. "Come inside and find out."

I would have said yes even if he told me he was feeding me animal crackers.

I follow him through the front door, stopping in my tracks as soon as I've crossed the threshold. Everything about the house is different than I remember.

Smiling at my surprise, he explains, "I renovated the place after my parents moved out. I had some extra money from the trust they set up for me for school." He gives me a side-eye that I know means his parents were not happy about him not going to school. That was always the plan. Jaxon would learn the family business, go to school to have a fallback plan, and then take over the business with all the right certifications. I don't let on that I know more than he's telling me—that he and his parents had a falling out that led to them leaving for good.

Jaxon takes me through the house so I can see the extent of the updates. Every room was touched in some way. The basement, which used to be his parent's theater room, is now a game room. The entire main floor has been updated with new floors, built-in cabinets, and a gourmet kitchen.

He takes me down the hall, skipping past the bathroom and the beautiful French doors leading to the den. We're standing in front of his bedroom at the end of the hall—or at least what used to be his bedroom. When he opens the door, I gasp.

The entire room is floor-to-ceiling art. Familiar canvases my brush once painted. *My art.*

My throat tightens, and I feel pinpricks in the back of my eyes as I try to control the emotion coursing through my body. I turn to Jaxon, my eyes officially watering, leaking tears of shock. "H-how?"

Every single canvas is one I thought I lost. Every single painting is one I painted with Jaxon as we wandered the woods, overlooking the waterfalls or exploring an abandoned cabin. For hours, we'd just paint. And then my father destroyed them all. Or so he said.

A strong arm wraps around my middle as his chin drops to the top of my head. I'm speechless. He waits, holding me as I try to regain my composure.

And then the tears fall. "He said he destroyed them all."

Jaxon squeezes my middle again. "He didn't destroy anything." He says the words through gritted teeth. "They were under your back porch, wrapped up in blankets. Lacey pokes around a lot under there, and I was curious one day and pulled them out. I only took them to keep them safe. They're yours, of course. This room—it's yours, Aurora."

I turn, my face falling into his chest as more tears build behind my eyes. I was not expecting this. Not at all. Seeing them again brings back one of the worst memories I ever kept. After my father took them, I experienced a pain I would never forget and hoped I would never feel again. A sob of sadness, happiness, and regret bubbles up in my throat and escapes before I can stop it. If there were anything Jaxon could do or say to show me he still feels a single thing for me, this is it.

My cheeks are streaked with tears and my chin quivers, but I don't care. I stand on my tip-toes to take his mouth with mine and give him everything I can possibly give in this moment. It's not enough. There will never be an equivalent to his love for me, but I will forever try.

Our mouths part as another sob leaves my throat.

"Babe, hey. Look at me," he says gently.

I peer up, my eyes wet and blurring my vision. I wipe them away and peer up again.

"You've always been with me, no matter what," he says. "This is the only proof I can give you. I brought you here to remind you of everything you've accomplished. You never needed permission to have passion. To do anything you ever wanted. We fought a lot because of it, because you never understood why I couldn't leave you to go overseas. To travel the world. You never understood." He leans in, kissing me softly and pulling away far too fast. "There's a reason. A reason you wouldn't listen to then, but I hope you do now. Aurora, there was no way in hell any of those experiences would have meant anything without you by my side."

Tears fill my eyes again, and I wipe them away with the back of my hand. "I thought you'd resent me if I was the reason you didn't go." Jaxon appreciates honesty, so I'll give it. "I thought you'd be waiting around for me and continue to fight with your parents about the property and hate me for it all. Jax, I was afraid that you staying would tear us apart, but I see now you only wanted to stay to keep us together. I'm sorry. Call me young and naïve, I guess."

Jaxon nods. "I know. I get it. And you know what? We could have worked through it, but things got…" He shakes his head, refusing to finish his truth, but I already know. "Timing was not on our side."

I swallow, understanding completely. "My father ruined it."

"Maybe," he says with a sigh. "But you were mad at me when you ran off into the woods that night. So I blame me for that, not your father."

"Jax, no." My heart squeezes, realizing that all this time, all the regret I feel, Jaxon has felt the exact same thing.

"And then you were upset that I betrayed your trust by confessing the truth to the cops and that courtroom," he continues. "But you know what? It's something I will never regret. I don't think I could have ever lived with myself if I hadn't spoken up. Whether your father did what he was accused of or not, what he did to you—to me—was unforgivable. Your father held a gun to my head, Aurora. He was unpredictable and hostile. Whether he meant it or not, he did and said what he did. That may have been something you wanted to keep to yourself, but it was for the wrong reasons. I wouldn't change a thing. And I'm sorry for how shitty that makes our situation."

Fuck.

"Okay," I say, accepting all the feelings, thoughts, and actions I once questioned. "I'm here now."

"Are you? Are you here to stay, Aurora? Because if you're not, tell me now."

Why does it feel like he's giving me an ultimatum? I hate that. He needs to understand that my being back isn't about him. And as much as I love that we've reconnected, I'm not sure if here is the best place for me to be in the end.

"I came here without a plan. I didn't even think you would still be here. I just—"

Jaxon's eyes bore into mine, both love and hate in his expression. I ruined us. He ruined us. There's no going back; there's only forgiveness.

"You just what?"

My fingers dig into his sides. "I just wanted to feel whole again. I thought it was this place that made me feel whole, but now I'm starting to realize it was you. I might not want to stay here, Jax, but I know I don't want to be away from you."

His lips crush mine, and then I'm in his arms. I wrap my legs around his waist, and he carries me from the room filled with my past, down the hall to the kitchen, and toward our future.

24

Aurora

The motorcycle ride back to my cottage is bittersweet. Jaxon takes his time getting there and starts his goodbye with a lingering kiss.

"I'm part of an art committee in Asheville," he explains as we stand at my door, my arms wrapped around his waist as I gaze up at him. "Every now and then they have fundraisers they ask me to be a part of. There's a three-day art fair they want me to judge. I walk around, schmooze, check out the pieces, ask questions, and then hand over my selections to the board. It doesn't pay much, but they let me promote my business for free."

I have to bite my tongue so I don't ask about Valerie. This sounds suspiciously connected to her. Will she be there? Will he see her? Trust was never an issue between us before. Then again, I was young and naïve, and there weren't any Valeries then.

"What's wrong?" he asks.

I shake my head. "Nothing." I smile. There's no way I'm going to divulge my insecurities about another woman after the day we've just had. "So, you'll be back Wednesday?"

He nods as he moves in for a kiss.

"See you when you come back," I whisper before his lips touch mine. But even as he kisses me, the words ache.

We've made a breakthrough in *us*, and it's not something I want to press pause on until he comes back to town. I already know the risk of waiting years, and I don't want to see what could happen in three days.

I watch with a heavy heart as he walks to his bike and throws his leg around it before revving the engine and giving me a wink. "I'll call you."

"When?"

He laughs. "Just have your phone on you, Waterfall Eyes."

I can't contain my grin. "Fine." And I feel that bubble in my chest. That nervous flit of excitement at the start of something new, something meaningful. It's life and love, exactly as it's meant to be.

I settle onto my couch, too restless to sleep just yet, too hyped up from the feels of today—the rushing falls and the memories that came with it. I can almost feel my hair whipping around me through the woods as Jaxon maneuvered us around the rough mountain terrain. It's all so familiar, but at the same time, it feels different. Better.

When we were young, everything had to be hidden. Kept a secret. But now that we aren't worried what anyone thinks, there's so much more I want to do with him.

I smile and pick up my phone again, finally getting to the messages that have been piling up over the last few days. Messages from Scott and Aunt Cyndi I've been avoiding for too long. I stop at Scott's messages, and even though I'd like to delete them and ignore the pain I must have caused him by leaving, I know I can't.

Tension wracks my gut as I read, every single message a polite plea to call or text back. I've been ignoring him for days even though I promised myself I would be a better friend. Just because I need to be selfish right now doesn't mean Scott deserves to be ignored.

Scott needs to know I'm okay in a different way than Aunt Cyndi does. Scott needs to understand that I'm happy, as painful as that might be for him to hear. But I can't bring myself to do any of that now. Not while I'm still figuring things out.

With a heavy sigh, I set down my phone and settle into the couch, close my eyes, and dream of the next time I'll see Jaxon.

Creek Café is bustling the next day. Luckily, Claire is here to open the store with me. There's some sort of hiking challenge happening this week, so all of downtown is teeming with people.

By the early afternoon, the crowd has finally thinned out and only a few stragglers remain. I'm cleaning the counter when Claire shimmies up to me with a wiggle in her brows. "Do I get three guesses to find out what that ridiculous smile is for?"

My face flushes as I shake my head. "Nope," I tease. I didn't even realize I'd been smiling like an idiot all morning, but now that she mentions it, my cheeks do hurt.

When her eyes burn lasers through me, I give up. There's no use hiding it anymore. "I spent the day with Jax yesterday, okay? Happy?"

"Oh yeah?" she says, her smile widening. "Mountain Look again?"

I shove off the counter and fold my arms across my chest, my cheeks flaming with heat. "Do you have to make this difficult? What do you want me to say? You know we have a past."

"Sounds like you have a future, too."

I groan and roll my head back. "It was perfect. Yesterday, the night before—"

"Wait, what happened the night before?"

Laughing, I shake my head. "You and your damn questions."

"I'm a mutual friend. I deserve to know what's going on between my business partner and employee." She grins again, and I smack her arm.

"You are horrible."

"Well, if it makes you feel better, Danny and I are excited to see it. To see Jax happy, anyway. We've had enough of his brooding to last a lifetime. And we're happy for you too, Aurora. Danny told me how hard things were for you back in the day. I hate everything you had to go through with your father and the town. And considering the people here are still being assholes, I'm glad you're sticking around." She pauses and bites her lips before speaking again. "You are sticking around, aren't you?"

I shrug. "I don't think I'm ready to have that conversation yet, Claire. As much as I love being back and being with Jax, I don't exactly want to make a home out of the cottage."

"You want to sell it?"

I sigh and nod, hating that I'm talking to Claire about this before Jaxon. He deserves to know my feelings too. "I think I do. Not right away, but I know I don't want to keep it forever."

Claire is about to speak when the door chimes, alerting us to another customer. We look up to find Tanner in full police getup strutting our way, his gaze aimed at me.

"Afternoon, ladies. Jaxon happen to be around today? Studio looks to be closed."

"Nope. He'll be back Thursday. Anything I can help you with, Tanner?" Claire asks, her curious eyes on him as she refills the napkin holder.

Tanner shakes his head, hardening his eyes on me. "Nah, just need to talk to your *boyfriend*." His brows shoot up. "Pops spotted his bike in the woods yesterday around Hollow Falls. Just wanted to remind him to be careful this time of year, that's all. Lots of tourists. I'd hate for someone to get hurt."

Heat flames my cheeks.

Tanner leans in closer. "And we can't have any funny business going on in the shops after hours, either. Pops said Jaxon wasn't alone the other night in the studio. Said he had to break something up."

"I'm not sure what you mean," I return with a swallow.

Tanner rolls his eyes and leans closer. "You know how pops gets when it comes to indecent exposure. Said he caught you and Mills out in the open back in the day. Don't be repeating history, June." Heat scales my chest at his accusation.

Claire moves between us before I can respond, forcing Tanner to look at her. "Is that all, Tanner? You can talk to Jax on Thursday if you want to stop by. Otherwise, we've got a business to run."

He winks at her. I get the sense he still loves stirring up trouble and that Claire is used to it. "That's all for now, darlin'." He flashes her his bright white smile and nods at the espresso machine. "I'll take a coffee while I'm here. My usual is fine."

Claire moves in front of the register with a sugary smile— too sugary to mean anything good. "Sure, Deputy. That'll be two fifty."

His eyes narrow. "I didn't bring my wallet."

She pouts theatrically. "Oh, my. That's unfortunate, isn't it? Come back when you have it, and I'll be sure to whip you up that coffee."

Tanner lets out a frustrated puff of air before turning on his heel. "I see how it's going to be. You ladies watch yourselves out there."

As soon as the door shuts behind him, I let out a laugh as Claire lets out a half-groan, half-scream.

"The *only* reason that asshole has a badge is because of his weird father," she says. "They think they're hot shit because the crime rate in this place is at a record low, but that's only because it was a ghost town for years. They're starting to panic now that tourists are returning in droves. Their luck is going to start running out, and they won't know what to do with themselves."

"That makes no sense. Shouldn't the growing tourism make them happy? Without people, they wouldn't have jobs."

She waves away my logic with a flip of her hand. "Oh, girl, yes. It should, but Tanner and Brooks have always preferred quiet around here. They want to keep things simple." Then a devilish smile takes over her face. "So, I take it you and Jax took a detour from the trail yesterday?"

I shrug. "We went to Hollow Falls. Nothing unusual. We used to go there all the time when we were younger. It's not flooded with tourists, so we always preferred it. Anyway, we thought someone was watching us and took off."

Claire makes a face. "You think someone was watching you? Why do you think that?"

I shrug. "We heard someone there. Whistling."

"That's creepy, Aurora."

I don't tell her the rest of my suspicious thoughts in fear of sounding too much like my father. But someone almost ran us off the road the other night, and while Jax and I thought it was a drunk driver, I'm starting to wonder what lengths folks will go to in this town to see me gone.

I shiver. I was too wrapped up in Jaxon yesterday to think much of all things combined. "Yeah, I guess the whistling was pretty weird. I just figured whoever it was wanted the falls to themselves. Teenagers trying to spook us … or something."

Claire shakes her head and goes back to refilling dispensers. "All I know is my Danny chose the strangest place to work. He could have gone anywhere. Anywhere at all, but no. He wanted to come back to his roots. He wants to be sheriff one day, you know." She sighs and leans against the counter again. "I tried to tell him that would never happen. Not with Tanner next in line." She narrows her eyes at me. "What is it with you people and this small town, anyway?"

I laugh. "I'll tell you as soon as I figure it out."

We say our goodbyes when Amber comes in to take over for us early in the evening, but instead of walking to the parking lot, I head down to the river and just walk. I used to love coming here and watching the sun set behind the mountain, so that's what I do.

It's a perfect night. Clear skies, orange hues fading into purple and blue. The gentle rhythm of the river sliding over the rocks. When the show is over, I walk back up the hill to the strip of shops and enter the small grocery store at the end of the block. I need to pick up a few things for the house—wine being at the top of the list.

I've just selected two bottles of my favorite red and started down the aisle toward the produce section when a familiar figure strolls around the corner pushing a grocery cart. Tanner stops when he sees me, appearing just as surprised as I am.

"What are you doing here?" I ask, my tone accusing as my heart beats triple-time in my chest. Obviously he's here for the same reason I am, but I'm still reeling from his attempt to intimidate me earlier.

Irritation stretches across his face. "What does it look like?"

I let out a sigh and tighten my grip on the cart's handle. "Look, Tanner. I appreciate you watching out for the town, but until I give you reason to find me a threat, get off my back, okay?"

His cheeks redden and his eyes narrow. "You don't seem to get it, so let me try this again. Since you've been back, the town's been on edge, and it's stirring Pops up. I don't like it. The June name is like a curse word around here, and you being here brings back unwelcome memories for everyone."

Something twists in my gut. "That's not fair, Tanner. This is my home too. The town doesn't get to just shoo me away because of something that happened seven years ago. Something I'm not responsible for."

He lets out a sigh. "Trust me, doll. I know you have a point, but that doesn't change what happened and who caused it."

My eyes darken as I leave my cart to step up to him. "Yet out of everyone still living in this town, I'm the only one directly affected by what happened. I was his victim, for Christ's sake."

"Which makes things even weirder. No one understands why you came back here, Aurora. And you lied to me."

"Lied to you? I have no—"

He scoffs, cutting me off. "There's no fiancé. Claire told me on Danny's birthday. You lied, Aurora. Why'd you need to go and do something like that?"

I want to scream. "I thought you'd be more inclined to give me my space if you thought I was here with someone else." It sounds stupid saying it out loud, but it doesn't matter anymore. I shake my head, frustrated. "Look, *Deputy*. If you hear anyone saying anything about me and how I don't belong, you tell them I'm not going anywhere until I'm good and ready. What do they care anyway? My dad is dead." My breathing comes fast and hard. I hate saying the words out loud.

There's a flicker of something in Tanner's eyes, and I think about how he was part of the search team that looked for the missing hikers and failed to uncover any sign of them except for the tree carvings.

He's bitter. Him and his father. That's what this is about, and I don't have to listen to it any longer. "See you around, Tanner."

Without letting him say another word, I stalk past him to grab the rest of my groceries. He doesn't follow, perhaps too stunned by my disobedience, but I don't care. He's not the voice of the town. He doesn't get to intimidate me into leaving again. And neither does anybody else.

The short ride home is quiet as I maneuver the dimly lit streets. It's not until I hear the crunch of gravel beneath my tires that I begin to breathe a bit steadier. When I reach the front door, I set down the bags to unlock it.

With a deep breath, I busy myself with putting away the groceries and opening a bottle of wine. I pour myself a glass and head straight for the back patio, not even bothering to put on my suit before I slip into the hot tub naked. My muscles instantly relax, and I inch down until my chin is just grazing the top of the steaming water. Opening my eyes, I look up to find the twinkling blanket of stars above, a comfort to my darkest thoughts. I trace the constellations I once knew so well.

My father was obsessed with the sky and all its intricacies. He liked to talk about our infinite universe, filled with black holes and asteroids. But that's not all the sky meant to Henry June. He looked at the sky as if it carried the answers to the universe. A universe that could be so perfectly solved just by tracing the stars with his eyes. It was his form of meditation.

"There will be times when the little things in life will steal your time. They'll catch you off balance and you'll lose your

way. You'll forget the entire reason you set out on your journey. When that happens, when you realize you've lost your way, look up, Aurora. The answers are in the stars."

So that's what I do now. I find the one that glows the brightest, and I focus on it. Breathe deeply. And suddenly, my anxiety begins to shrink, and my purpose comes back in a rush. I'm here to move my life forward. The town will be forced to accept that in time. All I can do is show them I'm not going anywhere.

My lungs fill with air. I find peace in the stars, just by doing as my father said. *Look up and breathe, Aurora.*

The nearby snap of a twig steals me from my meditation. I'm not sure how long I've been zoned out, but the sound has an instant effect on my heart. It stutters in my chest as I pull myself up from the water to look around. Soft and steady night sounds fill the air as a light breeze rustles the surrounding leaves. It's a beautiful night, one I wish Jaxon was here for.

Thinking of Jaxon, I grab my phone that sits on the back ledge of the hot tub. I could call him. See what he's up to. Tell him I miss him. I smile at how ridiculous my thoughts sound. No, I'm not going to call him. He said he'll call, and he will.

I sigh and I scroll through my messages, my eyes catching on the ones from Aunt Cyndi. I cringe as I press the call button, knowing I've put this phone call off for far too long. I won't be coming back to Durham, at least not for a while.

"Baby girl," Aunt Cyndi scolds as soon as she answers. "What on God's earth has gotten into you? Scott is a mess over your leaving."

I let out a breath. "Scott will be fine. He knows it's over, Aunt Cyndi." I don't mention that he's still been calling.

"I'm so confused by this whole situation. I hope you know what you're doing, Aurora. Scott loves you very much."

"I've thought long and hard about this decision, and leaving was the best thing for the both of us. He just doesn't realize it yet."

"That boy was good for you."

I know my aunt comes from a good place. She's been there through my worst, and Scott was right there with her. She's always been a fan of his, telling me he and I should be together long before anything happened between us. But she has a narrow view of our relationship and of my heart.

"I know, I know. I just—I can't say I'm good for him. I don't love him. Not in the way he deserves."

She sighs, and I can practically hear her heart breaking on the other end of the line. "I trust you think you're making the best decision. It just came as a shock; that's all. After your father passed away, I figured things would get better. I—"

"They *have* gotten better." I bite my lip, worried I'm saying too much, but I need to talk to someone. If I can tell anyone where I am, it's her. "My father left me something when he passed, Aunt Cyndi."

Silence fills the air for a few beats before she finally speaks up. "What did he give you, Aurora?" Her voice is stern, worried. She was never a fan of her sister's husband. Especially not after their separation, and definitely not when I was sent to live with him after my mother's death.

I pinch my eyes closed. "The cottage." She gasps, but I push on before she can interrupt. "He gifted me the deed to the cottage. In Balsam Grove. I'm here."

"Aurora, no," she scolds in a loud whisper. "Why would you go back there?"

I shake my head, wanting nothing more than to end the call and go back to my meditation. "Everything is fine. I'm okay. Being back here has been the best thing for me. I'm reconnecting with all the things I used to love but forgot. My painting, nature…" *Love.* But I won't dare bring up Jaxon.

"Oh, Aurora. You know all I want is for you to be happy, but there has got to be another way. The thought of you living in those woods where you…" I cringe at the words on the tip of her tongue. "God, Aurora. I can't imagine how that place is good for you. And what do you mean he gifted you the deed to the cottage? That's impossible."

I shake my head, confusion ringing between my ears. "What? It's not impossible. The deed was delivered after he passed. It came from his attorney, I assume as part of his will. It's in my name now."

"Aurora," she says firmly. "Your father lost everything when he went to that institution. He owned the place outright, but he couldn't keep up with taxes and property maintenance. The bank auctioned off the cottage last year. Your father's attorney gave me a heads up in case I wanted in on it, but I never said anything to you because honestly, Aurora, I didn't think you needed the reminder. Something's not right."

Another twig snaps in the woods and I jerk my head up, catching a rustle of bushes at the edge of the woods. *Shit.* My phone slips through my fingers, hitting the water with a splash before it starts to sink. *Fuck. Fuck! No.* I scramble to grasp it on its descent. It slips from my hand a few more times before I get a good grip on it and finally pull it from the water.

Just then, a whistle in the wind freezes me. Two long notes, just like what Jaxon and I heard yesterday at Hollow Falls. Chills rake over my body. Someone is out there.

I move quickly, climbing over the ledge of the hot tub and running inside, slamming the the door behind me. Panicked, I focus on locking the door and shoving the wooden cylinder in the slider. Making quick work of checking all the doors to ensure they're locked, I race up the ladder to throw some clothes on.

Back downstairs, I search the cupboards for rice in a desperate attempt to salvage my phone, but there is none, so I dry it off with a towel from the bathroom. It's no use. The damn thing won't turn back on, and I'm sure Aunt Cyndi is completely panicked.

"Damn it!" I scream into the air.

With tears in my eyes, I head back upstairs and turn on my laptop, sending her a quick email to assure her that I'm okay. Then I shower, using the steam to steady my heart rate and push away the lingering feeling that someone was watching me out there.

Should I call Tanner and Brooks? What would they say if I told them someone has been whistling in the woods? They'd laugh, or maybe they'd assume what I'm starting to fear. That someone is trying to spook me—away from Jaxon and away from Balsam Grove.

It seems to work, but I'm left with one cruel thought I can't ignore: the deed to the cottage, the thing that brought me here. I thought it was a gift from my father, but if someone bought it at auction, that's impossible.

I wrap myself in a towel and open my laptop again to search for more information. Aunt Cyndi has to be mistaken. If my father lost the cottage, then why are his things still here? Why would my father's attorney show up on my doorstep following his death with the deed in hand?

I locate the property online, and it only takes a second to find where the ownership history is listed. My father's name is there, above the original owner's and below another name. A name I never in a million years would have expected to see as the owner of the property I'm living in.

Jaxon Mills.

I gasp and cover my mouth as something hot pricks the backs of my eyes. According to this, Jaxon purchased the cottage last year from the bank and then recently gifted it to me.

How can that be? He would have told me. Right?

I think back to our conversation yesterday when I spoke about the deed. I swallow, shaking my head. No. There has got to be a mistake. Why would Jaxon buy my father's cottage and then give it to me without saying a word?

But the more I think about it, the more it all makes sense.

The cottage was far too clean and tidy for being abandoned for years. I remember feeling like someone had been here. And the fact that Lacey still came around seemed strange, but I know now it had nothing to do with me and everything to do with the fact that Jaxon probably brought her here all the time.

And finding Jaxon on my back porch in the middle of the storm on my first night here. He must have known I would come. Or maybe he came by my place every night.

But why? Why lure me here after my father's death? For a second chance? If so, that's a fucked up way of going about it.

I slam my computer closed and dress for bed, too furious to think about anything but the way Jaxon deceived me yet again.

The question is, what am I going to do about it?

25

Jaxon

"You have some fucking nerve showing up here tonight." Val's harsh voice at my back brings on an instant headache.

It's the first night of the art festival in Asheville, and a group of us walked to the corner bar and grill before retiring for the night. I've already said goodbye to the others, and I'm cashing out at the bar when Valerie approaches.

Her gravelly voice cuts like a knife, bleeding incredulousness at the fact that I turned her down. I can't imagine it happens to her often. She's an attractive woman with the confidence men love, and she offers no-strings-attached relationships. I'd be a liar if I denied the fact that she was a perfect fit for my needs at the time we were together. But that's over now. My needs have changed. And there's only one woman on my mind, now and forever.

I don't turn to look at Val when she leans against the bar and her arm brushes mine. "I'm here for work, Val. As are you. Let's keep it professional." There's an edge to my tone I couldn't extract if I tried. Just her presence puts me on edge.

She faces me, and in my periphery, I can see her eyes shooting daggers. "Professional?" she snaps. "A little late for that, don't you think?" She steps forward, too far into my bubble. I tense, turn my head to face her, and stand up taller. But she's not done, and she's not backing down. "You seem to have forgotten whose door you walked through to be here right now, Jaxon. Clearly, you have no respect."

I drop my head back and laugh, knowing every second of my amusement only antagonizes her to the core. Good. When I face her, she's all flustered. Her cheeks are pink, her eyes are wide with bewilderment, and she somehow looks smaller, deflated.

Now it's my turn to lean in. I drop my voice low, knowing it's the only way she will truly hear me. "Just because I won't *fuck* you doesn't mean I won't *respect* you. You're a great businesswoman, Val. I'm just in love with someone else."

Her eyes flare. Her body shakes like she's about to explode. Val has never been the tender-hearted type of lover, so I don't expect understanding from her now. She's a tiger, both in business and in the bedroom.

"She's the one, isn't she?" she sneers, unable to hold back. If she can't have me, she's going to try to hurt me. "The one who broke you."

A fire roars in my chest, hating how her words affect me. "The one and only," I say through gritted teeth.

Her lips curl up when she gets the reaction she wants. My frustration. My doubt. And I hate her for it. "She didn't want you then, Jaxon. Who's to say she wants you now?" Valerie's eyes flicker over my frame, pouting when she's done, her eyes landing back on my lips. "You know where to find me when she's through with you."

And with that, she turns back to the bar, still fuming, but I know there's a part of her that thinks she won. I step away from the bar just as the man behind it slides a pearl-colored martini to Val.

"Mm, that's just perfection. Thank you, Bernard," she purrs, leaning in to tip him with a view of her cleavage.

I roll my eyes and turn toward the exit.

Back in my hotel room, I slip off my shoes and shirt, then slide onto the bed with my phone. After messaging Danny to make sure he checked in on Lacey today, I dial Aurora, knowing she should be home from work by now. It's nice to have someone to call at night when I'm out of town. Loneliness hasn't been a feeling I've accepted with grace all these years. I've filled it with dishonorable choices, justified by the hole Aurora left in my heart. But everything feels different now.

I felt the shake of her body as I held her. Kissed her. Touched her. I heard the tiny noises that slipped from her throat, telling me I still remembered all the sweet places she loves to be touched. I relished in the way her fingers glided through my hair and the feel of her heat grinding on my cock. It was all too much, and it was all so perfect. I didn't want it to end, yet I was terrified to continue.

What would it be like to make love to Aurora again? I'm a hungrier man than I used to be. Demanding. Experienced. I know all the places I want to taste her, touch her, the things I want to do to her with my hands, my mouth. She has no idea the ways I've imagined taking her since she's been home. Hell, even when she was away, I'd think of every intimate moment we once shared. Each one special. Each one unique.

Her phone goes straight to voicemail, so I leave a message.

As I lie in bed, waiting for her to return my call, I fight the exhaustion settling over me and think of all the ways I want to make love to Aurora June.

26

Aurora

I'm driving home from the café in the late afternoon, exhausted from a lack of sleep, and still fuming about Jaxon gifting me the deed to the cottage without my knowledge. It's like he was trying to lure me here under false pretenses. With a dead cell phone, I can't easily reach him, and I'm not sure if I want to right now, anyway.

No. This conversation needs to happen in person.

It's not until I round the bend in the gravel driveway that I see a familiar white SUV parked under the carport. My heart lunges into my throat when I spot Scott standing at the front door of the cottage.

No, no, no.

I slam my foot on the brakes, spinning up gravel beneath my tires. But just as I'm considering putting my car in reverse and backing up out of sight, his head whips around and his dark eyes lock on mine through the windshield. I've been spotted.

Releasing my foot from the brake, I roll under the carport, park, and force myself to take a few deep, steady breaths before exiting the car and closing the distance between us.

Scott stands there, tall and handsome in his green button-down dress shirt and tan slacks that tell me he came straight from a business meeting. His sandy blond hair is combed over in a single wave. I think he's been styling it like that since first grade.

"Scott..." His name catches in my throat, and I smile through my unease. "I can't believe you're here." His arms are open so I step in for a hug, noting instantly the difference between Jaxon's strong hold and Scott's stiff one. We don't mold to each other. My blood doesn't warm beneath my skin. Our embrace is friendship and comfort, nothing more.

His smile is wide, as if the conversations we've had since I left Durham never happened. I let out a slow breath.

"I wanted to see you," he says. "You haven't returned any of my calls, and..." He looks back at the cottage, then turns to me. "So this is it, huh? Nothing like what I imagined when you described it when we were young. I was expecting something bigger. More...magical."

I laugh. "I guess this place felt much bigger when we were kids." I swallow, trying to figure out what to say next. God, this is awkward. "H-how did you find me?"

Aunt Cyndi. I know the answer already, but he dips his hands in his pockets and shrugs with a twist of his lips. "I think you know. She was worried, Aurora. And, I have to say I was shocked to find out you came *here* of all places. It's the last place I would have expected." His gaze moves over my face. "It's starting to make more sense now, though."

My heart drops into my stomach. "It is?"

He shrugs, seeming unfazed by his discovery. "Sure. You needed closure after your father passed away. What happened was traumatic, and you're trying to heal. I'm proud of you."

"You are?"

He nods emphatically. "You're facing your demons." His expression morphs into a mashup of confusion and disappointment. "You thought I wouldn't understand." His eyes lock on mine again like he's just made sense of the universe. "I was always so dead-set on you not coming back here. You didn't think I would approve. Is that it?" A glimmer of hope enters his gaze. "Aurora, if you're here, *I'm* here. You don't need to feel guilty for chasing your past. If you need that to move forward and find yourself, I'll help you."

"Oh, Scott." I sigh, the discomfort and guilt churning in my chest. When will he understand it's over? "Thank you. Really. You've always been there for me. And I know you would be if I asked. But I need to do this on my own. My entire life I've allowed others to take care of me. To know what's best for me. I'm doing it on my own now, and I feel stronger because of it."

And in a split second his expression changes from hope, to confusion, to sadness as he realizes what he came for is not just out of reach; it's never coming back. "Oh."

"I'm so sorry. I thought I made it clear when we spoke—"

Scott holds up a hand, his cheeks turning a shade of blush I've never seen on him before. "You did," he says with annoyance. "I guess I just thought you were reacting to your father's death. I thought you'd change your mind." His eyes flicker to mine. "You're not going to change your mind."

My insides crumble with guilt. "No. I'm not."

He steps back like he's lost his equilibrium and looks around us, taking in the woods, the cottage, the drive, like he's doing it for the first time. "But why did you have to come back *here*? Isn't it"—he looks around and shivers visibly—"creepy?"

I bite the inside of my cheek to keep from frowning. I was right. Scott wouldn't last a day in Balsam Grove. I shrug. "This is my home."

He breathes through the silence, and I know what he's thinking. He's never been the reactive type, and I've always appreciated that. Whenever anyone asked me to describe Scott, it was his thoughtfulness that came to mind first. He cared, and he showed that he cared. Even if he didn't care the way I needed him to.

"I'm happy here," I add, hoping it finally sinks in for him. "I have a job and old friends ..."

He sighs heavily. "I just—I don't understand."

I hang my head, unable to continue staring back into his sad, brown eyes. "This isn't for you to understand. I know that's not easy to hear, but you need to try to let this go. Let *me* go."

"I will never let you go, Aurora. Jesus, I've worried about you since I was six. Every cut on your knee. Every mean girl. Every broken heart. I've been there for you for everything. Driving you to and from doctor appointments. During your breakdowns after your father was convicted. You were doing so well with me. We were happy."

I shake my head and meet his gaze. "That's where you're wrong. I was numb, Scott. My medication—enabled me in forgetting what troubled me most. But in doing that, I lost so much of myself. I had no chance of being happy in Durham. Not when there were still pieces of me missing. I'd forgotten so much about myself."

"And you're finding them here?" he asks, incredulously. "How is that possible after what your father did?"

"I'm not my father. As much as you want to protect me from what you thought I would become, that's not me."

Scott lets out a frustrated breath. "Your father was a sick man, but he didn't start progressing until he was, what—in his mid-thirties?" He gestures to me with his hands. "You're still young. Prevention is the key."

My jaw drops, and every fear I've had since my parents informed me of my father's disorder comes crashing down around me. It's a flashflood of pain as I move from one emotion to the next. Shock, outrage, hurt... But in a way, I've always known Scott had this fear in the back of his mind. It was always on mine. But hearing him say it just cracks everything open.

"You think just because I left you—because I don't want to be with you—I'm some violent schizophrenic?"

He mutters something else under his breath before trying again. "I'm just saying we should check it out. Go back to Rohls. He'll run some tests. If anything is wrong, it's better to catch it and treat it early on, right? Maybe if your dad had been treated sooner, he wouldn't have..." He trails off.

"What?" I demand. My anxiety is one thing. But I never thought Scott questioned my sanity. "He wouldn't have let me bleed out as he held me in his arms, rocking me like I was a lifeless child? He wouldn't have been sent to a psychiatric facility where they couldn't help him? Where he refused to see his own damn daughter? And he wouldn't have *killed* himself because the voices in his head wouldn't shut up?"

"Stop, Aurora. Jesus Christ."

"No. *You* stop." My heart feels like it's about to explode from my chest. Maybe I do need to stop. Getting this worked up can't be good for me. Scott is coming from a good place. I shake my head, not wanting this conversation to end like this. "Trust me, Scott. I know the statistics. I've lived in this nightmare for far too long. And I may have issues, but I also know how strong I am. Strong enough to walk away from a situation that made me unhappy without letting you make me feel crazy."

"I don't think you're crazy."

"That's not what I'm hearing."

"Aurora," he pleads again, but I'm done having the same argument.

"It's too late, Scott. I have things I need to take care of. You shouldn't be here."

His face reddens with anger as he shifts in his stance. "I don't really have a choice in all of this, do I?"

I shake my head slowly, making sure there's no mistaking my certainty. Although the recent news about how the cottage came into my possession dampened my outlook some, it hasn't taken away from why I came. I'm still here for the right reasons. For *me*. To confront my past and move forward. To find myself again. To *love* myself again.

"It really is nice to see you." I try to soften the blow, but I also mean my words. I want Scott to be able to move on, too.

He deserves every ounce of happiness he thought he had with me and more.

He shakes his head, his expression telling me he doesn't believe me. "Yeah. Okay, Aurora." The crumpled look he gives me next presses heavy on my heart. He starts to walk toward his car, passing me without a word before he turns around, meeting my eyes again. Everything about him—his unsure stance, his sad eyes, and the tremble in his voice—crushes me.

I want to tell him I'm sorry, that he'll find someone else, but that's not what he wants to hear right now. I want to say goodbye and not have it mean forever, but I'm afraid it's the only way for him to let me go. I'm not just losing my ex-boyfriend. I'm losing my best friend. A lifetime of friendship. Not many people are lucky enough to have someone like Scott, and here I am, giving him up.

But none of it gets said as Scott climbs into his SUV, and disappears into the woods.

27

Aurora

I'm climbing down the ladder after my shower when I hear odd scratching and tapping noises coming from somewhere nearby. Swiveling my head around the space, I try to brace myself as a rush of adrenaline soars through me. It was just starting to sprinkle when I got in the shower, but the downpour is heavy now.

I turn, working my way in a slow circle as I listen closely for where the sounds are coming from. I'm facing the kitchen when I hear more scratching, followed by a whimper. I lean down to peer around the kitchen counter, spying the shadow behind the plastic entrance of the doggy door.

A breath leaves me in a relieved whoosh.

Lacey.

My stomach twists with emotions I'm too conflicted to make much sense of. I love that Lacey's here, that she knows she has a place to come to in the rain. I would never turn her away. But selfishly, I hate the fact that the reasons she's here are less about me than they are about Jaxon's deceit. He's been coming for the past year, at least. Maintaining the place, possibly even renting it out. Who knows how many others have been here in all my time away. Why didn't he just tell me?

It's still early in the evening, but the cloud cover makes it feel later than it is. With Jaxon still out of town until tomorrow, I'm glad Lacey knew she could come here. I go to unlock the doggy door for her, and she pushes her way in as if this is something we do every single day, her tail wagging happily behind her. I smile through fresh tears and find the dog food and water I purchased just in case she decided to visit me again. I set it out for her and pour myself a glass of wine.

I start a fire in the fireplace, bringing it to a perfect flame before curling up on the couch with my wine. My phone is dead, and I've made no attempt to replace it. What's the point? I'd rather not be that accessible, and I have internet access through my computer. I'll get a house phone for emergencies, and I have the café phone during the day if I need it.

Lacey pads over to the couch as if she can sense my anxiety, asking permission to join me with a nudge of her nose into my legs. I laugh and pat the empty spot next to me. She jumps up and wraps herself in a ball at my feet, her chin on my ankles and her beautiful blue eyes staring back at me.

"I've missed you too, baby girl." I scratch her head, watching her eyes fight sleep until they fall closed and stay there.

Time passes, I'm not sure how much, but the downpour outside is steady as I finish my wine and set the glass on the side table, too tired to get another and too wrapped up in all the reasons why Jaxon could possibly choose to omit something so incredibly important. I don't want to feel this way, like he's poisoned everything we've started to rebuild, blistering my already bruised heart. I don't want to question him after everything we've been through. But how else am I supposed to feel when the entire reason I'm back in Balsam Grove suddenly feels like a setup? I'm not entirely sure if I'm mad that he gifted the cottage to me, though. I guess it depends on his intentions.

A knock on the door startles me and wakes Lacey from her nap. I have every intention of ignoring it when I catch a glimpse of Jaxon's eyes peering in through the glass. He's drenched from head to foot, and he's pointing to the door to let him in. Did he ride on his motorcycle in the rain? From Asheville? He's not supposed to be back until tomorrow.

My heart pounds in time with his fist against the door, and then I hear his voice over the rain. "Aurora, it's me. Let me in."

No. After an odd look or two from Lacey, she leaps from the couch and walks lazily to the door, pressing her nose against it, then pawing at it. I take in a deep breath and follow her, debating my next move. I wasn't expecting him tonight. I thought I'd have more time to come up with something to say. To tell him I know about the deed and that I'm angry as hell that he kept it from me.

"It's not a good time right now."

"What? Why? I've been trying to call you since last night. I've been worried."

"I'm fine, Jaxon. And Lacey's fine, too. She can stay if she wants. Let's talk tomorrow, okay? It's late."

"Can you at least open the door? I've missed you." His voice cracks as he lowers his boom to something softer.

I let out a breath, slamming my lids together and holding onto my resolve a little bit longer. "No, Jax. Tomor—"

"Damn it." His fists slap the door, jolting me upright. There are a few seconds of silence before he speaks again. "If something is wrong, can you just tell me what it is? We don't need to play this game, Aurora. Not after everything we've been through, okay? Why are you avoiding me?"

With an angry breath, I pull the door open, letting it stop hard against the chain. "I have nothing to say to you right now."

His eyes grow wide, and his face twists in confusion. "What? Why?"

"You lied to me. Did you think I wouldn't find out?"

"What are you talking about?"

"The deed, Jaxon." His face crumbles instantly. "My father didn't give me the deed. He couldn't have. The bank repossessed it and auctioned it off to the highest bidder. To you." My eyes blur with tears, and I wipe them away angrily.

I watch his face morph from realization to guilt. I almost fall to my knees at the confirmation. "I can't believe you. You've been lying to me this entire time."

He shakes his head, throwing his hands against the door and then shoving off from it when he realizes he can't get closer to me. "It's not like that at all. Just let me in and I'll explain."

Hot tears fall from my eyes, and for a moment, I consider opening the door. Maybe I pause too long because he stands straighter and opens his mouth to speak.

"Fine. Keep me out, but I'm saying what I need to say before I leave. Christ, Aurora, is it so awful I wanted you to have your home back? Does that make me a bad guy? This cottage belongs to you. And I didn't tell you it was me who gave it to you because I wanted you to decide for yourself what to do with it. All I did was leave it in your hands. I didn't know you were going to come back here. Did I hope you would? *Yes.* Was I still fucking pissed at you for pushing me away years ago? *Yes.* Did my heart almost split open when I saw you that night in the storm? *Yes, goddammit, yes.* Because I didn't think you were real. I had convinced myself I would never see you again, but there you were, standing in the window like a goddamn ghost. You came back. On your terms. For your own reasons. All I did was hand you the keys to what already belonged to you. If you need to be mad at me, fine. You know where to find me if you want to talk."

He pushes off from the door again, his face flushed with passion.

It's so easy to trust him. To forgive him. I wish it could have been that easy years ago. Maybe he should have told me about the deed, but he's right. It doesn't matter how I got here. He didn't force me to come.

"Wait," I call. My hands move quickly to unlock the chain and open the door, leaving just enough room for him to walk in. He doesn't look at me as he slams the door behind him and kicks off his shoes, petting Lacey as she shoves her nose between his wet, jean-clad legs. I take his rain jacket from him and eye his black button-down shirt.

"You're back early."

He nods, jaw hard, like he knows I've forgiven him, but he's still pissed at me. "I tried calling you yesterday and today, and when Claire said you seemed upset and went home early today, I got worried. I thought maybe something happened." He swallows, and my heart drops to my feet.

A new reality dawns on me. "You thought I left?"

His stares at me, and his throat moves as he swallows. Then he looks away as if he's ashamed of his thoughts. "It crossed my mind."

I guess there was a part of me that considered it, so I can't fault him completely, but is this going to be the conclusion he jumps to every time he can't get ahold of me?

"I'm sorry for thinking the worst," I say quietly. "I just—I didn't understand why you would keep that from me. But that's not why my phone is off. I dropped it in the hot tub last night. It's done for." I cringe with embarrassment. "But I'm glad you're here."

"You are?" He looks doubtful.

"Yes, Jax. You should have told me about the deed, especially when I brought it up the other day, but I understand your reasons for gifting it to me." I swallow. "Thank you. It's actually pretty sweet of you." I catch a hint of his smile break through that gorgeous face of his.

My heart twists in my chest. It feels so natural to want to wrap my arms around him in a hug, but he's soaking wet. I laugh.

"Maybe you should take your clothes off." He raises his eyebrows in amusement, and my cheeks flush at my words. "I can throw them in the dryer," I add quickly, and then I point to the fire. "I have a fire going, so you'll be warm enough. And I just opened a bottle of wine. If you're hungry, we'll have to get creative, though. I don't really have anything—"

"Not hungry, but the rest sounds good," he answers gruffly, his eyes drinking in my body. I'm dressed in thin, dark gray sweats and an oversized white muscle shirt. Nothing sexy at all, but the way Jaxon's looking at me now makes me feel beautiful.

I clear my throat as he strips and, with a smug grin, hands his clothes over to me in a crumpled-up ball. I avert my gaze and take the two steps to the open door of the laundry room to toss his clothes into the dryer. When I walk back out to the living room, I find Jaxon moving some logs in the fire. Two fresh glasses of wine sit on the coffee table behind him.

He turns and greets me with a tired smile. I fight to keep my eyes from dropping down to take in more of his sculpted body and red boxer briefs. Ugh. Jaxon always did get my heart revved up when he wore red. It works well with his tanned skin, turbulent eyes, and wild hair. But now, standing in my cottage, which suddenly feels too small, he looks...dangerous. And not in a bad way.

We meet each other in front of the couch, and I wrap my arms around his waist. "I'm sorry," I say softly as I peer up at him. "It's just—when I'm around you I turn into, like, this teenage girl again. I'm just a bundle of nerves I have no clue what to do with."

He shakes his head, chuckling at my confession. "I should have told you when I saw you, or at least when you brought it up the other day. But you were adamant that the deed was some sort of sign. I didn't want you knowing that I gave it to you to change any of that, because it changes nothing, Aurora. I don't regret doing it. You needed to make the decision to come back on your own. I'm sorry you didn't find out the truth from me, though."

"So, we're even?"

He smiles. "I'd say we can call a truce."

I remove my hand from around his waist and offer it to him with a laugh. "Good. Truce, then."

He shakes his head, then tugs my arm forward and wraps it back around his waist with a grin. "I think we've moved past handshakes, don't you think?"

He doesn't give me a chance to respond before he kisses me, slow and sweet. And just like that, here in his arms, I'm transported back to the second time we ever kissed.

It was two long years after we first kissed on the rock at Hollow Falls. I was seventeen. We had met in the same spot on the bridge every single day for ten days, just the two of us. Catching up. Apologizing for how he'd pushed me away two years before because he was afraid of his own feelings for a girl too young for him to pursue. Playing with Lacey. And then one day, when I was laughing at something he said, he gave me a look that hit me deep in the chest. He leaned in until I could feel my heart crashing inside me. And then his lips touched mine.

I was buzzing. All I could feel was the spray of water coming off the rocks and a rush of adrenaline like I was leaping into the falls. I knew, without a doubt, he would be there to greet me after the fall. He still is.

I'm left winded when our kiss ends, and my cheek falls to his chest.

"You've changed so much," I say, my palms moving up and down against his back. I look up into his eyes and swallow, wondering if I'll ever get used to seeing Jaxon with a beard. I run my fingers over it, and something warms in my belly. Yes, I think I'll get used to it just fine. "As soon as I saw you on my back porch, I knew it was you. It was your eyes." My lips turn up shyly. "Other than that, nothing about you was the same."

"I thought I was dreaming," Jaxon confesses in return, his forehead dropping to mine as he pulls me tighter, closer. "I'd wished for you to come home for so long, Aurora. I thought my mind was playing tricks on me. But then I saw you in the café staring at our painting."

I smile, my heart skipping like rocks across a creek. "You always did call them ours. Those are *yours,* Jax. Your hard work."

He shakes his head. "Anything good I ever created was inspired by you."

"That's not true." I wish he wouldn't give me so much credit. Jaxon was painting masterpieces before anyone had ever seen his work, but he always insisted that I was the inspiration for everything he was proud of.

"It is true. I would have never had the courage to show my work to anyone if it wasn't for you. Every piece in Creek Café was inspired by you. I can't imagine creating anything great that you're not a part of in some way. Can't you see it when you look at them?"

I look at him with questioning eyes.

He breathes out and tries again. "You're the shadow in the falls, and you're the one who tipped over the canoe. It was your shoe that slipped off at the top of the mountain. And you were the one that picked that flower that fell in the creek. I've only ever been truly inspired to paint what you've already brought to life. I just tried to hold on to those memories the best way I knew how." A teasing smile flashes across his face. "It's a good thing you came back when you did. I was beginning to run out of memories."

The way he's looking at me now with such honesty fills my chest to the brim. They say before death, life flashes before your eyes. But what about before life begins again? Because in this moment, here with Jaxon, with our pasts wide open between us, it all comes back to me in a rush. The good parts of it, anyway. The first time we met, our adventures together, the way he looked at me when he knew he shouldn't. The first time he held my hand. Our first kiss. In a tortured youth filled with far more responsibilities than two kids should ever have, we found each other and fell into a deep, irreplaceable kind of love.

"I think I need my wine now." I laugh, feeling shaky from the gale of memories. It's like I've just been given legs after a lifetime of searching for a way to stand on my own.

He pulls us onto the couch and hands me my glass of wine. I curl up beside him, bending my knees so they fall over his lap, tucking my toes beneath me. His free hand rests on my thigh, tracing circles with his pointer finger as we drink our wine and stare into the flames in contented silence. Lacey pads around the couch to the fluffy rug outside my old bedroom, and it's just the three of us again.

Jaxon's fingers leave my thigh and weave through mine. "Hey," he says gently. I turn to meet his eyes.

"What is it?"

The look he's giving me now isn't comforting. I hold my breath for another wind to come in and sweep our newfound peace away.

He squeezes my hand with his. "I want you to know I saw Val last night."

My damn heart stutters, then restarts, telling me to trust him instead of jumping to conclusions again. "Okay." I let the word linger on my tongue.

"It wasn't planned," he assures me. "She was at the bar after the event. I was leaving, and she was getting a drink. She stopped me. She wanted to talk."

"Jax," I say, shaking my head. "You don't have to tell me anything. It's none of my business."

He tilts his head. "Bullshit, Aurora. I'm telling you because I don't want any secrets between us. A couple months ago, I found out she was married, and I ended things between us. She was angry because I've been avoiding her ever since, and Val doesn't handle being ignored well. That's why she came by the shop the other day. To confront me. She confronted me again in Asheville. And she didn't like what I had to say, but at least she knows where I stand." There's a pause while he exhales slowly. "We both have our pasts, Aurora. Good and bad. But I'm here with *you* now. I'm not going anywhere, and I sure as hell am not letting Val come between us."

A relieved breath fills my lungs. I smile and lean in, touching my forehead to his. "Thank you."

My hand falls to his chest a bit timidly. Being so close to Jaxon now is just as nerve-racking as the first time I touched him. Even after our day together at the falls, this seems more intimate—and not just because he's sitting beside me in nothing but his underwear, staring at me like he's imagining himself inside me. We've come a long way, the pain of all the years before us only making what we mean to each other so much stronger. I can feel it between us. The heat. The strength. But there's newness to it all, too. We aren't seventeen and twenty-one, making out behind trees and in abandoned cabins. He isn't taking my virginity in the dark basement of his house while muffling my screams of pleasure with his palms. It's been so long since those days, but unlike Jaxon, I haven't been intimate with anyone else.

My fingers skate across his chest on a mission to memorize every inch of its landscape, chiseled like the rock bed of a waterfall. He lets me have my fun until my eyes flick up to find his tortured ones. He clears his throat as if I've just walked in on him touching himself. Caught.

"Do me a favor." His plea is gruff, his breath hot against my neck.

"Anything."

He smiles. "Does that stereo work?"

I turn toward the bookshelf that holds my Bluetooth stereo and shrug. "Yeah. Want me to turn it on?"

He nods, then reaches for his phone on the coffee table in front of us. "We need some music."

I cross the room and power on the speaker. A few seconds later, an acoustic song I don't recognize pours out. I walk back to Jaxon, who takes my hand and pulls me between his legs, his long lashes batting against his brows as he peers up at me.

"That's better," he says with a smile. His fingers stroke my kneecaps for a moment, and then he continues up, skating up the thin fabric of my sweatpants. When he gets to my waist, his eyes light up and he looks back up at me. "I'm feeling a little underdressed here, Waterfall Eyes."

It's an invitation. A bold one that sends every inch of hair on my body standing on edge, begging for more of his touch.

The lump of nerves in my throat is thick, but I swallow it. He wants me to strip for him. I can do that, just as soon as I remember what underwear I put on after my shower tonight. A black lace thong, I think, with red polka dots. That'll do.

My insides clench with excitement. For the last seven years, no man has seen me naked, yet I'm about to strip down to my undergarments for Jax like it's nothing.

My fingers grip the bottom of my tank top in response. He sucks in a breath as I lift the cloth up and over my head, my hair dropping around my shoulders in long waves.

"Fucking beautiful," he says, tracing the lace of my demi cup bra with his eyes. I look down too. I want to know what he's seeing. My breasts fill the cups, threatening to spill with each heavy breath. It's no more revealing than my bathing suit from the other day, but there's no water to hide me now. There's no towel to wrap my wet body in.

My hands move to my sweats next, untying them and then hooking the elastic around my thumbs. My limbs shake and my breath catches, but I ignore it as I peel the fabric from my hips and slip it down over my hips, thighs, knees, and feet. My nerves are hard to hide now that I'm standing here in front of him, his eyes sweeping over every inch of me appreciatively, hungrily. But he makes no move to touch me. Not yet. I can almost feel the twitch of his palm. The need, fierce and heavy, hangs in the air between us.

The fire from the stove warms my skin as it sparks and crackles behind me. And then his hands begin to move. His fingertips, featherlight against my skin, float up my leg, skimming the lace fabric of my underwear before digging in at my waist.

"Turn for me." It's a demand, dark and controlling. Heat rushes to my belly as I turn for him, focusing on my breathing rather than what Jaxon's next move might be. I'm facing the fire, but my lids are pressed tightly together.

"I still can't believe you're really here." He blows out a breath. "I thought I'd go crazy never getting to touch you again. So many nights I'd lay awake thinking about those tiny earthquakes your body would make." A gentle pressure floats along my skin, the pads of his fingers dragging up the sides of my legs. I can barely breathe. "And the other day at the falls," he rasps, "I wanted to feel you again. I wanted to feel you tighten around my fingers until you had no choice but to erupt." A palm wraps a section of my ass and squeezes hard, dragging a moan up his throat. "I wanted to sit you on my cock and sink inside you so deep your cries would carry into town."

My knees tremble. I look over my shoulder, my lids feeling heavy with want. It's like he's drugged me with his words. But as doped up as I am, his eyes still pin mine in place.

"I need to touch you, Aurora. Do you understand?" His words are so desperate I almost fall to my knees.

Instead, I swallow and respond with a step backward. His legs widen for me, fitting me there so the backs of my calves hit the front of the couch. I have to press my knees together to keep them from shaking.

My next inhale is sharp as Jaxon's cool lips find the plump skin of my ass where he just squeezed. He swipes his tongue over the pressure, kisses it, then bites down. I moan at the feel of my skin between his teeth, his hot breath washing over me. It stings for a second—the good kind of sting. The kind that makes me want his teeth on every inch of my skin.

He curses again before squeezing my other cheek with his free hand. "Sit," his raspy voice demands.

I swallow and bend my knees, letting him guide me onto his eager lap. He's so hard beneath me, strained against his red briefs as he leans back on the couch, pulling me with him.

"You're making me crazy, Waterfall Eyes," he murmurs into my back before dropping soft kisses from my neck to mid-spine. Then he sighs, like he knows he should stop himself, and adjusts my positioning so that my legs fall over his and I'm pressed into the corner of the couch. I look up at him curiously.

He seems to be focused on something, deep in his thoughts as he watches the lick of the flames in front of us. The firelight whips shadows against the wall as the seductive smell of ash and burning wood scent the air. Jaxon's hand travels over my thighs and stomach, his touch light against my hot skin.

I try to breathe evenly.

I try to relax.

I try not to think of where I want him to put his hands.

He's obviously got something on his mind.

"Can I ask you something?" His voice awakens the silence, his tone husky with fatigue. "It won't change anything. I just thought I'd ask. You know about Val, but I haven't asked you about...you know. You said you've dated, but..."

My brows bunch together, hating that with every reminder of Scott, guilt comes along for the ride. "There's been no one else. Not in that way."

"Okay," he says with a squeeze of my thigh. "I don't need any other details. I was just curious."

I smile and let my head fall to his shoulder. "If it helps, I can't imagine another man's hands touching me." My eyes flicker to his lips. "Or another mouth kissing me."

He returns my smile as his fingertips tilt my chin to align our mouths. "That's really good to hear since I can't stop touching you." His fingers begin to trace circles around my navel.

Desire stretches through me, hitting every nerve, burning every surface. "Never stop touching me, Jaxon. Never again."

His eyes blaze before he leans in, pausing only a second before covering my mouth with his. Blood rushes through my veins like a wild river, causing my mind to swirl in a fog of endless bliss.

Jaxon's always been so gentle with me, like I'm fragile glass swept up in his hurricane— but instead of destroying me, he takes me along for the ride. He's needy in the way he touches me, testing his limits with soft kisses and vocal warnings about what he wants to do to me next.

His hand slides down from my navel, teasing the fabric of my panties before slipping his hand beneath them. My core aches, yearning for what was so rudely taken from us the other day at Hollow Falls. Nothing is stopping us now.

The fire crackles in the background as my head falls back and Jaxon's lips move to my neck. My skin burns hot beneath his kisses, his fingers still on the descent, brushing over my body like a paintbrush on canvas. And then he's there at my core, sweeping a finger down the center of my lace, slipping between my slick skin and teasing the magical bundle of nerves that reaches every part of me.

His mouth moves back to mine, swallowing my surprise as he pushes a finger inside me. I gasp at the fullness, breaking our lip-lock.

"How's that, babe? Good?" he rasps with eyes half-closed.

My hands move to his curls in response, grasping handfuls and tugging him deeper into another kiss. *More*, my hands say. *Deeper*, my tongue begs.

He manages to pull me onto his lap, his chest pressed to my back as he spreads me wider, his heels hooking onto my ankles. I let my head fall onto his shoulder, trying to focus on my breathing while his fingers continue to fill me like it's his job. His other hand grips my waist, rocking me against his stiff lap until every part of me is sparking, hot and alive.

We're sticks and friction, wind and smoke, and we fight our way to each other to feel what once was ours. I feel greedy nips and kisses on my shoulder and upper arm as he angles me back to curl his finger even deeper. Again and again, his pushes inside me like he knows I'm close and he's taking his time on purpose.

I relax against him, submitting to his touch, and that's when I feel the very first catch of the fire.

"Jax," I warn, my voice begging him for more. And he gives it to me.

His free hand moves to my breast, gripping it for leverage as he pumps against me while quickening his hand's movements. I arch and release my back, filling his palm with more of my chest while he stretches me with a second finger. I rub wildly against him, letting the fire build around us, just waiting to be doused in gasoline. I climb higher and higher with each lick of the flame until I'm finally exploding, shooting off wild and hot sparks, becoming featherlight as I continue to ride out my release on Jaxon's hand.

Finally, the smoke clears, and Jaxon's finger slips from me. He moves me to my back, lying beside me on the couch and pressing his lips to mine in a long, lingering, shaky kiss. I'm glad to know I'm not the only one affected by what we just did. Our breaths are as wild as the fire he just put out in me, and I feel his hard length pressed into my stomach.

"Stay the night." My invite probably wasn't needed, but I can tell Jaxon appreciates it when he nods into my mouth and smiles.

"Yes, ma'am."

His mouth moves to my neck, and I giggle when I feel the scratch of his beard against my sensitive skin. "What's so funny?" He nuzzles into my neck again, causing another fit of giggles to erupt.

"Your beard. I kind of love it."

"Kind of?"

I laugh again. "Kind of a lot."

He chuckles and nuzzles into me again. "Wait until you feel it between your thighs."

I smile as he lifts me from the couch. It's one single movement of strength and agility that makes me wonder how much time Jaxon spends working out. He was always strong, fit, and tall, but time has worked well for him.

He sets me down at the base of the ladder, never taking his lips from mine. He's still kissing me as I take the first step but releases me when I continue to climb toward the bedroom. "You're beautiful, Aurora June."

I smile over my shoulder. "There's a better view from up here."

He wastes no time climbing the ladder and moving me to the bed, lowering his body on top of mine. I crawl backwards as he follows in a short chase of cat and mouse. When my head is close to the window that acts as my headboard, he dips down to kiss me long and hard.

We're breathless when he sits up, his eyes scrolling over my body. "You're right. It's a much better view from up here."

I bite my bottom lip, taking Jaxon in too. He's so hard, and based on the way he grips his length through his briefs, I imagine it's becoming painful. And then his expression changes, and he groans, this time in frustration. "Please tell me you're on birth control."

I swallow and nod. "You don't have—?"

He shakes his head, eyes still shut. "I wasn't expecting anything to happen, and I came straight here from the show. I just wanted to see you and make sure everything was okay. I haven't been with anyone in months, and I'm clean. But we can wait."

My heart melts. Seriously, I feel my insides turn to mush. I sit up on my knees so I'm eye level with him. "Jax, it's okay."

"Are you sure? I've never forgiven myself for going in raw with you that one time. We got lucky, but it was stupid. So fucking stupid. I was selfish with you. I've always been selfish with you."

I let out a laugh, not because it's funny, but because Jaxon's version of what happened back then is completely different from how I remember it. "Jax, stop. We made that stupid decision together."

When he relaxes again, I smile and lean forward, pressing my lips to his. "Jax, I trust you. Will you please fuck me senseless? I've only been waiting seven years for this."

His lip curls before he presses his mouth to mine. "Since you asked so crudely. Your wish is my command."

28

Aurora

I've imagined taking Aurora so many different ways, and fucking her senseless—her term, not mine—is definitely on that list. But now that we're here, alone in her room, and she's wearing nothing but scraps of lace and the most beautiful smile, I think I'll feast on her slowly. Seven years is a long time. She deserves every bit of attention I gave her the first time, maybe even more.

The music is still flowing from downstairs, the fire still lit and crackling. Aurora's room is too bright, so I turn on the lamp beside her bed and switch off the overhead light. She's sitting in the middle of the bed, her legs bent and palms pressed into the mattress. She's watching me set the mood with that shy but eager gaze I love so much.

I step to the edge of the bed, reach for her ankles, and slide her to me in one swift pull so her legs are on either side of mine. She sits up as I sink to my knees and stare up at her with every bit as much adoration as I feel.

My Aurora. No distractions. Just us.

My palms cup her cheek as her lips part for me. It doesn't matter that we've been apart for years. Everything feels so natural when I'm with her. For the first time in years, I feel like my accomplishments mean something more than financial and professional success. I'm proud to show off who I am to Aurora. I still feel like she's to thank for all of it.

I pull her bottom lip between mine and suck until I hear one of those tiny moans fly from her throat. She can't hide the way she feels when we're intimate like this. Everything is a pant, a moan, a sigh, a scream. I fucking love every single sound, and I've barely even touched her since we've gotten upstairs.

"Jaxon, please," she whispers against my mouth, her hand snaking down to feel me, hard and so ready to give her what she wants. I want to tell her how much agony I'm in. How my cock, hard as stone, strains and fights against my briefs. I know she feels it as she squeezes me with her small fingers, her grasp firm and demanding as she strokes me.

"In time, beautiful." My hand stops hers mid-stroke. "There's something I want to do first."

With a gentle push, my hands splayed on her stomach, I press her into the mattress and pin her arms over her head with mine. "Don't move these." She nods, eyes wide, and I reward her with a chaste kiss before sinking back to my knees and grazing her body with my fingertips on the way down. I stop at her panties and brush a thumb against her center. She's still wet, her lace panties completely soaked. My cock flinches at the memory of her wrapped around my finger, hot and so fucking tight. I'll explode as soon as I enter her, I know it, especially if I'm bare. All the more reason to take my time now.

I hook the lace at one hip with a finger, and then I do the same with the other side. Her back arches as I peel the fabric from her body, my eyes transfixed on her beautiful offering of shaved, pale pink skin. For an instant, my chest puffs at the knowledge that no one else has ever seen her this way, bare and spread open. Just me. I'm a fucking king. And I can't wait another second to taste her.

My nose dips down first, catching her scent before I swipe my tongue against her center, pushing her hips back down as she jerks them in surprise.

"Ahh," she moans.

I smile and take another taste, this one just as quick, figuring I'll let her get used to me before I unleash on her completely. I can't fucking wait.

Using my hands to part her legs further, I let my thumb fall to her clit, massaging it as I inhale her sweet scent again, shivering on my exhale. She moans in response to my warm breath and arches her back again.

"Jax, more."

"Patience, Waterfall Eyes."

The next swipe of my tongue is slow and long, and I follow it up with the suction of my mouth on her clit. A gasp explodes from her mouth. Fuck, she tastes better than the wine we forgot to finish downstairs. I can feel myself start to unravel as I drink her in, my tongue lapping eagerly against her, my arms now hooked around her legs, pressing her hips down to keep them from bucking wildly against the sheets.

Everything about Aurora is so pure, so tight, and so reactive. This is new for us. This type of intimacy. We came close many times when she lay naked beneath me. My lips would travel down her body, exploring her uncharted skin, stopping just above her glistening center. She'd be jerking from my finger already inside her, moaning from the feel of my breath hitting her right there. But I never took a taste, too afraid that she was too delicate to handle all the things I wanted to do to her.

Now that I have a second chance, I won't let her down.

Her entire body is shaking, her breasts pressed into the air like she's a woman possessed, and she's crying out with a sound so guttural and filthy, I want to watch her come undone just as much as I want to continue devouring her.

But she wants more, and I'm not stopping until she gets it.

When her muscles begin to spasm around my tongue, I know she's letting go. Her fingers dig into the comforter, gripping and pulling. Her legs quiver. Her cry comes out a rasp. And when she finally starts to come down, she comes down slowly.

I release her from my mouth. She slides her fingers through my hair and tugs me toward her onto the bed. I land on my elbows with a grin, her juices still fresh on my lips. She attacks them, nibbles them clean while clawing at my back and reaching for my briefs. She pushes them down, and my cock springs free. She wastes no time. I inhale sharply as her hand grips me firmly, groaning at the feel of her palm stroking me like she's imagining me inside her.

I take the opportunity to unclasp her bra, releasing her supple breasts. They're perfect, firm and big enough to fill my palm. My mouth waters at the thought of tasting them again.

She releases me from her hold, grabs her bra, and flings it to the side. I chuckle at her impulse, loving this wild side of Aurora she never allowed herself to show me at seventeen— the woman I was only able to imagine in my dreams for so many years.

I roll to the side to slide my briefs off completely, letting myself breathe for a moment before attempting to climb back onto her. She seems to be doing the same. I peer at her, a smile spreading across my face when I take in her naked form. My petite girl with curves that drive me mad, with long hair strewn about in a messy tangle around her shoulders. I roll back on top of her, lifting my weight with my elbows as I gaze down. She stares back at me with a knowing smile.

Everything is perfect.

"I love you, you know?" I swallow against the nerves rattling my chest. I don't know why I'm shaking. We've made love before. I've heard her moans. I've watched her come apart for me, spine arched and neck stretched back as I filled her. But everything feels different now, like doing it again proves just how soul-crushingly real our love is.

Her eyes shine with emotion, and she cups my face with a small palm. "I love you too, Jax. I never stopped."

This time, when I kiss her, it's all heart and pent-up emotions I've been saving for her for seven years.

"That's really good news," I mumble against her lips. Then, I kiss her again, this time while her legs part and knees bend.

I push up on my arms to align myself just right and then guide myself into her snug opening. I push into her, edging my way in as she adjusts around me, squeezing me until my breath is coming in gasps.

I'm sweating by the time I'm halfway in, pumping my hips to push inside her as deep as her body will allow. Aurora isn't complaining as she presses her heels into my ass, more impatient than I am to feel all of me buried inside her.

"Are you okay?" I ask against her neck.

She nods, lifting her pelvis again to take more of me. "I'm sorry I'm so tight."

My laughter comes quick, pushing me the rest of the way in, and I groan before kissing her neck. "Baby, it's a good thing. Trust me."

I move slowly, desperate to feel every inch of her slide against every inch of me, grinding into her when I can't get any closer. She palms my ass. I flex, hitting her core and forcing her to slide further up the bed.

Her body was made for me. I know it. The way it moves with mine. The way she fists the sheets like her body is on fire. The way she arches her back, her beautiful tits bouncing in the air.

I pull her toward me so her back is still pressed against the bed but her hips are in the air, forming the perfect arch. I thrust harder, hit deeper, and growl when I see her wide eyes staring at the point where our bodies meet.

"Hey," I say gently to get her attention. "Eyes up here, beautiful."

Her long lashes flip up, and I almost come right there. "Switch with me."

I pull out of her with a wince and roll onto my back, fitting her on top of me with two hands on her waist. She holds me at her entrance before sliding down and rolling her head back with a gasp.

I love the way her hair falls to her ass. The way her curves are on display for me and me only. I scoot back toward the window so she can press her palms against the glass, and she does. How I would love to be staring up at her from outside that window, watching her hips roll with as much grace and power as a trained dancer. Her breasts are soft and heavy beneath my palms, her tips budding to a full bloom as I draw them into my mouth, nipping and sucking as she bobs up and down my shaft.

My hands skate down her ribs, grazing her ass before pressing her hips harder onto me. She picks up speed, nearing her release. Her breathing quickens, her abs tighten, and her muscles clench around me. That's all it takes to set me off.

We're both coming, a tangle of screams and grunts as we claw our way to each other's mouths for one last kiss as our release takes over.

And then we crash.

Aurora

Jaxon pulls me to his mouth as my release fizzles out, my body abuzz with sensations. I'm filled with air, my head buzzing in a haze spun from love and sex. I feel like I'm floating. I kiss him from his neck down to his chest, unable to get enough. He still loves me. After all this time.

I hear a familiar growl coming from downstairs, and I laugh into Jaxon's neck. "You think Lacey heard us?"

He smiles at the ceiling, teeth gleaming under the moonlight. "I think all of Balsam Grove's wildlife heard us." His eyes find mine as he sweeps my tangled web of hair over my shoulder. "You okay?"

My brows squish together in confusion. "Better than okay."

His smile fills my chest. "I mean, did I hurt you? Are you sore?"

Heat crawls up my neck. "Oh." I sit up and stretch my arms, testing them out and then letting them fall by my sides. I shrug. "I'm okay."

Jaxon's eyes shine with amusement. He moves a hand over my thighs and squeezes. "I mean here." He slips a hand to where we're still connected. "And here."

My blush deepens. "Oh. It's a little tender. But I'm okay."

This time his eyes narrow and his lip curls. He bucks his hips, and I gasp at the feel of him thickening inside me. "Let's fix that."

"Again?"

He bites his bottom lip and nods, eyes scanning my naked form. "I should have warned you. I have quite the sexual appetite. Don't plan on getting any rest tonight, Waterfall Eyes." His finger moves to my clit, and my entire body begins to tense all over again.

Another growl comes from below, this one so menacing that Jaxon stops his ministrations and turns his head. My pulse quickens.

"What's wrong with her?"

The cottage isn't soundproof in the least. We can hear every little sound coming from outside, so I've grown accustomed to the snapping of branches and the rustling of trees. But somehow, this feels different.

Lacey lets out another growl and then a sharp bark.

A light shines through the window, hitting my face and practically blinding me. "What the hell?" I scream and move my hands to shield my face as Jaxon pulls out and wrap his arms around me. He flips me around and pushes me onto the bed.

"Shit." His panicked expression feeds my own worry as he wraps me in the comforter, searching the night for whatever is out there.

Lacey's barks continue to grow louder.

"Was that a flashlight?" My voice shakes.

He looks over at me. "Sure as hell looked like it. Something spooked Lacey, too. I'm going downstairs to check it out."

"No! Wait, Jax." I don't want him to go anywhere. Not while Lacey is going nuts downstairs.

He kisses my head and tucks himself into his briefs. "It's fine. Probably a lost hiker who just got the show of his life." He grins, clearly not as horrified by that prospect as I am. "I'll just be a second. Don't get dressed."

I sigh and flip toward the window, keeping myself covered but moving close enough so I can scan the outside. Was someone watching us? A chill whips through me as I remember the whistling from the night before when I thought someone was watching me in the hot tub. *Jesus.* My heart pounds loudly in my chest at the possibility that someone could truly be watching me. Because there was someone in the woods at Hollow Falls, too. Jaxon was certain it was just a possessive local who wanted us gone from the falls, but maybe he was wrong.

Jaxon's heavy feet land on the wood floor. He's comforting Lacey, whose bark has turned into a light growl. Then I hear the sliding door open. Jaxon must be shining a flashlight into the woods because I see the spotlight moving steadily in a horizontal scan. He's out there for a few minutes, five tops, before I hear the door close again.

The clacking of Lacey's paws makes its way across the living room. I can hear her lapping up the water and crunching on the food in the kitchen as Jaxon climbs back up the ladder. He switches off the lamp on the nightstand, leaving us in solid darkness aside from the glow from the half-moon outside. No one will be able to see in now.

Jaxon climbs onto the bed, lifting the covers off me and moving his body over mine. I laugh as his chest practically crushes my front into the bed.

"Coast is clear," he murmurs into my skin, his beard tickling my back. He kisses me between the shoulder blades before lifting himself to my neck. "You tired?" he asks into my ear, pushing his hips into me so I can feel him thickening again.

"Never," I moan into the sheets.

"Good." In one quick movement, he lifts my hips to bring me to my knees, my hands and chest still pressed forward. I gasp as a finger brushes over my opening. "'Cause I'm wide awake."

29

Aurora

The chirp of my alarm comes too early the next morning. The worst part? I have to leave Jaxon, gorgeous and naked in my bed, to go to work, and I'm hating every second of it. Last night was both reward and punishment for seven years of missing the way his limbs entangled mine. I'm still lightheaded from the marathon our bodies took part in last night, and I'm still raw from "one more time" never being enough.

We passed out around five in the morning, giving me only a few hours of precious sleep before I have to get up for work. I move a hand over my face to cover the bright and burning sun. Birds are already chirping loudly outside the cottage walls. I'm still exhausted two coffees later.

Yawning my way through the first few hours of an unexpectedly busy day, I crave the instant I can be free from work and drive home to crash in my bed. I'm pretty sure I've been pouting since I clocked in, but I smile when Jaxon breezes through the door with narrowed eyes, telling me I'm in trouble.

I've just finished serving the last customer in line when he walks around the counter and pulls me into his arms, fusing our lips together as if nobody is watching. "Good morning, beautiful."

I blush. I will never get used to hearing him say that. "Good morning. And no PDA when I'm working." I make a lazy attempt to push him away, my grin revealing my truth.

He grins back and looks around the café with a sly glance before pulling me to him again. "There's barely anyone here. Besides, the boss—me—says I must grope the new barista."

I giggle and lift my eyes to his. "Well, in that case, you should really take the new barista home after her shift tonight. She's a little sore, but nothing a soak in the hot tub can't fix."

"Deal. But why didn't you tell me you had to work this morning?"

I bite back a smile. "And miss out on all the fun? No way." He grins and I shrug. "Amber couldn't come in today and I forgot I'd agreed to cover for her. Claire wasn't feeling so hot yesterday when she left the café."

"That's no good." He frowns before glancing back at me with a teasing smile. "Well, sorry about that. You can take out all your frustrations on me later." He winks. "I'm going to work in the studio today. I'm suddenly feeling inspired."

Another grin stretches my lips. It seems I can't stop smiling. "Glad to hear it. Rumor is the drought has been long and hard. The world is starved of Jaxon Mills originals."

Jaxon throws me a wink as he leaves for the studio, and I'm back to work. I call Amber to see if she wants to take my shift tomorrow, and she agrees, thank goodness.

It's about an hour before the start of Canvas and Wine night when I get my second wind. I'm not sure how it happens, really, although the three cups of strong coffee I've had and the extra pep in my step from last night might have something to do with it. There are only a few customers scattered around the café, so I fill the quiet time with cleaning.

The café door chimes as I'm dusting the frame of the bridge painting near the glass case. I smile before turning to welcome the new customer, but when I see who it is, the air freezes in my throat and my body goes stiff with dread.

Scott stands there in the same green button-down dress shirt and tan slacks he wore the other day. His hair is in complete disarray, his eyes are worn and bloodshot, and he smells like he hasn't showered in days. It looks like he hasn't slept, either.

"Scott? What are you doing here? I thought you went home."

He rubs his eyes and shakes his head, swearing under his breath. "Nope. Just grabbing some coffee. Didn't realize you worked here." *He's an awful liar.*

I scrunch my face. Why didn't he go home?

"Have you been staying at the hotel down the road?"

He looks down, ashamed. "Yeah, checking out today. I haven't been in the best state to drive. So, I…" His sad eyes wander over me and my heart drops to my stomach. "Well, it doesn't matter, does it?"

"Have you been drinking?" I can't hide the worry in my tone.

He shoots me a glare as his face twitches slightly. "Not really your business, now, is it?"

I didn't think it was possible for my heart to break over Scott, but it does. Not over love lost, but over the fact that I'm the one doing the breaking, and I can see it happening right in front of me. This isn't like him at all. What have I done? I've been so unfair to him for so long.

"Scott." My voice cracks.

He steps closer, then pauses, like he wants to reach out to me but knows he shouldn't.

My eyes catch on his shirt again, on a tear across his sleeve, and something hardens in my throat. He smells of whiskey beneath a shower of cologne, like he tried in vain to hide the stench. "You don't look like yourself."

His laugh is filled with sarcasm. "I don't feel it." He looks around the café, taking it in like a houseguest visiting for the first time. "So, this is the new job, huh? It's nice, Aurora." He sounds so deflated, but his voice still carries a twinge of sarcasm.

I look around too, combatting the conflicted emotions running rampant in my chest. Scott has never made me feel unsafe, but this confrontation is unsettling, to say the least.

"Thank you," I say carefully. "I'm loving it, actually." I continue to mask my anxiety with a small smile and steady exterior.

His gaze shifts to the front window where his SUV is parked. "Great."

I shake my head, trying to get his attention, but he's got a glazed look in his eyes. He's still drunk. Still holding out hope that I'll find my way back to him. To us. My heart clenches.

"Can I make you something?" I offer. "Maybe it will help."

Another laugh, this time louder, fills me with more unease. It feels...hostile. And Scott isn't hostile.

"Sure, Aurora." His eyes flicker to mine with a look that sends the final crushing blow. "I thought maybe..."

"Maybe what?" I'm hopeful this is it. Our closure. Just what we need to move on and go our separate ways.

He lets out a sigh and drops his head. "That maybe you'd call." He looks up again, his eyes pleading. "I've been up all night trying to figure out where it all went wrong. And I can't wrap my head around any of it. You're making a mistake. I get that you're going through something and you need to do this for you, but ending *us* because of it is just wrong. After everything—" His voice cracks.

"Nothing has changed since we last spoke, Scott." I'm not sure how to explain this anymore without hurting him further. But he needs to understand this isn't me being indecisive or impulsive. As much as it hurts, this needs to end. "I can't be with you. We can't be together. Not now, not ever."

He steps closer. "C'mon, Aurora. Twenty years." He stresses the words like I've forgotten.

"Twenty years of *friendship*," I clarify. "We can stay friends," I plead. "Always. We can still talk on the phone. I still care. I'd be devastated if we lost our friendship. But as for more...I just can't. And I won't change my mind."

He takes another step closer, and I instinctively take a step back. I bump into the glass case behind me just as he brings his fingers to my chin. I turn my cheek.

"Scott, stop it."

"I love you." His voice shakes with anger, causing a tear to spring from my eye. *What can I tell him to get him to understand it's over?*

But I don't have to. The sound of a door opening and then crashing against the wall makes Scott jump back.

"What the hell is going on?" Jaxon's deep voice radiates around us.

I slide out from between Scott and the glass case and move to stand between them, though Jaxon is far enough away for Scott to make a run for it if it comes to that.

I swallow. "Scott, please just go." I say it softly.

His eyes flash when he sees Jaxon. Recognizes him. His jaw hardens and twists like he's grinding his teeth, and I can already see him reading way too much into what this is. Or, considering all that's transpired since I got to Balsam Grove, maybe he's seeing it exactly as it is.

"*You.*" Dread settles on his expression. "You work here, too?"

"Scott—" I try, but he's already made up his mind.

His eyes burn a hole in my heart. "You came back for him." A breath leaves him in a whoosh, like he's finally put the last puzzle piece into place. "I don't know why I didn't realize it sooner. That's what this is about, isn't it? That's why you left me. To be with the asshole who broke your heart without any apologies? C'mon, Aurora. Tell me I'm missing something here."

I blink back tears, hot and prickly behind my eyes. "I didn't come back *for* him." I dart a glance at Jaxon, desperate for him not to take that the wrong way before I can explain. "I came back for me. But Jaxon and I—"

"*Don't* finish that sentence." Scott holds up a hand. "You realize how warped this is, don't you, Aurora? And to think a month ago I was planning to ask you to marry me." He twists his head with disgust. "But your dad had just died, and I knew you needed time, so I was going to give you time. Then I come home one night and all your things were gone. You just *left...*" His voice catches. "Is this some kind of game to you?"

I blink back tears. "No!"

He scoffs like he doesn't believe me, and my eyes dart around the room to see every customer gawking at us.

"I forgot to give these to you when I saw you the other day," Scott spits. My head swivels to watch him pull out the bottle of pills I left in his medicine cabinet in my rush to get out of town. "You're going to need 'em." He tosses them toward me, hard.

I'm not fast enough, and the pill bottle lands on the floor with a crash. It bounces once, and the impact is all it takes for the lid to pop off. Pills fly everywhere.

I don't even hear Scott leave. I'm on the floor, scrambling for the pills, my eyes blurred as I try to distract myself from what just happened. From what I might have just ruined.

At some point, I look up to face the silence. Jaxon is still there, swooping down to fill the bottle with the pills I missed during my hunt. He doesn't return my gaze. When he's done, he simply sets the bottle on the counter, helps me up off the floor, and then disappears into the next room without a word.

When Canvas and Wine ends and the doors shut, it's time to clean up. I make sure to do my part, wiping down the stations and cleaning the dishes before approaching him. I know we need to talk about Scott, but after working all day in a building bursting with tension, all I want is to go home and sleep. It's been a long fucking evening of Jaxon's clenched jaw and the unavoidable girls batting their pretty eyelashes at him.

What's worse, even if I wanted to avoid any of it, I couldn't. Jaxon fills a room in every way possible—his booming voice calling out instructions, the sound of his loafers moving across the tile floor, his confident strokes on canvas as he leads the class by example. I'm not sure if anyone else noticed anything beyond the rings of his reddish-brown hair, the turbulence in his eyes, and the gruffness of his voice. Anyone else would mistake those traits for focus. Passion. But I know the truth.

He's placing his freshly completed canvas against the front wall when I approach him from behind, wrapping my arms around his waist. He tenses, so I squeeze his middle and place my cheek against his shoulder blades. "Talk to me."

He shakes his head but doesn't say anything.

"Jax, please. You must have questions. I'll tell you anything you want to know. Just please, don't shut me out."

He swivels to face me, pushing me off him in the process. "Just like you talked to me when you found out about the deed? Or how you talked to me when you walked out of that courtroom with *him?*"

Jaxon shoves a chair out of his way, causing it to skate wildly across the floor before crashing into the wall. And then he walks forward, not stopping until he reaches the door.

"You're wrong, Aurora. I don't have any questions I don't already know the answers to. I don't want to talk about it. I just want to go. You ready?"

Even when he locks up behind us and walks me to my car, I have no idea if he plans on coming home with me tonight. We talked about it earlier, but after the run-in with Scott, I don't know what to think.

I watch in my rearview mirror as he follows me out of the parking lot and onto the main road, half-expecting him to turn off when we get to his driveway, but he doesn't. Instead, he follows me, leaving a glimmer of hope deep in my chest.

I park in the carport, scanning the heavy clouds rolling in above us and the tree branches lashing in the wind just a few feet away. I haven't checked the weather today since I no longer have a phone, but usually someone in a neighboring shop passes on a warning if it's looking bad enough to cause some damage. So I ignore the rise of anxiety in my chest and walk to Jaxon's bike as he stops behind my car.

"Come inside. I can pour us some wine. We can talk. Or not talk." I shake my head, knowing I sound lame. "Or we can paint." My eyes light up. It's the first time I've felt any sort of excitement over the prospect of painting again. Before, it just gave me anxiety. "I still have that blank canvas you gave me—"

Jaxon cuts me off with a shake of his head, and that's when I realize he hasn't shut off his engine. He won't even meet my eyes. "Not tonight, Aurora. I need to get home to Lacey. I just wanted to make sure you got home safe."

My face falls. "Oh."

He nods to the cottage. "I'll leave after you've locked up."

It takes me a few seconds to move, too disappointed to come up with anything that might change his mind, so I give in. I want to respect his space, and I definitely don't want to screw this up any more than I already have. I lean in, pressing my lips to his cheek, hovering there for a second to speak. "I love you." My eyes squeeze closed and I take a breath before continuing. "I wish you would talk to me, but I know I deserve this." And then I slide the back of my hand across my cheek, smearing the first fallen tear, and turn toward my house.

As soon as my door is locked, I hear the rev of the engine. I hear it a few times, in fact, like maybe he's debating whether he should leave after all. I stay by the door, praying for him to change his mind. But then I hear the crunch of dirt beneath his tires, and the engine's roar becomes quieter as he rides away.

30

Aurora

My canvas is no longer blank. At some point between Jaxon leaving and the first roll of thunder, I zoned out completely and started painting. Staring at the array of browns, oranges, blues, and greens on the canvas, I'm confused about how the painting got to this point.

Sure, I remember sitting down and mixing the colors, but I don't recall applying the first coat of primer. I always did skip the sketching part of the process since I usually had the landscape before me as my guide. But I also don't remember applying the paint to the canvas, layering light and dark until an image appeared.

Although somewhat abstract, the image looks like it's meant to be a cave. My eyes scan the canvas again—searching for what, I'm not sure. But as they scale the rock wall, I pay more attention to the subtleties that only a trained eye would look for. And I see intention. Whatever I was painting was meant to be dark. The lines of the rock are carefully drawn, creating a narrow arc in the center, and the shadows deepen around the bottom edges of the canvas, like a vignette.

It's only then that I see a full mane of carefully shaded, dark brown hair at the bottom of the painting, the end of it out of frame. It's the back of a girl's head. Her hair is the same color as mine, with light waves strewn about in a tangle, like her face is pressed into the ground.

The paintbrush I'm holding slips through my fingers and I stand, knocking the stool beneath me over. My inhale is sharp, the breath that follows shallow, and my heart pounds furiously in my chest.

The moment my legs gain strength again, I'm charging toward the ladder and taking the rungs two at a time before flying to the bathroom and reaching into the medicine cabinet for my pills. Once they're securely in my hands, I squeeze the bottle in my palm and stare back at myself in the mirror.

Do I really want to do this? Do I really want to toss away over two weeks of progress only to stifle every emotion, every sense I've regained since being back? Is it worth it?

No.

I toss the bottle into the sink with a growl and throw on my night clothes. My sheets are cool as I slip between them, my comforter soft and fluffy as I lay it over me. And as another bolt of lightning strikes the air, I curl my pillow up and over my ears, pressing them into the sides of my head, hoping it's enough to drown out the world, just for a little while. Just until I fall asleep.

Hope is a flickering shadow against the prison walls of my mind, revealing its presence with each burst of light. Heat waves roll in, and like yesterday and all the days before, air washes my skin with a humidity that leaves me clammy, hot.

Footsteps approach, a medley of rocks and sticks, much heavier than my own. The sound crescendos at a steady pace. They're heading toward me, and that's how I know this day is different from the rest. This time, someone is coming for me.

"It's time," the deep voice booms. His words echo and fade through the space, each soundwave reverberating against me. What is this cruel, dark hell I've somehow entered? Am I being punished for my sins?

Is this how my story begins? Or ends?

Somehow, over an indiscernible amount of time, the darkness has become my home. I remember nothing else. Not how long I've been here or how my body would feel free from the shackles that pin me in place. Not what put me here in the first place. But instinct ignites my remaining senses, telling me something is very wrong.

To have truth, one must find courage to seek light in the darkness. *The words cycle through my mind as if someone is trying to tell me something. But who? And what? And why? Who dimmed the lights? And what good is truth if my journey has found its end?*

Always carry your own light, Aurora. Never forget. *More calming words as the footsteps fall silent. My skin prickles as the man stands before me. He smells of musk and impatience. Of power and fear. My eyes search for him in the darkness until I find the white of his eyes, wide and firmly set on me. Waiting. Expecting...*

Jaxon

The sight of another man touching Aurora was a kick to my groin. Having that man be Scott was a blow to my gut. And it wasn't just the way he touched her. It was that he looked at her the way I look at her—eyes brimming with intensity and love. I knew before either of them said a word that there was something more than friendship between them. Something deeper.

Just when I've started to feel like she's mine again, I'm forced to remember how many years we spent apart. How much I still don't know about her life in all that time. And it drives me mad.

In that café, I felt the thin shell of our newly formed cocoon strip away, piece by piece, as it all came to light. As I realized who she was standing with and what they were to each other.

Scott. The best friend from Durham. The boy who would call and text her throughout the summers, sometimes for no reason at all. I knew then that he loved her, but she wouldn't listen. She called me jealous, and I couldn't disagree. I *was* jealous. Jealous and possessive and scared that at any moment our time together would be up.

But competing with the best friend from back home wasn't my only obstacle.

The odds had always been stacked against us, whether it was age or distance or our parents. But we got through it. We pushed and fought and found our way back to each other. And we were so close to forever. Close to her finishing high school. Close to leaving Balsam Grove together. Close to her getting her degree and us finding a place to live. Close to us traveling the world.

Our dreams were sandcastles in the sky. Detailed, inspired, and larger than life. They were also fragile, and one gust of wind or one wave was all it would take to destroy everything we'd built up in our minds.

I think of that day in the courtroom six years ago. Scott burst through the doors, and it felt like he came along and stomped all over our creation.

And then Aurora followed his lead when she walked out that door behind him.

So yeah, I'm pissed to fucking hell that he showed up in my café to talk to her, to look at her, to *touch* her. Aurora is no man's possession, but I know without a doubt in my mind and heart that she's mine to love for the rest of my life. And

I'm hers. We just need to find our way back to each other again.

Regrets, one by one, stack the deck in my mind, each one bringing the pile closer to spilling. I should have never left her tonight. The one thing Aurora and I were awful at when we were younger was hashing out our arguments together. One of us always walked away, and we both suffered for it.

Tonight, I should have looked past my blind rage to see those desperate eyes and listen to that heartfelt plea. She was trying to tell me everything I needed to hear, but I was too stubborn to listen. I was too stuck in the past.

I'm still lost in my thoughts as I turn out the lights for the night. The clock on the living room wall reads almost one in the morning. My head is foggy with exhaustion, my eyes are blurred and heavy, and my body moans its need for sleep. Yawning, I search the spot in the coolest, darkest corner of the room where Lacey always sleeps. She's not there.

Shit. Confusion breaks through the fog of exhaustion, and I walk to the hall to look for her. The door to the canvas room is still open from when I showed Aurora her old paintings the other day, so I search for Lacey there. Nothing. Just a room filled with colorful memories, mostly good, and that only adds another card to the pile.

Lightning crashes outside, and an internal groan rocks my chest. Of course there would be a storm tonight of all nights. Which means...

Lacey ran off.

Shit.

I turn away from the window, ready to make a mad dash for Aurora's house, when a flash of white outside catches my eye. At first I'm sure I'll find Lacey in mid-trot as she races off toward her old home, but then I realize the shape is taller, the figure softer. And my heart begins to crash against my chest.

It's Aurora, dressed in nothing but a white tank top and shorts, the thin cotton fabric plastered to her skin like papier-mâché. She's holding something flat and square, and I know instantly it's the canvas I gifted her. Panic kicks in my chest as I fear the worst. Maybe she's here to return it in a gesture that means far more than "no thanks." Maybe it's goodbye.

She walks at her normal pace, but something is wrong with her movements. I can't exactly place it right away, not until my eyes adjust.

And then I see it. Her face is expressionless, her arms hang limply by her sides, and her eyes look dark, empty. Like she's sleepwalking up the hill. She slows as she reaches the top of the cliff and stops completely to look up right where I'm standing. But I don't think she can see me. It's like she's in some kind of trance.

My past flashes before me. The night our lives went up in smoke. Our very last fight before the darkness stole our future.

Aurora came to me that night with the storm on her back and thunder rumbling around her. She had just learned I'd turned down the offer I'd received to travel the world. She stormed onto my parents' property like she was the storm herself, and I spotted her through the window of my old bedroom. Then I met her at the front door, and we fought with a vengeance.

Accusations were thrown, tears were shed, throats were hoarse, and hearts were battered and bruised. The funny thing was, every word we shouted was a desperate acknowledgment of our love for each other. She was fighting for my future, and I was fighting for hers. I didn't want to leave her in Balsam Grove, alone with her father. She feared that she was holding me back, and I tried to assure her I could never feel that way. I could paint anywhere. I could travel the world another time, with her right beside me where she belonged. Me turning down that offer wasn't going to make or break my career. I knew that, but I also knew why she fought so desperately for my future. *Our* future.

Whenever I look back on that day, I remember something feeling off. Not just because of the argument but because of the effort she put into pushing me away. Like there was something else going on, something just below the surface that I could only see hints of—the fear in her eyes, the hesitation before each new breath—something she didn't want me to know.

And then she left. She turned on her heels, her face red and tears spilling down her cheeks. And I let her walk away. Back into the storm. Back toward her cottage where she lived with her father. I was mad, upset that she would start a fight when all I was trying to do was protect our future. It was a misunderstanding that we could have worked through, and I had no doubt that we would. We just needed space and time to breathe.

That's where I got it wrong. Where I failed us both—especially Aurora.

Because that was the night she went missing.

It all hits me like I'm pushing replay, and I can't see straight. The next thing I know I'm slamming open the front door and leaping from the porch to the ground without bothering to use the stairs there. My heart pounds as I close the distance between us, because this is all too familiar, and I can't explain it, but I'm afraid our time is running out yet again.

She looks so tiny standing there on the cliff, her chin and eyes pointed up at my old bedroom— the room filled with memories of her. But her features are still a dark void, a total eclipse. Her hair is matted around her face. Now that I'm getting closer, I see that her night clothes are not only sopping wet but also torn like she snagged her tank top on a branch. I don't know what is going on with her; I just know I need to get her inside.

When I finally reach her side, I wrap my arms around her gently, just as her eyes seem to come to life. They land on me, and there's a flicker of recognition somewhere deep within them. "Jax." It's just a whisper, but it's enough to crash like symbols against my heart. I pull her feet off the ground and her body close to my chest, cradling her. I make sure I get a good grip on the canvas, too, which she's still clenching tightly in her small hands.

"I've got you, babe."

Just as quickly as the words leave my mouth, her eyes fall closed and Lacey trots up behind me, confirming my suspicion that she had run off towards Aurora's cabin. I kick the door shut behind me and head straight down the hall to my bedroom.

I lay her on the bed and begin to remove her wet clothes, starting with her sandals, then her shorts and underwear. When I move her arms to peel off her shirt, she squirms a bit. Her eyes pinch closed as she whispers something too soft for me to hear. I stop for a second and focus on her breathing, on the crease between her brows, on the shallow breaths that come out much too fast.

"It's so dark." Her words are quiet, but I can make them out now, enough to detect fear riding her breath. "Who are you?" Her breathing quickens, and she stirs. A moan tears through her throat as her mouth twists like she's in agony, and I can't take it anymore. I lean over her body, her wet shirt pressed into my damp one, and I place my lips to her ear. "It's just me, Waterfall Eyes. You're safe. You can go to sleep now, baby girl."

A sharp inhale comes next, followed by a peaceful sigh, and I know her nightmare is finally dissolving. At least, I hope it was just a nightmare. My chest rattles with an unsettled thought, one that I know will keep me up deep into the night as I watch over Aurora to make sure she stays in a restful sleep.

I can't get over the fear that her dream wasn't just a dream at all. Maybe it was a memory.

31

Aurora

Why does it feel like I've been hit by a bus? My eyes feel leaden with sleep, as if I've got miles to climb before I reach complete awareness. I sort through my thoughts like junk mail, trying to find something useful. Something to bring me back to the now.

Paint. The canvas. The cave. As I retrace my last memories, more puzzle pieces begin to fall into place. I remember how alone I felt last night. How I would have done anything to get Jaxon to understand. But the truth is, I'm not sure if I could understand if all was reversed. I was in a vulnerable place for years, and Scott knew that. And while Scott would have never taken advantage of that fact, he definitely waited for his opportunity to make his move. I can't fault him for trying. I can't fault Jaxon for being upset. But I can fault myself for allowing my vulnerability to hinder my decisions.

There were so many things I should have done differently, but how can I live like that? Hating myself for decisions I didn't understand the gravity of at eighteen years old feels a bit unfair. Living with a paranoid schizophrenic wasn't easy, and while I hate putting a label on it, that was our reality. Those are the cards my family was dealt, and we handled them to the best of our ability.

But last night, I gave in to the past and let my mind take me to where I'd never allowed it to before. It felt natural to be in front of the canvas again and let my mind speak freely through my art. I let the middleman in me go. The worrier. The gatekeeper to my darkest thoughts, and it gave me a cave—one I don't remember painting.

But I remember dreaming about it.

Fear clutches my chest. It felt so real.

Startled at the memory, I finally break through the fog of sleep and confusion. I sit up, suck in another deep breath, and open my eyes to find myself not where I expected to be at all. My eyes take a moment to adjust to the low light. Early morning warmth streams in from outside, but the window is different than the one I wake up to every morning.

Panic overtakes me. Where am I? I don't remember leaving my home.

A groan sounds from my side. I jump. My eyes dart down to find a tossing Jaxon, cheek down on his pillow, his arm searching the space where I just lay.

As my pulse begins to slow to normal, I lie back down and look at the man I love.

How did I get here? I sort through the night again, remembering Scott and the silence from Jaxon that followed. The way my heart ripped open when he refused to come inside the cottage. He rode away into the night, and I felt him slip through my fingers like I never fully had him to begin with. So how did I end up here?

Not wanting to wake him, I tiptoe out the door. I shower, then slip on one of his oversized muscle shirts. I find a new toothbrush in his medicine cabinet and brush my teeth, and then I walk down the hall, my aim the canvas room that holds so much of my past, along with the good and bad memories that come with it.

I peek my head into the room, and my chest warms as I scan the art. Each piece is a memory of my progress from the summer I was fifteen, along with what Jaxon stored for me when I returned two summers later and my father had forbidden me from painting ever again. I pause in front of a painting of Hollow Falls, I trace the brush lines with my finger, trying to remember the euphoria I often felt when painting.

"I love you when you think no one is watching."

I jump and turn at the sound of Jaxon's gravelly morning voice.

"I always did," he adds, his expression soft despite the odd circumstances.

"Do you know how I got here?"

Jaxon's fingers wrap the upper part of the door frame. "You walked here last night during the storm, Aurora. You don't remember anything?"

I shiver, hating the darkness that snakes through me at the thought of walking miles in a storm without any memory of it at all. Again. "No. Nothing." I swallow before looking up to meet his eyes. "But I painted last night. Before bed." My heart quickens when I catch sight of my painting sitting on an easel and canvas in the middle of the room. It's now destroyed, probably from my mindless journey last night. The girl I'd painted into the scenery is smeared into the floor of the cave, like it was always meant to be dirt. I decide now isn't the time to bring up the girl.

My eyes flicker to his in silent thanks for trying to save it, warmth spreading in my chest. But it's not only that. Jaxon was furious at me yesterday, for good reason. And despite it all, he still cared enough to bring me inside and tuck me safely in bed.

Maybe we're okay.

"You should have told me about Scott," he says, his jaw firm, eyes hard on me.

"I know." I say quietly, meeting his stare. "And you shouldn't have left me last night."

"I know."

Letting out a relieved breath, I nod, letting the silence hang in the air between us. *What now?*

He takes a step from the entrance toward me. "Six—seven years is a long time, Aurora," he says. "I had some time to think last night, and we both just need to face it. There are going to be things we learn about each other. Things maybe we don't want to know."

"That's true. Which is why we should talk about those things. There's something you need to understand about Scott and me." Jaxon moves a hand to stop me, but I cut in before he can. "I love him, Jax." I don't care how the words sound coming out of my mouth. He needs to hear this in all of its truth. "He's been a friend of mine for ages."

I can just see the anger working through Jaxon. I rush to continue. "But I'm not *in* love with him. We were friends, he was there for me, and he wanted to give us a try. I felt like I owed him a shot after everything we'd been through. And it was the wrong reason to date him. I've made a mess of things, but you need to know how deep my connection to you remained after all those years. It never went away. Scott knows that now. I think he's always known."

Jaxon's posture relaxes. "We were all just trying to move on." He takes the final steps toward me, cupping my cheeks in his hands and gazing at me softly. I can feel the heat radiating off his body as he brings his lips to mine. "Aurora, I just need to know you're here to stay. I can get over the rest. I just want time with you. I want forever. We've waited long enough, don't you think?"

The tension I've been holding in my body dissolves in a flash. "Yes." I close the distance, our lips locking firmly.

"Paint something for me," he whispers against my mouth.

The way he demands it is so desperate, so sweet. I nod, and when my eyes bat up to meet his, I smile. "Okay. Will you help me?"

"Of course. What can I do?"

"Just...sit behind me." I swallow, my heart already pounding inside my chest. "Like you used to."

Jaxon nods, a curly lock of hair spilling over his eyes. "You always got so intense when you painted."

"So did you. You still do."

He chuckles. "Yeah, but with you it was like you couldn't break out of it. Remember how I would loosen you up?"

Heat scales my neck and fills my cheeks. "Do it again."

His eyes shine with amusement as he nods. "Okay."

I take a seat at the easel in the center of the room and prepare my paint. When I start applying the first dash of green beyond the cave walls, Jaxon sits a safe distance from me in his stool. I fill in the ground with splotches of grass, then add bushes a bit further in the distance, followed by pine trees stacked along the edges. Ideally, I would be painting in front of my subject, catching each detail, each glint of light. But I don't have that luxury now. I'm painting strictly from what my subconscious tells me it sees.

I've traded colors to shade the rock inside the cave when Jaxon takes my arm and guides me, his hand closing over mine. "I always loved watching you paint. You picked it up so fast."

I smile. "From watching you so much."

"You were a natural. Art the way you create it can't be taught. It comes from here." He brings his palm to my chest, and warmth begins to spread in my belly. He leans down, dropping a kiss on my neck.

The moment his breath hits my skin, it unleashes something in me. Who knew all I needed was Jaxon's presence to remind me what it felt like to be free? And suddenly, the cave in the painting and my nightmare makes sense. It's a prison.

I straighten, still holding the brush, but I stare at my work with new eyes. With new understanding. "Do you remember that story we talked about a long time ago? About the prisoner who lived in a cave? He was stripped of knowledge. All he knew came from what was set before him in an experiment to show the difference between knowledge and reality."

Jaxon murmurs against my skin. "Oh, do I. You were obsessed with that story. You and your father went on about it for days. He loved that his daughter had his philosophical mind."

"He did?" I turn to Jaxon over my shoulder. His nod is unwavering. Despite my father's crimes, it still warms my heart to remember our connection before his mind began to deteriorate.

"The Allegory of the Cave," Jaxon confirms.

"From Plato's *Republic*." I smile. My father's old, leather-bound copy of the book is still on the bookshelf in the cottage. "I think that story influenced this painting somehow. I'm not sure how, but I dreamt about it last night. Before I came here, I guess."

"You dreamt about the story?"

I shrug. "A version of it. I dreamt that I was the prisoner, and there was a man approaching me. I couldn't see him, but he spoke to me. He said, 'It's time.' I got the feeling he wanted to help me escape."

Jaxon's breath stills on my back. "Escape what, exactly?"

I shrug. "I'm not sure. I mean, it makes sense now. There's a man in the story who helps the prisoner escape. He takes him into the light to fill him with knowledge and show him that his reality was false. Then the prisoner finally realized how much existed beyond the walls of the cave. Beyond the darkness. But in order for him to ever truly leave, he needed to be open to new knowledge. And once he was open to it, he was no longer a prisoner."

"And how do you feel now?"

"Hungry." I laugh. "But not for food. For knowledge. I want to experience everything. I want to paint. I want to travel the world." I glance at him over my shoulder and smile. "With you."

His lips brush mine. "You know how happy that makes me. Let's do it."

"We will."

He scoots closer so our bodies are pressed together, his front to my back. Then he dips his head to kiss my shoulder. "We'll do it all. Everything we ever wanted. We'll see the world. We'll paint. And we'll do it together."

I smile, feeling my chest balloon with excitement. Jaxon's hand moves mine, lifting it and taking it to the canvas in a simple stroke. "Don't stop painting."

My hand gets to work. The wildlife surrounding the cave begins to blossom, the light and dark tones shading the trees and bringing them to life. Jaxon's lips find my shoulder, his fingers peeling back the fabric at my collar to reach my skin.

"Remember this?" he asks, his words hot against my neck.

Shivers race down my spine as his fingers brush against me in perfect synchronicity with my movements. My mind swirls and my body warms.

"Yes." I swallow, never letting my brush leave the painting.

One day at Hollow Falls while we were painting from the bridge, he commended my progress. We had been sneaking around together for over two months, but I panicked, thinking that our time painting together was coming to an end. If he no longer thought I needed a mentor, what would that mean for us? Maybe he could sense it too, because he sat behind me, guiding my brush for a few strokes. And then his hand fell to my lap.

"Touch me," I whispered, sensing that he needed permission.

"Are you sure?" His knuckles turned white from gripping my skirt so hard.

"Yes, Jaxon. Please touch me." I turned to look at him over my shoulder, our eyes locking, then he nodded.

His breath hit my neck in a whoosh. "Do me a favor. Don't stop painting."

And I didn't. Not when he parted my knees. Not when his finger grazed against my center, soaked and still covered by my thin bikini bottoms. Not when he slipped the scrap of material to the side, exposing me. And not even when his finger stroked me, so soft, so careful.

But when that same finger pushed into me for the first time…I couldn't breathe. It was the first time I had ever been vulnerable like that for anyone, and here I was in the middle of the woods, being touched for the very first time.

"Keep painting," he reminded me as he pushed into me again.

Somehow I managed to obey. I was at the tip of my release, my heart beating fast at the feel of my muscles tightening and a fiery rush burning through me. He groaned into my back, bit into the skin at my neck—and at that moment, I happily lost the challenge.

The brush fell.

"Don't stop painting," he growls in my ear now, mimicking his command from years ago. But I don't know how I held out so long that first time. My eyes squeeze closed as he curls his finger inside me. My brush falls again. My palm slams into the canvas, smearing the new paint and knocking the easel over. Jaxon holds me tighter. Pumps me faster. My insides squeeze, heat rising in my core, and I cry out as my muscles tense to their peak and then liquefy in a hot rush inside me.

Desire has taken over. I stand, letting his finger slip from my core, turn, and strip his shirt from my body. He's already removed his briefs, and he's quick to wrap his arms around my waist and pull me down as he sinks into me, filling me faster than I'm ready for. Jaxon isn't about to be gentle, and I don't want him to be. My toes grip the bottom bar of the stool, giving me leverage as I rip the knit cap from his head and weave my brown-and-black-painted fingers through his curls, holding on tight as I ride his length.

His mouth falls to my neck, hot and wet. He keeps me balanced with his hands on my waist, gritting his teeth as he pumps into me, quickly bringing me closer to another release.

This is what I've been waiting for. This is why it took seven years to feel comfortable with the idea of sex again. Because to act on these urges, to give myself to a man so vulnerably, I need to do it with a full heart. And there's only been one man who has ever had mine.

My hips rock into him as he uses his grip to deepen each thrust. My skin is covered in a sheen of sweat. Sex fills the air with its sweet and tangy odor. I completely lose myself in this man, who I love more than anything.

"Wait for me, baby," he rasps.

My lungs fight for air as everything clenches below my waist. "Jaxon, I need—"

His mouth moves over the swell of my breast, covering it with his sticky warmth and sucking. Meanwhile the build climbs closer and closer to the peak.

Jaxon lifts his mouth, bringing me down hard on his lap as everything in me unspools. Every thread rips apart and I'm flying into an abyss, somehow both so full and so weightless that I'm not sure which way is up.

Finally, I land, and I chase my breath as he catches his own, our bodies shaking together, coming down together, breathing together.

God. I love him. So much.

32

Aurora

We spend the entire day around Jaxon's house. No more
hiding. No more anger. Just seven years of caged hunger for
each other and everything we've missed. Wrapped up in his
arms is my favorite place to be. Our conversation isn't heavy.
Our time together isn't even full of sex, surprisingly. It's just
us finally getting our chance to be a couple in every sense of
the word.

After lunch, Jaxon picks up his old backpack and fills it
with a canvas and supplies, and we walk to the pool of the
falls near his house. He's feeling inspired and wants to paint. I
let him be, knowing how rare that feeling has been for him.
I'm content to watch him as I sit on a patch of grass, my feet
stretched out and ankles crossed, my palms pressed into the

ground behind me. I angle my head up to face the sky, closing my eyes and smiling as the sun warms my cheeks.

It's such a beautiful day. Easy. Everything is just as it should be. Lacey pads over, a stick in her mouth, and we start to play fetch. I throw it farther away every time until she reaches the river's edge, pausing to stick her nose in the pool and lap up the water. I laugh as she pops her head up and shakes it, spraying water in every direction before she dips into it again.

Jaxon is completely focused. He doesn't even notice at first as I strip down to my birthday suit and dive into the river. Lacey follows, carrying her stick, and our game continues.

"A little distracting, don't you think?" Jaxon's voice reaches me from the edge of the river.

I laugh and bend my knees to sink deeper into the water. "You seemed pretty focused. I wasn't trying to distract you. I promise."

He grins and reaches behind him to tug off his shirt, revealing glistening, tan skin. His torn jeans move down his legs next, and then he's diving into the water and swimming toward me.

He runs a hand through his hair, now straight and darkened from the water. Beads of river drip from his beard while other droplets remain stuck there, glistening in the reflection of the sun. He scoops me up and pulls me toward him, and I smile as I wrap my legs around his waist.

"I've been curious." His tone is as light as his smile.

I bite down on my bottom lip. "I don't like the sound of that."

His smile widens. "Why in the hell did you work for a law firm after college? That seems so..." He trails off like he's afraid to offend me.

"It was kind of just the first opportunity that popped up. I wasn't planning to go to law school or anything like that. I just needed a job while I figured out what was next."

"How long did you work at the firm?"

Heat creeps up my cheeks. "Two years. Time just seemed to slip by me."

"I know that feeling."

I run my fingers through his hair, tousling it and watching some of his curls bounce back to life.

"Did you mean what you said about traveling the world?" I hear more than his question. There's fear of rejection trapped behind the gruffness of his voice.

My heart turns to putty at his words. "Yes, Jax. We can go now if you want. Anywhere you want."

He brings his lips to mine. "Right now?" he whispers, a playful smile tugging up the corners of his mouth. Water moves around us, and I realize he's walking me backwards. A few seconds later I'm pressed against a boulder, the slick surface and rough edges adding to the thrill of what we're about to do—and *where* we're about to do it. "Anywhere?" he asks, his beard tickling my jaw.

"Anywhere." My words float out on a breath just as his mouth crushes mine. Our lips are slick as we find our desperate rhythm. He lifts me from the water, aligning our bodies, and he pushes himself inside me in one quick thrust.

And there beneath French Broad Falls, we make love, marking a new beginning. One that doesn't have an end. At least, I can't feel one—not this time.

Jaxon is in his room getting ready for Canvas and Wine, and I'm in the art room looking at the smeared canvas from this morning. I bite back a smile just as the doorbell rings.

When I open the front door, I half expect to see Val or Scott standing there with accusing eyes. I feel almost guilty for spending the entire morning with Jaxon after Scott left the café hurt and angry yesterday. But guilt transforms into dread when I see a fully uniformed Tanner Brooks standing in front of me, a look of deep concentration written in his expression.

"Hey, Tanner," I say slowly. A million reasons for his being here trample through my mind, the first being the intimate swim Jaxon and I just shared beneath the falls. But there's no way he could know about that. Lacey would have sniffed him out if he'd gotten too close. No, something else is up.

"Why am I not surprised to find you here?" There's an edge to his tone that I can't quite read, like he's annoyed and disappointed all at once.

I shift in my stance, suddenly feeling as if I'm doing something wrong. But that's ridiculous. "Why are *you* here?"

"I need to talk to your boyfriend." His eyes pan over my head before locking back on mine. "And you."

I cross my arms, already sick of whatever power trip he's on. "He's getting ready for work. I can relay a message. What's got your pistol in a knot?"

Tanner's jaw ticks in irritation. "I'm happy to wait, Miss June. Or perhaps maybe I should just take you down to the station to have this discussion."

I freeze.

"Whoa, what the hell is going on?" a voice booms behind me. Jaxon approaches, pushing open the door to reveal himself. He's still wet from his shower and wearing only a towel around his waist. "Tanner? What are you doing here?"

"Sorry to stop in unannounced." Tanner tips back on his heels, pressing his eyes to the sky. "There's been a report."

"What kind of report?" My heart is already beating fast.

He looks at me pointedly. "A familiar report." Then he looks back at Jaxon. "I'm alerting all the residents in the area. We ask that you not wander around out there until our search is complete."

"Search for what?"

Tanner sighs and bows his head, whatever annoyance he held earlier dissolving into something that resembles defeat. Not even Tanner wants to give this news. "A man reported his girlfriend missing this morning. A female in her early twenties. They were scheduled to leave on a hike today. *Apparently*, they'd gotten in a fight at Franco's and she hitched a ride with another man. I managed to track down the man's car at the abandoned cottage near Hollow Falls, but so far, no trace of either of them." He lets out a heavy breath. "I need to ask you two a few questions while I'm here."

Now that I look at Tanner again, his eyes are red, his brows are turned down, and his face is a mask of unruly stubble. He looks exhausted, but I can hardly feel sorry for him as I'm plagued by his words.

A familiar report.

Another hiker gone missing.

"I thought you said Balsam Grove hasn't had a missing person in years."

"We haven't," he snaps. "Not until you decided to grace us with your presence again."

Fire roars in my chest. "Excuse me?"

Jaxon's strong hand squeezes my shoulder. "I know you're not accusing Aurora of having anything to do with this." He speaks in a level tone behind me, but I can feel the rumbled warning beneath his words.

"I'm not accusing anyone of anything. But I'm going to need to ask you a few questions."

"What questions?"

Tanner's jaw clenches. "I'd like to know where you both were last night between the hours of ten p.m. and four a.m."

My heart moves to my throat as I try to piece together my memories from last night. How did I get here? Did I really walk here during a storm? Why? The last thing I remember before going to sleep is staring at a half-finished canvas in front of me, convinced I had lost myself to my art so desperately I did it blind. It was a heavy night. I had just destroyed my friendship with Scott, and my future with Jaxon was on thin ice. It makes sense that I would want to forget and zone out. But it's not that simple.

A hiker went missing last night. A girl in her early twenties. Everything about the description Tanner painted awakens every tremor in my body. It's all too familiar. Why her? Why now?

"Aurora was with me last night. We got off work, closed the studio, and came back here. Afraid neither of us can help you."

Tanner cocks his head. "I seem to remember seeing Aurora's car parked in the lot next to the station last night, but now it's nowhere to be found. You sure that's the story you're going with, Mills?"

"What are you implying?" Jaxon's voice rumbles with anger, and I squeeze his arm to beg him to calm down.

"I'm not implying anything. Look, you're giving me every reason in the world to book you both right now. All I'm asking for is the truth, and what you're telling me doesn't add up. You get one more chance to tell me where you and Miss June were last night."

I squeeze Jaxon's arm again to have him let me speak, but he starts before I can even attempt it. "Aurora dropped her car off at her place, and I brought her here. We haven't gone anywhere except for around my property. Thank you for the warning. I hope you find your missing girl, Deputy."

"Can we help?" I ask, hoping to cut in before a dick-measuring contest breaks out. "With the search?"

Tanner eyes me hard, frowns, then releases a sigh as he shakes his head. "No, we've got a team coming in from the north. My dad and Danny are already out there searching other parts of the woods. Just go about your business and heed my warnings. Let's pray the girl turns up in the next eight hours or so."

I want to ask why in the next eight hours, but I think I already know. That would make it twenty-four hours since she disappeared. And if she's not found within the first twenty-four hours, chances are the girl, whoever she is, is dead.

We get to Jaxon's class just fifteen minutes before it starts. It's my fault, really. After Tanner's visit, I helped Jaxon take his mind off his anger at the deputy. I promised him everything would be okay. They would find the girl. This isn't the same town it was seven years ago when there was a serial killer on the loose. People get lost in the woods all the time, and it's rarely anything sinister.

"Thanks, babe." Jaxon kisses my head after the last of the canvases is placed around the room. The look in his eyes is so tender, so sweet. It's incredible how fast my heart pounds when he looks at me like that. Like I'm his entire world.

Peering over my shoulder, I see the crowd lined up outside the door, so I slide my hands down from his back to his ass and give it a squeeze, a grin of appreciation breaking across my face. "You're welcome."

He leans into my neck, a look of warning in his eyes. "Two hours, and then I'm throwing you on this desk and painting you while I fuck you," he growls.

A chill snakes up my spine. "Just remember to close the blinds."

"Oh, I—" Jaxon's tease is cut off by a moan coming from the café next door. At first it's so faint, we both kind of miss it. But then it comes again. "Jax," a strangled voice cries. We both turn toward the sound.

"Is that Claire?" But as I'm asking the question Jaxon is already jogging into the next room. I hurry behind him, my heart beating frantically in my chest. Something is seriously wrong.

I turn the corner and freeze in my tracks. All I see is blood. Blood on Claire's hands. Blood staining the front of her gray dress. Jaxon is just standing there, staring as Claire looks down at herself with one palm pressed into the counter like she needs help standing.

Her expression of shock and horror makes my heart shatter in my chest. *She can't lose that baby.*

A tear slips from one of her eyes, rolls over her cheek and drops to the floor as she looks up and catches Jaxon's eye. "Will you take me to the hospital? I can't get ahold of Danny. I-I think I'm losing my baby." Claire's face crumbles at her words as more tears stream out of her eyes. "I think I've already lost her."

33

Aurora

Jaxon moves quickly, catching Claire in his arms just as she's about to collapse. She leans on him as they walk.

"Will you lock up?" Jaxon asks. His voice is calm, but I hear the fear behind his words.

I open my mouth in protest. "Wait. I'm coming with you."

"Babe, someone needs to lock up and send everyone home. I'll be back to get you as soon as I can. Unless you know how to drive my motorcycle."

I fume, frustrated that I can't be there for Claire too, but this isn't about me.

Jaxon helps Claire around the counter. "Just send everyone home."

"Jax—" I cut myself off when I realize what I was about to say. What am I even thinking? But I want to do something. I want to help somehow. "We don't need to send them home. I'll shut down the café and teach class."

Jax turns to me in shock. "Really? You don't have to do that."

I wave him off, not wanting to give myself an opportunity to back out. Stepping up to Claire, I cup her cheeks, careful not to jostle her too much.

"Everything will be fine here, okay?" She nods as her eyes build with more tears. "Just take care of you and that baby."

"I'll call you as soon as she's situated," Jax tells me, his voice softer. I know he's appreciative, and maybe a little worried too, but this isn't the time to work through our feelings. "I'll keep calling Danny too," he continues, rambling as if to keep his mind busy. "I'm sure he's still out on that search."

"What search?" Claire looks up in confusion.

Jaxon's eyes dart to me and then her. "I'll tell you in the car. Nothing to worry about. He's just tied up."

Jaxon's eyes meet mine one last time before the two of them rush out to Claire's car, and I lock the door behind them. After turning the sign in the window to *Closed,* I make my way back into the studio to open the doors for Canvas and Wine.

"There was an emergency, so Jaxon won't be able to teach tonight," I inform the crowd, who eye me with a curiosity I completely understand. "I know, I know. I'm much better looking, but do me a favor and keep that between us." The crowd laughs, and I feel the tension begin to roll off my back.

"I'll be your instructor tonight," I say with a small smile. "If you want to leave, I completely understand. If you choose to stay, well, you'll have to be patient with me. It's my first time teaching. I've only ever been the student."

Miraculously, I'm able to teach the entire two-hour class without a panic attack. In fact, it's been the opposite. Maybe it's because I'm too busy thinking about Claire and her baby, the missing hiker and the boyfriend she left behind, and the accusing way Tanner glared at me this afternoon. For the first time in a long time, painting has become my distraction from the more stressful things in life.

I served two rounds of drinks without delaying class too much, and everyone has been loose enough to laugh and paint like they normally do with Jaxon. Maybe Val and Claire are putting too much stake in Jaxon's charm. Maybe it really is more about the art and the location.

I've just given the class their final instruction when the café phone rings. My heart leaps from my chest when I see Jaxon's name light up the screen.

"Hey," I answer in a hushed whisper. "How is she?"

There's a shaky exhale on the other end of the line before Jaxon's words race out of his mouth. "They're taking her for an emergency C-section. Something about her placenta rupturing. They won't give me a straight answer. She says she's okay, but I know she's trying to keep calm for the baby's sake. I'm still trying to get ahold of Danny. You almost done there? Shit, how's class? You okay?" He finally pauses for a breath.

"Don't worry about things here," I offer gently. "Everything is good. Just take care of Claire. Maybe try calling Tanner and have him radio Danny. He might be too deep in the woods to get any reception on his cell."

"Did that. Just waiting for him to call me back. I can't think straight right now. I'm just worried—about you, too. You sure you're okay? I'll come get you as soon as I get ahold of him—"

"Yes, Jax. I promise, I'm fine. Class has been great. They don't even miss you," I tease, hoping to offer some comfort. "Look, Claire needs you right now. I'll find a ride home to get my car and meet you at the hospital as soon as class is over. I'm sure I can get a lift from Meg or something. Do you know what time she closes up the bakery?"

"She'll already be gone by now, but her name should be on the directory under the front counter. I'll text her and let her know you'll be—shit," he curses in mid-sentence. "I forgot about Lacey. Can you—?"

"Yes, Jax. I'll take care of Lacey as soon as I get my car. Just sit tight, okay? Keep trying Danny. I'll be there as soon as I can. I love you."

"I love you, too, Aurora."

Those words coming out of Jaxon's mouth make all the craziness of the past two days a little less overwhelming. I practically float through the next half-hour, wrapping up class, closing the till, and cleaning up before finally giving Meg a call. The lights are off so as not to attract passersby, and I'm sitting on Jaxon's desk, facing the window with my feet on his chair.

Meg answers on the third ring. "Hey." The familiarity in her cheerful tone tells me she thinks I'm Claire.

"Hey, Meg. It's Aurora. I'm sorry to bother you, but I was hoping you could give me a ride home. Jaxon's at the hospital with Claire, and I'm kind of stuck at the shop until Danny gets to the hospital."

"The hospital? Is everything okay?"

"We don't know yet, but I'm sure it will be fine." I bite the inside of my lip, hoping that's true.

"Okay, I'm hopping in the car now. Give me two minutes."

A tap on the front door halts my response. A beam of light hits me next, and I have to cover my eyes and squint between my fingers to make out who's trying to get my attention. It's Tanner and his damn flashlight. Like father, like son, I guess.

What does he want now?

"Aurora? You there? I'm on my way." Meg's voice comes out in a rush.

"Uh, yeah," I say, without taking my eyes off the glass. I wave at Tanner to let him know I'm coming. "Thanks, Meg." I hang up and let out an annoyed breath.

Pulling the door open with a yank, I gesture for him to come inside, but he shakes his head. "Glad I caught you, Miss June."

"It's Aurora," I tell him, my tone leaking with annoyance. Why does he insist on being so formal after all the years we've known each other? I sigh. "What is it, Tanner? I need to get to the hospital."

His face twists. "Why?"

Now it's my turn to be confused. "Jaxon said he was calling you to tell you. Claire has been trying to get ahold of Danny. She's in the hospital, and I'm headed there now."

"Ah, yeah. That. Danny got the message. That's unfortunate news, but *you* aren't going anywhere."

"Yes, I am." What the hell is his problem?

Tanner's eyes narrow and he lets out a quick breath. "Not after what we just found. You're going to want to come with me, Aurora. This is serious."

My stomach drops. "Tanner, you need to stop being so vague and tell me what is going on here. I haven't done anything wrong."

He shuts his eyes and shakes his head. "We don't know that yet, do we?"

"Tanner," I plead. He needs to look at me, to see me and stop thinking the worst. That's all he's done since the moment I stepped into town.

"Aurora," he barks. "I just ran the plates on that SUV I found in the woods, and I have reason to believe the owner of the vehicle is with the girl who disappeared last night.

The room begins to spin. *SUV?* No, it can't be.

"Did you find her?" I swallow, avoiding his accusation entirely.

Tanner shakes his head, adding to the rising anxiety in my chest. "She's still missing. But the man she was with—" He pauses, eyeing me a little longer, as if readying to assess my reaction. Finally, he sighs.

"Aurora, do you know a Scott Turner?"

Jaxon

I've only felt gripping fear like this one other time in my life: seven years ago, when I found out Aurora was missing and I joined the hunt to find her. Most of the town had already proclaimed her dead by the time we started looking. None of the other bodies had been found; why would she be so lucky?

And then she was found, so close to death, and all I could do was wait by her side while she lay unconscious. Her aunt Cyndi arrived, and I was immediately thrown out of her hospital room. I never got to see her wake up. I never even got to see her at all until I showed up at Cyndi's, refusing to leave until I got a chance to speak to her. I was so angry. Angry at her father for what he'd done. Angry at her aunt for relaying the message that Aurora didn't want to see me. And angry at Aurora for kicking me out of her life, especially after everything she went through. I'd never wanted to be there for someone so much. Knowing she was okay and that I may never get to see her again was true heartache, and I promised to never allow myself to feel anything like that again.

But you can't plan for things like this. Claire has lost too much blood. Her baby's life is at risk, and the doctors have been prepping for emergency surgery for what seems like forever. What's worse, I've relayed a message to the station, but I'm not sure if Danny received it. He'll be gutted when he realizes what's going on.

So here I am on the other side of the door, the same one Cyndi kicked me out of years ago, waiting to see if my best friends are about to lose their baby.

And where the hell is Aurora? I've been trying to call Meg and the café for the last half hour, but there's been no response. She should have been here by now. There's got to be something I can do besides pacing these halls, waiting. Everywhere I turn, there are whispers. Rumors flying about the missing hiker and how history is repeating itself because Aurora June came back to town. As much as I hate that Aurora's name is part of the chatter, the coincidence is chilling.

A young woman.

On a hiking trip with her boyfriend.

Went missing during a storm.

All startling common denominators of mysterious incidents. But the eeriest similarity was found in the tree carvings scattered around the woods near where each girl was last seen by her significant other. Even Aurora has a carving, which is the strangest thing of all, because she was the only one of the girls found alive.

So of course everyone will jump to conclusions about Aurora being to blame for the latest event, like Tanner already has. In his mind, as a descendant of her father, she's sure to have the same instincts to kill.

They're all fucking crazy if that's what they truly think. Blaming Aurora is the easiest response to the news about the girl, but it's not logical. Anything could have happened to her.

Maybe she got lost. Maybe she slipped off a cliff or into the lake. Maybe a wild animal got to her. I shiver. Who the hell knows? But anything is more likely than Aurora June laying a finger on anyone.

I saw Aurora last night, the way she wandered onto my property completely zoned out and drenched from the storm. She was haunted by her nightmare. A nightmare that I'm sure had everything to do with what happened seven years ago.

I'm pacing the halls in front of a large waiting room window when a tall man in uniform darts around the corner, practically skidding to a halt when he sees me.

"Danny," I breathe out in relief. "We've been trying to get ahold of you all night. They kicked me out, man. I'm not family."

"Where is she?" His cheeks are flushed from running, and his bangs stick to his forehead as he tries to catch his breath.

"Just through there. Room 117. Go. I need to find Aurora, but we'll be back. Call me as soon as you can."

Danny curses and takes off running. "I will. Thanks, man."

And just like that, he's flinging open the emergency room doors and disappearing down the hall.

I breathe a little bit easier knowing Claire will have Danny by her side, but without knowing where Aurora is, my chest still pounds with worry. I slide into Claire's car and take the long, winding stretch of mountain road back to the café. Then I hop out and peek through the windows, trying the Creek Café phone again as I approach. It rings and rings, and through the windows, I see nothing but darkness.

I check all the doors. Locked.

She definitely left. So then, where is she?

"Jaxon?" My heart beats fast as I spin toward the voice. I know it doesn't belong to Aurora, but hope still fills my lungs.

"Meg, thank God." I look around. "I tried calling you. Did you talk to Aurora?"

She nods. "Yeah, that's why I'm here. I was going to give her a ride, but she was just leaving when I got here. I didn't realize you called."

"What do you mean she just left when you got here? She didn't have her car."

Meg looks toward the main road and shrugs. "I saw her get into Tanner's car. Maybe she got tired of waiting for me. I was only a few minutes later than I told her I'd be. I hope everything's okay."

My veins are too filled with adrenaline to take time to process what she's just told me. Instead, I call Tanner's cell, cursing under my breath when he still doesn't respond. Where the fuck are they? I take off running down the strip of shops until I get to the sheriff's station and throw open the door, only to find—no one. Not a soul. Just static from the scanner.

Leaving the station again, I find Meg standing there with her arms crossed and a worried expression. "Jax, what's going on?"

I shake my head, feeling just as confused as she looks. "Which way were they headed?"

"South, I think."

I nod. "Maybe he took her home to get her car. She was probably in a rush to get to the hospital and didn't want to wait. I'm going to drive up to her house to see if I can catch her. Do you mind waiting here for a bit? Just call me if anyone shows up. She doesn't have a phone, and I don't want to miss her if she comes back."

"Of course."

And I'm off again, jumping into Claire's car and flying through the mountain roads to Aurora's cottage. When I pull in to the driveway, my heart stops. The lights to her place are off, and her car is still in the same place she left it last night.

Tanner didn't bring her here.

She never came home.

I head for my house next. She mentioned she was going to check on Lacey. I sigh as soon as I pull up my drive. Once again, nothing. No sign of anything outside of the ordinary. As I shut off the engine, I hear a scratching sound coming from the inside of my house.

Sighing, I jog to the front door and unlock it, letting Lacey out. "I'm sorry, Lace. You've been locked up all night. Go potty, girl. But hurry. I need to find Aurora."

Lacey pushes past me. After being cooped up most of the night, she's feeling antsy. If it weren't for her incessant need to venture deep into the woods on her own, I'd let her do her thing without supervision, but I don't have time for any of her shenanigans right now.

Aurora probably had Tanner take her to the hospital and we just missed each other. I'll head back there as soon as Lacey takes care of business. I wait impatiently for her to find her favorite spot on the outskirts of the woods to relieve herself. As I guessed, she takes her time, probably sensing that she doesn't have much of it.

I'm checking my phone obsessively and redialing the café, Tanner, and the station without luck. Meg hasn't called either, so I know she hasn't spotted anyone.

All I can do is hope that when I show up to the hospital again, Aurora is there. Because I don't like this feeling. Not one bit.

34

Aurora

The car door jerks open, and I'm greeted by Tanner's wild eyes and flushed expression. "Let's go," he hisses, his tone gripping my chest in a vicelike hold.

I look around, refusing to move until I get some answers. It's dark outside, but we've somehow managed to drive through a narrow path in the woods, unpaved and clearly unfrequented. The headlights from the car illuminate the space in front of us, and I try to make sense of my surroundings. After a moment, it hits me where we are.

Why did he bring me here—to the abandoned cottage in the middle of the woods where I first saw Jaxon paint? Jaxon said he's purposely left it for the wild animals to roam. It's the one property in all the fifty acres that hasn't been maintained.

Surrounding it, all I see are trees and brush, but I know Hollow Falls is just over that hill.

"This is Jaxon's property," I say suspiciously. "Why are we here?"

"You'll find out in a minute, Miss June."

"It's Aurora," I say through gritted teeth.

It's not that I have a problem with my last name. I've always loved it, in fact. But the way Tanner is saying it is in direct correlation to how he feels about my father, and *that* I hate.

My eyes follow his flashlight as he moves it around the woods in search of something, I'm not sure what until it illuminates a white SUV positioned between two trees like it was put there on purpose. It's Scott's SUV, parked neatly with no sign of damage.

Ice fills my veins. Why would Scott venture into the woods? Why is he still here? Does Tanner think Scott has something to do with the missing girl? That's just—strange and wrong. Scott couldn't possibly have anything to do with that. If anything, he's still here because he's holding out hope for me. For us.

But his car is in the woods, Aurora.

"Tanner." I try to control the shake in my voice. "This has got to be a mistake."

His jaw hardens, and his eyes narrow. "Get out of the car, Aurora. You need to see something else."

Emotion clogs my throat, but I fight past it to ask what I need to know. "Is he okay?"

"We haven't found him. Get out of the car. Don't make me tell you again."

My pulse quickens, and my head grows light. My veins fill with dread, and I clutch the handle of the door. "Why? Should I even be out here right now? Aren't you all looking for that girl? Just take me back."

"Get out of the damn car!" Tanner reaches for my wrist, but I pull it away and slide to the other side of the seat.

"Don't you dare put your hands on me, asshole," I spit. "I'm not under arrest. You brought me out here, but I came willingly. And if I want to get out of this car, I will walk out on my own."

Tanner throws up his hands and steps back. "Fine. While you throw a princess fit in the back of the squad car, a young girl might be dyin'. Hell, I don't even know why I care. She's probably dead already."

He stalks off, and blood boils in my chest. I scramble out of the car after him, slamming the door behind me. Anger swirls around me like a tornado ready to annihilate anything standing in my path.

"Tanner, what the hell is going on?"

The glow of the headlights shines on him. His back is to me as he takes a deep breath and releases it loudly. He spins to face me, then places his hands on his hips. "Look. I'm just trying to get to the bottom of whatever the hell is going on out here, and I'm doing it my way. Not my father's or the town's. *My* way."

"Why?"

He shakes his head. "I can't tell you. But I need you to work with me. Trust me. I have a really bad feeling about all of this." He points to the SUV. "I ran the plates. You used to live with this guy? This Scott Turner?"

I nod without hesitation. "Yes. We lived together as friends." Tanner turns his nose down at me like he doesn't believe me. "We dated a little in the end, but it was nothing. We're just friends."

"Then why did he come to Balsam Grove, Aurora? Why do I have witnesses telling me he offered a young girl a ride at the bar last night after she stormed off from her boyfriend? And why the hell is his car here in the middle of the woods near our old stomping grounds?"

I swallow, scanning Tanner's eyes for any clue about what his theory is. "He was checking up on me. I didn't exactly tell him I was leaving Durham. It was shitty of me to do. He cares about me a lot, but I couldn't bear to say goodbye. So I left, and he found out where I was and showed up. I thought he left yesterday."

"Is that the last time you saw him? Yesterday? When?"

I exhale heavily, trying to remember. So much happened yesterday. "Um. He showed up at the café around seven p.m. It was before Canvas and Wine. He saw Jaxon, freaked out, and left. Like I said, I thought he left town."

"Did he leave angry?"

I open my mouth to respond. That's an easy answer. *Yes.* Scott was madder than hell, but I'm afraid of what Tanner's fishing for. "He was upset, yes, but wouldn't you be given the situation? He didn't yell or anything. He just left."

"But he didn't. He was supposed to check out of his room this morning. The hotel's been trying to call him, but nothing. He just—*poof*—disappeared. We've been investigating all out-of-towners and locals all day, but this isn't looking too good for your friend, Aurora."

"What do you think he did?"

"If anything happens to that girl, he's a suspect."

I whip my head to face him, my eyes stinging with new tears. "Scott would never hurt anyone. Ever."

"You said the same thing about your daddy, didn't you?"

I gasp, his words slamming me hard in the chest and pushing the emotion higher up my throat. "Go to hell."

Tanner lets out a frustrated growl. "What did I tell you about coming back here? It was a mistake. A big fucking mistake, Aurora."

I narrow my eyes at him. "How am I the enemy here?"

"Seven years," he says through his teeth, spit spraying from his mouth in frustration. "This town has been safe for *seven years*. Not a single missing hiker. Not a murder, not even a death outside of natural causes. You see how this looks, don't you?" He shakes his head. "I warned you this would happen."

My jaw drops, anger swirling inside me like a cauldron finally ready to bubble over. I've had enough. "And why would you have warned me to stay away when the murderer was caught and put away years ago? It makes no sense. The town wanted my father convicted despite the lack of hard evidence, and they got it. Y'all got what you wanted. Now he's dead."

"And now you're back—for what? For revenge?"

A half-growl, half-scream rips from my throat in frustration. "Jesus, Tanner. First you accuse Scott of hurting someone, and now you think this is all some sort of revenge plot? Did it ever occur to you that the girl's boyfriend had something to do with it? Or one of the other dozens of hikers that came out this week? No? Why not? Why are you dead set on targeting me and the people I care about? I can't make sense of it."

A cold hand grips my wrist, and before I can stop the force, I'm being yanked toward Scott's SUV. Tanner shoves me toward a tree on the left side of the car, so close that my nose is pointed into the bark just where the wood has been carved. The glow of the headlights illuminates the small space.

"What the fuck is that, then, Aurora? Who carved *that*?"

I gasp and jerk back against Tanner, who releases his grip on me.

"M.R.?" Her initials come out on a breath. I whip my head toward his, ice filling my veins. "Is that her? The missing girl?"

"M.R. Melody Roberts. Look at the tally marks."

A chill scrapes my spine as I turn again toward the tree. And there they are: eight familiar tally marks carved in the wood.

"Th-this doesn't make any sense. Are you sure this was just carved today?"

"Look down."

Tanner aims a flashlight at the ground where he wants me to look, and I see shavings everywhere.

"But how?"

He gives me a long stare before letting out a heavy sigh. "Let's just say I've been conducting my own investigation over the years. You said you have no memory from those three days you were taken, right?"

I nod, then swallow. "Nothing. It's all just…empty."

"Is there anything you've been able to remember since then? Anything at all? A motive, maybe?"

I shake my head before I even give it a thought. "No, I can't—"

"Think hard. Anything at all. A smell. A feeling. A moment. Something you never told anyone before."

Letting out another breath, I shake my head. When I think of those three days, all I see and feel is a darkness I can't seem to find my way out of. My eyes snap up to his. "Darkness." I swallow. "I remember the darkness."

Tanner lets out a sarcastic laugh. "Well, that's helpful."

Trying not to steam at his words, I think back to last night, which brought me closer to those three days of darkness than ever before.

I can't tell Tanner that I painted a cave because I don't remember doing it, and I'm not sure what it represents. And I definitely can't tell him that I dreamed about it, too. He'll just laugh at me again.

"Why, Tanner?" My voice rattles through my anger. "Why does any of that matter? It was so long ago."

His eyes move toward the woods. "I don't think your dad killed those girls. And I don't think he was the one that tried to kill you."

A laugh bubbles up my throat. Tanner always did have a thing for conspiracy theories—politics, natural disasters, you name it. He always wanted to believe there was something beneath the surface, which I probably would have appreciated if he hadn't been one of the voices in town accusing my father of the hateful things he was tried and committed for.

I've spent the past six years after my father's guilty plea convincing myself of what he was charged with. I thought I'd finally come to terms with what my father was, in fact, capable of, no matter how wrong it felt in my heart. And now, here's Tanner telling me it was all a lie. A setup.

"Okay," I say, throwing up my hands. "I'll bite. Who did it, Tanner? Who framed my father and murdered all those girls and hid their bones? Tell me. I'm *dying* to know."

Everything about Tanner should terrify me right now. The glow of the headlights that casts a halo around his lean, uniformed body. The seething look of hatred on his chiseled face when he stares down at me from his six-foot frame. The glint of satisfaction in his eyes because he knows he's gotten under my skin. The rough brush of his sweaty palms wiping against his pants. And the odd combination of musk and patchouli that brings a rush of familiarity and hits me right in the gut.

And then the whistling begins from behind me.

Fear could grip me. It could whisper irrational warnings in my ear. But I learned years ago that fear kills faster than courage. Something tells me I'm going to need all the courage I can muster tonight.

"Everything okay out here?"

My heart stops, and my head whips toward the familiar voice; toward where the whistling stopped. His voice is slurred, like he's come straight from the bar.

Sheriff Brooks.

"Everything is fine," Tanner cuts in as he grabs my arm, his other hand on his holster. "Get back in the car, Aurora." He looks up at his dad. "We're heading out now."

Brooks' eyes widen as he takes in the SUV Tanner and I are standing in front of. "How did that get out here?" Just the casual tone of his voice bristles the hair on my arms.

"It belongs to a Scott Turner, a friend of Aurora's," Tanner says, gripping my elbow again. "I was just questioning her, Pops, but we're done here for the night. Taking her to the station now. I'll be back for the search in the morning."

"Wait, you aren't searching for them tonight?" I jerk my arm away from Tanner again as I turn to face him. His eyes dig into mine, as if he's begging for me not to argue. I don't understand.

Brooks lets out a deep laugh. "Search parties take place during the day. You should be familiar with the process, Miss June. It's not safe at night for us to dispatch an entire rescue team into the woods at this hour. We've just got a private team out searching tonight."

A private team? What the hell is Brooks talking about?

"Just the deputies and myself, Aurora," he says in response to my confused face. "But seeing as you know the boy who's managed to park his car in our woods, perhaps you should join us. You tried calling him?"

"I don't have a phone."

Brooks' face twists in half-amusement, half-intrigue. "Well, ain't that unfortunate?"

"Alright, Pops, that's enough. I'll get Aurora back to the station, and I'll join you after she answers some questions. I'll radio you any leads I get. You good out here?"

Why does Tanner sound like he's in a rush to leave? The dynamic between him and his father has never been something that's made sense to me. Growing up, Tanner seemed terrified of his father, but that didn't stop him from constantly getting into trouble. Despite the issues between them, Brooks would somehow find every loophole in the book to get Tanner off the hook for his crimes.

"Actually, son, I think I'll take Aurora off your hands. You head on back to the station now."

Tanner's grip on my arm strengthens, making me wince. "Ouch," I hiss before shaking from his hold.

"Pops, you've been drinkin'. You shouldn't be out here. Let's all head back now, and we'll reassess the situation in the morning."

Brooks' eyes grow wild. "You don't give the orders around here, Deputy."

"Don't I have a say in this?" I cut in, staring between the two men. "Look, I'll call Scott again once I get to a phone, but right now I need to get to the hospital. Claire might lose her baby, and Jaxon's waiting for me."

And that's when I hear the click of a safety being unlatched, and I can almost feel the gun pointed at my back. I turn, despite the rise of panic in my chest, to see Brooks' holster empty, his gun raised in his hands toward Tanner and me.

My heart leaps up my throat.

"Pops, what the fuck?" Tanner yells.

"Move away from her, son." Brooks waggles his gun in a gesture for Tanner to move.

But Tanner doesn't budge. Instead, he yanks me against his chest. "Get in the car," he whispers through his teeth while reaching for his belt with one hand and pushing me behind him with the other. "Aurora's got people looking for her, Pops. She's leaving with me."

Brooks lets out a laugh, his back arched and protruding belly pointed outward. He eases his laughter as he shakes his head, the unsteady barrel of his gun still trained on us. "You don't seem to understand what's going on here, boy. Aurora and I have unfinished business to attend to. Now run along before you find a bullet between your pretty blue eyes."

I gasp, only getting a glimpse of Brooks over Tanner's shoulder. He wouldn't shoot his own son. But *unfinished business?* What does that—?

"What the fuck did you just say?" Tanner grabs his own gun from his holster. "You forget I've been putting up with your bullshit for twenty-eight years. No more. I'm not leaving here without Aurora."

"You know better than to sass me, boy. Maybe you won't leave here at all." Brooks' eyes narrow and his jaw hardens, and I swear I see his body sway slightly, bringing another image to mind.

It's now that I remember the odd friendship Brooks struck up with my father. The secrets between Jaxon and me that somehow made it to my father's ears. Brooks knew Jaxon took my virginity. He knew we'd been sneaking off together. Painting together. And on the night I went missing, my father confronted me about all of it.

Air stops in my throat as, piece-by-piece, memories surface and lock back into place. And just like that—I remember.

35

Aurora, Seventeen Years Old

I'd thought it was the flu.

The same day my rolling stomach began to send me to the bathroom earlier in the week, my father came home with news that Jaxon got the offer he'd put in for at the beginning of June. To travel the world. He'd done it. Just like that, he was accepted. So, I suffocated the selfish hurt in my chest at the fact that Jaxon didn't tell me the news himself, and I called to congratulate him on his acceptance. I was truly happy for him, despite my rising insecurity that I would be alone in Balsam Grove without anyone who knew me—who knew I wasn't the same drunken, unstable mess my father was. It was hard enough to make friends *with* Jaxon by my side. I couldn't imagine not having him there to bat away the narrowed eyes and upturned noses. Somehow, none of that mattered when I was with Jaxon.

But one week later, I had my answer. The rancid reaction in my gut wasn't a flu symptom. Not even close.

The room swirled as the walls closed in around me, the row of blue ducks decorating the wallpaper blurring into an indistinguishable mess. Woozy, I reached out to grab hold of something—anything—but before I could, I fell, my ass hitting the floor and my back slamming against the cold bathtub.

The indicator fell through my fingers and clattered to the floor beside me. I looked down, as if the three confirmations before it weren't enough. But there it was. Another blue plus sign.

I was pregnant.

At seventeen.

And I couldn't breathe.

My head fell back as I gulped in air, and a panic attack swept through me. I was done for. Not only had my father banned me from painting back in June, when I'd first arrived after my mother's death, but he'd warned me away from Jaxon as if my relationship with him was something I could just cut off like a dangling string.

He'd heard the rumors, that Jaxon and I were more than just friends. The lonesome artist with no future, four years his daughter's senior. Though I'd deny it at every opportunity, it didn't stop the rest of the town from stirring up drama, and anything related to Henry June was surefire entertainment. It made me a target. People quickly learned that any news to do with Jaxon and me made my father act out—publicly. And it all led to the worst night of my life.

When my panic ceased, I wrapped up the four pregnancy indicators and tucked them into my bra. I ran into my bedroom and hid them under my bed before my father could stop to ask me what was wrong—not that he was awake. He'd come home from an afternoon trip from the bar and passed out on the couch.

It was nearing eight o'clock, and being late fall, the sun had already set. I thought I could sneak out the front door rather than my bedroom window, but the moment the door creaked open, my father flew from his spot on the couch. He mirrored me, red-faced and still half-drunk. "Where the hell do you think you're going?"

I froze in place. "I-I was feeling better and wanted to get some fresh air. I'll be back in an hour."

He glared down at me, his eyes red and his unshaven face a cruel, twisted shade of flush. And he scoffed in my direction. "You think I don't know what you're up to running around the woods at all goddamn hours of the day and night? You ruin the boy's future and you think he still wants to see you?" My dad let out an evil chortle. "When are you going to stop fucking with everyone's future, Aurora? First your mom. Now Jaxon. You ought to be ashamed of yourself."

The terror from my newfound pregnancy dispersed in an instant and was replaced with a medley of confusion and dread. *What is he talking about?* As far as I knew, Jaxon was still planning on leaving at the end of December. We had plans. He would be back in six months, I would graduate high school, and we would move to Durham. There, I would go to college and he would paint, and then we'd travel the world together. As much as I knew I'd miss him for six months, I was happy with that plan—even when I realized there was a life inside me.

I'd be seven months pregnant by the time he'd get back. The way I saw it, that was still plenty of time for him to be with me during the pregnancy. And by then, maybe he'd have enough artwork to sell so we could finally leave this place together. We wouldn't have to scrape by.

"I haven't done anything." I reached for the door. Nothing would stop me from leaving this house. I'd deal with the consequences of my father's bad mood later—if he even remembered this conversation.

My dad glared. He'd been glaring for months, ever since that shipment of my paintings arrived from my mom's storage. It was like his patience, along with his mental health, was wearing thinner every day.

"If you hadn't forced your mom to go to your art show, she'd still be alive today." Anger tremored in his escalating tone. "But that wasn't enough for you, was it?" He fumed, breathing heavily through his closed mouth. "You had to go and stop that boy from traveling to fulfill his dream, too. Why is that, Aurora?" He tilted his head, an accusing look piercing my heart. "When will you stop?" Spit flew from his mouth as he screamed the last question.

My jaw dropped. My body shook. Jaxon wasn't leaving? Since when? He hadn't called. He hadn't stopped by. I was sick and promised I'd be by as soon as I got better, but why was I hearing this from my father?

"There's got to be a mistake. I need to talk to him."

And before my father could say another word, I flew from the house with Lacey at my heels. We ran as fast as we could into the storm and through the narrow path in the woods that joined my home with Jaxon's.

I had to see him. He had to know about the baby. Maybe then he'd go.

I stopped halfway to his house as rain battered down on me, realizing I needed a plan. I stood there for what seemed like hours. What would I say? How would he react? How could I get him to leave Balsam Grove to fulfill our plans so we could have our life together and take care of a baby?

Oh my God. What if he doesn't want this baby?

And that's where my mind stuck, repeating over and over like a broken record. Suddenly, I didn't know what I wanted anymore. My determination dissolved into second guessing everything, and every decision Jaxon and I had made together festered within me until I grew angry. Angry that he hadn't discussed such a life-altering decision without me. Angry that my father was the one to reveal such critical information to our future. Angry that there was a baby growing inside me, preparing to be born into the world of secrets and lies and mental illness that had ripped my family apart. And there was nothing I could do about it.

The rest of my journey to Jaxon's house was a blur, my mind a raging inferno. I was furious and ready to unleash. But I didn't expect to walk away in tears, without a resolution, in so much emotional pain it practically blinded me.

I fled Jaxon's house after the worst fight we'd ever had. The panic from earlier still swirled through me, my tears an endless cascade. I couldn't bring myself to tell him about the baby.

I knew I'd only be returning to my father's wrath. But I didn't realize he'd be digging through my things during my absence.

I didn't realize he'd find what I so foolishly tried to hide.

And I didn't realize he'd be ready for me.

Oh, but he was.

When I returned to the cottage, tears streaking my cheeks, I found him sitting in a rocking chair on the front porch, the buzzing light above him dim and flickering as it had been for days. I saw the silver metallic gleam of the label on his beer before I saw him, and I knew before I even saw his face that I should be afraid. His stillness halted me in my tracks, my heart thrumming triple time while the rain shower soaked me down to the bone.

I cowered into myself, not from the rain, but because of what he gripped in his other hand.

"Tell me this isn't what I think it is."

I couldn't tell him what he wanted to hear. My face was drenched with rain and tears, my eyes probably as red as his were. And there was nothing I could say or do to make any of it go away. To make any of it better.

From in front of me, Lacey growled something fierce, not liking my father's rage. That helped nothing. He stuck his face near Lacey's and growled back, unafraid of her shiny, white teeth that she bared in warning. She was ready to pounce, but just as she started to, my father's heavy boot slammed into her neck, tossing her from the porch as she yelped helplessly.

I screamed. I screamed bloody murder at him, then scooped Lacey up and fled. Away from my father. Away from Jaxon. Away from my pain, though it never seemed to leave me. I just kept running, praying for the pain to dissolve. For the Earth's axis to tilt back into my favor, to where dreams and plans didn't seem so damn impossible.

At first, I thought I'd run right into his trap because I was in the wrong place at the wrong time. But I'd learn later that I wasn't heading toward him. He had been watching, lingering. Just waiting for the perfect time to strike.

36

Aurora

A gunshot rings the air, forcing my palms to fly to my ears and my knees to hit the ground. Tanner takes a dive, landing with on the ground stomach-first. Brooks just laughs.

"What the hell, Pop?" Tanner screams, his ears still covered.

Brooks laughs again, waving his gun in the air like he's shooing Tanner away. "Go on. Get, son. If anyone asks, we've got a suspect in our sights, and I won't come out of these woods until she's cuffed or dead. Either way, she won't cause any more trouble."

Brooks steps forward and yanks me to my feet, giving me a wink as if he didn't just confirm my impending death. But how? Why? He rests a hand on my shoulder, gripping it firmly before turning me around with as much force as he's got, bruising my shoulder and causing tears to sting the backs of my eyes.

"Let's go for a walk, shall we?" Brooks voice is low now, menacing even.

I grit my teeth, refusing to let out a peep. I won't give him the satisfaction of knowing that he's hurting me.

Another shot rings through the air, and just as soon as it does, Brooks lets out a scream and releases his hold on me to reach for his foot.

"Goddammit, Tanner. What are you doing?" Brooks roars.

I turn just long enough to confirm that the barrel of Tanner's gun is aimed right at Brooks.

"Let her go, Pop," he says. "No one else needs to get hurt."

Brooks growls as he clutches his blood-soaked shoe. "The hell you talking about, son? Aurora is responsible, and I'll see to it that she pays."

"Pays for what?" Tanner challenges. His hand shakes, clutching the gun with a white-knuckled grip. "For being related to Henry June? The man you used to cover up your murders?"

Brooks lets out a heavy laugh. It comes straight from his belly. "You have some nerve, boy."

"It's true, isn't it?" Tanner demands.

Brooks responds by firing his gun, his aim low on Tanner. As the shot rings through the air and a howl rips from Tanner's throat, I take off through the woods, using all my strength to carry me as fast as possible toward the landmark I know is coming up over the hill. I'll go there and try to find a place to hide. Some brush, a boulder. Anything to duck behind and pray Brooks loses his way.

But who am I kidding? There's only one person who knows these woods better than Brooks, and that's Jaxon. And Jaxon isn't here.

Aurora

When I notice how far Lacey's taken me into the woods, I fume. Her nose is down along the path to the woods that lead to Aurora's, and she doesn't stop.

"Shit. C'mon, Lacey. Not tonight, okay? I don't have time for a walk right now." I jog after her, whistling and calling her name, but it does nothing to distract her from whatever mission she seems to be on. "Lacey, let's go!" I demand in a firm tone that always gets her attention. She would normally stop whatever she's doing to turn and give me those cute, ice blue eyes that tell me she hears me and I've just ruined her fun. But not this time. This time, she keeps going, moving faster and faster until I'm practically running after her.

"Where're you headed, girl?" I call after her. She doesn't stop to respond, her destination seemingly predetermined.

BANG.

A sound that eerily resembles the shot of a gun seems to freeze the air, echo through the windless night, and wrap the eerie calm of the woods. So much silence. The birds have lost their voice. Not a single rustle of a tree or snap of a branch.

Even Lacey halts in her tracks, her ears pointed toward the origin of the sound.

BANG. Another shot.

Lacey howls into the night, as if speaking to the sound. And then she takes off, faster than before. Panicked, I'm trying to follow her with only the flashlight on my phone to help me through the woods. But I can hear her, and I know these woods well.

BANG. A third shot.

What the hell is going on? It's then that my heart begins to pound fiercely in my chest. Because Lacey has only ever taken off like this once before: on the night I found out that Aurora had returned to Balsam Grove.

37

Aurora

Hollow Falls is just over the next hill. It hasn't taken much for
me to become accustomed to the woods again. Jaxon and I
practically lived in these parts back in the day, but there was
one thing I'd forgotten until now.

It's funny how memories return to you when the time is
right. When they're meant to play a part in your life again.
Everything I'd been sensing the past few days, from my
dreams and the eerie cave drawing I took to Jaxon's in my
sleepwalking state, all brings me to here, to this night, with
knowledge I'd suppressed for so long. But why?

I remember where he took me. Where I awoke, drifting in
and out like I'd been drugged, feeling as if I'd been hauled
through the mud and beaten to near-death. Where my world

had become nothing but wide-open darkness, bordered by the cold rock and dirt at my feet.

But what I don't remember is how I escaped. Why didn't Brooks stop me? Certainly, he was at an advantage. I'd obviously been out of it for three days, not that I realized it at the time. All I knew was that I was somewhere dark, somewhere cold, somewhere that housed the same familiar rush of water I'd heard day-in and day-out for months.

I press harder against my weakening body, adrenaline giving me speed I wouldn't normally be capable of. I know I need to run fast. I need to get somewhere. Anywhere, before the monster who stole seven years of my life can find me again.

The thought fuels my adrenaline again, causing me to shoot forward, but I miss my step. My toe slams on a fallen branch, sending me forward onto my elbows until I'm face-down in the muddy earth. My forehead slams into the jagged edge of a rock. My vision goes blurry as pain shoots through my right arm—the arm that took the most impact from my fall.

Shit. My throat burns from a thirst I didn't know I had. My head grows fuzzy as the fuel that sent me flying through the woods, away from my enemy, dies out. My body groans with each attempt to stand.

Time passes, but I'm not sure how much. I need to rest. Only for a few minutes.

A twig snaps behind me.

Then I feel it: a heavy boot pressing into my back, shoving me deeper into the mud.

"That's enough, you little bitch. Time to end what I thought I ended years ago."

And then, with a blunt force slamming the side of my head, my world dulls, rings, then turns to black once again.

Hope is a flickering shadow against the prison walls of my mind, revealing its presence with each burst of light. Heat waves roll in, and like yesterday and all the days before, air washes my skin with a humidity that leaves me clammy, hot.

Footsteps approach, a medley of rocks and sticks, much heavier than my own. The sound crescendos at a steady pace. They're heading toward me, and that's how I know this day is different from the rest. This time, someone is coming for me.

"It's time," the deep voice booms. His words echo and fade through the space, each soundwave reverberating against me.

To have truth, one must find courage to seek light in the darkness. *My father's words cycle through my mind as I fight through the darkness.*

Always carry your own light, Aurora. Never forget. *The calming words continue as the footsteps fall silent. My skin prickles as a man stands before me smelling of musk and impatience. Of power and fear. My eyes search for him in the darkness until I find the white of his eyes, wide and firmly set on me. Waiting. Expecting...*

But if it's intimidation he seeks, he'll be sorely disappointed. Darkness is no longer something I fear. Not when the light lives within me.

Because that's the thing about weaknesses. They somehow have the power to make you stronger.

I gasp and my eyes fly open, only to find myself suffocating in darkness. My head pounds, and my body feels like lead. Yet somehow, I'm aware of my surroundings, something I wasn't capable of seven years ago. The rush of Hollow Falls runs above me, taking its plunge to my right. It smells of stale air, plain but distinctive. But I can't see it. I can't see anything. It's so cold, my bones are shivering beneath my skin. My arms, stretched out like a T, ache, my wrists raw and bruised from friction against the cold metal that keeps them in place.

My head whips right, then left. So much darkness. So much coldness. Too many senses firing off simultaneously. My body screams in pain and aches with a need to utilize senses that have been stolen from me. I yank against the chains. They rattle as I let out an angry cry. I peer around the space, eyes open, but the darkness is all-consuming. My chest heaves as I try to take breath after breath, but nothing is working. Every bone, every organ feels as if a vice is holding me in place, tightening and squeezing without an ounce of relief in sight.

And then I hear his footsteps. Like in my dream. But these steps don't just sound heavy; I can almost hear their vibrato in the cold ground below me. And whoever it is, they're moving closer and closer. My body begins to shake.

The scent of musk and dirt clashes against the stale air of the space around me as I take my first breath. Just a sip, but it's something.

"We can't have you die just yet, Princess Aurora. That idiot son of mine deterred my plans just a bit, but we'll get back on track here shortly. You think you can breathe for me, sweetheart? As much as I love those panic attacks of yours, I need you coherent for this."

The last thing I want is to give Brooks what he wants, but I need to breathe. I've got to get ahold of myself so I can think clearly.

So I let go. I let the panic take over instead of fighting it. I allow it to course through my veins and blacken my mind, and almost as soon as I've let go, it begins to dissolve. I feel the pressure in my chest relax. My lungs expand, and I'm able to take in a breath that could very well save my life.

"There ya go. Wouldn't want you dying before we set the scene nice and pretty." Brooks chuckles, a deep laugh that shakes the air around us. "Oh, how I wish your daddy hadn't offed himself before getting out of that institution. It sure would have been great to see my old pal again."

I shiver, thinking about the stories I'd hear about Brooks and my father at Franco's. My dad would get trashed, and Brooks would drop him off on the doorstep at any odd hour of the day or night. I always thought he just had a soft spot for my dad and that he took care of him. Clearly there was something more to all of it.

"You framed him for murder." My words come out as a raspy whisper, but he hears me. As breathing becomes easier, I'm aware of the rawness in my throat. My words are sandpaper. I want to scream, but that would only make the pain worse.

"There's more to the story, darlin'."

"Use my name," I growl through my teeth.

Brooks laughs, a hearty laugh filled with venom and satisfaction. "Your father was a gullible son of a bitch, but he didn't kill anyone." Brooks lets out another deep chuckle.

"But they found me dying in his arms. He did nothing to stop it."

"The man was ragier than a bull seein' red, but he wouldn't have harmed a hair on your head. He thought you were already dead. He told you as much in court." Brooks' patronizing tone whips through me, but I tamper it down with my resolve to get information. Long, overdue information. Someone is finally filling in the blanks.

"So it was you who took all those girls? And you—" I swallow over the lump forming in my throat. "Killed them?"

He smirks proudly.

"Then why didn't you kill me?"

There's a heavy sigh, followed by a whimpered cry coming from somewhere behind him. My senses kick into high gear as I track the sound, trying to make sense of what I can hear. It's a girl. The moan sounds as if she's just awoken. My heart pounds fiercely in my chest.

Melody Roberts. She's still alive.

Brooks moves away from me, stepping to another part of the cave. Based on the number of steps he takes, I estimate it's about ten yards away. "Rise and shine, sweetheart. Not much longer now, but you're going to need to go back to sleep for me."

She cries, a tortured cry like she's gagged and unable to speak. There's a rustling of fabric against the dirt floor, a rattle of chains just like mine, and a soft grinding noise like the sound of the screw top of a lid. A second later, her cries escalate in volume before becoming muffled again. *He's holding something against her mouth like he's suffocating her.* My stomach rolls and my heart rate quickens.

More cries tear from her throat as her feet slam into the ground over and over like a kicking and screaming toddler. Brooks shushes her, whispering for her to be still in a fatherly tone, telling her everything will be okay. I can't see her. I can't see whether she'll be okay. But I don't believe him.

Eventually everything goes still again. *Did he put her to sleep?* Nausea creeps from my gut and up my throat. Then all the sounds I heard Brooks making before, replay in reverse, until he's stepping back over to me and leaning down. I can just see the glint of white in his eyes as he speaks.

"Sorry about that, princess. Where were we? Oh, yes. You wanted to know why I didn't kill you." He snorts. "Oh, I wanted to. I would have, but by the time I got back to the cave, you were gone."

Cave? Is that where we are now?

He lets out another breath before leaning in again so I can see the dim outline of his face. I clench my jaw and take a breath through my nose to keep the bile from rising.

"The cave is where I held all the naughty girls like you," he rumbles darkly. "You know the ones—the sluts who ran around the woods getting fucked by their boyfriends?" His breath blows over me, reeking of scotch like my father's used to. Brooks stumbles back a step, unable to keep his balance. "Your father's words, not mine, princess. Henry believed premarital sex was the ultimate sin. But you know that already, don't you?" Brooks laughs. "He talked about murdering all the little whores in town, like they were all made from the devil. It's what bonded us. What made us partners in a sense. And I'll tell you something. He wasn't too pleased when he found out his little girl was giving it up to the Mills boy on the other side of the woods."

Brooks leans in, placing his hands on my wrists, shaking each one as if to check that I'm still secured here. "You were never supposed to be one of them, though—" His warm, rancid breath makes my stomach coil. "I only offed the girls your daddy picked out. He'd spy on the kids fuckin' like rabbits—probably jacked off to the action, too—and then he'd run to me and spill all the details, along with how he wanted the little sluts to die for their sins. And lucky me. I had the pleasure of carrying out what he was too chicken shit to do—without him ever knowing."

I gasp, and Brooks chuckles, confirming what everyone had feared. Part of me never wanted to know what happened to those girls—what could have happened to me. Hot tears sting the backs of my eyes.

"What?" he challenges, pushing away from my chains. "You think any of them minded me showing them how it feels to get fucked by a real man?" He laughs, a deep, sinister laugh that pulls chills from my body. "They loved every second of it. And if that damn dog of yours hadn't shown up, you would have enjoyed it too."

Wait. *What?* "Lacey?" My heart rate quickens.

"What other mutt would I be talking about? She must have followed us here that night. Damn shit started yapping away like she was being mutilated. I went after her. Put up quite the chase, that one did. I never did find her. Woulda snapped her neck if I had."

I can't even think about his words. "And when you came back, I was gone?"

"That's right. Everyone was out looking for ya, but your pops found you first. Thought you were already dead, I guess. Poor stupid bastard didn't even think to call for help." Brooks lets out a chuckle in remembrance of his late friend.

"If he didn't help you"—I swallow—"kill them…then he wasn't your partner."

Brooks guffaws. "It was all his idea. Well, sorta. Those schiz episodes he had were no joke." Brooks shakes his head like he's amazed. "I might have fed him the booze to help inspire him a little, but he'd go off. Tell me everything the voices in his head wanted him to do. Gave me the perfect execution plan—how to hide the girls, what to do with 'em, how to dump 'em so no one would ever find them. That's half the job right there. Your daddy sure had a fucked up mind."

This, coming from the man who carried out the dark delusions of a schizophrenic.

"You're telling me he had no idea what you were doing?"

Brooks shakes his head. "Your daddy started to make a connection between the girls and himself in the spring before you moved here. Said he feared he was the one doing it all. I didn't argue with him. Why would I? When he found you that day, his guilt was my perfect escape. The perfect setup."

Something isn't adding up. "How did he know where to look for me, then?"

"We found the cave together on a hike around Hollow Falls a few weeks after you and your mom left him. Joked about what we could do with the space. I'm guessing when he was desperate to find you, he remembered this place."

Jesus.

"But there hasn't been another murder in seven years. Tanner said so much himself. You're telling me you just stopped killing, just like that?" I pause, answering my own question as I speak. "Or is that why you go out of town so much?" All the pieces of the puzzle are clicking together. "You aren't helping search and rescues in other parts of the state, are you? They don't even know you're out there. You're finding girls and cleaning up your messes before anyone is the wiser."

"You're a smart little whore, aren't you? I couldn't keep killin' in Balsam Grove, now could I? Not after your pops was put away. But seeing you again—" he moans low in his throat and fists the erection pressing through his trousers. Acid shoots up my throat and I spit it out to the side. He doesn't even notice, too turned on by wherever his thoughts have taken him.

"You should have seen the panic on your face when I almost ran you and Mills off the road. But it was when you spread your legs for your boy-toy at Hollow Falls that triggered my ache to kill again, just like old times, and I knew I could pin it on the crazy man's little girl if I had to."

"You're a sick bastard," I spit.

The back of his hand whips forward, stinging my cheek as the smack rings through the air, echoing off the cave walls. He steps forward, directly in front of my face, his nose practically grazing mine. Pain shoots down my throat, down my arms, and it lingers as his mouth begins to open. "Listen here, princess. I may not have finished what I started seven years ago, but you're sure as hell going to get it now. I'd watch that pretty mouth of yours. After watching that fuck-show you put on for me the other night up in your daddy's old bedroom…" He lets out a low growl, knotting my stomach and causing another sour taste to rise in my throat. "I'm more than ready to sit you right here in my lap—"

A bark sounds from beyond the cave. Distant, but I'd recognize Lacey's bark from anywhere. My pulse quickens. Brooks whips his head toward the entrance and curses low in his throat. "That dog of yours sure knows how to crash a party." He looks at me again with a sneer, eyeing my shackled wrists with approval. "It's time I finish that mutt of yours off once and for all. And this time you ain't goin' anywhere, sweetheart." He steps forward, pressing his oily cheek roughly against mine. "Wait right here, princess."

I'm so consumed with the visuals of what Brooks is capable of, with the disgust that slithers down my throat and winds my gut in a chokehold, that I don't even realize he's left until the rush of the falls over my head brings me back to the present. Back to the physical pain Brooks inflicted on me with just a slap of his hand.

He won't touch me again.

I yank my hands down, and the sharp, cool edges of whatever is wrapped around my wrists cut into me, slicing through my skin.

"Gah," I moan. The pain is intense, but I manage to keep my scream to a whisper. I'm in cuffs, that's for sure. But connected to what? Rock? I twist my body as much as the restraints will allow and try to feel around. My palm slides against a cool metal surface, a plate of some sort with a hook on it. Focusing on my right hand only, I shake my arm, seeing how far the chains allow me to move. Sure enough, after I've almost extended my elbow, I hear the crunching of rocks. I tug again, hope sparking in my chest. I'm hooked to a metal plate that's been secured to the wall. But the plate is small, and the rocks are giving way with each tug.

And just like that, I see the light.

38

Jaxon

Lacey's been on the hunt for what feels like hours. I know it hasn't been that long, but my adrenaline is pumping and my feet haven't stopped moving.

By the time we hit a clearing in the woods near the old abandoned cottage, I stop to catch my breath. Lacey is still moving, but even she has slowed down some as she takes her time to sniff around, tracing whatever scent she's picked up.

Three shots in the span of a few minutes. From two miles back, they were distinct but not loud. I'm not sure how Lacey knew which way to run. And what is she running toward, exactly? Maybe I should call it in, but what's the point? No one has picked the phone up all night.

A bark rips through my thoughts, calling my attention to where Lacey stands in place a few yards away, barking over and over. I aim my flashlight first at her, then in the direction she's facing. Dark brown mountain boots are all I see at first. There are two of them, crossed over each other, peeking out from under long blue pants cloaking a man's—at least, I think they're a man's—legs. I step closer to get a better look, careful not to move too fast. The last thing I want is to startle whoever it is in case it's a vagrant living out in the woods.

"Hello," I call out, softly.

The man's feet jerk, making me jump back slightly. I pan over him with the flashlight. My gut clenches as I get a glimpse of the man's shirt, tan with a gold badge on his pocket. My heart leaps in my chest.

"Tanner?" I dart forward, almost dropping my flashlight on the ground.

Falling to my knees in front of him, my eyes widen at the sight of blood drenching his trousers over his knee. "Jesus, man. What happened?" I'm not sure if he can hear me, but a moan slips from his throat as I search for his pulse. His skin is growing cold, but at least he's alive. I try to rationalize the situation. Maybe he's drunk. He could have fallen. Landed on a rock. But now I'm more certain than ever that those were gunshots I heard earlier.

"Buddy, wake up. You need to tell me what's going on here. Did you get shot?"

His mouth opens but no words come out. Another groan comes. Then he nods. The movement is slight, but unmistakable.

"Shit." My pulse quickens and I aim the light around the space to see if anyone else is there. I stop when I see a white SUV parked a few feet away. It looks familiar, but I can't place it at first, not until I see the Duke University sticker on the back window. My world begins to spin. That's the same SUV I remember seeing parked outside the café when I walked in to find Scott with Aurora—the same SUV I remember him peeling away in after he realized Aurora had already moved on without him.

Fear begins to grip me, inch by inch, as I sort through what I know.

Scott hasn't left town.

A girl went missing during a storm.

Tanner is unconscious in the middle of the woods.

Aurora is missing.

Scott has her. He must.

That bastard has her, and this is how he's going to try to get her back. But how? By abducting her just as she was taken seven years ago? By mimicking the actions of her father that sent her away to begin with? Because that's exactly what seems to be going on here.

Lacey's bark turns into a growl as she backs into me, her snarl now aimed in the other direction. I beam the light toward her dark enemy to find a man approaching.

"Brooks?" The man comes closer, and I get a better look. It's Brooks, alright, and he's looking between me, the car, and Tanner.

"What the hell is going on out here, Mills?" Brooks demands. "Why's my boy on the ground?" His hand moves to his holster and I stand quickly, backing away.

Lacey's fierce growl continues in one agonizing string of warning.

"Lacey, hush," I warn without taking my eyes from the sheriff. But she's relentless, and she keeps growling. "Lacey found him. He's alive, but looks to be in pretty bad shape. I think he was shot."

"Shot?" Brooks asks incredulously.

My head tilts a little. "Surely you heard those gunshots, sheriff. I heard them all the way back at my place, and Lacey took off toward the noise. That's how we got here." I nod in the direction of the SUV. "That car belongs to Aurora's ex-boyfriend. He's got her, Brooks. You need to help me find her."

Brooks releases his hold from his holster and squints at the vehicle. My stomach churns as I realize he still hasn't checked to see if Tanner is okay. Like he expected to find him here.

"We ran the plates on it earlier," he says. "Came up as a Scott Turner. Haven't been able to find him, and it's a little late tonight to start a hunt."

"You think Scott Turner might be to blame for the hiker girl's disappearance?"

"Ah, I'm afraid I can't speculate with you, son. Why don't you run on home? Take your mutt, too. This is no place to be alone at this time of night, no matter how experienced you are with these woods. It's dangerous right now. Killer on the loose and all."

Air freezes in my lungs. Did he say "killer on the loose"? How would he know there's a killer? Have they found a body? I think back on the news from Tanner earlier today. A young woman went missing last night during the storm. A strange coincidence since that's how Aurora and all the others were taken years ago. That doesn't mean there's a killer in the woods. Unless—

I run the flashlight over Tanner, giving him another once-over. *Why isn't he more worried?* "Sheriff. He's losing blood, and fast. We need to get him to the hospital. Now."

"You're such a good boy, Mills, but I'm sure you and Lacey need to run along. Let me deal with Deputy Tanner here. We'll have the rescue teams out here in the morning if you want to join us on the hunt for the missing girl. Like old times."

I cringe at his statement as discomfort snakes through my body. Swallowing, I call for Lacey to stand by my side. She does, never once taking her eyes off Brooks.

Brooks looks down at Lacey with a smile that seems to hurt. I frown before poking the bear further. Something is off with Brooks, besides the fact that he's clearly been drinking on the job. There's nothing unusual about the drinking bit, but his mannerisms are off. He's almost…too casual for the situation.

More growling from Lacey. She's never taken to the old sheriff, but her aggression toward him now is more intense than ever. I take a moment to scan his body, from the annoyed look on his face to his dirty and wrinkled clothes, to his boots—one of them caked with blood. At least, it looks like blood.

"Looks like you're hurt, too."

"This?" He shakes his foot. "It's nothing, just a stumble. Don't you worry."

"Okay, Sheriff," I say, despite my growing suspicion—of what, I'm not exactly sure. "Well, Lacey and I are still looking for Aurora, but we'll get out of your way."

I step forward, moving the Sheriff into my periphery. Almost as soon as I do, I know it's a bad idea. He lifts the gun in his hand slowly, deliberately, aiming it at my head. Lacey's facing him, her growl fierce and rising in volume.

Freezing, I lift my hands and turn slowly to face the barrel of the gun that's aimed straight at me.

"There a reason you don't listen to orders, boy? This isn't the time or place for you to be running around searching for your girlfriend."

"I'm not leaving here without Aurora." There's no hesitation in my tone, but maybe there should be. Maybe I should have tried to hold Brooks off longer. He's losing his fucking mind.

"That's the second time I've heard that tonight." The corner of his mouth curls as he narrows his eyes. "Didn't go so well for my son."

The click of the gun's safety causes me to jump.
Shit.

"Sir," I try again, but Brooks takes a step toward me, jabbing his gun in my direction.

"Don't you 'sir' me. I told you. To get. The hell. Out," he spits. "I have enough to deal with tonight. But now—I'm afraid you're in the wrong place at the wrong time, and you've seen too much."

I look down at Lacey, feeling like she's my only hope. She whimpers up at me, letting out a weak bark, asking me to come with her. "Go on, girl. Get," I say again. "Go find Aurora."

Lacey whimpers again, but this time she begins to back up, still hesitant to leave without me.

Brooks coughs out a laugh to my right. "Oh, no you don't, you little shit."

The metal gun whips toward Lacey, and my heart leaps up my throat. "Go!" I scream at Lacey. This time she takes off. Brooks aims—and shoots. Every inch of my body lights up. Fear tranquilizes me, but only for a second as the bullet blasts against the rock where Lacey's feet just were, bursting a small boulder into shards that shatters against my jeans. Lacey is already running past Brooks in the direction of Hollow Falls.

"No!" Brooks growls, moving his flashlight around to find her. "Not again."

Not again? I scramble backward, then duck behind the SUV, which separates me from the sheriff.

Brooks swings back around to find me. I can see his light waving in front of him, but he can't see me as I crouch on the other side of Scott's SUV. If Aurora's out there, Lacey's going to find her, and I'm going to buy them both some time. Somehow.

I don't have time to stop and fear the man with the gun. I'm determined to get to Aurora one way or another. Sliding around the front of the SUV, I wait until Brooks starts his approach on the other side of the car, widening the space between us, and then I turn to run after Lacey's tracks.

Almost as soon as I do, another shot rings through the air, and the last thing I feel is my face slamming into the earth before my world fades to black.

39

Aurora

There's blood everywhere. It's running from my wrists, where the grind of the cuffs has cut through my skin, onto my palm and down my arms in long streams. And it's not by accident.

I clench my teeth harder as I try to use the sticky, red lubricant to slip my hand through one cuff. "Argh!" I scream. It's still too tight. Yanking again against the rock, I feel more of the base where the metal plate is secured to the wall crumble.

Oh my God. Did I do it? Elation flits through me. Looking up, I yank on the cuffs again, then again. Each time, more rocks fall, until it feels like the plate is hanging on by a thread. One more tug, and it comes loose completely.

My heart pounds as my hand, which is still attached to the cuff and plate, falls to my side, pulling on my arm with its weight. I groan and pull the limb up as I face my other arm. Using the weight of the metal as a hammer against the other base, I detach it quicker than the first one.

Both my hands are now free, but the heavy metal plates are slowing me down. I moan and cross my arms, grabbing the plates with opposite hands to free myself from the heavy objects tearing at my wrists. Shuffling around, I try to find a way out. The terrain is flatter than I imagined, but I stumble over several objects on my path. Rocks, plastic bags, tools—at least, I think that's what I see in the dark, but I don't stop to take to a closer look. My goal is to get the hell out of here, get help, and come back for the girl.

I use the wall to feel my way in one direction, moving slowly but still stumbling along the way. And then I see it. A tiny sliver of dim moonlight filtering into the dark space. And then another. And another. I realize I'm no longer staring at a rock wall, but a thin sort of curtain I can't quite make out.

As I near the light, my senses come back to me in a rush, and I realize where I am now. It's the cave from my drawing, but the entrance, which was wide open in my dream, is now covered with what looks like a curtain of vines. A few feet more, and I'm there.

A loud bark from just outside the entrance makes me halt my tracks. "Lacey?" Hope and panic fill my lungs as I clamp a palm to my mouth with regret. If Brooks hears us, we're both dead.

I can see her, just a faint outline, but she's staring right at me, as if unsure at first. My heart jumps into my throat and I fall to my knees, dropping my shackles to the ground. "It's just me, baby girl. C'mere," I say softly.

Lacey lets out a cry and then pads over, licking my face and nuzzling into my neck. "You found me again," I whisper with a smile. "This time I won't forget. I promise."

"Where are you, you little shit?" a voice roars from deep in the woods. But it's close enough for me to begin looking for an escape plan. We could make a run for it. That might be our only hope. We could try to find a place to hide. But where? I look around and remember the girl still unconscious in the cave. We'll come back for her. First, we need to escape Brooks and get help.

Then something dawns on me as I'm scratching the backs of Lacey's ears. "Where's your daddy, huh? Where's Jaxon?"

Lacey whimpers in reaction to my words. My heart does a deep dive into the pit of my stomach. He better be okay. But one thing's for sure; if Lacey's here, Jaxon's nearby too. Her whimper morphs into a growl as the vines covering the cave entrance part to reveal Brooks. His flashlight catches Lacey almost immediately, blinding us both, but a second later I hear his footsteps charging toward us at full speed.

"No!" I scream.

It's enough to make him look up. To give us time. I cross my arms and grip the metal plates again so I can stand without the weight bearing down on me.

Then everything happens so fast.

Brooks nears me and wraps his hands around my neck. Lacey charges Brooks with a growl and jumps onto his back. And then I swing my left arm up, bashing the side of his skull with the metal plate.

He falls back, and Lacey's snout opens in a snarl before her bright white teeth, dripping with saliva, chomp down, piercing

Brooks' neck. His yell is so loud that it seems to reverberate off every surface of the cave.

I reach down and fumble for his flashlight, which went dark when it hit the ground. If I can find it and it still works, it will help us get out of here much faster. Mud and rocks scrape against my knees as I crawl until my palm hits hard plastic. The object rolls against the ground, and I chase it. The moment my fingers wrap the circumference I let out a deep breath. With a lightness in my chest, I successfully flick on the light and leave it facing the front of the cave. It's emitting enough light that I can leave it here to guide us out, thank God. I don't think I could carry the flashlight too.

I turn to the battle between Lacey and Brooks just in time to see Brooks backhand Lacey the same way he did me earlier. A yelp tears through the cave, echoing off every wall as my heart howls in response.

"Don't touch her!" I scream, my voice no longer my own. I've been possessed by the seventeen-year-old still kicking around inside me. She never died. There were moments when she wanted to, but she continued to float until the time was right to fight back against the current. She's not going to let history repeat itself.

Lacey doesn't waste a second as she pounces on Brooks again. Before he can hit her, I roar and shoot forward, slamming the plate in my right hand against his head. He grunts, stunned by another blow, but he's focused on Lacey, who's now got a good grip on his leg. She sinks her teeth into it, and his pants darken as blood seeps through the cloth.

He mewls, and I charge forward again just as another figure approaches the entrance to the cave.

"Jaxon," I gasp, my throat thick with a multitude of emotions that all but strangle me in this moment.

Jaxon is standing in the path of the flashlight's beam, and he doesn't look right. He's cloaked in blood, but I can't tell where it's coming from. His eyes are glazed over, like he's not quite awake.

"Jax," I say again, fighting through the emotions to try and get to him. To get him to hear me. As I stumble toward him, my foot kicks the flashlight, turning it in the opposite direction.

Another tortured yelp escapes Lacey's mouth. Horror ricochets through my chest when I see her lifted in Brooks' grip. He's holding her by the neck, dangling her in the air, and his gun is pointed directly in her mouth. A roaring heat licks at the inside walls of my chest, thawing whatever kept me frozen, then feeds my adrenaline like gas on a fire.

"Come and get her, asshole," Brooks sneers at Jaxon. "She'll die first. You'll die second. And this little bitch behind me goes last. You ready? 'Cause I sure as hell am."

Jaxon's face twists in angry determination just as a cry slips past my throat, just as I turn my head in the wrong direction and see Scott lit up by the only glow in the cave that's now pointed at him, his lifeless body propped up against the rock wall, his tongue pinched between his teeth. Dead.

A gasp slips from my throat and acid crawls up behind it, stirring a liquid poison in my belly. A sob comes next as guilt wraps its ugly scales around my still-beating and undeserving heart. Scott is dead. He's dead, and it's all because of me.

Another shot fires; I vaguely hear it, but I don't know where it comes from. I'm frozen in grief at the sight of my oldest friend and the circle of blood soaking through the shirt that covers his chest.

For the first time in seven years, my world doesn't go blank. There's no panic attack or amnesia to blame. Clarity washes over me. So much clarity now that even in the darkest cave I can see. I can hear. I can feel it all. And this time, I just want to forget.

Jaxon

The shot flies past my ear. I can feel the whoosh of air before the bullet hits its target: Brooks.

I swirl around to find the gunman. I should duck, but I can barely move as it is. When Brooks shot his gun at me, I was already on my way to the ground. His bullet may not have struck me, but that big rock sure as hell nailed me in the chest and arm as I hit the ground. By the searing pain radiating through my arm, I know it's broken.

Broken or not, I'm not letting Brooks touch another hair on Aurora's head.

Limping through the entrance of the cave comes Tanner, one knee bloodied, his eyes hard and trained on his father as he shoots him again and again, closing the gap between them.

"Thanks for confirming everything I already knew, Dad. You dirty fuck," he yells like he's fighting back a different emotion—guilt, grief, I'm not sure.

I don't count the gunshots, but I know Tanner finishes his round, signaled by the click-clicking of his gun before he tosses it to the ground. His face is still hard as Brooks stares back at him, eyes wide and unbelieving. Brooks' mouth opens as if to speak, but all that comes out is a gurgle of blood as Brooks chokes on the thick liquid filling his throat.

The gun that nearly shot Lacey falls from his hand as he teeters off balance, and Aurora jumps for it, grabbing it and kicking it to me. Then she scrambles to Lacey and wraps her in her arms, cradling her as she whimpers in pain. Aurora's wrists are still shackled and the metal plates attached to the chains are prohibiting her from doing much more than that, so I move quickly to their side, just as Brooks faceplants into a large rock.

Tanner falls with him, landing on his ass with a thud. His eyes glaze over like he's in shock at what he just did, watching his father's blood pool around his dead body.

Tanner's face crumbles, twists, and then a heart-wrenching sob tears from his throat.

THREE WEEKS LATER

40

Jaxon

A stage sits in the main parking lot, a podium at the center with six chairs behind it. It's standing room only, stretching from one end of Main Street to the other, as five hundred twenty-eight members of the Balsam Grove community, as well as families of the victims, gather for the press conference the town has been waiting for since the disappearances began ten years ago.

Acting Sheriff Daniel Andrews stands at the podium wearing a somber look that matches the crowd's. Dressed in brown slacks, a matching button-down shirt with a gold badge pinned to his pocket, and a wide-brimmed hat, he looks every bit the part. Danny has been ready for this moment since we were playing cops and robbers in elementary school. His confident eyes scan the sea of faces, commanding our attention.

The locals were shocked when they found out the truth about what happened to the hikers. Everything they had been certain of for the last seven years since Henry June's arrest was false. Instead, the true abductor—and now confirmed murderer—had been right under their noses the entire time, living among them, breathing their air, ruling their town. Sheriff Brooks was adored by many. Despite his comfort with bending the rules and covering up the odd crime here and there to maintain the town's squeaky-clean reputation, he seemed as sane as the rest of us.

"Thank you all for being here today," Danny starts, his voice projecting through the speakers set up along the sidewalks. I squeeze Aurora's hand, but she doesn't need my comfort. If I've learned anything over the past three months, it's that Aurora June is the strongest woman I know. Her jaw is set, pointed straight ahead at Danny, ready for the closure I know she's been seeking for years.

"I want to start off by acknowledging the men and women sitting behind me who have worked tirelessly over the past three weeks to uncover the information I know you all are waiting to hear. I would also like to take this opportunity to thank my fellow deputy, Tanner Brooks, who has taken a leave of absence due to personal reasons. His family asks that everyone respect his privacy during this devastating time." He continues to scan the crowd as he speaks, but there's not even a stir as everyone awaits the closure they came for.

This part, Aurora and I already know.

It took close to three weeks for the homicide detectives to explore the entire cave and locate all six missing bodies. After finding a stash of trash bags, tools still caked with dried blood, zip ties, and stacks of cement blocks, it didn't take long to piece everything together—especially after they found a manmade window at the other end of the cavern. Brooks used it to deposit pieces of the bodies into the deadliest part of the waterfall when he was done torturing, raping, and dismembering them.

Brooks was one sick fuck. He'd befriended Aurora's father—sat with him at the bar, loaded him with shots, then drove him home like the great sheriff he wanted the town to believe he was—and learned all facets of Henry June's personality—the stable ones and the delusional ones. He became a trusted ally just by being present when everyone else turned their cheeks. He egged on Henry's delusions of devil worshipers, of sinners who had premarital sex, and shared fantasies for how they should be punished. He planted the idea for Henry to stalk Brooks' potential victims—all females between the ages of seventeen and twenty-four, all unmarried, and all from out of town, except for Aurora. And over his bar chats with Brooks, he'd report back, unknowing of Brooks' plans to carry out what Henry had only ever imagined. The tree carvings were, in fact, trophies of Brooks' Balsam Grove killings.

Sadistic fuck.

After an investigation to put the final pieces of the puzzle together, it was confirmed that each of the girls had what he considered inappropriate relations with someone they were in town with—a boyfriend, a friend, a fiancé. He'd bragged about his conquests to Melody Roberts when he was tying her up. She was supposed to be next.

Detectives were there to question Melody when she woke up in the hospital. Disoriented and scared, it took a few visits to get the information out of her. Information that answered many questions regarding why Brooks started killing in Balsam Grove again, using the same methods that made Henry June the prime suspect seven years ago. And between Brooks' confessions to Aurora and Melody, the detectives were finally able to close the case.

Danny clears his throat after delivering the key findings to the crowd, giving them everything they need to understand what played out over the last decade. "Wrongful convictions cannot be taken lightly," his voice booms. I swallow, my pulse racing because I know what's coming next. "And so while it deeply saddens me that Henry June is not here to accept my sincerest apologies for the crimes he was accused of, I would like to take this opportunity to extend my regrets on behalf of the Balsam Grove community to his daughter, Aurora June." Danny's eyes lock with Aurora's.

My heart twists in my chest as I look over at the love of my life, the wind blowing back loose strands of her dark brown hair, her chin raised high, a sad smile lifting her rounded cheeks, and a glossy mask of tears filling her big, beautiful, light blue eyes. She nods up at my best friend, accepting his apology, and then she looks at me and squeezes my hand.

Aurora wholeheartedly forgave me for the fact that my testimony was one of the key pieces of circumstantial evidence to help arraign Henry June, an innocent man under the law. His actions leading to the murders were still questionable. Still immoral. But one thing's for certain. Henry June is innocent of all accused crimes, except for doing nothing about his daughter dying in his arms. But now that the facts are out in the open, his actions on the day he found her escaping the cave come down not to malice, but to poor judgement based on a mental disorder he couldn't control. He never had a part in the killings—not knowingly, anyway. And the voyeurism Brooks accused him of may not be true at all. That's something we'll probably never know for sure.

Danny goes on to recognize the dozens of victims outside the county whose bodies are now being uncovered at the bottom of various waterfalls. His method of killing seemed to remain the same, though his tree markings were reserved only for the girls he took in Balsam Grove.

"And the final Balsam Grove victim, Scott Turner, who, after extensive investigation, we concluded was simply guilty of giving a friendly ride to someone in need, will be sorely missed by his loved ones."

I know this statement hurts Aurora most of all. Scott shouldn't have been driving that night. He was as drunk as Melody Roberts was when he pulled off the road and headed down the trail, deep into the woods. They were just trying to wait out the storm.

While there may be closure with her father and the crimes he was accused of committing, she's working on forgiving herself now. Scott's death will be a hard one for her to recover from. She may never fully heal from losing her childhood best friend, and that's something I'll learn to deal with, too. For Aurora. For Scott. Because the only thing Scott was guilty of was loving her, and I can't be angry at that.

In the end, I'm thankful Aurora can finally put her father to rest. Because although Henry June had a mental disorder that made him a less-than-pleasant man in his final years, she was right. He wasn't a monster.

THREE MONTHS LATER

41

Aurora

Puffs of white float lazily through the sky, adding to the layers of sparkling powder that blanket the landscape. Water moves fluidly in the stream below, crashing over boulders and rocks in a rush toward the cascade. A crisp, wintery breeze whips a strand of loose hair against my frigid cheeks, and I move it with a leather-gloved fingertip.

I lived in Balsam Grove for ten summers and one fall, but until now, I've never seen it in the winter. And this year, it came early. I've heard people talk about it, the majestic sight of cottages wrapped in white and the quiet that cloaks you in its calming embrace. But now, seeing it, it's a whole different thing.

It's only been three months since I stepped out of that cave realizing I'd never really left it. It had been my prison for seven years. I was chained in darkness, starved from the truth, gutted and heartbroken by events I never quite understood, and robbed of a future for too damn long. But not anymore.

Gloved hands wrap my center as Jaxon hugs me from behind. His bearded cheek moves against mine. "You ready, Waterfall Eyes?"

My belly flips at the name, and I smile. It will never get old. "I think I am."

I shiver when I turn to face him, not because I'm cold or because his eyes are still the most beautiful storm I've ever seen, but because I can feel it—the long-awaited ending of the final chapter, an epilogue inevitable—and it's happening now, as I say goodbye to my childhood summer cottage for the final time.

It's been sold, and the new owners, a family of three, close on the home tomorrow. Jaxon and I decided it was best to sell as part of our plan to start over. It's time to let go completely of the past and move on together. So far, we've made great strides. For the first time since I can remember, I don't mind making plans. Plans give me something to look forward to as I continue to heal from the physical and mental trauma of it all.

Scott's death hit me hardest. The grief and guilt filled my every vein with a poison I'm still trying to drain. The worst part was making the phone call to Aunt Cyndi to let her know what had happened. She considered Scott to be like her son, and hearing her pain was like learning about his death all over again. Scott's memory is like an excruciating wound that can't be bandaged, threatening to haunt me for the rest of my days.

Jaxon turns to me, wincing a bit at his own residual aches and pains, then gives me a small, supportive smile. "You sure you want to do this?"

Releasing another breath, I nod, knowing this is the right thing to do. I've had my time with the cottage. Years' worth of memories. The happy days, the sad days, and everything in between. It's time to let it go.

"I don't have any doubts," I confirm. "Not a single one."

His forehead presses against mine before our chilled lips warm each other's. I love how gentle Jaxon's been with me lately. And since he's been recovering from a broken arm, our need for each other has become a raging fire, roaring hotter with each glance, each embrace, each kiss. While he would have risked his recovery to be close to me, I wouldn't allow it. I couldn't. It would have only added more guilt to all that already weighed on my mind.

He moans. "Damn. Maybe Claire and Danny can bring the baby over another time. I'm missing you," he growls low against my lips. "A lot." He presses against me, letting me feel his truth.

I bite back a laugh and graze my lips against his. "I want to see the baby." My eyes connect with Jaxon's, a serious look making him understand right away.

Claire's delivery scare was a part of our nightmare when we left the cave that night. So much light entered my world after that moment, powerful knowledge of a reality I'd kept hidden seven years before. The light drove out darkness that was so much more than a cold, empty prison cell. It was the feeling the loss of blood seeping into my clothes and just knowing that I'd lost our baby. The doctors never even noticed.

That night in the hospital, I told Jaxon everything I'd remembered. The entire fight with my father, learning about my pregnancy and Jaxon's decision to stay in Balsam Grove.

We cried together. At the loss. At the secrets. At the devastation of it all. I felt like I was losing the baby all over again. I'd forgotten that I was pregnant. After making a visit to my therapist in Durham, he confirmed what I suspected—that bleeding out from the miscarriage in that cave was ultimately the trauma that triggered my amnesia. Of course, the events surrounding it didn't help, either.

One good thing came from the discoveries. Jaxon had always blamed himself for my abduction that night. No one knew that I'd gone home after our fight. No one, not even me, knew about the altercation with my father and the fact that Brooks was tracking me like game, just waiting for the right time to strike.

Jaxon helps me into his white truck, an older, beat-up vehicle he keeps hidden in his garage for the winter months when the roads are too dangerous for his motorcycle. Lacey hops in behind me, pushing me to my spot in the center. I laugh and nuzzle her soft, white fur that makes her look just as majestic as the snowy landscape. Her light blue eyes shine back at me above that long-hanging smile, her panting every bit as energetic as it was when I took her on her first walk.

"What do you say, girl? You think we can all finally live together now?" Lacey laps me with her wet tongue, making me giggle as Jaxon hops into the driver's seat. He reaches over and pats Lacey's head, then grabs my knee, leaving me with a smile before he starts the truck and backs up.

"What are you two giggling about?"

I smile back down at Lacey, nuzzling my nose with hers. "Oh, nothing. We were just agreeing that you're outnumbered now, buddy. Two females and one male."

Jaxon chuckles. "Yeah, well. We'll have to even that out one day, don't you think?"

My heart flutters in my chest. He spoke the exact words I was just thinking. "I think I like the sound of that."

The rest of the short drive is silent as Jaxon takes the highway to his—*our*—driveway and pulls up to the garage to find the new blue truck already parked outside.

"Lila's here!" I gush, spotting the carrier in Danny's hands as he steps out of the car.

We got to meet little Lila through the incubator she was stuck in for the first six weeks of her life. Once Danny and Claire were finally able to take her home, they wanted to get settled a bit before inviting anyone over. Yesterday when they called, Claire said they were stir-crazy and needed to venture out.

We rush them all inside to get out of the cold, and Jaxon takes Lacey downstairs. We aren't sure how she'll react to a baby, but we'd rather not test out our luck today.

Lila is still low on the scale at nine pounds, fourteen ounces. But as Danny gently pulls her from the carrier and into his arms, I can see how perfect she is. Dressed in a light blue onesie jumper, matching socks, and a pink cap wrapped around her tiny, fuzzy head, she's the most beautiful sight, a perfect blend of Danny and Claire.

I hug Claire first. "You look amazing," I say, a smile growing wide on my face and my heart filling up my chest.

Her eyes glisten with the same emotion as she laughs. "Yeah, well, thanks to Danny I manage to get some sleep in between the feedings and medication." Her eyes glisten as she stares at Lila. "But she's just the most amazing little thing."

I grip Danny's arms instead of crushing the baby between us in a hug. "Good job, Deputy Danny," I whisper, emotion still gripping my words as they escape.

Tanner took a leave of absence to spend time with his mom somewhere far away. They never told anyone where they went. But when they came back, they immediately packed their things and left again.

Poor Meg had no clue what to think of the horror that swept through the town and carried Tanner away. But Antonio Garcia, the new artist Jaxon hired to cover his Canvas and Wine classes, has already swooped in and stolen her heart. Just like that, in a matter of months.

Danny smiles down at me. "Thanks, Little A. How are you doing? Healing okay?"

I nod. "Yes, and I don't want to talk about any of that right now. I want to hold that baby."

Danny laughs. "Deal. But go wash your hands first. You smell like wet dog."

Rolling my eyes, I do as he says, coming right back and approaching him with my arms out and ready. "All clean. Hand her over."

Danny places her in my hands, making sure her tiny head is rested comfortably in the crook of my arm. I bob her gently, the way I saw Danny doing it, slowly, careful not to jostle her too much. Her gray eyes are sparkling up at me, stealing my heart like no other being in this world could.

"Hi, baby girl. I'm your auntie Aurora. And you have the sweetest pink cheeks I've ever seen," I coo ridiculously. "Yes, you do."

Laughter fills the room—Claire's, Danny's, and Jaxon's, who I didn't realize had come back upstairs. I look up, and he's standing there wearing the most beautiful smile as he watches me. Our eyes latch, and in that moment, my heart fills with so much love.

And so much light.

Jaxon takes Lacey outside for a walk before bed as I shower and slip on one of his old shirts. I'm already lying on my stomach, half-asleep by the time Jaxon climbs into bed beside me, but the feel of his chilled body against my warm one brings me to eager alertness. He's moved my hair to expose my neck, and he kisses it softly before lifting the bottom hem of my shirt up and over my head.

He sighs before dropping kisses down my spine, alternating a peck for a brush of his lips, a hand feathering down the side of my ribcage, then slipping to my belly button and moving down to where the friction burns. Brushing lightly against my center, he nudges me with his legs to turn me over. I turn willingly and stare up at him, smiling at his seriousness as he scans me with his eyes.

With one look, I feel him between my thighs when he's not even touching me there. I feel him under my skin. I shake from the inside out as my nipples come alive and the ache between my thighs takes over my mind, reminding me what I've been missing for too damn long. Three months too long.

My palms run the length of his front from his waist up to his chest, slowing down over the faint bruising that remains, then widening to his shoulders. "Are you sure this is okay?" My eyes flick up to meet his again.

Jaxon sits up, a wicked smile on his face. My hands begin to fall from his shoulders, but he catches them in his, bringing them back to his chest and pressing them there. "We've been patient long enough, don't you think?"

He guides my palms down with his until they reach his naked length that sits hard in his lap. Wrapping my hand around his girth, he squeezes before beginning to move my palm around him. I can feel his firm vein as I bring pressure to his tip with each stroke.

I look up to catch his eyes falling closed, then his deep swallow at the pleasure. "We can take it slow," he says with a deep rasp.

Once I've found my rhythm, he releases his hold on me. I keep a firm grip on him as I stroke, remembering the way he taught me when we were younger. He responds to the pressure with a groan, and I smile with pride at how I can make him feel. My eyes find his again and they're burning with desire. I adjust myself to sit on my knees and lean over his thick muscle. My mouth moves around him, my tongue stroking the underside of his skin as my lips wrap firmly around the tip of his shaft. He gasps in surprise, and places his palm on the back of my head, pressing me down until I can feel him in the back of my throat.

"You have the sexiest goddamn mouth, Aurora," he rasps. "You have no clue what you do to me, do you?"

I'm humming with pleasure as he rocks into me over and over, his hips quickening until a curse flies from his mouth.

He can't take it anymore. Pulling out, he pushes my back onto the bed and leans over my body, my hand moving between us to stroke him again. He kisses me hard, then soft, as if remembering we're supposed to be taking things slow and he's fighting against his natural urges for more. With gentle hands, he removes my grip and presses my palms into the bed above my head while our tongues tangle together.

Three months of missing the way his body fits in mine... I sigh, and my thighs tremble at the memory of him inside me, stretching me, filling me, and bringing me to life.

His lips move from mine, and he's staring down at me now. A heavy breath. A weighted stare. His tongue darts out and wets his lower lip as he reaches for my knees and pulls them apart. He moans at the sight. I can't see myself, but I can sure as hell feel it. I'm so wet for him.

His eyes pinch shut as he collects his breath, and then they're back on me. He slides his thumb against my core, once, twice, until he's moving down my body, his mouth hovering over me and swiping my clit with his tongue.

I moan and lift my hips, hitting his mouth in a desperate plea for more. He chuckles and grabs my waist, holding me still while he swipes me again with his tongue before covering me with his mouth and sucking. *Shit.* There's a swirl of chaos inside my chest, sparks light within the depths of my belly, and I'm held prisoner by Jaxon's hands as he tortures me to a rising climax.

Just as he takes me to the edge of the cliff and threatens to toss me off, he tears himself from my aching core and climbs back up my body, his mouth crushing mine just as a finger sinks into me. I scream into his mouth as the sensation returns. My legs spread wider.

He adds another finger, and then he's curling them over and over until I erupt. Heat spreads, hot and wet, moving like a stream of lava through every vein, every limb, every organ. I'm a bundle of nerves, unraveling as they shoot off, zinging through the air and eventually sizzling out. But the after effects leave me in a haze with an intense desire to return the favor.

Jaxon rolls me over so I'm on top of him now, my legs straddling his belly as my mouth finds his. Kissing Jaxon gives me back every breath he just took. His hands cup my cheeks, fingers hooking behind my head as he moans against my mouth. "Put me inside you. I need to feel you. Every inch. Go slowly."

My breath catches as I nod and obey, wrapping my hand around his hard muscle and guiding him to my entrance. I gasp at the feel of his wide tip nudging my opening. As I sink around him, my body adjusts to accommodate his thickness while squeezing around him.

My belly flips at the thought of how new this feels all over again. But one thing remains the same: the connection that flows around us, between us, through us. Different rivers blending into the same stream. Bending and coursing over rock and whatever debris may fall on a timeless journey through every storm, every cave, and every waterfall. We're unstoppable, unbreakable, yet ever-changing.

He was the wild rush of the creek barreling by, a force powerful enough to alter even the sturdiest of landscapes, and he halted me with his eyes. Icy gray orbs with a stormy finish. And I wanted to fall. To let his rapids carry me and take me over the edge.

I wanted to live in his waterfall.

So I did.

EPILOGUE

THREE MONTHS LATER

Jaxon

Aurora slips out from between the sheets and glides across the hardwood floor of our hotel room, wearing the soft smile I've become addicted to. Pink stains her cheeks, her dark brown hair is still wet from her shower, and her naked body glistens with evidence of our lovemaking. I tuck a pillow in the crook of my arm and turn to my side, watching as she slips on a short peach dress with flowy sleeves, a perfect contrast to the golden bronze of her tanned skin.

Perhaps lovemaking is too gentle a term for what we've been doing the entire day. Our five-day stay in Brazil has been the highlight of our month-long South American journey. We've spent the days hiking all the angles of Iguazu Falls, including a day trip to the Argentinian side of the natural phenomenon, and painting until the stars took over the sky. But today was different. Today, our hunger for the sights was replaced by our hunger for each other. It's the last day of our long-awaited vacation, and we've spent the entire day in bed. Tomorrow, we begin the trip home, and as much as we both love the adventure, we're missing Balsam Grove.

I'm surprised by how much I miss it. Aurora and I have spent months making a home together, caring for the properties, managing the café and canvas shop, playing house with Lacey, and filling our world with everything we always wanted—together.

My eyes flick to Aurora, who smooths the front of the chiffon material before walking toward me and sitting at the edge of the bed with her back to me.

"Can you get that button at the top?"

It's just a single pink pearl that I fasten at the top, leaving the rest of her back bare. My hand drifts down, my fingers gliding over her satin skin. She's so soft...and I'm so hard. Again.

I clear my throat to give myself a distraction. "Is that the dress you bought in town yesterday?"

She sneaks a look at me over her shoulder, catching my gaze glued to her sexy back. With a teasing smile, she stands. My hand falls away from her skin, and I narrow my eyes at her cruelty.

"It is." She twirls slowly. "You like?"

I resist the urge to pull her back into bed, giving her a nod instead. "I love it."

Her eyebrow lifts. "Aren't you going to get ready? I thought we were going to watch the sunset before dinner."

I pout and nod. "We are. I just need a minute. I can meet you at the spot if you don't want to wait for me."

She hesitates, assessing me further, and then drops her shoulders in defeat. "Okay, fine. But don't take too long."

"Thirty minutes tops," I promise. And then I lunge for her hand before she can dart away. Knowing Aurora, she was planning to walk out that door without another word, leaving me with an incentive to take the world's fastest shower. Who am I kidding? I will anyway.

She gasps as she's pulled toward me and falls onto my chest. I lock my arms around her waist as she struggles to get off, kicking her heels in the air and pushing against my front with a laugh.

"You're like a gorilla," she shrieks.

I chuckle.

She giggles again, and then I flip her onto her back and dive for her neck, tickling her with my beard as she squirms below me.

"Jax, stop." Her voice is breathless through her laughter. "You're going to wrinkle my new dress." She tries again, but my mouth won't leave her skin. We both know she doesn't give a damn about a dainty dress.

"You smell like me." I smile into her neck.

She laughs and bucks her hips again. "I smell like sex, but there's no way I'm taking another shower. We both know what happened last time I did that."

I groan in frustration and release her, allowing her to sprint from my hold. She moves quickly to the closet, sliding on her sandals before turning back to me with her finger in front of her face. "Thirty minutes."

Then she blows me a kiss and walks out the door, letting it shut behind her.

God, I love that woman.

Aurora

God, I love that man.

I leave him with a smile plastered on my face, a fluttering in my chest, and a soul filled to the brim with contentment. I've never felt so light, yet so full at the same time. Full of life and love. It's all I've ever wanted, and I've wanted it with him.

Heat scales my cheeks as I remember the way I left him in the room. Hot, hard, and frustrated. But we made a pact on this trip. A pact that we'll watch the sunset every night in a different spot. No matter where we are, no matter what we're doing. It's been the easiest promise to keep.

There's no better excuse to stand still with Jaxon's strong arms around me as light shifts to darkness. So many promises live inside those silent moments—promises that never need to be spoken—of a forever filled with an unconditional love that will span time and leap solar systems.

I take my time walking around the hotel property, burning every inch of its plush, green landscape and elegant décor into my memory. I'm going to miss this—waking up to paradise every day in the home of one of the seven natural wonders of the world. But the more time we spend away from Balsam Grove, the more I miss it. And the more I want to get back home to continue the life we've started together.

Still, things will be different when we get home. There'll be no more heavy work hours for either of us. With Jaxon's new property manager tending to the rentals and the small staff at Creek Canvas bringing in more people than ever with nightly Canvas and Wine classes, we'll have more time to spend on other things. Like finally setting up the art gallery in the empty suite we bought beside Creek Café. We figured if we don't make any money selling art, it will still serve a purpose as an art studio.

The powerful rush of water intensifies upon my approach, and my lungs fill with air as I rest my hands on the balcony overlooking the falls at the edge of the hotel property. I'm not sure Jaxon could have picked a more beautiful location for our final stay. We planned most of our month-long journey together, but he wanted the final stop to be a surprise. And it was. Imagine my shock when we arrived at the same spot my finger landed on when I flipped to a random page in *Art World Magazine* months ago.

With over two hundred seventy-five falls combined, the tallest at two hundred sixty-nine feet, the falls span nearly two miles across three countries: Argentina, Brazil, and Paraguay. We've ventured around most of it, hiking through the park in Argentina, going on a jungle tour in Brazil, and taking a boat ride to get closer to the falls. And almost every day, we set aside time to paint the beauty around us.

A monarch butterfly lands on the rail beside my hand. I smile at the fearless winged creature that reminds me so much of myself. It wasn't long ago I was secluded in darkness of my own making. But it was me who set myself free, who found the light and made a home there. I was just fortunate to have Jaxon standing there waiting. Always waiting.

I hear his footsteps before his hands slip around my waist, the fresh scent of his aftershave and deodorant the most delicious complement to my serene thoughts. His front presses against my back and his nose dips to my neck, his scruff tickling my sensitive skin. Chills spread over me, and my smile stretches from ear to ear.

"Good evening, Mr. Mills. I take it your shower was satisfactory," I tease.

He growls from deep in his throat as his lips press into my skin. "Not as satisfactory as it would have been if you were with me, Miss June." He pulls back slightly, his focus moving up toward the horizontal landing at the top of the falls. "Did I miss anything?"

I shake my head, my heart beating like mad in my chest. He still does this to me, makes me breathless. I love him. I just can't believe he's actually mine.

"No," I say as his lips graze mine. "It's just about to start."

So we face front, wrapped in each other as we watch the orange blaze of the sun reflect hues of purple and pinks against the nearby clouds until it dips behind the falls. I let out a deep breath, a bundle of emotions swarming my chest as I bid farewell to the sun, marking our final night in the most magical place on the planet.

I take a step back from the balcony. I hadn't even realized Jaxon stepped away until now. My head turns left, then right in search for him. Then I turn around, my eyes locking with his. They're the first thing I see, those perfect storms, hovering near enough to know something is brewing beneath them. I feel it in my chest.

There's something he's been keeping from me.

And then he kneels.

My heart stops.

Or maybe it starts.

I'm not sure I could tell the difference. He hasn't taken his eyes off me. He hasn't spoken a single syllable, yet the tears are already streaming down my face, so fast they could rival the waterfall behind me. My hand flies to my chest, as if it could stop my heart from crashing through it.

Jaxon smiles. "Aurora June," he says with a calm, sexy confidence.

My entire body is quivering. I'm sure he can see it, and it only makes his smile grow.

"You came into my life like the fastest river, unsure of where you would end up. And then you leapt—from that rock at Hollow Falls when you were fifteen years old. You leapt and you crashed into my world. Even then, I saw you. I didn't realize what it meant—I wouldn't allow myself to figure it out—but I could feel it."

My tears are unstoppable, but I've given up clearing them from my face. I wasn't expecting this. Not at all. I knew it would happen one day, and I hoped it would be soon, but after a few weeks of our month-long getaway passed, I figured it just wasn't our time.

"Aurora." He reaches into his blazer pocket, and I shake harder when I see the ring box in his hand.

This is really happening.

"You're the only woman I've ever loved—the only one I want to sit through a million sunsets with. I've loved you for as long as it matters, and the easiest promise I'll ever make is to continue loving you. Waterfall Eyes, will you spend forever with me?" He blows out a breath, and it's then that I realize, deep down, he's nervous too.

Now it's my turn to smile. I step forward and reach for his hand to pull him up. My arms wrap around his neck, my lips crash into his, and I kiss him harder than I ever have before. I kiss him until my head clears and I realize I never did respond. I pull away and wipe my eyes one final time, and then nod, emphatically, until my words begin to work again.

"Yes, Jaxon. I will spend forevers and eternities and infinities with you. That's the silliest question you've ever asked me."

He smiles before pressing another kiss against my lips and lifting me from the ground. "Good thing I don't have to ask it again."

I squeal before our lips find each other's again and we lose ourselves in the roar of the waterfall—and in each other. Forever.

The End.

SURPRISE! The extended epilogue can be found here:
www.smarturl.it/WE_ExtendedEpilogue

For My Readers

I hope you enjoyed Aurora and Jaxon's story! If you have a few minutes to spare, please consider leaving a review on Amazon and Goodreads. Reviews and sharing your love for our stories mean the world to an author. You can also connect with me on social media and sign up for my mail list to be sure and never miss a new release, event, or sale!

Join the Waterfall Effect Discussion Group:
www.facebook.com/groups/WaterfallEffect
Website & Blog: www.KK-Allen.com
Facebook: www.Facebook.com/AuthorKKAllen
Goodreads: www.goodreads.com/KKAllen
Twitter: www.Twitter/KKAllenAuthor

Join

K.K.'S INSIDERS GROUP, FOREVER YOUNG!
Enjoy special sneak peeks, participate in exclusive giveaways, enter to win ARCs, and chat it up with K.K. and special guests ;)

JOIN HERE

www.facebook.com/groups/foreveryoungwithkk

Want More?

You do not want to miss what K.K. is working on next ;)
Sign up for new release alerts to never miss a thing!

SIGN UP HERE
smarturl.it/KK_MailList

Thank You!

My first thank you is to YOU, the reader, for giving *Waterfall Effect* your time when there are so many amazing choices out there. As a reader myself, I know how difficult selecting a book from your teetering TBR pile can be. Your time is so precious, so valuable. Thank you for dedicating some of that time to my words. It means the world.

To all the bloggers and bookstagrammers who came out swinging to support me this release. THANK YOU will never be enough. You all do so much for this community and ask for nothing in exchange. I'm honored to be included in your feed, whether it's a share or a review. Authors would be nothing without you supporting us.

To my family for being ridiculously supportive of my work, my long hours, my travel, and for suppressing your eye rolls every time I mention I have a deadline. Jagger, I love you to "invictory." Mom, Ed, T, Dad, Corey—love you all to pieces and pieces.

Now, onto the heavy stuff. I first read Plato's *Allegory of the Cave* in my college western philosophy class. The concept of human perception intrigued me to no end, and for some reason— around the same time I was plotting *Up in the Treehouse*—I also started plotting a story about a girl who suffered from an altered reality due to manipulation from a parent. When I finally sat down to finish plotting this story more than one year later, I struggled. I struggled a lot. After some time, three books later, and thanks to some brave sounding boards, I was able to reshape *Waterfall Effect* to make it what it is today.

So, to my parents, Ed and Helene, who were the first to listen to my crazy ideas yet have no recollection of this brainstorming period—you get my thanks, because I love you. Ashleigh Wilson, I'll never forget that conversation in Chili's when you crushed all my dreams and told me none of my ideas were original (haha). Thank you for that. Seriously, thank you. And

Becca Hensley Mysoor with Evident Ink, who I hired to help me get out of my head. Girl, you took on that mission like a champ. You understood what needed to happen from that first conversation, and then you waved your magic fairy wand and set me on a new path. The right path. THANK YOU!

Now, to the folks who helped me once the first draft was done. My Rock Star Beta Team. My Dream Team. You three mean more to me than Starbucks' chocolate croissants. Forrrreals. I've never had so much fun during a Beta read, but it's your honesty that I value the most. Thank you Sammie (bestie), Cyndi (love you so hard I named a character after you), and Richard (thanks for all the laughs!).

To my Alpha Team, who, let's face it, didn't get to read much because I still had a ton of work to do. Kim Lorraine and Joy Eileen. Adore you both.

A huge shout-out to my PA, Lindsey Truman, AKA "Boss of K.K. Allen." I LOVE you, girl. You stepped up at a time when I didn't realize I needed you, and you just did the damn thing. I'm so grateful for you and cannot wait for the day we finally meet in person. I will squeeze you so hard, xoxo.

To all my author friends who have been my rocks these past seven months. Some of you were there for my meltdowns, and some of you were just there. Thank you. Your friendship means everything. Alyson Santos, Kim Lorraine, RC Boldt, Kate Farlow, Kim Holden, K Langston, Stephanie Kneese, Nicole Davis, Ginger Scott, my Do Not Disturb ladies, After Hours Book House ladies, and the Minxes. And there are so many more! Just, thank y'all from the bottom of my heart for being true friends with the best hearts. I adore you all.

Let's face it: a lot of you picked up this book because of THE COVER. The most beautiful cover ever, and it was perfectly designed by the amazing Sarah Hansen of Okay Creations. You nail it, girl, every single time. But this one is pure magic.

I'm just saving the best for last, aren't I? Shauna Ward, your amazing ability to take my writing and work your editing genius while never changing my tone. It's a gift. And I love you so much for your honesty and support and encouraging words, and I know there are way too many "ands" in this sentence. Anyway, you're the best, and I couldn't think of a better co-pilot to work on my babies.

To my amazing reader group, FOREVER YOUNG. Y'all are the BEST GROUP EVER. I've never felt so supported in my entire life. But you're behind me every single day, watching my random live videos, and filling me with so much encouragement. YOU remind me every day why I'm here, why I'm doing this, why I pour my heart and soul into these books.

And for the ones with the graphics talent who make the most beautiful teasers that I get to share with the world. Kcee Bomer with Unbound Book Reviews, Bianka with InBookEden Book Blog, and Yvette @booksandbandanas. Mwah!

To my Angsters <3—my street team with major cred. Can't wait to watch us grow. Adore you all!

To my publicist, Linda Russell, with Foreword PR & Marketing. It's been one year, babe, and we're still doing it. Thank you for slapping me around when I need it, and filling me with hope when I need it, and reminding me every day that this journey is mine. No one can take that from me. I love you.

And finally, to those of you who suffer from mental health issues or know someone who does, please know this story was not written lightly or purely for entertainment. All my books are influenced by real people or experiences in my own life. And when I can't claim to be an expert in something, I research the hell out of it.

To everyone, thank you so much for reading.

Much Love,

Books

by K.K. Allen

Sweet & Inspirational Contemporary Romance
Up in the Treehouse
Under the Bleachers
Through the Lens (Coming in 2018)

Sweet & Sexy Contemporary Romance
Dangerous Hearts
Destined Hearts

Romantic Suspense
Waterfall Effect

Young Adult Fantasy
The Summer Solstice Enchanted
The Equinox
The Descendants

Short Stories and Anthologies
Soaring
Echoes of Winter
Begin Again

Up in the Treehouse (Chloe and Gavin's Story)

I wanted to tell him all my secrets,
but he became one of them instead.

K.K. ALLEN

UP
IN
THE
TREE
G+C
HOUSE

I wanted to tell him all my secrets, but he became one of them instead.

Chloe Rivers never thought she would keep secrets from her best friend. Then again, she never imagined she would fall in love with him either. When she finally reveals her feelings, rejection shatters her, rendering her vulnerable and sending her straight into the destructive arms of the wrong guy.

Gavin Rhodes never saw the betrayal coming. It crushes him. Chloe has always been his forbidden fantasy—sweet, tempting, and beautiful. But when the opportunity finally presents itself, he makes the biggest mistake of all and denies her.

Now it's too late ...

Four years after a devastating tragedy, Chloe and Gavin's world's collide and they find their lives entangling once again. Haunted by the past, they are forced to come to terms with all that has transpired to find the peace they deserve. Except they can't seem to get near each other without combatting an intense emotional connection that brings them right back to where it all started ... their childhood treehouse.

Chloe still holds her secrets close, but this time she isn't the only one with something to hide. Can their deep-rooted connection survive the destruction of innocence?

Under the Bleachers (Monica & Zach's Story)

Under the Bleachers (Monica & Zach's Story)

One kiss can change everything.

Fun and flirty Monica Stevens lives for chocolate, fashion, and boys ... in that order. And she doesn't take life too seriously, especially when it comes to dating. When a night of innocent banter with Seattle's hottest NFL quarterback turns passionate, she fears that everything she once managed to protect will soon be destroyed.

Seattle's most eligible bachelor, Zachary Ryan, is a workaholic by nature, an undercover entrepreneur, and passionate about the organizations he supports. He's also addicted to Monica, the curvy brunette with a sassy mouth—and not just because she tastes like strawberries and chocolate. She's as challenging as she is decadent, as witty as she is charming, and she's the perfect distraction from the daily grind.

While Monica comes to a crossroads in her life, Zachary becomes an unavoidable obstacle, forcing her to stop hiding under the bleachers and confront the demons of her past. But as their connection grows stronger, she knows it only brings them closer to their end.

It's time to let go.

To have a future, we must first deal with our pasts. But what if the two are connected?

Dangerous Hearts (A Stolen Melody, #1)

His heart beats for the music. She's his favorite song.

Lyric Cassidy knows a thing or two about bad boy rock stars with raspy vocals. In fact, her heart was just played by one. So when she takes an assignment as road manager for the world famous rock star, Wolf, she's prepared to take him on, full suit of heart-armor intact.

Wolf is the sexy lead singer for the hottest rock band around with a line-up of guaranteed one night stands. Lyric Cassidy isn't one of them. That's fine with him. Women like Lyric come with fairytale expectations, so it should be easy to stay away. Too bad she's hot as sin with a fiery temper and a mouth that drives him wild.

She's also got something to hide. Something he discovers. Something he wants ...

Sharing a tour bus, neither of them are prepared for the miles of road ahead and the fierce attraction they feel toward one another--a dangerous combination.

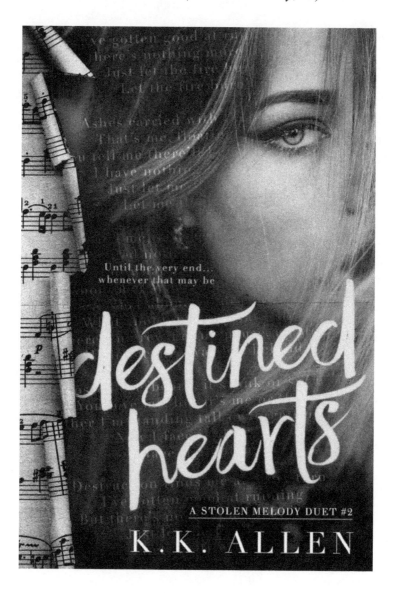

Destined Hearts (A Stolen Melody, #2)

He stole her lyrics, and then he stole her heart.

Lyric Cassidy is off the tour, lost as to what her next career move will be, and certain that she'll never love again after Wolf. All because of a social media scandal that left her with no choice but to pack up and face the consequences. When she learns that the fate of her career is in her hands, she has a difficult decision to make. Step back on the tour bus with Wolf and deal with the mess she left behind, or end her contract early and lose her job at Perform Live?

Wolf's shattered heart finds no resolve in giving Lyric a chance to come back on tour. He can never be with her again. Not after she walked away. Conflicted with wants and needs, he struggles to remember who Wolf was before Lyric. That's what he needs to become again. Maybe then his heart will be safe. Or maybe there's no hope for the damaged.

But with stolen dreams, betrayals, and terrifying threats—no one's heart is safe. Not even the ones that may be destined to be together

Soaring (a short story)

On an Alaskan cruise in the dead of winter, Emma and Luke find each other under the aurora borealis, a phenomenon that bonds them in the most unlikely of ways. While Luke teaches Emma what it means to soar, she gives him a reason to stay grounded, but as their journey nears its end memories of a forgotten past surfaces, challenging their future—if a future for them still exists.

About the Author

K.K. Allen is an award-winning author and Interdisciplinary Arts and Sciences graduate from the University of Washington who writes Contemporary Romance and Fantasy stories about "Capturing the Edge of Romance." K.K. currently resides in central Florida, works full time as a Digital Producer for a leading online educational institution, and is the mother to a ridiculously handsome little dude who owns her heart.

K.K.'s multi-genre publishing journey began in June 2014 with the YA Contemporary Fantasy trilogy, *The Summer Solstice*. In 2016, K.K. published her first Contemporary Romance, *Up in the Treehouse*, which went onto win RT Book Reviews' 2016 Reviewers' Choice Award for Best New Adult Book of the Year. With K.K.'s love for inspirational and coming of age stories involving heartfelt narratives and honest characters, you can be assured to always be surprised by what K.K. releases next.

More works in progress will be announced soon. Stay tuned for more by connecting with K.K. in all the social media spaces.

www.KK-Allen.com

CPSIA information can be obtained
at www.ICGtesting.com
Printed in the USA
FSHW010529060520
69871FS